"She even got her own band going," Gabe went on. "They managed to clear out a few nests around town: giant spiders, some old carrion wyrm down in the sewer that everyone forgot was still alive. But I hoped—" he bit his lip "—I still hoped, even then, that she might choose another path. A better path. Instead of following mine." He looked up. "Until the summons came from the Republic of Castia, asking every able sword to march against the Heartwyld Horde."

For a heartbeat Clay wondered at the significance of that. Until he remembered the news he'd heard earlier that evening. An army of twenty thousand, routed by a vastly more numerous host; the survivors surrounded in Castia, doubtless wishing they had died on the battlefield rather than endure the atrocities of a city under siege.

Which meant that Gabriel's daughter was dead. Or she would be, when the city fell.

Clay opened his mouth to speak, to try to keep the heartbreak from his voice as he did so. "Gabe, I—"

"I'm going after her, Clay. And I need you with me." Gabriel leaned forward in his chair, the flame of a father's fear and anger alight in his eyes. "It's time to get the band back together."

KINGS OF THE WYLD

KINGS of THE WYLD

NICHOLAS EAMES

www.orbitbooks.net

Copyright © 2017 by Nicholas Eames

Excerpt from *Bloody Rose* copyright © 2017 by Nicholas Eames
Excerpt from *The Dragon Lords: Fool's Gold* copyright © 2016 by Johnathan Wood
Cover design by Lisa Marie Pompilio
Cover illustration by Richard Anderson
Cover copyright © 2017 by Hachette Book Group, Inc.
Map by Tim Paul Illustration

Orbit
Hachette Book Group
1290 Avenue of the Americas
New York, NY 10104
orbitbooks.net

First Edition: February 2017

Orbit is an imprint of Hachette Book Group.
The Orbit name and logo are trademarks of Little, Brown Book Group Limited.

The Hachette Speakers Bureau provides a wide range of authors for speaking events. To find out more, go to www.hachettespeakersbureau.com or call (866) 376-6591.

Library of Congress Cataloging-in-Publication Data
Names: Eames, Nicholas, author.
Title: Kings of the wyld / Nicholas Eames.
Description: First edition. | New York : Orbit, 2017. | Series: The band
Identifiers: LCCN 2016038141 | ISBN 9780316362474 (paperback) |
ISBN 9781478946625 (audio book cd) | ISBN 9781478915355
(audio book downloadable)
Subjects: LCSH: Mercenary troops—Fiction. | BISAC: FICTION / Fantasy /
Epic. | FICTION / Action & Adventure. | GSAFD: Fantasy fiction.
Classification: LCC PR9199.4.E15 K56 2017 | DDC 813/.6—dc23
LC record available at https://lccn.loc.gov/2016038141

ISBNs: 978-0-316-36247-4 (trade paperback), 978-0-316-36246-7 (ebook)

Printed in the United States of America

LSC-C

10 9 8 7 6 5

For Mom, who always believed.
For Rose, who always knew.
And for Dad, who will never know how much.

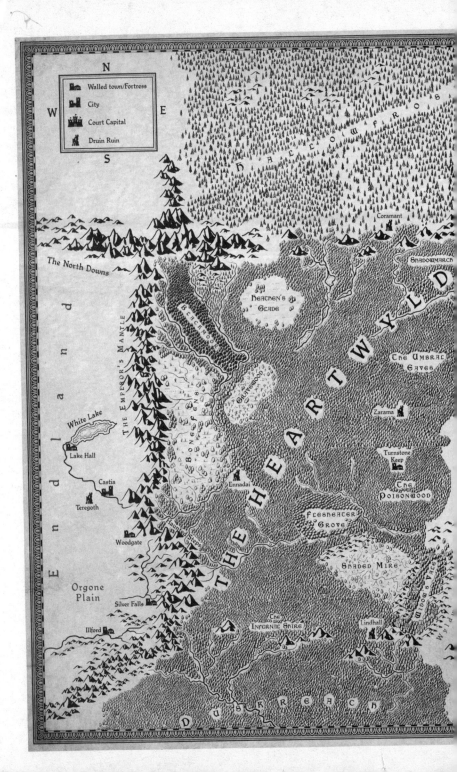

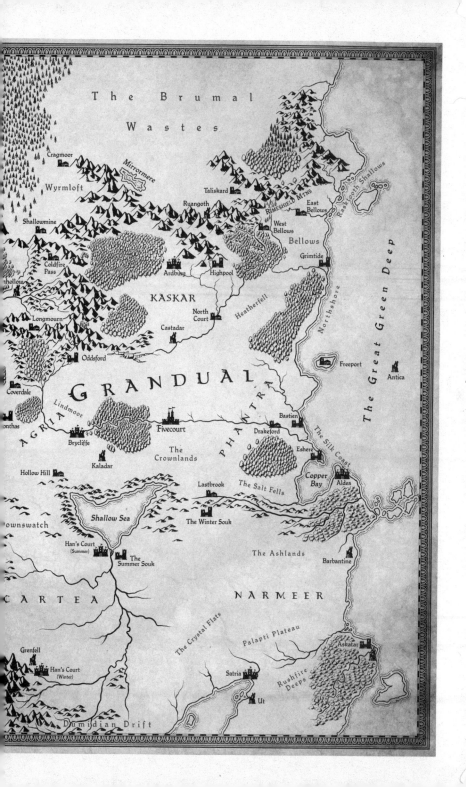

Chapter One

A Ghost on the Road

You'd have guessed from the size of his shadow that Clay Cooper was a bigger man than he was. He was certainly bigger than most, with broad shoulders and a chest like an iron-strapped keg. His hands were so large that most mugs looked like teacups when he held them, and the jaw beneath his shaggy brown beard was wide and sharp as a shovel blade. But his shadow, drawn out by the setting sun, skulked behind him like a dogged reminder of the man he used to be: great and dark and more than a little monstrous.

Finished with work for the day, Clay slogged down the beaten track that passed for a thoroughfare in Coverdale, sharing smiles and nods with those hustling home before dark. He wore a Watchmen's green tabard over a shabby leather jerkin, and a weathered sword in a rough old scabbard on his hip. His shield—chipped and scored and scratched through the years by axes and arrows and raking claws—was slung across his back, and his helmet ... well, Clay had lost the one the Sergeant had given him last week, just as he'd misplaced the one given to him the month before, and every few months since the day he'd signed on to the Watch almost ten years ago now.

A helmet restricted your vision, all but negated your hearing, and more often than not made you look stupid as hell. Clay Cooper didn't do helmets, and that was that.

"Clay! Hey, Clay!" Pip trotted over. The lad wore the Watchmen's green as well, his own ridiculous head-pan tucked in the crook of one arm. "Just got off duty at the south gate," he said cheerily. "You?"

"North."

"Nice." The boy grinned and nodded as though Clay had said something exceptionally interesting instead of having just mumbled the word *north*. "Anything exciting out there?"

Clay shrugged. "Mountains."

"Ha! 'Mountains,' he says. Classic. Hey, you hear Ryk Yarsson saw a centaur out by Tassel's farm?"

"It was probably a moose."

The boy gave him a skeptical look, as if Ryk spotting a moose instead of a centaur was highly improbable. "Anyway. Come to the King's Head for a few?"

"I shouldn't," said Clay. "Ginny's expecting me home, and..." He paused, having no other excuse near to hand.

"C'mon," Pip goaded. "Just one, then. One drink."

Clay grunted, squinting into the sun and measuring the prospect of Ginny's wrath against the bitter bite of ale washing down his throat. "Fine," he relented. "One."

Because it was hard work looking north all day, after all.

The King's Head was already crowded, its long tables crammed with people who came as much to gab and gossip as they did to drink. Pip slinked toward the bar while Clay found a seat at a table as far from the stage as possible.

The talk around him was the usual sort: weather and war, and neither topic too promising. There'd been a great battle fought out west in Endland, and by the murmurings it hadn't gone off well. A Republic army of twenty thousand, bolstered by several hundred mercenary bands, had been slaughtered by a Heartwyld Horde. Those few who'd survived had retreated to the city of Castia and were now under siege, forced to endure sickness and starvation while the enemy gorged themselves on the dead outside their walls. That, and there'd been a touch of frost on the ground this morning, which didn't seem fair this early into autumn, did it?

Pip returned with two pints and two friends Clay didn't recognize, whose names he forgot just as soon as they told him. They seemed like nice enough fellows, mind you. Clay was just bad with names.

"So you were in a band?" one asked. He had lanky red hair, and his face was a postpubescent mess of freckles and swollen pimples.

Clay took a long pull from his tankard before setting it down and looking over at Pip, who at least had the grace to look ashamed. Then he nodded.

The two stole a glance at each other, and then Freckles leaned in across the table. "Pip says you guys held Coldfire Pass for three days against a thousand walking dead."

"I only counted nine hundred and ninety-nine," Clay corrected. "But pretty much, yeah."

"He says you slew Akatung the Dread," said the other, whose attempt to grow a beard had produced a wisp of hair most grandmothers would scoff at.

Clay took another drink and shook his head. "We only injured him. I hear he died back at his lair, though. Peacefully. In his sleep."

They looked disappointed, but then Pip nudged one with his elbow. "Ask him about the Siege of Hollow Hill."

"Hollow Hill?" murmured Wispy, then his eyes went round as courtmark coins. "Wait, the Siege of Hollow Hill? So the band you were in..."

"*Saga,*" Freckles finished, clearly awestruck. "You were in *Saga.*"

"It's been a while," said Clay, picking at a knot in the warped wood of the table before him. "The name sounds familiar, though."

"Wow," sighed Freckles.

"You gotta be kidding me," Wispy uttered.

"Just...wow," said Freckles again.

"You *gotta* be kidding me," Wispy repeated, not one to be outdone when it came re-expressing disbelief.

Clay said nothing in response, only sipped his beer and shrugged.

"So you know Golden Gabe?" Freckles asked.

Another shrug. "I know Gabriel, yeah."

"Gabriel!" trilled Pip, sloshing his drink as he raised his hands in wonderment. "'*Gabriel*,' he says! Classic."

"And Ganelon?" Wispy asked. "And Arcandius Moog? And Matrick Skulldrummer?"

"Oh, and..." Freckles screwed up his face as he racked his brain—which didn't do the poor bastard any favours, Clay decided. He was ugly as a rain cloud on a wedding day, that one. "Who are we forgetting?"

"Clay Cooper."

Wispy stroked the fine hairs on his chin as he pondered this. "Clay Cooper...oh," he said, looking abashed. "Right."

It took Freckles another moment to piece it together, but then he palmed his pale forehead and laughed. "Gods, I'm stupid."

The gods already know, thought Clay.

Sensing the awkwardness at hand, Pip chimed in. "Tell us a tale, will ya, Clay? About when you did for that necromancer up in Oddsford. Or when you rescued that princess from...that place...remember?"

Which one? Clay wondered. They'd rescued several princesses, in fact, and if he'd killed one necromancer he'd killed a dozen. Who kept track of shit like that? Didn't matter anyway, since he wasn't in the mood for storytelling. Or to go digging up what he'd worked so hard to bury, and then harder still to forget where he'd dug the hole in the first place.

"Sorry, kid," he told Pip, draining what remained of his beer. "That's one."

He excused himself, handing Pip a few coppers for the drink and bidding what he hoped was a last farewell to Freckles and Wispy. He shouldered his way to the door and gave a long sigh when he emerged into the cool quiet outside. His back hurt from slumping over that table, so he stretched it out, craning his neck and gazing up at the first stars of the evening.

He remembered how small the night sky used to make him feel. How *insignificant*. And so he'd gone and made a big deal of himself, figuring that someday he might look up at the vast sprawl of stars and feel undaunted by its splendour. It hadn't worked. After a while Clay tore his eyes from the darkening sky and struck out down the road toward home.

He exchanged pleasantries with the Watchmen at the west gate. Had he heard about the centaur spotting over by Tassel's farm? they wondered. How about the battle out west, and those poor bastards holed up in Castia? Rotten, rotten business.

Clay followed the track, careful to keep from turning an ankle in a rut. Crickets were chirping in the tall grass to either side, the wind in the trees above him sighing like the ocean surf. He stopped by the roadside shrine to the Summer Lord and threw a dull copper at the statue's feet. After a few steps and a moment's hesitation he went back and tossed another. Away from town it was darker still, and Clay resisted the urge to look up again.

Best keep your eyes on the ground, he told himself, *and leave the past where it belongs. You've got what you've got, Cooper, and it's just what you wanted, right? A kid, a wife, a simple life.* It was an honest living. It was comfortable.

He could almost hear Gabriel scoff at that. *Honest? Honest is boring*, his old friend might have said. *Comfortable is dull.* Then again, Gabriel had got himself married long before Clay. Had a little girl of his own, even—a woman grown by now.

And yet there was Gabe's spectre just the same, young and fierce and glorious, smirking in the shadowed corner of Clay's mind. "We were *giants*, once," he said. "Bigger than life. And now . . ."

"Now we are tired old men," Clay muttered, to no one but the night. And what was so wrong with that? He'd met plenty of *actual* giants in his day, and most of them were assholes.

Despite Clay's reasoning, the ghost of Gabriel continued to haunt his walk home, gliding past him on the road with a sly wink, waving from his perch on the neighbour's fence, crouched like a beggar on the stoop of Clay's front door. Only this last Gabriel wasn't young at all. Or particularly fierce looking. Or any more glorious than an old board with a rusty nail in it. In fact, he looked pretty fucking terrible. When he saw Clay coming he stood, and smiled. Clay had never seen a man look so sad in all the years of his life.

The apparition spoke his name, which sounded to Clay as real as the crickets buzzing, as the wind moaning through the trees along the road. And then that brittle smile broke, and Gabriel—really, truly Gabriel, and not a ghost after all—was sagging into Clay's arms, sobbing into his shoulder, clutching at his back like a child afraid of the dark.

"Clay," he said. "Please . . . I need your help."

Chapter Two

Rose

Once Gabriel recovered himself they went inside. Ginny turned from the stove and her jaw clamped tight. Griff came bounding over, stubby tail wagging. He gave Clay a cursory sniff and then set to smelling Gabe's leg as though it were a piss-drenched tree, which wasn't actually too far off the mark.

His old friend was in a sorry state, no mistake. His hair and beard were a tangled mess, his clothes little more than soiled rags. There were holes in his boots, toes peeking out from the ruined leather like grubby urchins. His hands were busy fidgeting, wringing each other or tugging absentmindedly at the hem of his tunic. Worst of all, though, were his eyes. They were sunk deep in his haggard face, hard and haunted, as though everywhere he looked was something he wished he hadn't seen.

"Griff, lay off," said Clay. The dog, wet eyes and a lolling pink tongue in a black fur face, perked up at the sound of his name. Griff wasn't the noblest-looking creature, and he didn't have many uses besides licking food off a plate. He couldn't herd sheep or flush a grouse from cover, and if anyone ever broke in to the house he was more likely to fetch them slippers than scare 'em off. But it made Clay smile to look at him (that's how godsdamn adorable he was) and that was worth more than nothing.

"Gabriel." Ginny finally found her voice, though she stayed right where she was. Didn't smile. Didn't cross to hug him. She'd never much cared for Gabriel. Clay thought she probably blamed his old bandmate for all the bad habits (gambling, fighting, drinking to excess) that she'd spent the last ten years disabusing him of, and all the other bad habits (chewing with his mouth open, forgetting to wash his hands, occasionally throttling people) she was still struggling to purge.

Heaped upon that were the handful of times Gabe had come calling in the years since his own wife left him. Every time he appeared it was hand in hand with some grand scheme to reunite the old band and strike out once again in search of fame, fortune, and decidedly reckless adventure. There was a town down south needed rescue from a ravaging drake, or a den of walking wolves to be cleared out of the Wailing Forest, or an old lady in some far-flung corner of the realm needed help bringing laundry off the line and only Saga themselves could rise to her aid!

It wasn't as though Clay needed Ginny breathing down his neck to refuse, to see that Gabriel longed for something unrecoverable, like an old man clinging to memories of his golden youth. *Exactly* like that, actually. But life, Clay knew, didn't work that way. It wasn't a circle; you didn't go round and round again. It was an arc, its course as inexorable as the sun's trek across the sky, destined at its highest, brightest moment to begin its fall.

Clay blinked, having lost himself in his own head. He did that sometimes, and could have wished he was better at putting his thoughts into words. He'd sound a right clever bastard then, wouldn't he?

Instead, he'd stood there dumbly as the silence between Ginny and Gabriel lengthened uncomfortably.

"You look hungry," she said finally.

Gabriel nodded, his hands fidgeting nervously.

Ginny sighed, and then his wife—his kind, lovely, magnificent wife—forced a tight grin and reclaimed her spoon from the pot she'd been tending earlier. "Sit down then," she said over her shoulder. "I'll feed you. I made Clay's favourite: rabbit stew with mushrooms."

Gabriel blinked. "Clay hates mushrooms."

Seeing Ginny's back stiffen, Clay spoke up. "Used to," he said brightly, before his wife—his quick-tempered, sharp-tongued, utterly terrifying wife—could turn around and crack his skull with that wooden spoon. "Ginny does something to them, though. Makes them taste"—*Not so fucking awful*, was what first jumped to mind—"really pretty good," he finished lamely. "What is it you do to 'em, hun?"

"I stew them," she said in the most menacing way a woman could string those three words together.

Something very much like a smile tugged at the corner of Gabe's mouth.

He always did love to watch me squirm, Clay remembered. He took a chair and Gabriel followed suit. Griff trundled over to his mat and gave his balls a few good licks before promptly falling asleep. Clay fought down a surge of envy, seeing that. "Tally home?" he asked.

"Out," said Ginny. "Somewhere."

Somewhere close, he hoped. There were coyotes in the woods nearby. Wolves in the hills. Hell, Ryk Yarsson had seen a centaur out by Tassel's farm. Or a moose. Either of which might kill a young girl if caught by surprise. "She should've been home before dark," he said.

His wife scoffed at that. "So should you have, Clay Cooper. You putting in extra hours on the wall, or is that the King's Piss I smell on ya?" *King's Piss* was her name for the beer they served at the pub. It was a fair assessment, and Clay had laughed the first time she'd said it. Didn't seem as funny at the moment, however.

Not to Clay, anyway, though Gabriel's mood seemed to be lightening a bit. His old friend was smirking like a boy watching his brother take heat for a crime he didn't commit.

"She's just down in the marsh," Ginny said, fishing two ceramic bowls from the cupboard. "Be glad it's only frogs she'll bring home with her. It'll be boys soon enough, and you'll have plenty cause to worry then."

"Won't be me needs to worry," Clay mumbled.

Ginny scoffed at that, too, and he might have asked why had she not set a steaming bowl of stew in front of him. The wafting scent drew a ravenous growl from his stomach, even if there were mushrooms in it.

His wife took her cloak off the peg by the door. "I'll go and be sure Tally's all right," she said. "Might be she needs help carrying those frogs." She came over and kissed Clay on the top of his head, smoothing his hair down afterward. "You boys have fun catching up."

She got as far as opening the door before hesitating, looking back. First at Gabriel, already scooping at his bowl as if it were the first meal he'd had in a long while, and then at Clay, and it wasn't until a few days after (a hard choice and too many miles away already) that he understood what he'd seen in her eyes just then. A kind of sorrow, thoughtful and resigned, as though she already knew—his loving, beautiful, remarkably *astute* wife—what was coming, inevitable as winter, or a river's winding course to the sea.

A chill wind blew in from outside. Ginny shivered despite her cloak, then she left.

"It's Rose."

They had finished eating, set their bowls aside. He should have put them in the basin, Clay knew, got them soaking so they wouldn't be such a chore to clean later, but it suddenly seemed like he couldn't leave the table just now. Gabriel had come in the night, from a long way off, to say something. Best to let him say it and be done.

"Your daughter?" Clay prompted.

Gabe nodded slowly. His hands were both flat on the table. His eyes were fixed, unfocused, somewhere between them. "She is... *willful*," he said finally. "Impetuous. I wish I could say she gets it from her mother, but..." That smile again, just barely. "You remember I was teaching her to use a sword?"

"I remember telling you that was a bad idea," said Clay.

A shrug from Gabriel. "I just wanted her to be able to protect herself. You know, stick 'em with the pointy end and all that. But she wanted more. She wanted to be..." he paused, searching for the word, "...great."

"Like her father?"

Gabriel's expression turned sour. "Just so. She heard too many stories, I think. Got her head filled with all this nonsense about being a hero, fighting in a band."

And from whom could she have heard all that? Clay wondered.

"I know," said Gabriel, perceiving his thoughts. "Partly my fault, I won't deny it. But it wasn't just me. Kids these days... they're obsessed with these mercenaries, Clay. They worship them. It's unhealthy. And most of these mercs aren't even in real bands! They just hire a bunch of nameless goons to do their fighting while they paint their faces and parade around with shiny swords and fancy armour. There's even one guy—I shit you not—who rides a manticore into battle!"

"A manticore?" asked Clay, incredulous.

Gabe laughed bitterly. "I know, right? Who the fuck *rides* a manticore? Those things are dangerous! Well, I don't need to tell you."

He didn't, of course. Clay had a nasty-looking puncture scar on his right thigh, testament to the hazards of tangling with such monsters. A manticore was nobody's pet, and it certainly wasn't fit to ride. As if slapping wings and a poison-barbed tail on a lion made it somehow a *fine* idea to climb on its back!

"They worshipped us, too," Clay pointed out. "Well *you*, anyway. And Ganelon. They tell the stories, even still. They sing the songs."

The stories were exaggerated, naturally. The songs, for the most part, were wildly inaccurate. But they persisted. Had lasted long after the men themselves had outlived who (or what) they'd been.

We were giants once.

"It's not the same," Gabriel persisted. "You should see the crowds gather when these bands come to town, Clay. People screaming, women crying in the streets."

"That sounds horrible," said Clay, meaning it.

Gabriel ignored him, pressing on. "Anyhow, Rose wanted to learn the sword, so I indulged her. I figured she'd get bored of it sooner or later, and that if she was going to learn, it might as well be from me. And also it made her mother mad as hell."

It would have, Clay knew. Her mother, Valery, despised violence and weapons of any kind, along with those who used either toward any end whatsoever. It was partly because of Valery that Saga had dissolved all those years ago.

"Problem was," said Gabriel, "she was good. Really good, and that's not just a father's boasts. She started out sparring against kids her age, but when they gave up getting their asses whooped she went out looking for street fights, or wormed her way into sponsored matches."

"The daughter of Golden Gabe himself," Clay mused. "Must've been quite the draw."

"I guess so," his friend agreed. "But then one day Val saw the bruises. Lost her mind. Blamed me, of course, for everything. She put her foot down—you know how she gets—and for a while Rose stopped fighting, but..." He trailed off, and Clay saw his jaw clamp down on something bitter. "After her mother left, Rosie and I . . . didn't get along so well, either. She started going out again. Sometimes she wouldn't come home for days. There were more bruises, and a few nastier scrapes besides. She chopped her hair off—thank the Holy Tetrea her mother was gone by then, or mine would've been next. And then came the cyclops."

"Cyclops?"

Gabriel looked at him askance. "Big bastards, one huge eye right here on their head?"

Clay leveled a glare of his own. "I know what a cyclops is, asshole."

"Then why did you ask?"

"I didn't . . ." Clay faltered. "Never mind. What *about* the cyclops?"

Gabriel sighed. "Well, one settled down in that old fort north of Ottersbrook. Stole some cattle, some goats, a dog, and then killed the folks that went looking for 'em. The courtsmen had their hands full, so they were looking for someone to clear the beast out for them. Only there weren't any mercs around at the time—or none with the chops to take on a cyclops, anyway. Somehow my name got tossed into the pot. They even sent someone round to ask if I would, but I told them no. Hell, I don't even own a sword anymore!"

Clay cut in again, aghast. "What? What about *Vellichor*?"

Gabriel's eyes were downcast. "I . . . uh . . . sold it."

"I'm sorry?" Clay asked, but before his friend could repeat himself he put his own hands flat on the table, for fear they would ball into fists, or snatch one of the bowls nearby and smash it over Gabriel's head. He said, as calmly as he could manage, "For a second there I thought you said that *you sold Vellichor*. As in the sword entrusted to you by the Archon himself as he lay dying? The sword he used to carve a fucking doorway from his world to ours. *That* sword? You sold *that sword*?"

Gabriel, who had slumped deeper into his chair with every word, nodded. "I had debts to pay, and Valery wanted it out of the house after she found out I taught Rose to fight," he said meekly. "She said it was dangerous."

"She—" Clay stopped himself. He leaned back in his chair, kneading his eyes with the palms of his hands. He groaned, and Griff, sensing his frustration, groaned himself from his mat in the corner. "Finish your story," he said at last.

Gabriel continued. "Well, needless to say, I refused to go after the cyclops, and for the next few weeks it caused a fair bit of havoc. And then suddenly word got around that some- one had gone out and killed it." He smiled, wistful and sad. "All by herself."

"Rose," Clay said. Didn't make it a question. Didn't need to.

Gabriel's nod confirmed it. "She was a celebrity overnight. Bloody Rose, they called her. A pretty good name, actually."

It is, Clay agreed, but didn't bother saying so. He was still fuming about the sword. The sooner Gabe said whatever it was he'd come here to say, the sooner Clay could tell his old- est, dearest friend to get the hell out of his house and never come back.

"She even got her own band going," Gabe went on. "They managed to clear out a few nests around town: giant spiders, some old carrion wyrm down in the sewer that everyone forgot was still alive. But I hoped—" he bit his lip "—I still hoped, even then, that she might choose another path. A bet- ter path. Instead of following mine." He looked up. "Until the summons came from the Republic of Castia, asking every able sword to march against the Heartwyld Horde."

For a heartbeat Clay wondered at the significance of that. Until he remembered the news he'd heard earlier that evening. An army of twenty thousand, routed by a vastly more numer- ous host; the survivors surrounded in Castia, doubtless wishing they had died on the battlefield rather than endure the atroci- ties of a city under siege.

Which meant that Gabriel's daughter was dead. Or she would be, when the city fell.

Clay opened his mouth to speak, to try to keep the heartbreak from his voice as he did so. "Gabe, I—"

"I'm going after her, Clay. And I need you with me." Gabriel leaned forward in his chair, the flame of a father's fear and anger alight in his eyes. "It's time to get the band back together."

Chapter Three

A Good Man

"Absolutely not."

It was not, apparently, the answer his friend was expecting. Or at least not as emphatically as Clay put it. Gabriel blinked, the fire inside him snuffed out as quickly as it appeared. He looked confused more than anything. Disbelieving. "But Clay—"

"I said no. I'm not leaving town to go running off west with you. I'm not leaving Ginny behind, or Tally. I'm not going to track down Moog or Matrick or Ganelon—who very probably still hates us all, by the way—and go traipsing across the Heartwyld! Tits of Glif, Gabe, there's more than a thousand miles between here and Castia, and it ain't paved with stone, you know."

"I know that," said Gabriel, but Clay spoke over him.

"Do you? *Do you*, Gabe? Remember the mountains? Remember the giants in those mountains? Remember the birds—the fucking *birds*, Gabriel—that could snatch those giants up like they were children?"

His friend grimaced at the recollection; the shadow of wings that spanned the sky. "The rocs are all gone," said Gabriel, without conviction.

"Sure, maybe," Clay allowed. "But are the rasks gone? The

yethiks? The ogre clans? How about the thousand-mile-wide forest? Is that still there? Do you remember the Wyld, Gabe? Trees
that can walk, wolves that can talk—and hey, do you know
if the centaur tribes are still trapping people and eating them?
Because *I* do, and they are! And that's not even mentioning the
bloody rot! And you're asking me to go there? To go *through it*?"

"We did before," Gabriel reminded him. "They used to
call us the Kings of the Wyld, remember?"

"Yeah, they did. When we were twenty years younger.
When our backs didn't ache every morning and we didn't
wake up five times a night to piss. But time did what it does
best, didn't it? It beat us up. It broke us down. *We got old*,
Gabriel. Too old to do the things we used to, no matter how
good we were at doin' 'em. Too old to cross the Wyld, and too
old to make any difference at all if we did."

He left the rest unsaid: That even if they managed to
reach Castia, somehow evaded the encircling Horde, and made
it into the city itself, there was every chance in the world that
Rose was already dead.

Gabriel leaned in. "She's alive, Clay." His eyes were steel
again, but his assurance was belied by the threat of tears. "I
know she is. I taught her to fight, remember? She's as good as
I ever was. Maybe better. She killed a cyclops by herself!"
he said, but sounded as though he were trying to convince
himself as much as he was Clay. "They say four thousand survived that battle and made it back to Castia. Four thousand!
Rosie made it. Of course she made it."

"Maybe, yeah," said Clay, mostly because there was nothing else to say.

"I have to go," Gabriel said. "I have to try and save her, if I
can. And I know I'm old. I know I ain't what I used to be. Not
even a shadow," he admitted sadly. "I guess none of us are.
But I am her father—a shitty one, yeah, to have let her go off
in the first place, but not so shitty I'll sit here moaning about
my sore back while she's trapped and probably starving in a

city half the world away. But I can't do it alone." He laughed sourly. "And even if I could afford to hire mercs, I doubt I could find any willing to go."

He has that part right, thought Clay.

"You're my only hope," Gabriel said. "Without you—without the band—I'm lost. And so is Rose." There was a silence after he spoke, weighted with expectation. And then he added, quite unfairly, "What if it were Tally?"

Clay said nothing for a long while. He listened to the creaking boards of his house. He stared at the empty bowls, the wooden spoons resting against the rim of each. He gazed at the tabletop. He looked across at Gabriel and Gabriel looked back. He could see the other man's chest rise and fall, rise and fall, his heart hammering as Clay's own thumped quietly on, and he wondered if so simple an organ (just a fist-sized, blood-slick muscle) might not have some premonition of what the mind, perhaps, did not yet know.

"I'm sorry, Gabe."

His friend just sat there. Frowning at first, and then smiling that strange, withered smile.

"I *am* sorry," Clay said again.

Another while passed, and Gabriel...Gabriel just looked at him, tilted his head ever so slightly, and said, after what seemed like forever, "I know you are."

He stood. The sound of his chair scraping back was as loud as a falcon's screech after the long silence between them.

"You can stay," Clay offered, but Gabriel shook his head.

"I'll go. I left my bag on the step. There's an inn in town?"

Clay nodded. "Gabriel," he began, intending to explain... he didn't know what, exactly. That he was sorry (again). That he couldn't risk losing Ginny, or leave Tally without a father if he went off west and the worst should happen (and it *would* happen, he was sure of it). That he was *comfortable* here in Coverdale. Content, after so many restless years. And that deep down the thought of crossing the Heartwyld, of going anywhere *near* Castia and the Horde that surrounded it, scared him shitless.

I'm afraid, he wanted to say, but could not.

Gabriel, mercifully, cut him short. "Tell Ginny the stew was delicious," he said. "And tell your daughter Uncle Gabe says hello. Or good-bye, whichever."

Offer him boots, some part of Clay's mind insisted. *A cloak, at least. Water, or wine, for the road.* He said nothing instead, just sat there as Gabriel opened the door. Cool air. The wind rustling in the trees outside. The chorus of a hundred thousand crickets in the tall grass.

Griff looked up from his mat, saw that Gabe was leaving, and promptly fell back asleep.

Gabriel stalled on the threshold, looking back. *Here it comes*, thought Clay. *The final plea. The scathing remark about how if it were the other way round he would do it for me. Vellichor* notwithstanding, words had always been Gabe's most potent weapon. He'd been their leader, back when. The voice of the band. All he said, though, before walking out and tugging the door closed behind him, was "You're a good man, Clay Cooper."

Simple words. Kind ones, even. Not the knife he'd been expecting. Not the piercing sword.

They still hurt, though.

His daughter insisted on showing him the frogs the moment she came in the door. She spilled them out on the table before her mother could stop her. One of the four, a big yellow bugger with the nubs of wings not yet grown, made a break for freedom. He leapt off onto the floor, but froze when Griff came at him barking. Tally scooped him up and gave him an admonishing smack on the head before setting him back down with the others. He stayed put this time, too dazed or afraid to move.

"You'll scrub the table before you go to bed," Ginny warned.

Their daughter shrugged. "Yep. Daddy, guess how many frogs I found!"

"How many?" Clay asked.

"No, guess!"

He eyed the four frogs on the table. "Umm...one?"

"No! More than one!"

"Hmm...fifty?"

Tally cackled, moving a hand to head off one of the frogs as it neared the edge of the table. "Not fifty! I got four, silly. Can't you count?"

She proceeded, with the glowing pride of a horse trader showing off her stable of prized stallions, to introduce her amphibious prisoners one by one, pointing out the peculiarities of each and announcing them by name. She held the big yellow in two hands and thrust him up for Clay to see.

"This one is Bert. He's yellow and Mom says he'll have wings when he grows up. I got him for Uncle Gabriel." Tally looked around, as though just now realizing Uncle Gabriel was nowhere in sight. "Where is he, asleep?"

Clay shared a brief glance with Ginny. "He left. He said to say hello."

His daughter frowned. "Is he coming back?"

Probably never, he thought. "Hopefully," he said.

Tally spent a moment digesting this, staring down at the frog in her hands, and then she grinned great big and wide. "Bert will have his wings by then!" she announced, and the nubs on Bert's back twitched as if in demonstration.

Ginny came over and smoothed Tally's hair the same way she did Clay's. "Okay, whelpling, time for bed. Your friends can wait outside while you sleep."

"But, Mom, I'll *lose* them," Tally protested.

"And you will no doubt find them again tomorrow," said her mother. "I'm sure they'll be very happy to see you."

Clay laughed and Ginny smiled.

"They will," their daughter assured them. One by one she picked up the frogs and walked them outside, bidding them farewell and giving each a kiss on the brow before setting them free. Ginny winced with every kiss; Clay was just glad none of them turned into princes. He'd had enough of company tonight, and there wasn't stew left anyway.

After Tally had scrubbed the table clean she left to wash herself. Griff scampered off behind her. Ginny sat down at the table, took one of Clay's big hands in both of her own, and squeezed. "Tell me," she said.

So he told her.

Tally was asleep. The lantern beside her bed, shuttered by a metal blind cut with star-shaped holes, cast a flickering constellation across the walls. Her hair glimmered in the soft light, veins of her mother's gold amidst the plain old brown she'd inherited from her father. She had insisted on a story before bed. She wanted dragons, but dragons were forbidden because they gave her nightmares. Tally asked for them anyway, of course. She was brave that way. He offered her mermaids instead, and a hydrake, which he realized midstory was sort of like seven dragons at once, and he hoped she wouldn't wake up screaming.

It was a true story for the most part, though Clay embellished it somewhat (told her he himself struck the fatal blow against the hydrake, when in fact it had been Ganelon) and left out a few details his nine-year-old daughter—or her mother, for that matter—didn't need to know. Suffice it to say the mermaids had been very gracious afterward, which explained Clay's fairly comprehensive knowledge of the famously mysterious mermaid anatomy. Truth be told, though, he still didn't quite understand it.

He let the story trail off when Tally's breathing deepened to indicate he was speaking only to himself. Now he sat looking at her face—her tiny mouth, her blushing cheeks, her small, porcelain-perfect nose—and marvelled that Clay Cooper, even with Ginny's evident contribution, could have produced something so extraordinarily beautiful. He reached out, unable to help himself, and took her hand in his own. Her fingers tightened instinctively on his, and he smiled.

Her eyes fluttered open. "Daddy?"

"Yes, angel?"

"Is Rosie going to be okay?"

His heart froze. His mouth opened and closed as his mind groped for a suitable response. "You were listening earlier?" he asked. But of course she'd been. Eavesdropping had become a favourite habit of hers since overhearing him and Ginny whispering one night that they were getting her a pony for her birthday.

His daughter nodded sleepily. "She's in trouble, right? Is she going to be okay?"

"I don't know," Clay answered. *Yes*, he should have said. *Of course she is*. You could lie to children if it did them good, couldn't you?

"But Uncle Gabe is going to save her," Tally mumbled. Her eyes drooped shut, and Clay hesitated a moment, hoping she had fallen back asleep. "Right?" she asked, eyes open again.

This time the lie was ready. "That's right, honey."

"Good," she said. "But you're not going with him?"

"No," he said softly. "I'm not."

"But you would come if it was me, right, Daddy? If I was trapped by bad guys far away? You would come and save me?"

There was an ache in his chest, a seething rot that might have been shame, or sorrow, or sickening remorse, and was probably all three. He was thinking of Gabriel's broken smile, the words his oldest friend had uttered before walking out.

You're a good man, Clay Cooper.

"If it was you," he said in a voice still fierce for how quietly it spoke, "then nothing in the world could stop me."

Tally smiled and tightened her tiny grip. "You should save Rosie too, then," she said.

And just like that he cracked. Clamped his teeth shut on a sob that threatened to choke him, closed his eyes against the well of tears, too late.

Clay had not always been a good man, but he was certainly trying. He'd curbed his tendency toward violence by signing on with the Watch and using his particularly limited skill set for the greater good. He did his best to be a man worthy of a woman like Ginny, and of their daughter, his darling girl, who was his most precious legacy, the speck of gold siphoned from the clouded river of his soul.

But there were . . . measures of goodness, he figured. You could set one thing against another and find that one, if only by the weight of a feather, came out heavier. And that was just it, wasn't it? To make a choice between the two—the *right* choice—was a burden few had the strength to shoulder.

To sit idly by—no matter the reason—while his oldest, most cherished friend lost the only thing he'd ever truly loved wasn't what a good man did. Whatever else he knew, Clay knew that.

And his daughter knew it, too.

"Daddy," she asked, her brow furrowed, "why are you crying?"

He imagined the smile he put on looked something like the one Gabe had been wearing earlier on the outside step, brittle and broken and sad. "Because," he said, "I'm going to miss you very much."

Chapter Four

Hitting the Road

He said good-bye to Ginny on the hill that overlooked the farm. Clay figured she would wave him off at the door, or turn back where the lane ended and the long road began, and he'd dreaded the moment like a man waiting for the black-hooded executioner to wave him onstage—*Your turn, pal!* But instead she led him on, speaking quietly of small things as they walked hand in hand up the slope. Before long he was nodding away, chuckling at something he wouldn't be able to recall when he tried to later that night, and had very nearly forgotten he might never hear her voice again, or see her hair catch fire in the morning sun, as it did when they reached the summit and saw the world span gold and green beyond it.

Hours earlier, both of them still awake in the grey dark before dawn, Ginny had warned him she wouldn't cry when she said good-bye, said it wasn't in her nature, and that it didn't mean she would miss him any less. But on the hill at sunrise, after telling him again what a good man he was, she went ahead and wept anyway, and so did he. When their tears dried she took his face in both hands and looked hard into his eyes. "Come home to me, Clay Cooper," she told him.

Come home to me.

Now that he *would* remember, right up to the end.

*   *   *

Gabriel hadn't rented a room above the King's Head, but the barkeep, Shep, who was such a permanent fixture behind the wood Clay sometimes wondered if the man even had legs, mentioned he'd offered an empty stable to a shabby old bard in exchange for a few stories. "And bloody good ones," Shep added, rinsing out pitchers in a sink of cloudy water. "Friends becoming enemies, enemies becoming friends. Described a dragon so real you'd have thought he fought the thing himself! Sad stories, too. Real poignant stuff. Bugger even made himself cry a few times."

It was Gabe in the stable, sure enough. The once-lauded hero, who had shared wine with kings (and beds with queens), was curled up around his pack on a pile of piss-soaked hay. He cried out when Clay nudged him awake, as though roused from the clutches of some terrible nightmare—which was very probably the case. He dragged his old friend inside and ordered breakfast for both of them. Gabriel fidgeted till it arrived via one of Shep's mild, dark-haired daughters and then attacked it as ravenously as he had Ginny's stew the night before.

"I brought you some fresh clothes," Clay said. "And new boots. And when you're done eating I'll have Shep fill the tub for you."

Gabe grinned crookedly. "That bad, eh?"

"Pretty bad," said Clay, and Gabriel winced.

After that Clay picked slowly at his meal, wondering if maybe he'd done enough. He might just send Gabe on his way with a full stomach and fresh clothes before wandering back home. He could tell Ginny there'd been no trace of his old friend in town, and she'd say *Well, at least you tried*, and he'd say, *Yep, I sure did*, and then he'd slip back into bed alongside her, all cozy and warm, then maybe...

Gabriel was watching him as though Clay's skull were a fishbowl and his thoughts plain to see swimming round and round. His eyes floated to the heavy-looking pack on the bench across from him, and then to the rim of the great black shield strapped to Clay's back. Finally he stared down at his empty plate, and after a long silence he sniffed once and swiped a soiled sleeve across his eyes.

"Thank you," he said.

Clay sighed and thought, *So much for home.* "Don't mention it," he said.

On the way out of Coverdale they stopped by the watch-house so Clay could turn in his greens and inform the Sergeant he was leaving town.

"Where ya headed?" asked the Sergeant. His real name was a mystery to everyone but his wife, who had died some years earlier and taken the secret to her grave. He was a man of high integrity, little imagination, and indeterminate age, with a face like sun-ravaged leather and an iron-shot moustache; its ends, thick as horse tails, drooped halfway to his waist. As far as anyone knew he'd never served in an actual army, or fought as a mercenary, or done anything but stand guard over Coverdale his entire life.

In no mood to explain their quest in all its hopeless detail, Clay simply answered, "Castia."

The men posted on either side of the gate fairly gasped in surprise, but the Sergeant only stroked his great moustache and stared at Clay through the puckered creases that served him as eyes. "Mmm," he said. "Long way off."

Long way off? The old man might have just remarked that the sun was *way up high*.

"Yeah," Clay replied.

"I'll take your greens, then." The Sergeant held out a callused hand, and Clay passed over his Watchmen's tunic. He offered up the sword as well, but the old man shook his head. "Keep it."

"There's been folk robbed on the road south," said one of the guards.

"And a centaur spotted out by Tassel's place," supplied the other.

"Here." The Sergeant was thrusting something into Clay's hands. A brass helmet, shaped like a soup bowl, with a flared nose guard and a leather skullcap sewn inside. The gods knew Clay hated helmets, and this one was uglier than most.

"Thank you," he said, and tucked it beneath his arm.

"Why don't you put it on," said Gabriel.

Clay levelled a baleful glare at his so-called friend. He'd spoken earnestly, but Clay could see the corner of his mouth twitch in wry amusement. Gabriel, too, knew how much Clay despised wearing helmets. "Sorry?" he asked, pretending not to have heard.

"You should try it on right now," Gabe urged, and this time his voice betrayed him, skirling up at the end with the effort of keeping a straight face.

Clay looked around helplessly, but he and Gabe were the only two in on the joke. The men at the gate watched him expectantly. The Sergeant nodded.

So Clay put the helmet on, shuddering as the sweat-moulded leather settled onto his head. The front guard pressed painfully against his nose, squashing it, and Clay blinked as his eyes adjusted to the bar of black between them.

"Looks good," said Gabriel, scratching his nose as an excuse to cover his grin.

The Sergeant said nothing, but something—a glint in those crow-sharp eyes of his—made Clay wonder if the old man wasn't fucking with him after all.

Clay smiled tightly at Gabriel. "Shall we?" he asked.

They passed beyond the gate. About fifty yards out the path curved south behind a stand of dense green fir. There was a gulch on the far side of the road, and the moment they rounded the bend Clay tore the helmet from his head and sent it spinning out into the sky. It bounced twice on the hillside, careening in a long arc on its rim before skidding to rest. There were numerous others littering the ground around it, rusted by rain, overgrown by lichen, or half buried in the muck. A few were home to some critter or another, and even as the bronze bowl settled on the mud-slick grass a wren landed lightly on its wide rim, deciding then and there it had found a perfect spot to nest.

Clay and Gabe walked side by side down the dirt path. A forest of tall white birch and squat green alder hedged either side of the road. Both men remained silent for the first while, each lost in the dismal maze of his own mind. Gabriel bore no weapons at all and carried what appeared to be an empty sack. Clay's own pack was stuffed near to bursting with spare clothes, a warm cloak, several days' worth of cloth-wrapped lunches, and enough pairs of socks to keep an army's feet warm. The Watchmen's sword was belted on his hip, and *Blackheart* was slung over his right shoulder.

The shield was named for a rampaging treant who had led a living forest on a monthlong killing spree through southern Agria. Blackheart and his arboreal army had wiped out several villages before laying siege to Hollow Hill. Though a few stalwart defenders remained to protect their homes, Clay and his bandmates had been the only real fighters in town. The ensuing battle, which lasted for almost a week and claimed the life of one of Saga's numerous unlucky bards, was the subject of more songs than could be sung in a day.

Clay himself had cut down Blackheart, and from the treant's corpse had hewn the wood from which he'd fashioned his shield. It had saved his life more times than all his bandmates together, and was Clay's most cherished possession. Its surface told the story of countless trials: here gouged by the razor claws of a harpy broodmother, there mottled by the acid breath of a mechanized bull. Its weight was a familiar comfort, even if the strap was starting to chafe, and the top lip kept scraping the back of his head, and his shoulders ached like a plough horse hitched to a granite wagon.

"Ginny seems well," said Gabriel, shattering the long silence between them.

"Mmm," said Clay, doing his best to repair it.

"How old is Tally now?" Gabe pressed. "Seven?"

"Nine."

"Nine!" Gabriel shook his head. "Where did the time go?"

"Someplace warm," Clay guessed.

They trudged on quietly for a while longer, but Clay could see his friend growing restless. Gabriel had never been one for keeping to himself, which was essentially the reason he and Clay had become friends in the first place.

"You still living in Fivecourt, then?" If they were going to talk, Clay decided, then he could at least steer the subject away from his wife and daughter, whom he was already beginning to miss with a longing he'd never imagined possible.

"I was," said Gabriel. "But, well, you know how it is."

Clay didn't know, actually, but he got the sense Gabriel wasn't planning to elaborate.

"I left the city maybe two years ago now. I lived in Rainsbrook for a while after that, took on some solo gigs to pay the rent and put food on the table."

"Solo gigs?" Clay prompted, shuffling sideways to avoid a treacherous pothole. All through spring and summer wagons burdened with fresh-cut timber ran the road south to Conthas, leaving deep ruts and gaping holes that no one ever bothered to restore.

"Nothing I couldn't handle," Gabe was saying. "A couple of ogres, a barghest, a pack of werewolves that turned out to be, like, seventy years old in human form, so...they went down pretty easy."

Clay found himself torn between horror, amusement, and

genuine surprise. Generally the closer you got to Fivecourt, which was pretty much the dead centre of Grandual itself, the fewer monsters you tended to find. "I wasn't aware Rainsbrook had a monster problem," he said.

Gabriel's lips twitched toward a smirk. "Well it doesn't anymore."

Clay rolled his eyes. *You walked into that one*, he told himself. Then again, it was nice to catch a glimpse of Gabe's old self-assurance beneath the humble façade. *There may be a blade beneath that rust, after all.*

"That's where I saw Rose last," said Gabriel, and just like that a sombre cloud returned to darken his mood. "She came to visit on her way out west. I tried to talk her out of going and we ended up getting into this huge fight over it. We yelled at each other half the night, and when I woke up she was gone." He shook his head, chewing his bottom lip and squinting at nothing in particular. "I wish..." he said, and left it at that. Eventually, he asked, "What about you? What was the plan before I came along and fucked it all up?"

Clay shrugged. "Well, we're hoping to send Tally to school in Oddsford when she's old enough. After that...Ginny and I were thinking of selling the house, opening up a place of our own somewhere."

"You mean like an inn?" asked Gabriel.

Clay nodded. "Two stories, a stable out back, maybe a smithy so we can shoe horses and repair tools..."

Gabriel scratched at the back of head. "School in Oddsford, an inn of your own...who knew standing a wall paid so well? Maybe I should ask the Sergeant for a job when we get back. I've always thought I looked pretty dashing in a helmet..."

"Ginny trades horses," Clay divulged. "She brings home five times the coin I do."

"Ah. You're a lucky man," he said, glancing over. "Gods,

your very own inn! I can see it now: *Blackheart* mounted on the wall, Ginny pouring drinks behind the bar, and old Clay Cooper sitting by the fire, telling any with an ear to listen how we had to walk uphill in the snow to slay dragons back in our day."

Clay chuckled, swatting at a wasp buzzing in front of his eyes. Considering that most dragons he'd ever heard of lived on the tops of mountains, walking uphill in the snow in order to kill one seemed like a forgone conclusion. He was pondering this when Gabriel stopped so abruptly Clay nearly ran him over. He was about to ask why when he took note of where they were.

Beside the road, the remnants of a modest house lay overgrown by decades of tangled brush and waist-high yellow grass. An arching oak grew among the ruins, shedding a steady rain of vibrant orange leaves. Its grasping roots curled around soot-blackened stones as though attempting to drag them, season by turning season, into the ground below.

It had been several years since Clay had last laid eyes on what remained of his childhood home. He rarely had cause to travel this far south of town, and even then he tended to ignore it, or avoid the place altogether. Standing here now, Clay told himself he couldn't smell ash on the breeze, or feel the heat of flames buffeting his face. He couldn't hear the screams, or the dull slap of pummeling fists—not really—but he remembered them vividly. He could *feel* those memories clutching at him like roots, threatening to pull him under.

He nearly jumped when Gabe laid a hand on his shoulder. "Sorry," Clay mumbled distractedly, "I..."

"You should go see her," said Gabriel.

Clay sighed, staring at the ruins. His eyes tracked the spinning descent of leaves, falling like embers toward the shaded earth. Another wasp, or the same one, droned in the air around his head. "I won't be long," he said finally.

Gabriel's assuring smile came and fled like a gust of wind. "I'll wait here."

Clay's father had been a logger by trade, though he would often brag of his brief stint as a mercenary. Leif and the Woodsmen were a band of little renown until they'd taken down a banderhobb that had been snatching children outside Willow's Watch. Unfortunately, the creature's acid bile did a number on the frontman's legs, and Leif was left crippled, unable to walk without a stumbling limp. His band, known afterward as simply the Woodsmen, rose to fame without him.

Clay's mother, Talia, had supervised the kitchen at the King's Head. She was an artist when it came to food, and her husband often complained she provided better meals for strangers than she did for her own family. On one such occasion, she pointed out that Leif spent more time drinking at the pub than he did with his son. This was her way of calling him a drunk without actually calling him a drunk, and though Leif wasn't quick enough to catch her subtlety he didn't much care for her tone, so he hit her.

Rankled by his wife's words, Leif had brought his son with him to the woods the following day. It was bright and cold—a winter wind had come prowling down the mountains and turned the leaves crisp, so they crackled beneath Clay's boots as he scampered along behind his father.

What are we looking for? Clay remembered asking.

And Leif, carrying the axe he sharpened every night before bed, stopped where he was and peered at the trees around them—white birch, red maple, pine still cloaked in green. *A weak one*, he declared finally. *Something that won't put up a fight.*

Clay had laughed at that. He hated that he'd done so, looking back.

They found a narrow birch, and Leif put the axe in his

hands. He showed Clay how to plant his feet and set his shoulders, how to grip the axe low on the haft and put all his strength into a swing. Clay's first chop was a feeble thing. It sent a jolt up his arms and left his elbows aching. The birch was barely scratched.

His father snorted. "Again, boy. Hit it like you hate it."

Eventually the tree fell, and Clay got a rough slap on the back for his effort. Leif led him home afterward; the birch was left where it lay.

And there it remained, though almost forty harsh Agrian winters had come and gone since that brisk autumn day. The tree was white as bone beneath the dappling sunlight. Clay knelt, setting his pack aside and shrugging *Blackheart* to the ground. The scent of the forest filled his lungs, a comfort. He reached out and placed his hand on the trunk, picking idly at the curling bark, grazing the tips of his fingers over its rough knots and creases.

No one else besides Gabriel and Ginny knew that Clay had buried his mother here. He had meant to bring Tally around one of these days, but hadn't quite summoned the courage to do so just yet. His daughter was insatiably curious; she would want to know how her grandmother died, but there were some things a nine-year-old girl had no business knowing.

There was nothing to mark the grave, no headstone upon which Talia Cooper's single mourner might lay a wreath, or set a candle. There were only the words *be kind* carved into the birch's brittle skin, as if whoever did so had been crying, or a child, or both.

Chapter Five

Rocks, Socks, and Sandwiches

"So where are we headed?" Clay asked, shortly before they were robbed on the road to Conthas.

"First things first," said Gabriel. "I need to get *Vellichor* back."

"You sold it, you said?"

Gabe nodded. "Basically, yeah."

Clay could scarcely believe they were having this conversation. Gabe's old sword, *Vellichor*, was perhaps the most treasured artifact in all the world. Several thousand years ago (or so the bards generally agreed) a race of rabbit-eared immortals called druins had narrowly escaped the cataclysmic destruction of their own realm by using *Vellichor* to carve a path into this one, which, at the time, was a land of savage humans and wild monsters. The druins had little trouble subjugating both, and quickly set about establishing a vast empire known as the Dominion.

The druins were led by their Archon, Vespian, who disappeared into the Heartwyld when the Dominion, many centuries later, was overrun by its own monstrous hordes. When Saga encountered him close to thirty years ago, the Archon had been searching desperately for his estranged son. Shortly after, Clay and his bandmates had found Vespian again—mortally wounded, he'd confessed, by the very son he'd been pursuing. The dying druin had given his sword to Gabriel upon one condition: that Gabe use it to kill him.

Gabriel did so, and the Archon, with his final breath, had said something too quiet to hear, in a language too ancient to comprehend. Whatever those words were, Clay was fairly certain they hadn't been *Sell this if you need to.*

"Basically?" Clay could feel his anger rising, "So who did you *basically* sell your magic sword to?" Clay asked, attempting to sound less exasperated than he actually was.

Gabriel glanced over, obviously embarrassed. "Um...Kal has it."

"Kal?"

"Yeah."

"Wait—as in Kallorek? Our old booker, Kallorek? The one Valery—"

"The one Valery left me for, yes," Gabe finished. "Thanks for reminding me. And I didn't exactly *sell* him the sword. I was into some people for a fair bit of coin, and Kal offered to bail me out, only I had nothing to offer up as collateral. He said the sword would square us up, but that if I ever needed it to come and ask. So I'm gonna go ask."

Clay hadn't seen Kallorek in almost twenty years, and he wouldn't have said he was looking forward to reacquainting himself with their old booker once again. Kal was loud, brash, and abrasive—sort of like Gabriel, except louder, brasher, and much more abrasive, without Gabe's natural charm and disarming good looks to offset it all.

From what little Clay knew of the booker's sordid past, Kal had been a goon-for-hire on the streets of Conthas before trying his hand at booking, which, it turned out, he had a knack for. It had been Kallorek who had introduced them to Matrick and convinced Ganelon to join the band, Kallorek who booked the gig that led them to Moog. If not for Kal, there'd have been no Saga.

Still, the man was as mean as a murlog with a mouth full of nails.

Clay wondered if Valery knew yet that Rose had gone to Castia. He hoped so, for Gabriel's sake. If there was anything scarier than a Heartwyld Horde, the wrath of a vengeful ex-wife might just be it.

"So how about the others?" Clay asked. "Have you talked to Moog about this? Or Ganelon?"

Gabriel shook his head. "I came to you first. Figured you and I together would have an easier time getting the rest of them on board. They trust you, Clay. More than they trust me, anyway. This isn't the first time I've tried to re-form Saga, remember."

"Yeah, well, you wanted us to fight in an arena," Clay reminded him. "Against the gods-knew-what, with ten thousand people watching."

"Twenty thousand," Gabe amended.

"But what for? What's the *point*?"

"I don't know!" said Gabriel. "That's just how it's done these days. People want excitement. They want blood. They want to *see* their heroes in action, not just hear about it from some bard who's probably making up half the story anyway."

Clay could only shake his head in disbelief. Didn't people know that stories, and the legends that inevitably sprang from them, were the best part? The gods knew that bards weren't good for much besides getting themselves killed and telling lies, but they were undoubtedly masters of both. Clay had lost count of the times he'd bumbled his way through a messy, bloody, terrifying brawl, only to hear a bard convince a crowded tavern it had been the greatest, most glorious battle ever waged between man and beast.

In stories there were marches without weeping foot sores, swordfights without septic wounds that killed heroes in their sleep. In stories, when a giant was slain, it toppled thunderously to the ground. In reality, a giant died much the same way anything else did: screaming and shitting itself.

A part of Clay had always suspected the world beyond Coverdale was worsening day by day, but since he hadn't planned on having much to do with the outside world—aside from pouring drinks and renting beds to folk passing through—he really hadn't bothered to care. But now that he was rushing headlong back into it...well, he had a feeling things had gotten worse than he'd thought.

"The point is," Gabriel went on doggedly, "if you tell the others we can cross the Heartwyld and bring Rose home, they'll believe you."

"If you say so," Clay said. He saw a bird, or some other bright thing, flit between the trees in his periphery. When he turned to look, though, it was gone. "So what are the others up to?" he asked, eager to change the subject. "I mean besides Matrick, who I assume is still the king of Agria."

Before Gabe could answer, a woman sauntered onto the road ahead. Her long brown hair was a mess of loosely bound braids exploding into frizzy tangles. Her clothes were in little better condition, but what they lacked in quality they made up for in quantity, layered upon one another with seemingly no regard for pattern or colour. A longbow was slung over her shoulder, and a single arrow dangled loosely in one hand.

"Mornin' boys," she said. "Lovely day for a stroll, ain't it?"

"Or a robbery," muttered Clay, scanning the forest to either side. Sure enough, he spotted half a dozen others hidden among the trees. All of them women, garbed in the same haphazard fashion as the one who'd blocked their path, and all of them armed, as it were, to the tits.

"Ya think?" she asked, with the lazy drawl of a Cartean plainswoman. "I prefer rain for a robbery. Not a downpour, mind you—more of a light drizzle. Suits the mood, I think. You ask me, it's a shame to spoil a sunny day like this with something so crass as petty thievery." She made a helpless gesture, and then leveled the arrow she was carrying at Clay's chest. "Yet here we are: pettily thieving."

"We have nothing you'd want," said Gabriel, spreading his hands.

The brigand flashed a smile. "Oh, we'll see about that. Now if you'd be so kind as to introduce your weapons to the road and have what's in those packs out for us to see?"

Clay complied, flinging the Watchmen's sword to the ground and upending his pack.

The girl whistled, stepping close to examine the contents. "Ooooh, socks and sandwiches! It's our lucky day, girls! Come collect!" A chorus of hoots and howls answered from the trees, and her women poured onto the road like a pack of patchwork coyotes. They circled the two men, making threatening gestures with knives and spears and half-drawn bows. Gabriel, flinching with every feinted thrust, turned his own pack upside down.

To Clay's surprise, it wasn't empty. To the surprise of everyone else, it contained only a handful of rocks that clattered to the road at Gabriel's feet.

The clamour died almost instantly, and for the first time since she'd appeared the leader of the bandits seemed genuinely displeased.

"By the Heathen's hairless balls!" she swore, kicking one of the stones in the grass beside the road. Gabriel started forward as if he meant to dive after it, but the woman's glare stopped him cold. "*Rocks*? Are you bloody serious? Can't be sapphires, or rubies, or fat silver ignits."

"Ingots," Clay mumbled, but the woman wasn't listening.

"The gods forbid we waylay some fool with a pack full of diamonds, oh no! But rocks! And socks! And...what's that there on those sandwiches?"

"Ham."

"Ham," the woman growled, as though uttering the name of a bitter enemy. Her knuckles went white on the haft of her bow.

"What about that there shield?" asked one of the bandits. She pointed to *Blackheart* with the tip of her spear.

"Looks fancy," said another. "Probably worth a court-mark or two."

Clay didn't bother addressing them. Instead, he fixed his gaze on their leader. "The shield's not going anywhere," he said.

The woman blinked. "Ain't it now?" She stepped around him, holding her bow like a walking stick and casting one more disdainful glance at Gabriel's pitiful pile of stones. "Last I checked you weren't in no position to...to..." She trailed off. "Well, I'll be a kobold's cock ring—is that what I think it is?"

"Depends what you think it is," Clay answered.

"I *think* it's the shield what belongs to the one they call Slowhand, also known as Clay Cooper," she said. "I *think* it's godsdamned *Blackheart*!"

"Well, in that case you're right," Clay said. It had been years since anyone had called him *Slowhand*, a nickname he'd earned thanks to his propensity for getting hit first in almost every fight.

"So it *is* fancy," exclaimed the bandit who'd suggested so earlier. "We'll have it off ya, then." She reached for it, and Clay said a prayer in his head to whichever of Grandual's gods was in charge of forgiving men who broke women's wrists before punching them in the throat.

"Leave it be," said the woman in charge.

For a moment the two bandits glared at each other, like predators standing off over a fresh kill, but eventually the leader prevailed, forcing the other to look sullenly away.

"This shield," she explained, "was hewn from the heart of a vicious old treant who killed a thousand men before this one"—she pointed at Clay, nearly jabbing his eye out with the arrow in her hand—"chopped him to firewood. This here is Slowhand Clay Cooper. He's a real live hero!"

"And we don't rob heroes?" one of the bandits said.

"Of course we rob heroes," said the woman, and with the tip of her arrow sliced neatly through the purse at Clay's waist. Twenty silver coins spilled onto the dusty road, and the bandits scrambled to recover them.

The woman raised her voice to a pitch fit for proselytizing. "A sandwich belongs to whoever eats it; a sock to whoever wears it; a coin to whoever has it to spend. But some things are not for the taking. Like this." She grazed her fingers across *Blackheart*'s blistered surface as though laying hands on the tomb of someone sacred. "This here belongs to Clay Cooper and none other, and I'll grow a tail out my arse before I stoop so low as to rob him of that."

She stepped away, shouldering her bow and resuming her place on the road ahead. "*Sock up, girls!*" she yelled, and the bandits leapt to action, pulling off boots and pulling Ginny's handmade socks over whatever they were already wearing. After that they divvied out the sandwiches, then scurried back to the edge of the woods.

One of them plucked up Clay's sword as she went. "Does *this* belong to Clay Cooper?" she asked.

"Not anymore," said the leader.

Gabriel watched the brigands disperse with obvious relief. The leader, looking at Clay, jutted her chin in his direction. "Who's this tagalong, eh?"

Clay scratched at his beard. "Uh . . . that's . . ."

"Gabe," his friend answered for himself, straightening a little as he gave his name.

The woman gaped. "You mean *Golden Gabe*?" Gabriel nodded, and she shook her head in disbelief. "Well, you ain't what I expected, I'll tell you that for free. My daddy told me you were fierce as a lion and cool as a Kaskar pint. My mum used to say you were the prettiest man she ever saw—'ceptin' my daddy, o'course. But look at you here: meek as a kitten, and so damn—" she frowned like a farmer assessing an ear of rotten corn "—*old*."

Clay shrugged. "Time's a bitch," he said.

The young woman laughed. "Yeah? Well she clearly has it in for the pair o'you." She squinted up at the sun. "Anyhoo, my girls and I have some silver to spend, so I'll thank you for that."

Clay managed a wan smile. Despite the fact that she'd left them without food, coin, weapons, or with any foreseeable means of keeping his feet warm in the long, cold months to come, Clay couldn't quite bring himself to dislike the woman. She'd been affable enough (for a brigand, anyway) and she'd had the good grace to leave *Blackheart* alone. So there was that.

"What do they call you?" he asked.

Her grin grew wider. "I've been called many things," she said. "A thief. A harlot. A spittin' image of the goddess Glif herself. But when you tell this tale beside the hearth tonight, you can say it was Lady Jain and the Silk Arrows who took your stuff."

"You're a band?" Clay asked.

"We're band-*its*," she answered. "But I like to think there's hope for us yet." She scampered off, and the Silk Arrows melted into the forest behind her.

Clay let out a breath he didn't know he'd been holding and looked on despairingly while Gabriel knelt to collect the stones he'd emptied from his pack.

"Seriously? Is there a reason you're bringing a handful of rocks on this fool's quest of ours?"

Gabriel went to the roadside. When he found the stone Jain had kicked into the grass he examined it as though seeing it for the first time. "These belonged to Rose," he said. "She used to bring them up from the beach when we lived in Uria. I thought I'd bring them in case sh—"

"She won't want them," Clay snapped. "She won't care that you brought her a handful of rocks from halfway across the world, Gabe. She's not a little girl anymore, remember?"

"—in case she's dead," Gabriel finished. "I thought maybe I would put them on her grave. She'd like that, I think."

Clay shut his mouth. He felt, at this particular moment, like an asshole.

Before long they were shouldering their packs, and to

Clay's very great surprise he found a sandwich still wedged in the bottom of his. He handed half to Gabriel, who raised an eyebrow.

"That's lucky."

Clay snorted. "If you say so. I sure hope this incredible good fortune of ours holds up all the way to Castia."

"And back," remarked Gabriel, too intent on eating to have noticed the sarcasm in Clay's voice.

Within minutes Clay swallowed the last of his sandwich, and with it the aching memory of the woman who'd made it. "And back," he said eventually, without any conviction whatsoever.

Chapter Six

The Monster Parade

As a man who'd once made a living exploring decrepit ruins with the intent of killing whatever lurked inside, Clay knew more than most about the Old Dominion. The ancient empire of druinkind had, once upon a time, encompassed all the known world, from Grandual in the east to Endland in the west, as well as the sprawling expanse of the Heartwyld Forest in between. The druins were brilliant craftsmen and powerful sorcerers, who ruled with the liberty of gods over the then-primitive tribes of men and monsters. But as with anything that grows too big for its own good—ambitious spiderwebs, for instance, or those giant, late-harvest pumpkins—it became something altogether monstrous, and eventually collapsed on itself.

The Exarchs in charge of governing the cities of the Dominion rebelled against the ruling Archon, and a civil war erupted. Though immortal, the druins were relatively few in number (Moog had once told Clay that druin females could give birth to but a single child), so they bolstered their armies with monsters, which the Exarchs had bred for generations to be more fierce and feral than ever before. The creatures proved too wild to control, however, thus giving rise to the first great Hordes: vast hosts that swept unchecked across the Old Dominion and brought it to ruin.

An Exarch named Contha built an army of massive golems hewn from stone and bound to thralldom by runes that ... well, in truth Clay had no idea how the runes worked, and most of the golems he'd encountered while touring had been masterless, rampaging juggernauts. At any rate, Contha's golem armies were smashed to rubble by the ravaging Hordes, and so the Exarch abandoned his fortress and fled underground, never to be seen or heard from again.

Some said the immortal Contha had since returned to wander the crumpled ramparts of his citadel and bemoan the fall of his beloved Dominion, while others suggested he remained belowground, reduced to a gibbering troglodyte that dwelled alone in the smothering dark.

Clay figured he'd just fucking died. The druins were so long-lived as to seem immortal, but they could be killed— Clay had *seen* one killed—and there were a lot of nasty things living down there in the darkness.

The ruin of Contha's fortress had served as a rallying point during the War of Reclamation. In the shadow of its walls the Company of Kings had driven the remnants of the last Horde back into the Heartwyld Forest. Eventually a settlement sprang up around it, a place where those brave enough to enter the Wyld could gather and supply, and for those who returned to spend their newfound riches or drink away the memory of the horrors they'd barely escaped.

Before long Contha's Camp grew into a proper town. Someone built a wall, and when the town swelled into a big, bloated city, someone built a bigger wall. Somewhere along the way the name was shortened to Contha's, then eventually to Conthas, though it was also called the Free City, for although it was technically within Agria's borders, the king (in this case, their old bandmate Matrick) laid no claim to lands so near the savage border. There were no taxes there, no tariff on goods that passed through. Conthas was a bastion of enterprise and opportunity: One of the last wild places in an ever more civilized world.

That being said, Conthas was a shithole, and as far as Clay was concerned the sooner they were rid of it the better.

It was half past noon on the third day since he and Gabe had set out from Coverdale. They were road weary, dust cloaked, and so hungry that Clay's mouth watered when a man outside the gate offered him what appeared to be charred rat-on-a-stick.

The last meal they'd eaten was two days earlier, when a sadistic old farmer had tossed them each an apple for doing push-ups on the road. Clay had found a turtle scrabbling up the muddy slope of a creek bed yesterday, but while he'd busied himself starting a fire Gabe had wandered off with the turtle and set it free. He'd placated Clay with assurances that Kallorek would feed them like kings once they reached the city, and Clay passed those same assurances on to his growling stomach. Sadly, his stomach was less susceptible to bullshit than his head.

Conthas was the same old circus he remembered. No king meant no law; no guards to keep the peace or discourage violence before it got out of hand. No taxes meant no one to clean gutters or lay down stone for roads, and so Clay and Gabriel sloshed through what they hoped was mud as they passed through the wide-open gates into the city whose parents had hired a prostitute as a babysitter and never come home.

The main strip ran along the defile between two hills. The city crawled up either slope like a mould, cloaked in a mantle of cloying grey smoke. Clay could see several fires burning unchecked, but no one seemed overly concerned, and certainly no fire brigade was rushing to put them out. To the north loomed the sealed fortress of Conthas itself, clenched like an iron-shod fist against the glaring sun. Some sort of temple was under construction on the southern hill, unfinished and shrouded in scaffolding.

It was said the Free City drew all sorts, but mostly it drew all sorts of bad. Bright-eyed adventurers from all over Grandual came to Conthas with dreams of joining a band and touring the Wyld, and inevitably those dreams were distorted, like something reflected in a mirror made of shoddy glass. That, or they had the mirror broken over their heads.

You couldn't throw a rock without hitting an adventurer, or a thief, or a thief catcher, a bounty hunter, a smoke wizard, a wandering bard, a claw-broker, a storm witch, a sell-sword—or else those who came to profit off this bunch: armourers and ironmongers, harlots and haruspices, dice men and card sharks. Scratch peddlers skulked in alley mouths, while the addicts on whom they preyed slouched in the mud with knives in their hands, bloody gouges on their arms, and blissful grins on their haggard faces. On every corner was a merchant selling magic swords and impenetrable armour, or an alchemist pawning potions of enchantment, or water breathing, or invisibility. Clay even spotted one labelled IMMORTALITY.

"How much for that?" he asked the old woman selling it.

"One hundred and one courtmarks," she announced. "No refunds."

Clay frowned down at the vial. "Looks like grass and water."

The woman glared at him until he moved on.

On the Street of Shrines they passed temples dedicated to each of the Holy Tetrea. Clay heard screams drifting from the barred windows of the Winter Queen's austere refuge, and moans of pleasure behind the silk curtains of the Spring Maiden's sanctuary. There was a lineup outside the temple of Vail the Heathen. Farmers, he assumed, come to pray for a fair harvest. Many of them carried squirming calves or mewling lambs to be offered up as blood sacrifices to the Autumn Son. One desperate-looking man clutched a mangy cat in his arms. The animal had guessed its fate, apparently, since the farmer's arms and face bore a network of angry red scratch marks.

Priests clad in the red-and-gold vestments of the Summer Lord were shooing a beggar from the steps of their church. The poor wretch was draped in soiled grey robes, and Clay nearly gasped when he spotted the beggar's char-black hands, one of which was reduced to little more than a flailing stump.

A rotter. He grimaced, unable to suppress a shiver. Aside from the more tangible horrors lurking among the poisoned eaves of the Heartwyld, anyone entering the black forest risked being afflicted by the Heathen's Touch, more commonly known as the rot. What began as a dark stain on the skin soon hardened into a black crust that clung to the flesh like barnacles to a boat's hull. Scraping it off was impossible without tearing away swathes of flesh, and it didn't matter anyway, since the crust would grow back regardless. Inevitably it would spread, or manifest itself on some other part of the body. Affected limbs would rot through until they crumbled away, until at last the disease laid claim to the victim's throat, or some vital organ. If they were especially lucky, this happened sooner rather than later. Clay had heard of rotters living for years in restless agony before death finally claimed them.

There were, allegedly, many ways of forestalling the disease—anything from drinking tea brewed from a dryad's eyelashes to visiting an oracle somewhere high in the Rimeshield Mountains—but despite the efforts of Grandual's greatest minds there was no known cure. The rot was a death sentence, plain and simple.

"Clay, look. It's Moog." Gabriel tugged at his sleeve, pointing to a wall plastered with posters. A number of them depicted the wizard, badly drawn but instantly recognizable. He was grinning from ear to ear, one eye closed in a knowing wink.

Clay squinted to read the words scrawled beneath: "Magic Moog's Magnificent Phallic Phylactery. Zero to Hero with just one sip. Satisfaction guaranteed!"

Clay scanned some of the other posters on the wall. One offered a bounty for the toxic breath of a rot sylph, another called for bands willing to kill Hectra, Queen of Spiders. He was wondering whether Hectra was actually a spider or merely a woman who styled herself their monarch when the noise around him disrupted his thoughts.

There were men moving up the street, four abreast and three ranks deep, armed with cudgels and oval shields. They hadn't resorted to violence yet, but had managed to clear a good length of street behind them with iron glares and those big shields. Behind them walked a man in soiled leathers with a wolf's pelt draped over his head. He raised his arms and called out to the crowd.

"Good people of Conthas! Hear me!"

Clay searched the crowd for good people and came up short, but Wolfhead went on nevertheless.

"Make way for the Stormriders, only just returned from a daring tour of the Heartwyld." He waited for the rising babble to subside before going on. "They will be preceded by the Sisters in Steel, who have subdued the goblins of the Cobalt Caverns and their fearsome Warchief, Sicklung!" Wolfhead and his shield-bearing goons pressed on, forcing a path where some were slow to make one.

There was a commotion farther down the street. Peering west, he saw a column meandering down the mudded thoroughfare. The Stormriders—a band, Clay presumed, though he'd never heard of them—would have paid out-of-pocket for a parade through Conthas. And as the procession drew near it became clear that those pockets were very deep indeed.

A cadre of drummers led the way. They were clad in long gowns sewn with strips of bark and hats that sprouted tufts of green foliage. Children scampered among them dressed as wood sprites, gossamer wings trailing behind as they ran. Behind them waddled a huge hulk of a man. Half his face was painted blue, in likeness to the Feral Men who called the black forest home and lived on a diet of flesh and blood—or so the stories went, anyway. Clay had met more than a few cannibals who preferred a well-roasted chicken over the fleshy rump of some hapless adventurer, but chickens (unlike hapless adventurers) were notoriously hard to come by in the Wyld.

The brute was draped in exotic fur, with a horn slung over one shoulder that might once have been a dragon's tooth before someone hollowed it out and made an instrument of it. He jeered at the crowd, working them into a frenzy, and then blew long and deep on the horn. Its call reminded Clay of the wind moaning through high places, or the sound of something wounded wailing in the dark.

Next came the goblins. Two rows of six, each with their hands bound, linked to one another by chains that slithered like iron snakes through the mud. They were a sickly looking bunch, scrawny as beggars, but lively enough. They snapped and screamed gibberish at the crowd, and didn't seem to mind when someone lobbed a bloated tomato or a rotting fish their way.

They're probably starving, Clay reckoned. *Wait till they get a sniff of rat-on-a-stick.*

Behind them came their warchief, Sicklung, limping in his fetters, sporting a face so battered and bruised he looked ugly even by the notoriously low standards of goblinkind.

The Sisters in Steel were not at all what he'd expected. Clay had fought alongside plenty of women warriors in his day, but these three looked nothing of the sort. Their hair was done up in ringlets and tied with bright ribbons. Their eyes were thick with smoky kohl, their lips painted red as roses. And their armour! It looked brittle as porcelain, designed to show off skin instead of protect it from a sword's edge or an arrow's piercing tip. They cantered along on a trio of pristine white mares whose silver barding gleamed like mirrors.

A man out front whistled at one of the Sisters as she passed. *Uh-oh.* Clay winced, preparing himself to see a man trampled into the mud. Instead she smiled and blew him a kiss.

"What in the *fuck*?" Clay heard himself ask of no one in particular.

Beside him, Gabriel bobbed his shoulders. "That's how it is now, man. I told you. So much spectacle, so little substance." He snorted, nodding in the direction of the goblins. "They probably bought those poor buggers at an auction."

The column marched on. Now came the spoils reaped by the Stormriders during their tour of the Wyld. A squad of men marched by bearing relics of the Dominion: blunted swords and rusted scale armour recovered from ancient battlefields.

Next came an ox-drawn cart loaded with the crumbled remains of one of Contha's rune-bound automatons. The pieces were fitted together so observers could apprehend how massive the golem had been in life.

"That's impressive," said Clay. "Those things go down hard."

Four heavily armoured men escorted a lanky troll weighed down by heavy iron manacles. The thing's arms had been severed at the elbow and capped with silver studs to keep it from regenerating new limbs. Two of the men bore torches and used them to corral the beast whenever its coal black eyes lingered too long on someone it thought looked particularly appetizing.

An enormous ape striped like a tiger came after. The woman who held its leash was smiling and waving, occasionally reaching up to stroke the ape's fur. It grinned whenever she did this, evidently besotted by its handler.

A strange hush had come over the crowd. Looking right, Clay saw another cart approaching. It was as wide as the entire street, hauled by six oxen and rolling on ten stone wheels. The steel bars of the cage it carried were as thick as a man's leg, and in the shadows within he saw something—a glimpse of coarse fur, the metallic glint of scales...

"Frost Mother's Hell..." Gabe put a steadying hand on Clay's shoulder.

And then Clay saw for himself what the Stormriders had brought back from the Wyld. It was a chimera. And it was *alive*.

He swallowed hard. Felt a pang in his gut that might have been fear, or exhilaration, or both. Either way, he'd felt nothing quite like it in a long while. He'd once heard someone (Gabe, probably) say that while most things were born to live, an exceptional few were born, instead, to kill. Chimeras were very much the latter.

This one was obviously drugged. Its movements were slow and sluggish. Its serpentine tail hung limp between the bars of its cramped prison. Wings that would throw a house into shadow were folded against its back. Of its three heads—lion, dragon, and ram—only the dragon seemed to take interest in its surroundings. Its jaw was clamped shut by an iron muzzle, and smoke plumed from its nostrils, obscuring the slitted yellow eyes that peered through the bars as if it were the one on the outside looking in.

"Why not kill it?" asked Gabriel.

Clay, who had been thinking the same thing, could only shake his head in wonder. "Spectacle," he said.

At last the Stormriders rolled in. There were five of them standing on a curtained flatbed heaped with treasure. Open chests spilled over with jewels and gemstones, coins glittered in hillocks at their feet. In case the band itself (all of whom were armed) weren't enough to discourage the mob from rushing the cart, there was a full escort of pikemen whose scowls and long spears served to keep the crowd at bay. There were a number of women dressed as nymphs—which was to say they were pretty much naked—who scooped bronze coins by the handful from the wagon's edge and tossed them to the roadside. Clay noted that the gold and silver coins were conveniently piled closer to the centre.

The band looked young to him at first, until Clay remembered he'd been barely eighteen when he and Gabe had first set out on the road. Their armour, at least, looked functional, if a little garish, and Clay suspected they were wearing more makeup than the Sisters in Steel. He also couldn't help but ne large number of young girls who had found their way to the edge of the street and were screaming hysterically as the boys went by.

Clay found himself smiling, recalling the first time he and his bandmates had paraded the spoils of their own Heartwyld tour down this very same street—not that there was much to recall, since they'd all been blind drunk at the time. Moog had slept through most of it; Matrick had fallen from the wagon into the crowd and was missing for three days.

"I've seen enough," said Gabriel. He looked annoyed, suddenly, and Clay wondered if it wasn't jealousy that had soured his mood. "Let's get out of here before this crowd breaks up. Go pay Kallorek a visit."

Clay rolled his neck to work out the kink from looking westward for the past half hour. "Sure thing. Where's he at?"

Gabe nodded toward the southern hill, at the temple under construction at its summit. He scowled like a man gazing up at the noose meant to hang him. "Up there."

Chapter Seven

Swimming with Sharks

There was a pond in the middle of Kallorek's house. The water was so clear Clay could see the tiles that checkered the bottom, blue and white. There were no fish or frogs that he could see. No lilies, or rushes, or dragonflies skimming the surface. There was just . . . empty water.

"What the fuck is the point of this?" he asked.

Gabriel didn't answer. He'd gone meek again, sitting in a wicker chair near the edge of the pond, bullied by his own thoughts. Fair enough, Clay supposed, since he'd come here to beg Kallorek for his sword back, which would have been awkward even if their old booker hadn't also been in possession of something else that had once belonged to Gabe: his wife, Valery.

They hadn't seen her yet, but they'd heard her voice as a servant led them here to wait. Gabriel had frozen at the sound like a mouse cringing at an owl's screech.

One of the many knacks his own wife had instilled in Clay was seeing the bright side in any situation. To know that however bad things seemed there was always someone, somewhere, who had it worse. One look at the slump of Gabe's shoulders, or the small, worried movements of his fingers in his lap, and Clay couldn't help but feel like the most fortunate man in the room.

At least until Kallorek arrived. The booker swept in wearing a deep blue robe of silk so fine it flowed like water over the brink of his voluminous gut. Several heavy-looking gold chains were slung around his neck. Rings set with gaudy gemstones twinkled on every finger and pierced both ears. Clay had seen kings buried with fewer trinkets on their person.

"My boys!" Their host managed to pull Clay and Gabriel both into an awkward hug. His grey-shot beard, once as coarse as a horse brush, was now soft with scented oil and carefully braided. His ruddy skin wafted the scent of sandalwood and spring lilac above the earthen tang of sweat. He had an underbite so vicious that some folk had (out of earshot, of course) dubbed him "the orc."

Kallorek released his grip at last, holding each at arm's length and grinning widely. "Golden Gabe and Slowhand himself," he said wistfully. "Legends in the flesh! Kings of the bloody Wyld, right? You're looking fit as a fresh horse, Cooper. And you, Gabe, look tired. And *old*! Gods of Grandual, man, what's eating you? Not booze again? Or scratch? Don't tell me you've got the bloody rot."

Gabriel tried for a smile and failed spectacularly. "I'm just tired, Kal. And old. And..." He faltered, going a shade paler than he'd already been. "I need to speak to Valery, and to... ask you a favor."

Kallorek looked momentarily suspicious, but his grin quickly returned. "In time, yes? When you've kicked the dust off your boots! Let's open a keg first, and eat. Are you hungry?"

"Starving!" Clay blurted.

"Of course you are!" Kallorek clapped his meaty hands together. "You two hit the pool. I'll have some grub ready when you've had time to freshen up a bit." When his guests made no move he gestured toward the pond behind them.

Clay glanced over his shoulder and back. He shrugged.

"The pool," said Kallorek, pointing. "The pool, right there."

"You mean the pond?"

"I mean the *pool*," growled the booker. "Get in. Swim." He accompanied these words with effusive gestures that set his jewellery ringing.

Clay examined the pond. "Swim to where?" he asked.

"What do you mean *swim to where*?" Kallorek's brow deepened.

"Is it a healing spring?" Gabe asked. He flexed his arm, wincing as he extended it fully. "Because I think my elbow—"

"Listen, fuck your elbow!" Kallorek blew up. Clay had forgotten how short the booker's fuse was. That big toothy smile one moment, and the next... "It ain't a spring, or a pond, or a godsdamned sea nymph's bathtub. It's a fucking *pool*. Just a pool! You swim around in it to relax."

Clay was wise enough to know that suggesting Kallorek make use of the pool himself would only provoke him further, but Gabriel wasn't—and so the moment he opened his mouth Clay shoved him hard into the water, where he splashed and spat and scrabbled like a dog for the shore.

Kallorek's rage dissipated; he burst into a fit of laughter that left him wiping tears from his eyes.

"You're right," said Clay. "I feel better already."

Say one thing about Kallorek: The man was as vile as a two-headed toad. But say another and it was this: That fat bastard sure knew how to eat.

The meal lulled Clay into a near-euphoric daze for which he was doubly grateful, since Valery (in a daze herself) had opted to join them at the dining room table. She didn't say much, but loosed a lot of long sighs, and giggled here and there at something only she found funny, like when two of her maple-glazed sprouts stuck together, or the sound her knife made when she clacked it again and again and again against the honey crisped skin of her rolled pork loin.

Clay's eyes were drawn time and again to the scars

half-hidden by her shirt sleeve. He'd heard from Gabriel that Valery had been dabbling with scratch—a drug made from the venom of dazeworms and introduced to the system by cutting tiny nicks in the soft skin on the underside of one's arm. It looked as though she were using still, since a few of those wounds were raw and red.

Watching her now, Clay could hardly believe this was the same woman Gabe had fallen in love with so many years ago, the woman many claimed was singlehandedly responsible for breaking up the greatest mercenary band in Grandual's history. She wasn't, of course—that had been a different woman altogether—but although Valery hadn't been responsible for sinking the ship, she sure as hell had punched a few holes in the hull.

Gabe and Val first met at the War Fair, a triannual festival held among the ruins at Kaladar, the ancient seat of Dominion power. For three riotous days in late fall, every band, bard, and booker in each of the five courts gathered to fight, fuck, and drink themselves blind. Valery, however, had been attending in protest. She'd been part of a faction called the Getalongs, who held the idealistic—if unpopular—opinion that humans and monsters could peacefully coexist. As a roundabout means of getting their point across they decided to set fire to Saga's argosy, the house on wheels the band used as a base of operations.

The Getalongs were driven off before any harm could be done, but Valery was taken captive by Gabriel, who insisted she attend the party he was hosting within. Clay remembered how absurd she'd looked sitting amidst so many rowdy, hard-bitten mercenaries: tall and wisp-thin, with ivory skin and hair like fine-spun gold. She'd been wearing a dress that was little more than a shift, and there'd been a wreath of flowers on her brow. Like a princess in the company of orcs, Clay had remarked at the time, though he was quite sure no one heard him say so.

At any rate, she and Gabriel had been at each other's throats right from the beginning. Clay had heard it said that some couples were like fire and ice, but although Gabe and Val held opposing ideologies they were more like identical clashing swords. On fire. In an ice storm. What had begun as a playful interrogation by Gabriel for the amusement of his guests became an intense discussion, then a heated argument, then a violent shouting match, during which Valery made a second attempt at burning down Saga's war wagon by hurling a lamp at Gabriel's head.

By morning they were madly in love.

Val left the Getalongs, which proved a timely decision, since a week later they accepted an invitation to feast with a tribe of wild centaurs without realizing they were intended as the feast. She accompanied Saga on their following tour, often clashing with Kallorek when it came to determining which gig they would tackle next. More and more often Gabriel conferred with Valery on matters that concerned the entire band, which suited Moog and Clay just fine, but didn't sit very well with Matrick, or Ganelon, who endured her condemnation of his violent nature the way a mountain endures a goat scampering up its backside—until, that is, the first flower showed up in Gabriel's hair...

The sharp nudge of Gabe's elbow in his ribs prompted Clay to realize he'd been asked a question. "Yes. No. What?" he asked, effectively covering all his bases.

"How old is your little girl now?" Kal repeated. "Talyn, was it?

"Tally. She turned nine this summer."

"Tally? That short for something?"

"Talia," Clay told him.

"Mmm." Kallorek appeared less interested in Clay's answer than in heaping beef gravy onto a slab of thickly buttered bread. "And how about yours, Gabe?"

Gabe, positioned opposite the booker, sat straight-backed with his hands in his lap, having barely touched his food at all. "My what?" he asked.

"Your daughter," said Kallorek around a sloppy mouthful. "Her and that gang of rejects she calls a band came round, what, seven or eight months ago? Said they had a huge gig lined up—but didn't need a booker, mind you—and were looking for handouts. Asked if I could spare some gear."

"Rose was here?" Gabe asked.

Kallorek licked gravy from his fingers. "I told her I'd think on it, but I ain't running a charity, you know. I'm a collector. A curator of rare and beautiful things." Perhaps unconsciously—but perhaps not—he took Valery's hand in his own. She blinked and smiled as though a butterfly had flitted past her nose, but said nothing. "Anyway, the little runt stole a few priceless relics and took off in the night. Haven't heard a peep from her since."

Gabriel looked over pleadingly, but Clay was in the midst of a long, lingering sip of wine that he planned on stretching out for as long as it took his friend to explain what had happened to Rose and what they planned to do about it.

As Gabe did so, Clay watched over the lip of his cup as Kallorek's bushy brows climbed toward his greasy scalp. Valery listened in silence, her expression unreadable, occasionally rubbing at the cuts on her arm. At the mention of Castia her eyes widened, and for an instant there was *something*—a glimpse of grief, faint as the wail of a prisoner echoing up dungeon stairs—before her gaze drifted off into nowhere. When Gabriel had finished Kallorek sighed and tugged at his braided beard, while Valery fashioned a placid smile and murmured to no one in particular, "That's nice."

Poor Gabe looked as though he'd been stabbed. Clay half-expected that disbelief to boil over into anger, but Gabriel just shook his head and returned his attention to the untouched plate before him.

Kallorek called for a servant to take Valery to her room. The three of them ate dessert (a chocolate pie topped with chopped almonds and whipped cream) and sipped sweet red beer in mildly uncomfortable silence. Afterward, Kal offered to show them around his estate, which had originally been intended as a grand temple to the Autumn Son.

"They sunk a lot of coin into it," he told them, "but were halfway finished when someone had the bright idea of putting one right down in the gutter." *The gutter* was what those who lived on the slopes in Conthas called the valley bottom. "And there's no sense walking up a hill to talk to a god when he can hear you at the bottom just fine, now is there?"

"Why build the temple at all?" Clay ventured. "Seems cheaper just to shout at the sky."

Kallorek looked at him as though Clay had suggested putting out a fire by tossing a few logs on it. "Shout at the... What the fuck are you on about, Slowhand?"

"Nothing. Never mind."

"At any rate," Kal went on eventually, "the priests up here went bankrupt, so I swept in and bought the place for the price of the nails."

They toured an open garden, following a stone path between apple trees heavy with fruit. There were guards patrolling the compound walls—a necessary deterrent, Kallorek explained, since the chapel now housed his increasingly valuable collection of rare memorabilia.

"You still handling mercenaries?" Clay wondered.

"Of course," Kal assured him. "But it ain't like the old days. The whole operation is too big to handle myself, so I assign an agent to each band. They book the smaller gigs—goblins and whatnot—while I give the big contracts to those I think can handle it. My cut is half, the agent takes ten, and the band splits whatever's left over."

Half? Clay would have choked had he still been eating. Things had changed drastically since he'd been touring. Back then, Kallorek had split a 15-percent share with Saga's five other members. The remaining ten was supposed to have belonged to their bard, but since none of Saga's bards lived long enough to collect their share, it was chiefly used for what Gabe had called "adventuring essentials"—which was to say booze, tobacco, and the company of indiscriminate women. Considering what mercenaries were paid nowadays, it was little wonder Kallorek could afford to live as he did now.

"So who do you book for?" Gabe asked as they neared a pair of tall bronze doors. "Anyone we'd know?"

Kallorek chortled at that. "*Everyone* you'd know. I've got agents all over Agria. There ain't a band west of Fivecourt doesn't owe me a slice. Well, except your old pals Vanguard, actually."

"Vanguard's still touring?" Clay asked.

"Most of 'em," said Kal, without bothering to explain what that meant.

Vanguard. Now *there* was a name Clay hadn't heard in a long while. Barret Snowjack and his eclectic bandmates—Ashe, Tiamax, and Hog—had been friendly rivals of Saga back in the day. To hear they were still on the road, still fighting after all these years . . . well, it made Clay's back hurt just to think of it.

"If someone runs a gang of kobolds out of a sewer," Kal was saying, "I make all my cupboard-handles silver. If they turn in the bounty on a basilisk broodmother, well, I add a new wing to the house."

"Or put a pond in it," said Clay.

"You mean a pool," the booker was quick to correct.

"What did I say?"

"You said *pond*—"

"Where's my sword?" Gabe interrupted.

Kallorek scowled. "What's that now?"

"*Vellichor*. Where is it?"

Kal's face was hard to read. He looked like a parent deciding how best to discipline an unruly child. They'd arrived at the massive bronze doors, and the booker hauled one open, beckoning Clay and Gabriel to follow him inside. "This way," he said.

Chapter Eight

Vellichor

He led them into a vaulted chapel lit bright with mirrored lamps. The pews had been removed, and the stone floor was laid with rich carpets. The hall itself was in disarray, haphazardly cluttered with shelves, display cases, weapons racks, overflowing chests, and wooden dummies half-clothed in armour scraps.

"Excuse the mess," said Kallorek, surveying the room. "I'm still sorting it all out. Hey, look at this." He plucked a helmet off a dummy's head. It sported a pair of long cheek guards that jutted like poison-laced mandibles. "This belonged to Liac the Arachnian. Poor Liac got devoured by a crypt slime a few years back. This here was all that remained." Kallorek replaced the helm and ran a hand over the coat of red mail beneath it. "The *Warskin*," he said reverently. "The impenetrable armour of Jack the Reaver. No sword or spear can pierce it, they say, but syphilis got through all right. Poor Jack."

He waded farther into the room, pointing out artifacts as he named them. "There's the *Witchbow*, and here are the gauntlets of Earl the One-Handed." Kallorek waved at a bookshelf set against one wall. "Those were written before the fall of the Dominion. And these boots were worn by Budika, the Sea Wolf of Salagad. So many precious treasures!" he exclaimed. "But none so prized as this..."

He gestured toward a raised dais at the end of the hall, where a statue of the Autumn Son towered in the gloom. The statue's face had been crudely altered to resemble Kallorek, and though it bore Vail's characteristic torch in one hand, the sickle in his other had been replaced with...

A sword, Clay realized, in the same moment he heard Gabe speak softly beside him.

"Vellichor."

From this distance the blade glowed faintly blue-green. A subtle mist rolled down the weapon's length, drifting from the tip like smoke from an extinguished candle.

If his friend had seemed unsettled by the sight of his ex-wife, he now looked positively dumbstruck, his expression a mix of awe and shame, like a father gazing upon the face of a child he'd been forced by poverty to sell into bondage. When he spoke his voice was unsure, wavering. "You said I could have it. You said if I ever *really* needed it—" He swallowed, and Clay saw the sheen of tears in his eyes. "I need it now, Kal. I really do."

Kallorek was silent for a long time, idly fingering one of the heavy medallions on his chest. "Did I say that?" he asked, affecting an air of abashed innocence. "It sure doesn't sound like me. If I remember correctly I paid a princely sum for that sword. Enough to clear your debt with the Mercenary's Guild. I'd say I've a fair claim to it. In fact, I'd say it's well and truly mine."

"You said if I—"

The booker waved dismissively. "Yeah, yeah, you said what I said already. But like I *also* said, I've grown rather fond of it since then. Druin swords don't exactly grow on trees, you know, and that brat daughter of yours stole a pair of 'em from me. Doubt I'll be seeing those blades ever again."

"Kal, I promise—" Gabe began, but Kallorek rolled on over him.

"And now you'd have me lend you what is, quite possibly, the most coveted weapon in all of Grandual so...what? So you can take it into the bloody Heartwyld? It might be years before someone stumbles across your bones and brings it back to me." He crossed his hairy arms. "No. Best it remains right where it is, I think."

The barest flicker of anger lit Gabriel's face as he started toward the booker. "Listen, you—" he said, before a pair of broad-shouldered constructs came plodding from the shadows of nearby alcoves. Each of the golems were half again as tall as Clay, though much smaller than the one they'd seen during the Stormriders' parade. Both were the matte black of old basalt, with runes carved into their eye sockets that pulsed a vibrant green as they answered to some unheard command. The glass of display cases rattled as they moved to intercept Gabriel. They were two strides away when Kallorek raised a hand.

"Hold on," said the booker, and Clay noticed he was clutching the medallion he'd been toying with earlier. A rune identical to that in the golems' eyes blazed there. The automatons stopped dead. "How's this then, Gabe? If you can take it, *Vellichor* is yours."

It took Gabriel a moment to tear his eyes from the nearest golem. "Really?"

"Really truly," said Kallorek, stepping aside with a flourish. He was grinning again, but there was no mirth in it. He'd been a common criminal in his youth, Clay remembered. His brutish nature had served him well as a booker who occasionally needed to extort payment from those who reneged on a contract. As grateful as Clay had once been for the ruthless flavour of Kallorek's past, it was beginning to taste awfully bitter now.

"Go ahead," Kallorek urged. "Take it."

Gabriel slunk forward warily. He tripped over the corner of a gilded sarcophagus and barely caught himself.

The booker sniggered. "Careful. Kit the Unkillable's in that thing. Dead as a doornail, but he walks and talks just the same. Talks a little too much for his own good, actually. I locked him in there for a reason."

Gabriel climbed the steps of the dais one at a time. When he reached the top he turned and looked back. At a loss for inspiring words, Clay could only nod. He didn't think for a moment Gabe could wrest the sword from the statue's grip, and it was quite obvious Kallorek didn't, either.

Then again, the fact that Clay was here at all instead of at home with his wife and child was testament to the fact that Gabriel was, if anything, full of surprises.

Gabe gave the blade a quick tug first. When it didn't budge he stretched his shoulders and cleared his throat. He placed a bracing hand on the statue's elbow and gripped the hilt just under the guard, trying to push the blade forward. Long seconds passed. Gabriel stopped, flexed his fingers, and tried again. Kallorek and his golems watched in silence. The booker was clearly amused; the golems didn't appear to give a shit. Clay found he'd stopped breathing. He prayed silently that *Vellichor* would slip suddenly free, waited to hear the clang as it struck the floor.

Instead he heard a low whine, so quiet it seemed to come from a long way off. The whine grew louder, finally stretching into a long and lingering squeal as Gabriel poured all his strength into pushing the weapon loose. At last he gave up and stood panting, staring down at his own right hand as if it had somehow betrayed him.

"So, Slowhand." Kallorek turned his way, good-natured once again. "I see you've got *Blackheart* still. Can't be much use for a treasure like that standing on a wall up north, can there? How about I buy it off you, eh?"

"It's not for sale," said Clay, really not liking the direction this was going.

"Oh, come on, now. I'd say a relic like that is worth... let's call it five hundred courtmarks? A man in your position has more use for gold than for a ratty old shield, does he not?"

Five hundred courtmarks! Clay tried to keep his face impassive. Kallorek had never been one for bartering when he could bludgeon instead. With five hundred gold coins Clay could buy himself a whole new life. He could send his daughter to a proper school in Oddsford. He could give up the Watchmen's Green and open that inn he and Ginny had so often discussed. Of course he'd always imagined mounting *Blackheart* in a place of honour above the hearth, but he could find something else to put there instead. A painting, maybe. Or a stag's head. Who didn't enjoy the glassy stare of a severed animal's head gazing down at them as they ate supper?

Kallorek took note of Clay's hesitation and kept on, his voice sweet as syrup. "You're on a fool's errand, Slowhand. You'll be lucky if that shield is all you lose." He waved toward Gabriel, who was now suspended off the floor, trying desperately to pry the statue's stone fingers apart. "Do you really want to risk crossing the Heartwyld? If the monsters don't kill you the Feral Men will. Or the rot..." He shook his head. "And you think the others will drop whatever they're doing and tag along? Moog's got a thriving business to keep him busy, and Matrick's a king—ain't no way he'd give that up, not for all the icicles in hell. And Ganelon... well, I reckon he has a mighty hate-on for the lot of you—and for good reason."

"Ow!" Gabe had somehow cut himself on *Vellichor*'s edge. Clutching his bloodied hand to his chest, he aimed a few sad kicks at the flat of the blade, hoping to jar it loose.

Somewhere, thought Clay, *poor dead Vespian is rolling in his grave*. He couldn't help but smirk to imagine it. *Kick this if you need to...*

Kallorek laughed. "There's an enchantment on the statue," he told Clay. "It'll never come loose unless the spell is broken.

Can't have someone slipping in here and just taking the thing, now can I?"

Clay sighed. He'd have to tell Gabriel eventually, though it would shame his friend to hear it. Kallorek, meanwhile, mistook Clay's reaction for resignation. "I knew you'd come around, Slowhand. You were always the smart one. Frankly I'm surprised Gabe managed to drag you this far, but lucky for you he did. Now, let's have that shield of yours and I'll go count out your coin, eh?"

Clay smiled politely. "I don't think so, Kal."

The booker's toothy grin withered like a cock in cold water. "Oh, you don't think so?" When Clay started toward the dais Kallorek imposed his bulk before him. "Rose is as good as dead," he growled. "I know it. Valery knows it. You two clowns are the only ones this side of the Wyld who haven't clued in yet. She's *dead*, and so is Gabe if he's fool enough to go after her." The booker was close enough that Clay could smell the foul waft of his breath. "The offer's changed on that shield, by the way. One hundred courtmarks. One hundred and I *don't* dress you and this sorry sack of shit up in plate armour and toss you both into the fucking pool. How's that sound?"

"What's a pool?" Clay asked, and when Kal took a breath to berate him he grabbed hold of the medallion the booker had used to compel the golems and punched him hard in the face. Kallorek staggered back, tripping over the gilded sarcophagus of Kit the Unkillable as the chain around his neck snapped free in a spray of broken ringlets.

"New offer, Kal," said Clay, inspecting the medallion. It seemed to vibrate in his hand, and was curiously warm to the touch. "You run away as fast as you can, and I give you a five-second head start before I tell these boys—" he motioned at the two looming sentinels "—to make you the meat in a golem sandwich."

Kallorek's face was a mess of dark red blood. He fingered a

tooth as if he thought Clay's punch might have broken it. "You son of a bitch! I swear by the Winter Queen's frozen tits—"

"Four..." Clay began counting.

"Clay, please," the booker said, trying a different tack. "I was kidding! It was all in fun, right? Surely you—"

"Three..."

"Wait, what about—"

"Two..."

Kallorek bolted. Clay waited until his heavy footfalls receded and then moved to the dais. Gabriel was slumped at the foot of the statue. His arms hung limp at his side. Blood coated the fingers of his right hand, spattering drop by drop on the stone floor.

"Gabe—"

"Do you think he's right?"

Clay blinked. "Sorry?"

"About Rose. Do you think she's dead?"

She might be, Clay thought, but didn't say. "We'll find her, Gabe. But we need to get out of here now. Kal's gone to fetch his guards."

He could hear the booker shouting beyond the chapel's heavy doors. From nearby, though, came the growl of grinding stone. Glancing around, Clay saw the heavy lid of the sarcophagus Gabe and Kal had each tripped over sliding ajar. A pair of desiccated fingers scrabbled around the edge, seeking purchase.

Whatever Kit the Unkillable was—and Clay was fairly certain it wasn't necessarily *alive*—was about to break free. He decided to be far away from here when it did.

He held up the medallion that controlled the golems, unsure if it mattered that they could see it. "Pick him up," he ordered, and one moved to obey. He addressed the other, pointing at the wall. "Make a door here, please."

Saying please to a golem, Cooper? Wouldn't Ginny be proud...

The construct's rune-scribed eyes burned green. It obliged

by using its shoulder to ram a hole in the brick, then battering away with its fist until the portal was wide enough. It was dark outside. The night breeze carried only the faintest scent of the city below; smoke and the sour pong of humans mucking about in the mud.

"Let's go," Clay said. He followed the first golem out while the other plodded after, bearing Gabe in its arms.

Chapter Nine

The Heathen's Touch

Around noon on the next day they came across a farmer whose wagon had collapsed beneath the weight of several enormous bales of hay. One of his sons had joined a band in the summer, he told them. The other had gone into Conthas to watch the parade and was late coming back. Clay presented the man with Kallorek's medallion and explained what he knew of how it worked.

"I'd wait until dark to use them," he warned, indicating the towering sentinels with a thumb. "There'll be a very ugly, very angry, very dangerous man looking out for these over the next few weeks."

The farmer's gratitude was profuse. His first command to the pair of golems was that they wave good-bye to Clay and Gabe as they set off down the road. So that was pretty weird.

"There it is."

Gabe pointed to a ruined tower on a forested hill, stark against the white autumn sky. It reminded Clay of a crooked finger, or a broken fang, until he remembered the posters he'd seen in town for Magic Moog's Magnificent Phallic Phylactery—and then it reminded him of something else entirely.

"Looks like he's home," said Clay, nodding at the torrent of blue-green smoke steaming from a hole in the crumbling roof.

The door was the only part of the building that seemed in good repair. It was sturdy oak, with a brass knocker moulded into the wizened face of a satyr with a ring set into its mouth. When Gabe gave the knocker a desultory clack its features sprang to life.

"Yeth?"

Gabe scratched the side of his head. "Sorry?"

"Thtate your bithineth with my mathter," said the knocker.

"What?"

"Why are you here?" it asked, carefully enunciating each word around the ring in its mouth.

Gabriel looked back at Clay, who answered with one of the numerous shrugs in his repertoire. "Uh . . . to see Moog?"

"To thee Moog!" the face repeated, hampered by its lisp. "And who, may I athk, ith calling?"

"Gabriel. And Clay Cooper."

"Exthellent. Pleath wait here. My mathter will be with you mo—"

The door was suddenly thrown open, and there was Moog. He was wearing what looked to Clay like one-piece pyjamas: tiny moons and stars scattered across a dark blue sky. He was skinny as ever, and his long beard was white as cotton. He'd gone bald up top, but the fringe that remained was long and wisp thin. His eyes were the same startling blue beneath bushy white brows.

"Gabriel! Clay!" The wizard cackled delightedly and did a little dance that only reinforced the fact that he was dressed like a child, then threw his spindly arms around both men at once. "Tits and Tiny Gods, how long has it been?" He scowled at the brass knocker. "Steve. Have I not told you a thousand times we don't keep friends waiting outside?"

"Exthcuthe me, thir. But theeth are the firtht friendth you've had vithit."

"The first? Well I suppose they are, but..." He raised an admonishing finger to the face in the door. "Bad start, Steve. Bad start."

The knocker managed a frown despite the ring in its mouth. "Ath you thay, thir."

"Yes, well, never mind it. Come, come!" He beckoned his guests to follow him inside. As Clay had feared, there was a buttoned flap in the rear of the wizard's garment. "You've come at the perfect time!"

Moog's home was much as Clay imagined it would be. The majority of the tower floor was given over to counters crowded with glass alchemical globes and an assortment of dangerously unlabelled decanters. There were shelves along one wall crammed with books and a fairly typical collection of wizardly reagents—grinning skulls, bundled herbs, jars filled with everything from floating eyes to what was either a milky-white dragon embryo or a calcified yam.

Against the opposite wall were perhaps a dozen stacked cages of various size, each home to some creature or another. He recognized a few of them—there was a badger in one cage, a skunk in another—but some of the others, like the dog-sized elephant or what looked to Clay like an eight-legged weasel with heads on both ends of its sleek body, were unsettlingly new.

Also unsettling was the long wooden table basked in slanting light, upon which something vaguely humanoid was draped in a white shroud.

The wizard crossed to the table, motioning on his way toward a steaming cauldron hunkered below the fireplace mantle. "Are you two hungry?"

Clay thought of the blue-green smoke they'd seen from the road. Whatever was in the pot looked like soup but smelled like burning hair. "Just ate, thanks. For what?"

Moog looked back, frowning. "What?"

"The perfect time for what?" Clay prompted.

The wizard whirled and favoured them both with a rueful smile. "To witness a miracle," he told them, taking hold of the shroud.

Don't be a corpse, Clay prayed under his breath. *Please, don't be a corpse.* Moog had been a staunch enemy of necromancy his entire life, but when you left lonely old wizards in ancient towers for too long, it stood to reason they'd start meddling with dark and unfathomable powers sooner or later.

Moog tore away the sheet with a dramatic flourish. What lay beneath was not, thankfully, a dead person. In fact, it wasn't a person at all. It was a treant, like the one Clay had killed and carved up for the wood to make his shield, except that Blackheart had been a hoary old oak ten times the height of a man and strong enough to tear a bull in half. This creature was a small, scrawny-looking ash. And more to the point: It wasn't dead.

It was, however, very angry. The moment it saw Moog the treant began thrashing against the cords binding it to the table. The branches too small to serve as limbs all strained toward the wizard, seeking to grasp hold of him. Though this creature looked far too frail to threaten a full-grown man, Clay was reminded again of Hollow Hill. The treants there had been huge and hale, capable of swallowing men whole or snapping them, ironically, like twigs.

There was something odd about this one, though. Its flesh, or bark, or whatever you called the skin of a tree that wasn't really a tree, was dappled with dark lichen. The fungus was spread over much of its torso and face. A few of its limbs seemed affected as well; the leaves that clung to these were withered and grey-brown, like parchment rescued too late from a fire.

"Why do you—" Gabe began, but cut off abruptly when the tree snapped what passed for its face in his direction. It shrieked at him, a sound halfway between a gargle and a snore.

Moog laid a calming hand on the creature's trunk, commanding its attention once again. Its gnarled boughs scrabbled weakly against his arm.

"Shhh. It's okay, Turing. It's okay. These are my friends. Gabriel and Clay. I've told you about them, remember? They've come to watch me cure you."

Turing seemed decidedly uninterested. One of his blackened branches made a weak stab for Moog's eye, but the wizard casually swatted it away.

"Cure him of what?" Gabriel asked, and Clay wondered briefly if Turing the treant had come to reap the "restorative" benefits of Magic Moog's phylactery.

The wizard looked up. The mirth had drained from his bright blue eyes and left them as cold and hard as a shallow pond in winter. "The rot," Moog said.

Wizards were obsessive by nature, and Moog was no exception. There were two things about which he'd been passionate for near as long as Clay had known him.

The first of these was the owlbear, a mythical creature that no one alive had ever seen but whose existence Moog (along with a pathetically small society of owlbear enthusiasts) staunchly asserted.

The second was the rot, which had claimed the lives of a great many fellow adventurers, including the man Moog had loved more than anyone in the world: his husband, Fredrick. Even before Fredrick found himself afflicted by the Heathen's Touch, Moog had nursed an interest in curing the infamously incurable disease. Afterward he became increasingly (and understandably) preoccupied by it. When the bonds that bound Saga began to fray, the wizard fairly leapt at the chance to quit the band and devote himself entirely to fighting the illness.

Alas, the rot had proved too implacable a foe for both Moog and his husband alike. Fredrick succumbed within months of Saga's breakup, but Moog, apparently, had not yet given up on overcoming their old nemesis, which had taken everything from the wizard and, as yet, given nothing but grief in return.

Turing was dead.

Night had fallen, and Clay could see stars peeping through the roof beyond the crumbling second storey. Gabriel hauled the cauldron out of the hearth and got a real fire going, and Clay, rummaging through the tower's pantry, found a loaf of stale bread, a basket of overripe tomatoes, and a brick of hard cheese. So he made sandwiches.

Moog had, throughout the course of the afternoon, moved from sulking over the treant's corpse to sulking amidst the clutter of laboratory equipment to sulking while sitting on the steps to the upper floor. Currently he was curled up and hugging his knees in a huge armchair, sulking.

"It's hopeless," he muttered, as he had done every few minutes over the past two hours. His bony fingers clutched at his long white beard, and his eyes darted frantically, like a man who'd poisoned his wife and was expecting her ghost to appear any minute and cuss him out.

"You did your best," said Gabriel, though even he sounded unconvinced by the platitude.

Moog didn't bother responding, except to mutter "Hopeless" again beneath his breath.

Clay spent a good while ruminating on his sandwich and chewing on what to say next. Direct consolation seemed a wasted effort, and it had never been one of Clay's strengths anyway. He opted for a different tactic, one that he used now and again on Tally when she was being obstinate: distraction.

"Those creatures in the cages, they all have the rot?" He got a brooding nod in response. "Did you collect them yourself?"

The wizard stirred, glanced sullenly toward the stacked cages, and then nodded. "Most of them, yes."

"Is that wise?" Clay prodded. "The Heartwyld's a dangerous place."

Moog rubbed at his eyes with the back of one hand. He really did look like a child in those ridiculous pyjamas. "I bought a few of them, like Turing, off of mercenaries. But not many mercs are brave enough to dare the Wyld anymore. The Renegades do. And I hear the Stormriders just wrapped up a successful tour. Which reminds me: They have a parade in Conthas tomorrow."

"It was yesterday," said Gabriel.

Moog only blinked. "Oh."

Clay swiped crumbs from the front of his shirt. "Do you hire bodyguards, at least?"

That drew a scoff from the wizard, who gestured at their humble surroundings. "I can hardly afford to pay off goons every time I need a specimen," he declared. "Alchemy is a costly hobby, I fear. I barely make ends meet selling my phylactery. Frigid Hells, if it wasn't for the limp dicks of Conthas I'd be flat broke! Besides, I'm careful about setting foot in the forest. I *am* a frigging wizard, after all, not some street magician peddling cantrips for silver shillings! I can handle a few monsters!"

Moog's dogged good cheer was making its inevitable return, but Clay's concern was mounting as well. "It's not monsters I'm worried about," he stated. "What if you—"

It was the look on Gabriel's face that cut him short, and Clay cursed himself for a fool. The wizard had been grieving all evening. Reminding him of Turing's death, or of Fredrick's for that matter, was both counterproductive and cruel. Moog, however, loosed a chuckle that bore only the barest trace of bitterness.

"If I what, Clay? If I get the rot, you mean?"

"Well, yes. Exactly."

"I've already got it."

Chapter Ten

Through the Looking Glass

"Listen, you don't—" Clay faltered. "If you—" and faltered again. "What? No. Just . . . no," he repeated, like an idiot.

Gabriel looked dumbfounded, like a man who'd found himself stuck on the pointy end of a centaur's lance.

The wizard, meanwhile, lifted his left foot and removed his slipper, so that Clay could see the black crust sheathing his two smallest toes. "Don't worry," he assured them, "it's not contagious. There's only one way to get the Heathen's Touch, and that's to be cracked enough to spend time in the forest."

Clay considered a number of responses, many of which involved calling Moog a bloody fucking fool, but then he tossed them aside and settled on "Why?"

"Why put myself in danger?" Moog asked, replacing his slipper and sitting up in his chair. "Because I needed specimens, like Turing, who were actually infected. I needed to see what didn't work at all, and what almost worked, and then figure out how come."

"Why not ask"—*rotters*, he'd almost said—"people who are already infected? We saw one in Conthas."

The wizard shrugged his bony shoulders. "I couldn't afford to feed them. And besides, with people . . . there's too many emotions involved. Theirs and mine. I mean, you see how upset I am over Turing, and he was a tree! He tried to strangle me in my sleep once, you know." Moog smiled wistfully. "I'm going to miss that cheeky little bugger."

"And what if there is no cure?" said Clay. "What if you're wasting your time? What if you've thrown your life away for nothing?"

The wizard's melancholy smile remained firmly in place. "Yes, well, what choice do I have? I've devoted nearly half my life in search of a cure for this damnable disease, and I'm no closer now than when I started. I'm not married, I have no children. You have a little girl, right?"

"I do, but—"

"You *both* do," said Moog. "And Matty's got, what, five, six kids now? *And* he's the Glif-kissing king of Agria! And Ganelon...well, he's frigging Ganelon, isn't he? But me? What sort of legacy will I leave behind? I've got no family, no friends, except for you guys. What have I done that's *worth* anything?"

"Well..." Clay looked desperately at a crate stamped with Magic Moog's winking visage.

"Ah, yes, I *do* have erectile dysfunction by the throat!" He gave a derisive snort and curled his fingers around the imaginary neck of...well, Clay let that image slide right on out of mind. "No," said Moog finally. "The rot has defined my life for so many years. It might as well define my death as well. Unless, of course, I find a cure. Now who wants hot chocolate?"

Clay opened his mouth and closed it. They could be at this for hours, going round and round in the ruts carved out by earlier arguments, but he knew it was no use. Moog was stubborn as a bugbear on its birthday when he set his mind to something—this business with the rot was evidence of that—and had always dealt with grief in his own unusual way.

And besides, Gabriel had raised his hand. "I wouldn't mind some," he said.

Moog bounded to his feet. He poured water from an ewer into a brass kettle and hung it over the fire, then went to a cupboard and withdrew something wrapped in cloth that turned out to be a brick of black chocolate. "So what brings the two of you here?" he called over his shoulder. "Don't tell me Matty invited you and not me to the Council of Courts?"

"The what of the what?" Clay asked.

The wizard pared off a slab of chocolate and used a mortar and pestle to grind it into powder. "Oh, it's got something to do with that Horde laying siege to Castia. They say a druin's the one who got all those monsters riled up in the first place. He arrived in Fivecourt a few weeks ago and demanded a meeting with the high and mighty of Grandual."

"A druin?" Clay said.

"Where's the meeting?" asked Gabriel.

Moog looked from one to the other. "A druin, yes. He calls himself the Duke of Endland."

Clay used his tongue to ferret a tomato seed from between his two front teeth. "Since when does the Republic have dukes?"

"It doesn't," said Moog. "I doubt this druin has anything to do with the Republic. In fact, I'd say it's clear he doesn't like them very much. It's possible the 'duke' thing is for the benefit of the courts. It's a familiar title, regal enough to command their attention, but not as overtly pretentious as, say, Supreme God-Emperor of the City Formerly Known as Castia."

"Fair enough," Clay said with a shrug.

"Or maybe he's just an asshole," suggested Gabriel.

"Maybe," Moog agreed, chuckling. "As for the council, it's being held right here in Agria."

"And all of Grandual's monarchs will be there?" Clay asked.

The wizard nodded. "Those who are able will no doubt attend, and those who aren't will send emissaries in their stead. Whether or not he's an actual duke, having a hundred thousand monsters at his command gives the fellow a fair bit of clout. That, and it's not every day you see a real live druin."

True enough, thought Clay. He'd only seen a handful in his life, and they'd all been hiding out in the Heartwyld.

Although the druins were rare enough to be considered harmless, they tended to steer clear of human populations, since most people tended to harbour a certain animosity for immortal beings who had once treated their kind as chattel.

It also didn't help that scrubbing one's scalp with a druin's blood was said to cure baldness—this dubious fact alone made them fair game for bounty hunters the world over.

"Will the courts send an army, do you think?" Gabe sounded hopeful, and Clay, too, felt hope flutter in his gut. If the kings and queens of Grandual decided to send a professional army against the Heartwyld Horde, maybe he could go home after all.

Stow the thought, Cooper, he told himself. *How long will it take for a host that big to gather? How long to march that many men and women through the Heartwyld and over the mountains beyond? Months, at least. Half a year, maybe. And how long do you think Castia can hold out?*

"Beats me," said Moog, answering Clay's unasked question along with Gabriel's inquiry. "Agria and Cartea are at each other's throats these days. The Narmeeri tend to keep to themselves, and the northerners hardly get along with one another, let alone the rival courts." He spooned the chocolate powder into a pair of cups. "As for the Phantrans . . . well, they've got all of Grandual between them and the forest, and I hear the fishmen have started raiding their coasts."

"You mean the saig?"

The wizard shrugged. "I think *fishmen* sounds cooler."

"It doesn't," Clay assured him.

When the kettle began whistling Moog crossed to retrieve it, then poured its scalding contents into each mug and began stirring. "You never answered the question, by the by. What brings you two to my humble tower?"

Clay looked over at Gabriel, who was busy gazing up at the stars beyond the second floor. *Guess this is up to me, then,* he thought with a sigh. "We're headed to Castia."

Tink-tink-tink . . . The stirring spoon fell silent.

"What? Castia? Frigid Hells, *why*? It's about to be wiped off the map by the biggest Horde on record since the Reclamation!"

"Yeah, we know. Gabe's daughter is inside."

The wizard's face dropped. "Ah . . ."

"So we're . . ." Clay swallowed. *Just say it, Cooper.* "We're getting the band back together. Or hoping to, anyway." He lapsed into silence and waited for Moog to fill it with excuses. He had his phylactery business to think of, an elusive cure to find. Who would look after his animals? He was too tired, too old. He would rather die slowly over several years than trek across the black forest and get torn apart by monsters. Of all the reasons Moog might offer in his refusal, this last reason seemed the most likely. Clay certainly wouldn't blame him for using it.

"Fantastic! Well, not the bit about Rose," said the wizard. "That's awful, Gabe. Just awful. But yes! Yes! Saga reunited? The old boys together again? Are you kidding me?"

"So . . . you'll come with us?" Clay asked.

"Of course I'll come! What kind of friend would I be otherwise?"

Clay found himself baffled, recalling the emphatic *no* he'd given Gabriel when he'd first come calling. "What about your research?"

"It'll be here when I get back. This is Rosie we're talking about! And besides, it's not like I need to worry about catching the rot while we're in the forest, right?" He glanced between Clay and Gabe, both of whom wore the same stricken expression. "Too soon?" he asked. "Too soon. Never mind. Anyway, I'm in!"

He strode over to Gabriel and offered up one of the mugs. Clay could smell the hot chocolate as it wafted past, and was beginning to regret not having raised his hand earlier.

"To Saga," he said, clinking his cup against Gabriel's. He was about to take his first sip when a heavy knock rattled the door and they heard Steve ask in his ring-hampered lisp, "Thtate your bithineth with my mathter."

The rumble of low voices, and then a recognizable one spoke up. "Arcandius! Moog, you in there, pal? It's Kal."

Clay and Gabriel shared a look of panicked terror.

Moog wheeled toward the door. "Kallorek? Hi! I'll be right—"

Too late, Clay clapped a hand over the wizard's mouth.

"We went to Kal to try and get Gabe's sword back," Clay said as quickly and quietly as he could. "He threatened to kill us instead."

"You mean *Vellichor*? Why does Kallorek have *Vellichor*?" Moog asked.

"We'll explain later," said Clay, when it looked like Gabriel was preparing to do so.

"You got company in there, Moog?" Kallorek's voice was chummy as could be. "Our old friends Slowhand and Gabe, perhaps? How about you open up and we can all three of us talk things over, eh?"

Steve chimed in again. "Thir, would you pleath thtate your bithineth with my—" The door thundered as someone hit it with something heavy. The knocker's customary politeness evaporated. "You punthed me!? You thon of a—"

Another thud shuddered the door, louder this time, and Steve went quiet.

"Moog?" Kallorek's voice was losing affability like a wineskin with a hole punched in the bottom. "Open the door."

The wizard squirmed out of Clay's grip and rushed to a nearby counter, where a crystal ball rested on a swathe of dark velvet. The orb contained nothing but grey-white fuzz, but when Moog set his mug aside and touched his fingers to the surface an image began to materialize within a swirl of purple smoke. An instant later the image faded, replaced by static fuzz.

"I bought this off the witch that lived here before me," the wizard explained hurriedly, hitting the orb a few more times without success. "Damn thing doesn't work half the time. I swear it's enough to drive a man to *read*." He put his nose to the glass, muttering an incantation too quiet to hear. When that failed he swore and slapped the glass with his open palm. "Fucking piece of junk..."

The picture came suddenly clear, and Clay felt his gut curl up like a man pounced on by a bear. He saw Kallorek, dressed in scale armour beneath a cloak trimmed with black fur. He was surrounded by no less than sixteen armed guards. One of these, an especially big, brutish-looking bastard, was lurking just outside the door with a torch in one hand and a heavy maul in the other. Of the brass knocker there remained only a mangled ruin.

"Oh, poor Steve," Moog whimpered. "When did Kal get so *mean*?"

Clay suspected the booker had bullied the midwife that pulled him from the womb, but there wasn't time to speculate now. "We need to get out of here," he said. "Is there a back door? An escape tunnel?" He looked around, seeing evidence of neither. "Any way of getting out of here?"

The wizard thought for a moment, and then slowly began to nod. "There is a way. It's risky, though."

It's risky. Clay could remember Moog saying those words half a hundred times. More often than not they'd preceded some sort of wild debacle, but occasionally the wizard came up with something truly miraculous.

Clay blew out a sigh. "Let's hear it," he said.

"Go upstairs!" Moog pointed to what remained of the second storey. "I just need to grab some stuff first." The first thing he went for was the crystal ball, hastily wrapping it in velvet cloth before dropping it into a bag. Next he collected a number of vials, tossing them into the sack without regard for whether or not they might break. "Go!" he urged them. "I'll be right behind you."

Clay started for the stairs, Gabriel hot on his heels. When they gained the second floor he looked around frantically for a means of escape. The tower's roof had crumbled away, and a carpet of bright stars glittered above them. By their light he saw a single bed against one wall, another bookshelf, a nightstand, and no way out at all. Even the windows were too high to reach.

Gabriel, meanwhile, was gazing up at the night sky in open-mouthed shock.

"What?" Clay asked. He glanced up, saw nothing out of the ordinary, and then asked Gabriel, "What is it? The sky? The stars?"

"Not stars," Gabe whispered.

"What do you mean—?"

Not stars, Clay grasped. *Spiders*. Thousands upon thousands of faintly glowing spiders, a scuttling constellation spread across the firmament of an undetectable web. For a moment neither he nor Gabriel moved, each of them rooted where they stood by primal, paralyzing fear.

Would you look at us, Clay thought scathingly. *We, who might once have faced down a dragon and only stopped to ask how it preferred to get its ass kicked, baulking at glow-in-the-dark spiders!*

A few of the critters came sliding down for a closer look. Clay did his best to ignore them, calling down the stairs behind him. "Moog!?"

"Coming!"

Peering onto the lower floor, he saw the wizard cramming a few last-minute items into his quite-obviously-enchanted bag: a staff, a wand, a rod, a dagger studded with gemstones, an onyx cat statue, half a dozen hats, a few books, a pipe, two bottles of brandy, a pair of ragged slippers—

There was a loud crunch, like the sound of a tree's back snapping, and the door buckled inward.

At exactly the same time hundreds more spiders began descending to see what all the fuss was about. The effect was unnerving, since a part of Clay's mind still thought the spiders were stars, and it was shrieking at him that the sky was falling. He supressed the urge to vomit for any number of reasons and yelled at the top of his lungs, *"Moog!"*

"On my way!" the wizard shouted. He'd been setting his menagerie of rot-infected animals free. As the dog-sized elephant went scampering toward the door, Moog, with a word and a gesture, set a fire beneath the largest glass crucible. He tossed a vial of red liquid inside before taking the stairs two at a time. When he gained the second floor and saw the horrified expression on Gabriel's face the wizard looked up.

"Ah, you've spotted my pets!"

"Pets?" Gabe sounded incredulous. "Moog, they're *spiders.*"

The wizard waved off his concern. "They're harmless! Well, mostly harmless. One took a nip of me once and I turned invisible for a week. Remarkable, yes, but it was bloody hard to buy groceries! Anyway, they eat the bats." He thrust his bag into Clay's hands. "Hold this."

Kneeling beside the bed, he reached beneath it and hauled out a mirror near as long as Clay was tall.

Gabriel pointed at the thing. "Is that—"

"Yes, it is," Moog confirmed without waiting for Gabe to finish. "I just hope it still works!" He dipped a finger into it, as if testing the temperature of stew. Ripples spread from his touch, distorting the reflection of Clay and Gabriel peering down in concern.

The mirror had a twin, and both were enchanted, so that you could step into one and out of the other, no matter the distance between. The band had used them once before as a means to rescue Matrick's wife, Lilith, who was then the princess of Agria. She'd been abducted on her eighteenth birthday by a suitor turned kidnapper—a minor lord hell-bent on becoming king. They'd accessed the mirror through the maid's quarters and appeared in the royal bedchamber barely in time to stop the lord from robbing the young princess of her precious maidenhead.

A lucky thing, too, or she'd have been unable to offer it up to Matrick later that night.

The door to the tower gave in, smashed to splinters as Kallorek's gang ploughed through, led by the brute with the maul.

Moog shook his head. "Shit, I thought—" There was a flash of light, and the crucible downstairs exploded in a cloud of bright orange smoke. The wizard waved frantically toward the mirror. "In! Get in!" he screamed.

"What was that?" Gabe asked, covering his mouth as the smoke roiled up to envelop them. It stung his eyes and filled their nostrils with a sickening sweetness, like fruit on the cusp of going bad.

"My phylactery! Go!" Moog shouted over a chorus of hacking coughs and glass-shattering chaos below.

Since no one else made a move, Clay did. He shook his head, cursed himself for a fool, and jumped into the mirror as though leaping to his death from a high cliff.

Chapter Eleven

The Cuckold King

He came out sideways, unsure of when he'd begun screaming at the top of his lungs.

A man spun at the sound, and Clay caught a glimpse of widening eyes above a drawn veil before he inadvertently performed what could aptly be described as a flying drop-kick to the poor man's face.

He and his unintended victim hit the ground together. Clay had barely begun his litany of apology before the man turned on him with hot eyes and a bloody snarl, at which point Clay noticed the wickedly curved knife in his hand.

He tried to scramble backward, but his legs were trapped beneath his assailant. He could hope the first strike didn't kill him, or that the man concluded in the next half second that Clay meant him no harm, which didn't seem likely at all.

Gabriel came through the mirror in a head-first roll, as though he'd been pushed. He landed directly on top of Clay, which didn't improve their chances of not getting stabbed, but then Moog hurtled overhead, hooting like a child on a playground slide. The knife-bearing man took another accidental kick—to the jaw this time—and went out like a candle in a hurricane.

"Oh, my!" The wizard scrambled to his knees. "Sir, I am so—"

"Leave it, Moog. He's out." Clay jutted his chin toward the knife still clasped in the man's limp hand. "Also, he tried to kill me."

"Oh. How rude."

"I'd say so," Clay agreed. *Though I did technically kick him first.*

Gabriel rolled onto his back, swiping hair from his eyes. "Where are we?"

For a moment they took stock of their surroundings: an expansive room, expensively furnished. The walls were hung with paintings and rich tapestries, the ceiling painted with a mural depicting a scene from the War of Reclamation, when mankind had scattered the Heartwyld Hordes feasting on the carcass of the Old Dominion. Against one wall was a huge bed shrouded by diaphanous white curtains.

"We're in Brycliffe Castle," said Moog. "This is the same room as the last time: the king's bedchamber."

"Which means..." Clay began.

"Matrick is here," said Gabriel.

Clay frowned. "What? Why do you say that?"

A shrug. "Because he's the king of Agria. And because that's him there." Gabriel pointed toward the bed. Sure enough, there was Matrick. The king, who had put on considerable weight since Clay had seen him last, was sprawled amidst a tangle of silk sheets, fast asleep and snoring.

Moog whirled. "Matty?" He dashed to the bed and leapt through the gap in the curtains, pouncing on their old bandmate like a boy determined to wake his parents on the morning of his birthday. "Matty, wake up!"

The foul-mouthed, booze-guzzling, whore-mongering, and wholly unscrupulous thief who was now the ruler of one of Grandual's five great kingdoms awoke with a start.

"What? Who?" He rolled away from the wizard, flailing

as he ran out of bed and fell into a heap on the floor. Then he screamed, "Assassins!"

The double doors to the chamber burst open and a pair of guardsmen rushed in, swords drawn. At the same time someone tumbled through the mirror, wreathed in trails of orange smoke. It was one of Kallorek's thugs—the big brute with the hammer who had smashed Steve's face to smithereens.

Clay looked despairingly between the guards and the hulking newcomer. His first instinct was to size the man up, but when his gaze flitted downward he froze. "Um, do you... need a sec?"

The big brute scowled, and then followed Clay's stare to the very obvious bulge in his breeches. He half-turned, suddenly embarrassed, though the side profile did little to help matters.

Clay got as far as opening his mouth before Moog cut him off.

"It's the phylactery," he explained. "I threw it, remember? The explosion, the smoke..." he chuckled, wearing a grin that was equal parts sheepish and smug. "Zero to hero. As advertised."

"That would explain this then." Gabe motioned toward the rise in his own trousers.

"Ah, me too, now," said Moog. "Look here!"

Clay didn't look. Didn't need to. He had a fair idea as to what the wizard was referring.

Another silence followed, infinitely more awkward than the last. Finally, one of the guards spoke up. "Sire, what should we... Sire?"

The king was doubled over, clutching his gut as if he'd taken a wound. Clay heard a wheeze, then a snort, and then Matrick threw his head back, howling in laughter. Kallorek's brute began growling like a threatened dog. His big fists tightened on the haft of his maul.

That was all the warning Clay needed. In one motion he

shrugged *Blackheart* free and caught the grip as it fell. He was already moving as the brute hefted the heavy iron hammer and lurched toward Gabriel, who was preoccupied with trying to adjust himself. The blow pounded the shield with a deep *thunk*, glancing off. The force of it sent a jolt down Clay's arms, and pain arced like lightning across his shoulders. It had been months since he'd got into a scrap of any sort, years since he'd fought anything with a legitimate chance of killing him.

Better blow the dust off fast, Slowhand, he told himself. Clay saw the hammer rise again and this time met the swing with strength, driving the weapon wide. He'd just decided to throw a punch when the man's boot kicked him square in the chest. He hurtled backward, crashing painfully into one of the bed's thick posts.

The king's guards hadn't moved, still unsure who their enemy was—a dilemma Clay could scarcely relate to. The brute had recovered and was hefting his maul like a lumberjack stepping up to the tree. There was no time to reach for anything—a candelabra, or an especially heavy bedside tome—that might constitute a weapon, and he couldn't simply step clear or he'd leave Gabriel helplessly exposed, so Clay rushed instead.

The hammer came swinging in from the left. Clay put his shoulder into *Blackheart*, leaning hard into the blow so as to not be thrown to the ground by the immense strength behind it. He ducked a clumsy backhand swing and then launched himself into the air, slamming the warped wooden face of his shield into that of his opponent. The brute stumbled back a step, then another. Clay pressed the advantage and levelled a kick of his own, forcing the man back into the mirror. It rippled like water in his wake.

Clay wheeled on the bed. "Moog, how do I stop him from coming back?"

The wizard spread his hands. "Poke your head through and ask him not to?"

"Moog..." Clay felt his patience rapidly fray; his nine-year-old daughter was easier to manage than this senile old sorcerer.

Thankfully, Gabriel had his wits about him. He stepped forward and tipped the mirror facedown onto the floor.

"Thank you," said Clay. Gabriel flashed him a tight smile and quickly looked elsewhere.

By now the torrent of Matrick's mirth had drained to a trickle. He was still giggling as he stepped between his guardsmen, urging them with a touch to sheath their swords.

"Gods of Grandual, what are you guys doing here?" He approached them warily, as if they were a trio of deer he'd caught drinking from a forest pool and any sudden move might startle them to flight.

Clay swiped hair from the sweat beading his forehead. The fight, brief as it was, had left him winded. "It's complicated," he said.

Moog was sitting on the bed, hands on his knees. "Gabe's daughter is trapped in Castia. We're going to rescue her and we want you to come."

Clay shrugged. "That about sums it up."

Matrick paled. "Castia? What was Rose doing in Castia?"

"Now that really *is* complicated..." Clay began.

"She's in a band," said Gabriel. He was wringing his hands again, like a pauper on a chapel doorstep. "When the Republic asked for help in fighting the Horde, she went."

"Okay, yeah," Clay agreed. "That's pretty much it exactly."

"We're getting the band back together!" Moog exclaimed. "Think of it, Matty! It'll be like old times! The five of us reunited, setting out across the Heartwyld!"

Matrick groaned, rubbing at his eyes with the palms of his hands. The years, despite having been spent in obvious luxury, had taken their toll on the king of Agria. His black hair was streaked with grey and receding rapidly; his whiskers were salted white on a jowly chin. He looked tired, but Clay supposed that might have been due to the fact that he'd been fast asleep when four men had burst into his room through a magic mirror and started swinging at one another with shields and hammers and absurdly incongruous erections.

"Matty? Whaddaya say, man?" Moog seemed genuinely confused by the king's lack of enthusiasm.

"I...can't, Moog. I just can't. I'm sorry."

Moog looked utterly crestfallen. Clay, however, thought that Matrick was the first among Saga's old crew to show a lick of good sense, and it was a moment before he recognized the cold stone settling in his gut for what it was: dejection.

Clay realized he had been *hoping* that Matrick would have said yes. A part of him had believed (without any good reason, to be sure) that if *he* could be convinced to drop everything and follow Gabriel on his mad quest to Castia, then surely the other members of the band would do the same. He had his doubts about Ganelon, of course, but not Matrick, who loved Gabriel like a brother, and had once been the most adventurous of them all.

It was to Gabriel that the king now spoke. "I really *am* sorry, Gabe. There's just a lot on my plate here. I've got Lilith and the kids to think about, you know. Not to mention a kingdom to run, a border war that seems inevitable, and this damnable council tomorrow. If I wasn't—"

"The Council of Courts is tomorrow?" Gabe asked, suddenly alert.

Matrick ran a hand back over his vanishing hairline. "It is, yes. At Lindmoor. And that horse fucker Obolon Han will be there. He and I nearly came to blows the last time we met, and tensions with Cartea have been higher than a scratch addict ever since. I'll tell you, this 'Duke of Endland' chose an orc-shit time to stage this...well, whatever the fuck it is he's up to."

Gabriel listened, gnawing anxiously on a knuckle and peering at nothing in particular. When the king finished griping, he asked, "Can we come? I'd like to get a look at this duke myself. Maybe we can convince him to release Grandual's mercenaries."

"Um...well, sure," said Matrick. "I don't see why not. I mean, I'll have to run it by Lilith first, obviously."

As though she were some malevolent spirit conjured by the utterance of her name, the queen of Agria stormed into the room. She wore nothing but a bare slip of a nightgown, and although she'd aged many years and given birth to several children since Clay had seen her last, neither had done a damn thing to diminish her stunning—if severe—beauty. Nor did the fact that she looked extremely pissed off at the moment. She was trailed by a tall, heavily muscled man who was, somewhat curiously, not wearing a shirt. He was, however, wearing a protective frown and carrying a very large sword.

"What in Vail's name is going on here?" Lilith demanded to know.

"Lilith!" Matrick took a step toward his wife, but drew up short when the queen's shirtless guardsman stepped between them. "There was an assassin, but the boys here—well, you remember the boys?"

She cast an icy glare at the three men who had risked their lives to rescue her some twenty-five years ago. "What are they doing here?"

The king wrung his hands in much the same way Gabe had earlier. "Uh, they came through the mirror there, actually." Matty's voice had found a tone that balanced on the blade's edge between pleading and placating. Clay imagined it was what a talking dog might sound like while explaining to its master why it had shit all over the rug.

"I didn't ask *how* they arrived, dear," said Lilith, sweet as poisoned honey. "I asked *what* they were doing here."

"Of course, yes. Well, they're on their way to Castia."

"Castia?" The very word seemed repellent to her. "Why?"

"Oh, um . . ." The king threw a nervous glance at Clay.

"It's complicated," Clay said.

At the pub in Coverdale there was a dish known as the King's Breakfast. It consisted of two watery eggs burnt to the bottom of a cast-iron skillet, doused heavily with black pepper and a thick red sauce Shep referred to as tomato blood. It was served with a slice of blackened toast and, if you were lucky, a few slices of pear more bruised than a bad bard's ego.

Unsurprisingly, when it came to what a king *actually* ate for breakfast, Shep had missed the mark by a fair margin. Highlights from Matrick's table the next morning included tottering columns of fluffy gold pancakes drenched in maple syrup, steaming loaves of mouth-watering bread alongside delicate porcelain dishes of salted butter, perfectly browned toast served with a staggering variety of jam—blueberry, strawberry, raspberry, blackberry, apricot, grape, fig, and something called marmalade that Moog couldn't pronounce regardless of how many attempts he made to do so. There were slabs of pork belly, plump sausages, and eggs so airy and fresh Clay swore he could hear hens in labor beyond the kitchen door.

To drink there was fresh-squeezed juice—apple, orange, cranberry—and crisp white wine; a tea made of fragrant, flowery leaves; cool water flavoured with tart southern limes; and even strong Phantran coffee that Matrick gulped down as if it were the antidote to a poison burning through his veins.

Clay might have dubbed it one of the very best breakfasts of his life—or it had been, anyway, until Lilith, who was seated opposite the king at the far end of the long table, went ahead and spoiled it all by announcing she was pregnant.

The king, caught entirely by surprise, had a mouthful of

pancake at the moment and Clay had to wonder whether the timing of the queen's confession had been artfully planned. Around the table drinks froze on their way to lips and clattering forks fell silent, excepting those of Matrick's five children, all of whom continued eating and talking with one another, as children did when adults said whatever it was adults said.

Besides Clay and his bandmates, there were several others in the hall as well. Servants bustled in and out of an arched doorway, clearing away dishes and setting down more as fast as the king and his guests could finish them. Soldiers stood at attention between the tall windows on one side of the room, and the queen's personal guard cut an impressive figure standing a few feet behind her. A northman by the look of him, the same one who had appeared shirtless in the king's bedchamber the night before. He was younger than Clay had first perceived, but seemed a capable sort, if a touch too handsome for his own good. His nose, like those of a great many Kaskars Clay had met, was hooked like a falcon's beak, and his eyes had been rapturously fixed on Lilith all morning.

Clay was fairly certain he was fucking the queen, which made her declaration just now all the more interesting.

Moog broke the silence with a slow clap that left an even more uncomfortable silence in its wake.

By then, at least, the king had managed to swallow both his pride *and* his pancake. "That's . . . wonderful news, honey."

"Isn't it?" Lilith's grin was frosted with spite. "The augurs tell me it will be a boy. You're going to have a new little brother," she said, addressing the quintet of children seated along one side of the table.

Clay watched each of them react in turn. The twin boys were the youngest; they simply giggled at each other and kept on eating. Lillian, whose nut-brown skin contrasted the vibrant blue of her eyes, looked unimpressed, probably dreading the prospect of yet another brother to harass her. The fat one, Kerrick, wore a look of surprise. His jaw had dropped so low Clay could see the food still in his mouth. The oldest, Danigan, red-haired and freckled, simply nodded without looking up.

"But I don't *want* another brother," said Kerrick.

"Neither do I," Lillian added her voice in protest.

Their mother regarded them coolly. "Well I didn't want to give birth to a twelve-pound monstrosity, or to a girl at all, for that matter. But life isn't fair, is it? Kerrick, share some of those peas with your sister. You've had more than enough, I think, and she's skinny as an urchin boy, I swear."

Clay felt his own mouth sag open. Needless to say, both Kerrick and Lillian began crying at once, which in turn set the twins to bawling. Only the eldest remained silent, spooning eggs into his mouth with evident disinterest.

Matrick swiped a hand through his thinning hair. "Now, children, your mother didn't mean to upset you. She just..." He looked despairingly down the length of the table. "It's the baby," he said. "It just makes her cranky, is all. Isn't that right, dear?"

"That must be it," said Lilith. "And dreadfully tired. I think I'll have a quick...nap before we leave for the Council. Lokan, would you be so kind as to escort me to my room?"

"With pleasure," said her guardsman, in a tone that all but confirmed Clay's earlier suspicion.

The two of them left arm in arm, but if it bothered Matrick at all he didn't let it show, concerning himself instead with placating the children. "Go ahead and finish your peas, Kerrick, they're good for you. Lil, can you please pass your little brother his juice before he knocks it over? That's a good girl."

He managed to cajole the kids into cleaning their plates, and Clay watched throughout with utter fascination. The Matrick he'd used to know had been devious, foul-mouthed, and drunk more often than sober. He'd had a different woman on his arm every night—or on either arm, if he was feeling especially ambitious. He'd been a master thief and a vicious killer, wielding *Roxy* and *Grace* (the knives he'd named for the prostitutes to whom he'd lost his virginity) as though they were a pair of bloodthirsty fangs and the entire world his prey.

Who'd have thought he'd make a good father? Or a competent king for that matter? By all accounts, Agria was a flourishing kingdom, and even without Lilith's help he seemed to be raising some half-decent children. Each one of them asked to be excused and kissed him good-bye before being trundled off to their tutors.

Matrick asked the guards to leave as well, and after the servants refilled the coffee he dismissed them as well. Clay looked on in horror as Moog upended half a bowl of sugar into his.

"I like it sweet!" said the wizard.

Matrick produced a flask from somewhere and spiked his own drink, and for a while just stirred it idly and stared at nothing. Moog finished his cup and began transferring sugar from the bowl directly to his mouth with a saliva-dampened finger.

"Well Matty," said the wizard, "I sure wish—"

"Shhh!" The king cut him off with a raised finger, glancing quickly back at the kitchen door before leaning across the table and whispering, "Get me the fuck out of here."

Gabriel blinked. "What?"

The king mouthed the words again with exaggerated slowness. "Get me. The fuck. Out of here."

Moog looked puzzled. "Why? Matrick, you're the king! You said yourself you had lots on your plate. The kids—"

"—aren't mine!" finished Matrick. "Did you get a *look* at them? I love the little bastards like I love free cake, but I sure as hell had no hand in making them!"

"Are you," Clay began, and then lowered his voice. "Are you saying—"

"I am saying I was fishing in Phantra when the twins were

conceived. I'm saying that Lillian has her father's eyes—*and mine aren't fucking blue*! I'm saying Kerrick is bigger at ten than I was at twenty, and Danigan, well…" Matrick made a frantic gesture that encompassed his head in general. "You'd think the red hair would tip me off, wouldn't you? But oh no, it took me four more kids to realize they all looked a bit like Lilith and a little like the castle librarian, or the ambassador from Narmeer, or the bloody rose gardener—who I thought was gay, by the way. No offense, Moog."

The wizard popped the finger out of his mouth. "Why would I—"

"And now she's pregnant again?" Matrick's laugh was a bitter thing. "I'll bet my kingdom that boy comes out tall as a tree and as hungry for his mothers' tits as noble Sir Lokan, that flea-bitten Kaskar whoreson!" Matrick was fairly screaming by now, unconcerned whether anyone lingering in the kitchen might hear.

"Then why don't you just leave?" asked Gabriel.

"I've tried!" Matrick moaned. "The guards won't let me. They're fiercely loyal to Lilith—I have no idea why."

Clay had some idea why. "What's the point of keeping you here?" he asked.

"She's worried I'll go off and father a legitimate heir. She said she'd kill me if I ever managed to get away, and now it looks like she wants me out of the picture for good. Remember that man in my room last night—the one you kicked when you came through the mirror? Well, that was one of her assassins. It wasn't the first one she's sent after me, and as sure as Hell is cold it won't be the last if I stick around this place. I need to escape, and I need your help to do it. No way Lilith'll find someone stupid enough to follow me into the Heartwyld."

Moog beamed. "Wait, so does this mean you'll come to Castia?"

"Of course I'll come," said Matrick. "You shits are the only real family I've got."

There it is, thought Clay, *that warm, fuzzy feeling again . . .*

"The problem is getting away. It will have to be after the council, obviously."

"We could use the mirror," suggested Gabriel, but the king shook his head.

"Lilith had it confiscated. She claims it's a threat to castle security. Which it is, I suppose. By the Unholy Dead, I'd forgot the thing was a portal at all, or I'd have jumped through it long ago."

"So we can't leave out the front gate," Moog reasoned. "And doubtless she'll have the rest under guard . . ."

"Believe it," said the king.

"What about that bag of yours, Moog?" asked Gabriel. "You can fit anything in there, right? Matrick could hide inside and we could smuggle him out of the castle."

The wizard shook his head. "It's a vacuum."

Gabe frowned. "A what?"

"A void. There's no air. He wouldn't survive longer than he could hold his breath. Trust me. I had a cat once that—" He broke off. "Just . . . no."

"You could kidnap me," Matrick suggested. "Disguise yourselves, knock me out, fight your way past the guards. We could leave a ransom note . . ."

"Lilith would assume it was us," said Clay. "Also, I'd rather not kill anyone if we don't have to."

Their cups rattled as Moog slammed his hand on the table. "I have it!" he shouted. All eyes turned toward him. The wizard grinned and spared Clay a rueful wink. "It is risky, though."

Chapter Twelve

The Council of Courts

It was something like four hundred years since the Company of Kings had defeated the last of the Heartwyld Hordes at Lindmoor and brought an end to the War of Reclamation, but the place still looked like a battlefield. Each spring the groundwater surged up and transformed it into a stinking fen. By summer's end it had mostly dried out, save for a few fetid pools here and there, and the muddy ground was littered with dredged-up relics: shattered arms and rusted armour, the mould-sheathed bones of monsters great and small. It was bordered, distantly, by spruce forests east and west, farmlands to the north, and the broad, slow-flowing river to the south. Beyond the river, on a clear day like today, you could see the squat blue shadow of Matrick's castle in Brycliffe.

At the centre of the broad peatland rose a grassy hillock known as the Isle of Wights. It was upon this rise (or so Matrick informed them as the king's mounted entourage made its meandering way toward it) that Agar the Bald did battle with something called an Infernal, which, as Clay understood it, was akin to a champion among the Hordes of old. He'd never seen one except in paintings or tapestries, and though no two artists rendered an Infernal quite the same, they all tended to agree that it stood on a giant pile of corpses and looked like the worst, most terrifying monster imaginable.

"Agar managed to kill the demon," Matrick explained, "but died of his wounds. His grandson, Agar the Beardless, went on to become the first king of Agria. Ever since then, whenever the five courts meet to discuss something of great importance, they meet right here on the Isle."

Lilith, wrapped in an ermine-trimmed cloak and mounted on a brilliant white mare beside him, affected a loud and lasting yawn.

"Why *isle*?" asked Moog. "Looks like a hill to me."

Matrick glanced over at his wife before answering. "In the spring this whole place floods—the isle's the only dry spot for miles. And as for the rest of the name, Agar the Bald was buried beneath the hill, and each night the spirits of those who fell here at Lindmoor come to pay him homage."

"Really?" Gabriel sounded skeptical.

"Really!" Matrick said proudly.

"Really . . . ?" Moog stroked his chin, intrigued.

"*Really*?" snapped the queen. "I swear by the Summer Lord's beard, I have laundry maids who talk less than you three." She gestured at Clay with a white-gloved hand. "Kale, at least, knows when to keep his mouth shut."

"It's Clay, actually."

Lilith pouted haughtily. "And you were doing so well."

The hill was surrounded by a crowd of gawkers gathered in hope of laying eyes on a real live druin. They'd laid out blankets, unpacked picnic baskets, and were generally making a day of it. Someone was selling skewers of roasted chestnuts, and one enterprising woman was hawking what she referred to as "authentic druin dolls." Moog bought one for five coppers, and the thing turned out to be little more than a stuffed sock puppet with buttons for eyes and a pair of flimsy cloth rabbit ears sewn on top. The wizard seemed pleased with his purchase nonetheless.

Upon reaching the Isle and climbing its gentle slope they found two delegations already waiting by the wind-scoured monument up top. The king's retainers set about erecting an open-walled tent around a massive cedar table they'd hauled by wagon all the way from Brycliffe, while Matrick and his clutch of Agrian nobles mingled with their foreign guests.

The company from Phantra was entirely female. The Salt Queen's kingdom was matriarchal: the sailors, soldiers, and laborers were commonly men, while women formed the core of the merchant class and held most of the senior positions in both the government and the military. Though their country was a fractious one—rival merchant houses rose and fell near as often as the tide—the easterners liked to remind the rest of Grandual that they had never lost a war against a neighbouring realm.

Their delegation was led by a young woman who introduced herself as Etna Doshi. She was short, stocky, and walked with the telltale Phantran swagger that was one-quarter useful for staying balanced on a ship's deck and three-quarters cocky bravado. Her skin was sun bronzed, her face weathered as sailcloth, and her garish attire—bright scarves, draping sashes, an abundance of gaudy jewels—reminded Clay of the brigand "Lady" Jain, who had robbed them on the road to Conthas. She bound her black hair in a silver net adorned with sparkling sapphires and bright blue seashells. A puckered scar at the corner of her mouth made it look as though she were constantly sneering.

"Doshi?" Matrick asked as he clasped her hand. "Any relation to—"

"My mother," she said before he could finish.

"Ah, splendid! How is that blind old bat?"

Etna seemed momentarily taken aback by the king's frankness, but her scar-torn sneer stretched into a grin. "Still blind," she said with a wink. "And still the finest Admiral in the Salt Queen's illustrious navy."

"Did she ever find that lost island she was always on about?"

"Antica, you mean?" Etna shook her head. "She's still searching, the old fool, though I told her she'd have better luck finding an honest man in Low Tide."

Matrick laughed, bracing his belly with a steadying hand. The rogue-turned-king had always felt right at home on the Phantran coast, where even the grandmothers could be charitably described as gutter-tongued swindlers. He'd gotten along especially well with Etna's mother, who Matty used to claim had taught him everything he knew about ships and most of what he knew about women and knives.

"Slowhand."

Clay turned and found himself eye to eye with Maladan Pike, the First Shield of Kaskar. Pike had been a mercenary once, the frontman of a band called the Raiders. He'd had a pair of older brothers—twins—destined to rival each other for the right to inherit their father's throne, but both had died at the hands of an especially mean (and prodigiously ugly) ogre chieftain named Ikko Umpa. Pike had begged his father for the opportunity to avenge his fallen siblings, but the northern king, unwilling to risk the life of his only remaining heir, refused and hired Saga to kill the ogre instead. They'd done so, and ever since, the reluctant prince of Kaskar had treated Clay and his bandmates with an admixture of mild resentment and grudging respect.

"Pike," Clay said by way of greeting.

"Heard you were dead."

"Close. Married."

The First Shield snorted. "Kids?"

"One. You?"

"Seven." Pike's chest swelled a little. "The oldest is near tall as me already and could strangle a yethik with his bare hands. And yours? I'll bet my horse he's a stone-cold killer, same as his father."

Clay stifled a shudder while plastering on a smile of his own. "A girl, actually. She collects frogs."

"Oh." The northman looked troubled as he smoothed his grey-shot beard against the six-fingered bear-claw embossed on his studded leather cuirass. "I was just kidding about betting my horse, obviously."

"Obviously," said Clay.

The First Shield's gaffe was overshadowed—literally—by the arrival of a rapidly descending skyship.

Clay tried to hide his astonishment from those around him as the galleon dropped out of the grey sky. He and the band had discovered the wreckage of many such vessels during their touring years—most often amidst the ruin of Dominion cities—but those had been derelict, their sails torn and their hulls reduced to splinters. He'd heard rumours these past few years of skyships being found more or less intact, but had dismissed them as false until the day he'd glimpsed one sailing the clouds above Coverdale. Even still, Clay had never thought to see one up close.

"The Second Sun," said Moog, sidling up beside him. "The flagship of the Sultana herself."

It looked to Clay like any other ship, except the sails were shaped a bit like leaves and braced with spanning metal struts that crackled with blue electricity. Also, it was flying.

"Flagship?" he asked. "You mean Narmeer has a whole fleet of those?"

The wizard laughed. "Well, no. They might have one or two more, actually, but I'd be surprised if there were thirty skyships in the whole world that are actually airworthy. *The Second Sun* was found buried in the sand near Xanses. The Salt Queen of Phantra has one as well, I hear. All the really cool monarchs have them."

"I can hear you, you know," said Matrick. He was gazing covetously at the hovering galleon, which had cast a pair of huge anchors to the ground. Narmeeri soldiers scrambled deftly down nets draping the hull, and there was a curtained palanquin being lowered over one rail.

Clay's eyes were nailed to the ship as well. "How?" was all he managed to say.

Moog scratched the bald crown of his head. "How does it fly, you mean? You see those metal-looking orbs on either side?"

Clay nodded. There were two near the prow of the ship, and two near the stern, each one surrounded by a haze of fine mist. "Sure."

"Tidal engines," said the wizard. "They're actually a series of spinning gyres made of pure duramantium and powered by static electricity trapped by the sails."

Clay had never heard of tidal engines, and he sure as shit didn't know what a "gyre" was supposed to be. As for duramantium, he'd always half-believed the metal was a myth devised by merchants to sell you a sword for ten times its worth. "So basically magic," he mumbled.

Another chuckle from Moog. "Not magic exactly, but close."

The palanquin the Narmeeri had unloaded from the ship was borne to the hilltop by eight hulking Kaskars in bronze-plated lamellar skirts and calf-strapped sandals. Northmen, especially those with blond hair and bright eyes, were paid a princely sum to serve as elite bodyguards to Narmeeri nobles. Most who did so were criminals or outcasts, and Clay noted that the Sultana's guardsmen were careful to avoid the First Shield's gaze as they lowered their burden and took up places on either side. Their mistress, the enigmatic ruler of the southernmost court, remained ensconced within the palanquin while a trio of ministers with plaited beards and patterned robes conferred with one another in hushed voices.

It was late afternoon before the Carteans turned up at last, plodding across the ancient battleground on sturdy steppe ponies. The yellow-and-blue pennants of the High Han drifted limply down below, but by the time they reached the summit they streamed and snapped in the crisp autumn breeze.

"My Queen!" The lead horseman, who Clay assumed was Obolon Han, called out to Lilith from the back of his mount. "See how my banner stiffens when you are near!" His remark drew a round of guttural laughter from the men around him and brought an oddly gratified smirk to the queen's lips. Clay glanced between Matrick and her bodyguard—the one she'd called Lokan at breakfast—and couldn't decide which of the two looked more affronted.

The Han dismounted with the practised ease of a man getting out of a chair and advanced at a saunter. He was flanked by two of the Ravenguard, denoted by the wings tattooed beneath their collarbones. All three men bore a black stripe painted over their eyes and the bridges of their broad noses, and each shouldered a horn bow and carried a naked sabre on his hip.

Obolon was a short man but sturdily built, with broad shoulders and muscles packed beneath a meaty frame that bespoke a man who loved eating and drinking just a little bit less than he loved riding and fighting. His battle-scarred arms, like those of the men behind him, were browned by long days beneath the sun. His head and cheeks were shorn clean, though he wore a wispy beard on his chin that Clay thought looked pretty stupid, all things considered.

The Han's narrow, heavy-lidded eyes were hauntingly familiar, and Clay was trying to decide whether or not he'd met the man before when Gabriel, standing on his right, sucked in a breath.

"Holy shit"—his whisper carried a note of disbelief over Clay's shoulder—"the fat one."

Clay frowned. He didn't . . . *Sweet Maiden's Mercy.* He tried to keep his jaw from hinging open as Gabriel's words clicked into place. This man, the warlord who ruled the Cartean tribes, was very obviously the true father of Matty's son, Kerrick. *Little wonder Matrick loathes the man*, he thought. *Let's just hope the two of them can stay civil long enough to get this council over with.*

Obolon stopped before the king and spread his beefy arms like a man expecting a hug. "Old King Matrick! Long time, no see. How's my boy doing?"

Clay sighed. *Or not.*

To his left, Moog's bushy eyebrows climbed halfway to the back of his head.

A few of the king's guards exchanged furtive glances, but Matrick did nothing but clamp his lips and force a smile. "I have no idea what you're talking about."

The Han kept on, undeterred. "Hungry little bastard, ain't he? Runs in the family. Is that why you can't afford to defend your borders against my raids? Have you emptied your coffers feeding that brat o' mine?"

Matrick pretended to ignore him, but Clay saw the king's fingers twitch, itching for the pommels of knives he wasn't carrying, at least not visibly. After all, if the king wanted someone full of holes there were a dozen guards around him happy to oblige.

"And who is this stallion?" The Han's shit-eating grin grew wider as he took stock of Lilith's bristling bodyguard. "Looks like it won't be long before we welcome another little warrior into our happy family!"

Lokan, being possessed of more pride and less sense than Matrick, drew his sword.

Obolon, growling, drew his.

And Matty, who had indeed been hiding a pair of knives, brought them spinning out.

A breath later the Ravenguard put arrows to string, Maladan Pike and his fur-clad northmen brandished axes, and Etna Doshi's silk-clad pirates tore scimitars from their scabbards. The Sultana's blond brutes levelled long spears and hard glares at everyone, including Clay and his bandmates, who were among the few people on the Isle left unarmed.

And thus stood the Lords and Ladies of Grandual as the shadow of a wyvern's wings fell upon them all.

Chapter Thirteen

The Duke of Endland

Clay had once tried describing to his wife the difference between a wyvern and a dragon. They were each vaguely reptilian, he'd admitted, and covered with metallic scales. They shared commonalities like razor-sharp fangs and claws that could punch through an iron breastplate as though it were made of eggshell. They both had leathery wings and sinuous necks, and were equally capable of shearing a man in half with a snap of the tail. Ginny had stopped him there to point out what a piss-poor job he was doing of differentiating the two, whereupon Clay was forced to concede that there was essentially no difference between them whatsoever.

Although now, as a wyvern touched down on the hillside before him, a few notable distinctions sprung to mind. For starters, a wyvern's front arms were built into its wings, with curved spines flaring from the elbow and a joint spiked with curling talons. On the ground, wyverns plodded along on their knuckles, like apes. Their long tails were barbed on the end, and could inject a poison strong enough to paralyse a plough horse in seconds flat.

Unlike dragons, they weren't especially cognizant. A dragon could plan and plot; it could speak, although no one (not even Moog) could decipher their draconic tongue. A dragon could, if given sufficient reason, *hate* you—something Clay and his bandmates knew all too well.

A wyvern, on the other hand, was a predator, compelled by instinct to hunt and to kill. It was a beast, and like any beast its will could be broken, its instincts subverted by the understanding that it was not, after all, the most dangerous thing in the world.

At least that was Clay's assumption, or else why in the Frost Mother's Frozen Hell would a wyvern permit someone to *ride on its fucking back*?

The "someone" in question was a druin, as Moog had mentioned yesterday. He slid down the wyvern's black scales with a grace that mirrored Obolon Han dismounting his pony.

The Duke of Endland wore a long leather coat that was either burnished brown or bloody crimson, and carried three distinct swords in three distinct scabbards across his back. He was tall, like many of his kind, and thin, with skin pale as cream. His hair was the colour of a late autumn leaf, or a freshly minted copper coin, and but for a few strays the wind had plucked loose it was swept back against his skull. His features were typically druin: severe, all hard angles and jutting lines. He had a strong, sylvan nose, thin lips, sharp teeth, and long ears tufted like a rabbit's and sheathed in fine white fur.

An old scar sliced through his left brow. It wasn't obvious from where Clay stood behind the bristling crowd of Matrick's guards, but he knew it was there.

Because he'd met this particular druin before. Knew his name even before Matrick said it out loud.

"Lastleaf?"

Lastleaf, son of Vespian, from whom Gabriel had inherited *Vellichor.*

Lastleaf, who had tried and failed (hence the scar) to take the Archon's sword from Gabriel many years ago.

Lastleaf, the Duke of Endland, master of the Heartwyld Horde.

Clay found himself wondering what the Council of Courts etiquette was regarding vomiting your breakfast onto your boots. He suddenly wished he were elsewhere, anywhere—or better yet, someone else entirely. A simple man doing simple things. A cobbler, maybe. Cobblers rarely, if ever, made enemies of vengeful immortals, or so he figured.

The druin stopped where he was. He didn't appear to notice the king had spoken. The wyvern craned its neck and lowered its head so the druin could stroke the glossy scales along its jaw. Clay assumed the beast was a matriarch, since it was twice the size of most wyverns he'd seen, and he'd seen quite a few. The creature emitted a sound like ten thousand cats purring at once, and the ribbed fins along her neck and below her chin vibrated in pleasure.

Clay made a note to congratulate himself later for not shitting himself right then and there. The same could not be said for the horses, however. At a word from the king—and a gesture from the Han—the skittish mounts were led away, off the hill and into the babbling throng. The great good fortune of seeing a druin *and* a wyvern on the same day had created a fair bit of excitement down below. Clay saw one fellow setting up an easel and mixing water into a bowl of dry paint—no doubt he'd have the whole affair framed and hung on a brothel wall by tomorrow.

At last the druin turned and addressed the king of Agria in a measured voice. "Hello...Matrick, was it?"

The queen turned on her husband. "You know this creature?" she asked, which seemed to Clay like a piss-poor way to begin what was supposed to be a negotiation.

Though they were here at Lastleaf's demand, Matrick had explained last night that the Council's aim was to convince the self-proclaimed "Duke of Endland" to abandon his siege and disperse the Horde he claimed to lead. Though the kingdoms of Grandual had few—if any—ties to the faraway Republic of Castia, it seemed unwise (and somewhat callous) to sit by and do nothing while a horde of monsters wiped an entire city of humans off the face of the world.

"We've met before, yes," Matrick told his wife. "It was a long time ago."

"Not so long," said Lastleaf, whose kind counted the turn of seasons as though they were hours in an endless day. "Not for me, anyhow, and yet I barely recognized you. You have grown old, and fat, and judging from the crown on your head it appears someone was foolish enough to make you a king."

Obolon sniggered, and Matrick shot the Cartean ruler a glare before he replied. "I'm the king of Agria, yes." The old rogue tried puffing out his chest but was forced to settle for thrusting out his gut. "And you look ... exactly the same. Except the scar, of course," he added with a decidedly undiplomatic wink. "That's new."

The scar had been dealt by *Vellichor*'s edge on the day Lastleaf, along with a few sylf henchmen, had ambushed Saga shortly after Gabriel had inherited Vespian's fabled sword. The sylfs—druin-human halfbreeds most often shunned by everyone but their mortal mothers—were killed or driven off, and when Clay had last seen Lastleaf, the Archon's son had been curled in agony around Ganelon's boot, blinded by blood, heaping promises of retribution upon Gabe and his bandmates.

Just now the druin's face remained impassive, which Clay found troubling for a number of reasons. Lastleaf touched his thumb to the pale scar beneath his left eye. "It suits me, don't you think?"

Before the king could answer, Maladan Pike cut in. "Excuse me, Duke, but I didn't come here—"

"*We*," said Etna Doshi with a pointed look.

The First Shield of Kaskar sighed. "Fine. *We* didn't come here to listen while you and Old King Matrick swap stories. We came because—"

"—you want me to lift the siege of Castia," finished Lastleaf.

"Well, yes," said Pike. The northern prince was still holding his axe. In fact, members of several delegations hadn't bothered to resheathe their weapons since the wyvern landed. Clay had a moment to wonder if putting everyone on edge had been the Duke's intention in the first place.

"And my Horde?" wondered Lastleaf with feigned naivety. "Should I disband it? Bid my monstrous minions return to their forest lairs? Crawl back to their caves? Retreat to the deep, dark places of the world and wait patiently for some glory-hungry adventurer to come and claim the bounty on their heads?"

Pike wasn't the sharpest sword in the armoury, but he knew when he was being toyed with. "Sounds like a plan," he grated.

The ghost of a smile haunted the druin's lips, but quickly vanished. "What's done is done, I'm afraid. The arrow has left the string. Castia will fall, and soon. I could no more resurrect the Dominion than rescue the Republic from the doom that awaits it."

The Phantran delegate shook her head. She'd slung her cutlass back into the sash at her waist, but her fingers lingered on its jewelled pommel. "What does the Old Dominion have to do with any of this? Who are you, even? Where did you come from?"

The druin regarded Etna Doshi as if she were a mouse that had poked its head out of the salad he was partway through eating. "I am from the forest. You may call me Lastleaf, or Duke—whichever you'd prefer. And as for the Dominion..." His long ears twitched. "We are each what the past has made of us. You would do well to remember what has come and gone before. Time is a circle, history a turning wheel. Though I can hardly expect a human to understand. Your memory is as limited as your mind is narrow."

Doshi was on the verge of an angry retort when Lastleaf spoke up again. "I mean no insult to you personally, of course.

I am merely pointing out the fact that humans are short-lived, short-sighted, and prone to repeating the mistakes of both your ancestors and mine."

The Admiral's daughter looked decidedly unimpressed by the Duke's apology. "Since when was Endland a duchy then?" she asked sharply.

Lastleaf grinned, just as sharply. "When Castia is mine— and it *will* be mine very soon—I may remake of it whatever I wish. Why not a duchy, with myself as its duke? Or would you rather I chose a more...ostentatious title? Shall I call myself king, or emperor, or archon?"

Moog was right, Clay found himself thinking. *The whole duke thing is for our benefit, a way to make him seem less threatening to the kings and queens of Grandual.* Which seemed unnecessary, he thought, considering the druin commanded a force that was larger and substantially more terrifying than what any of the courts could muster on their own.

While Lastleaf was speaking, Clay saw a white-gloved hand push aside the silk curtains shrouding the Sultana's palanquin. He caught the barest glimpse of a gold mask in the gloom as the occupant spoke with one of the three ministers, who then turned and cleared his throat before addressing Lastleaf.

"My Esteemed Lady, the Sultana of Narmeer, Bride of Vizan the Summer Lord, Mistress of the Scorching Throne, Herald of the Devouring Wastes, Scourge of the Serpent Clans, Bane of the Giants of Dumidia, Eternal Enemy of the Palapti Centaurs, bids me ask you this: How is it you control the Heartwyld Horde?"

"I do not control them," said Lastleaf. "I compel them."

"There's a difference?" asked Obolon Han.

"The Horde cannot be controlled," the druin replied. He had an odd manner of speaking, Clay noted. He opened his mouth very little, as though ashamed of his serrated teeth, or else reluctant to put more effort than necessary into the act of conversing. "My own kind learned this lesson long ago, and far too late. But it can be coaxed, threatened, provoked—"

"Well how about you *provoke* them into leaving Castia the hell alone?" asked Doshi.

Lilith leaned in and whispered harshly into Matrick's ear. The king blinked and started like a man roused from a peaceful nap. "Ah, yes, how about we adjourn to the—"

"I will not sit," said Lastleaf. Behind him, the wyvern's wings shuddered with a sound like wind-cracked sails.

"Fair enough," said the king, earning himself one of Lilith's many and varied scowls. The queen would be tired, of course, but to sit alone in this company would be seen as a sign of weakness from a woman who had very serious aspirations of ruling as Agria's lone monarch before long.

The druin turned to face the First Shield, and when he did Clay got a good look at the scar left by *Vellichor* above his eye. The catlike pupil beneath it had ruptured, swelling to encompass the iris around it, which lent the druin an odd, unsettling gaze. "Imagine you lead a host of bloodthirsty warriors into the country of a bitter rival. You face their army on the field of battle and vanquish them."

"Who says *vanquish* anymore?" Moog breathed.

People who vanquished things, Clay supposed.

"Your enemy retreats behind their walls, and though you cannot breach them it is only a matter of time before their refuge becomes a grave. But your army, too, grows hungry. They have been promised blood, or coin, or flesh. And more: They crave the immeasurable joy of seeing a mortal foe brought to ruin and all they have loved turned to ash."

"Been there," quipped the Cartean Han, to the amusement of no one but his own clansmen.

"The Horde is an army like no other, and I have promised them Castia. Were they but men, then perhaps I could call them off. But they are not men." He said these words very carefully, and seemed to savour each as they left his mouth.

"They are wild things, fey creatures. They are everything you fear and many things you would fear to know, and they will not be turned back. Not even by me."

The First Shield's face had gone stern as a stormcloud. Doshi shrugged and shared a helpless glance with her fellow Phantrans, while the Han growled something over his shoulder to the Ravenguard warrior behind him. Matrick's head was bowed as Lilith grumbled into his ear. Clay looked over at Gabriel, who was staring through the soiled mess of his hair as if the druin were a puzzle he was determined to solve. The Duke had yet to recognize any more of Saga's members, standing as they were behind the screen of Matrick's guards.

I don't imagine he'll be happy to see Gabe again, he figured, and wondered—not for the first time—if attending this council had been a wise idea after all.

The palanquin's curtain shifted again, and again the gold-masked Sultana uttered something to her attending minister, who nodded, smoothed out his robes, and turned. "My Esteemed Lady, Sultana of Narmeer, Bride of Vizan the Summer Lord, Mistress of the Scorching Throne, Herald—"

"Ask your question," barked Lastleaf, his long ears quivering impatiently.

The druins, Clay knew, possessed something Vespian had referred to as "the prescience," which gave them insight into the very near future. It meant they often knew your mind a moment before you spoke it, and made even the kindest druin seem impatient, since they sometimes replied to something you hadn't quite finished saying.

And of course it made them real nasty fuckers in a fight.

The Narmeeri minister, caught between a rock and the very hardest of places, gave his mistress an inquiring glance. The mask dipped in acquiescence, and the man sighed, obviously relieved. "The Sultana would have me ask: Why summon us to council if not to negotiate? What is it you hope to achieve? Or have you come simply to gloat?"

Lastleaf raised his chin and wet his lips. His ears shivered, and his fingers opened and closed as though longing for the grasp of a sword. He appeared profoundly uncomfortable, and Clay wondered how long it had been since the druin had dealt with something other than a monster.

"I have a—" Lastleaf paused, as if rummaging his archaic vocabulary in search of a suitable word "—request of my own."

"And that is?" asked Matrick wearily.

Lastleaf spread his hands. His smile might have been charming were it not full of daggers. "Do nothing," he said.

No one spoke. The wind picked up; Clay could smell smoke on the evening breeze. Below, a few people had already begun trickling toward the river, where boatmen would be waiting by the dozen to ferry them across before dark.

Eager to be first back to Brycliffe with this story, Clay figured, his eyes drawn to the pale Duke and his great black wyvern. *But is it over yet?*

It was Etna Doshi who broke the silence at last. "You wanna clarify that?" she asked.

"I am aware that you plan on sending an army to Castia," said Lastleaf. "I am telling you to reconsider."

"Requesting, you mean." This from Obolon Han, who had not so casually placed the palm of one hand on the pommel of his sabre.

Clay saw Gabriel steal a nervous glance toward Matrick's back. Matty had explained on the way here that the courts were, in fact, marshalling an army with the aim of liberating Castia, or at least eradicating whatever monsters inhabited the city by the time it arrived. Endland was a fair and fertile land, shielded from the Heartwyld by a range of daunting mountains. The Castian Republic, which had been founded by the fleeing remnants of Grandual's short-lived Empire, had thrived there for more than three hundred years. Several prominent members of Castia's ruling senate had fled their city and found asylum in Fivecourt before the siege began. They had promised great rewards to whichever of Grandual's monarchs delivered their city from the Horde's clutches.

"Think of the cost," said Lastleaf, "to equip this army of yours, to feed them, to pay them wages worth facing a Horde for. The Heartwyld, even by the straightest path, is more than a thousand miles across. And beyond the forest lies the Emperor's Mantle."

A modest name for a wall of ice-clad stone infested with as many horrible creatures as the forest it borders, Clay mused.

"It will take several months for an army to reach Castia. How many soldiers will you lose along the way? The woods remain home to terrible things—things even I dare not approach. How many of your people will fall prey to the flesheater tribes, or to the hungry mouths of the trees themselves? How many will succumb to the rot, I wonder?"

Moog stirred at that. He glanced sidelong at Matrick, who they hadn't yet told of the wizard's condition. *Condition*, of course, being a gracious term for *inevitable and exquisitely painful death.*

"By the time your army reaches Endland, weary and depleted, Castia will have fallen. My Horde, whose size even now would beggar your imagination, will have grown larger still, swollen with scavengers come to feast on the city's corpse. If you challenge us, you *will not win.* I defeated the Republic's army, bolstered though it was by a legion of your famed mercenaries, and I would defeat you as well. Next time, however, there will be no more walls to hide behind, nowhere to run. If you face me on the battlefield, you risk annihilation."

The sun had dropped behind the druin, throwing his shadow like a spear through the heart of the assembled delegates. There was a cold bite to the wind now. The Agrian guardsmen were growing visibly anxious, and Clay abruptly remembered what Matrick had said earlier about the wights that flocked to the Isle after dark.

"How many could each of you send? Five thousand? Ten? Even still, it will not be enough."

That may be true, Clay thought. The Heartwyld Horde might lack the cohesion of a professional army, but it was rumoured to be a hundred thousand strong. By the time Grandual's forces reached Endland they would be tired and footsore, battered from the months-long trek across the forest, over the mountains. They would be outnumbered, he knew, and likely outmatched. Common soldiers—even the rugged warriors of Kaskar—weren't the same breed as mercenaries. Mercs spent their whole careers hunting and killing monsters. A soldier's life, especially since the courts had been at peace for decades, consisted primarily of marching, standing, sleeping, and occasionally throwing dice or playing cards against other soldiers who weren't busy marching, standing, or sleeping.

A court soldier might know one end of a sword from the other—hells, there may even be a few handy fighters among them—but they weren't likely to know that a cockatrice's gaze could turn flesh to stone, or that bugbears, for whatever reason, couldn't see the colour yellow. Knowledge like that could be exploited. It could save your life. No, Clay reasoned, pitting regular troops against a Heartwyld Horde was likely to result in disaster, as it had for the Republic.

The council knew this, and so did Lastleaf.

"All those precious lives," he said blithely, "will vanish, like smoke. Who among you can afford to lose so many soldiers?"

"It tastes like a mouthful of seawater," said Etna Doshi, "but the 'Duke' here has a point. Castia may be far from here, but it's a damn sight farther from Aldea. My queen won't likely see the sense in sending so many west with little to no chance they'd ever come back."

Clay saw Gabriel flinch as though struck.

Matrick, his hands balled into fists, whirled on her. "We can't just let all those people die!"

"Of course we can," snapped Lilith. "Be practical, Matrick."

"I'm with the king on this," said Maladan Pike. "A lot of good mercs went west. I'm not of a mind to give up on them. And besides, any one of my warriors is worth ten bloody goblins. A hundred, even. I'd bet my horse on it."

At the rate the man wagered horses, Clay was surprised the First Shield had found a mount to carry him to Lindmoor.

The High Han was shaking his head at Matrick. "It hurts like a horse's cock to say it, but I stand with Old King Matrick as well. If Agria goes west, Cartea rides with 'em."

Lastleaf turned on Maladan Pike, a sneer pulling at his mouth. "And who will remain to defend the north should the yethiks emerge in force from their winter caves?" The First Shield glowered, and looked poised to voice an angry retort, but the druin wheeled on Doshi first. "Who will be left to guard your coasts if saig raiders storm ashore by the thousand? Who will keep the serpent kin from despoiling your precious oases and cutting off trade with the north?" he asked the Narmeeri ministers, who began clucking to one another behind raised, ring-adorned hands.

These aren't probabilities, Clay thought, *they're threats*. His gaze roved among the assembled delegates, who were wringing their hands and muttering worriedly.

Lastleaf said to Matrick, "Your borders are plagued by centaurs, yes? Stealing children, killing farmers here and there? Let us hope they do not grow emboldened while your soldiers are away in the west. They might start wiping out whole villages, putting entire towns on the spit." At last he looked to Obolon Han.

"Oh, fuck off," said the Cartean. "I get it. We attack you, you attack us. I can see the clouds without you telling me rain is on the way."

"And if we leave you alone?" inquired Lilith, no longer content to use Matrick as her mouthpiece. "If we shun the Republic and abandon Castia?"

Another grin from Lastleaf, autumnal this time—all light and no warmth.

He has what he came here for, Clay thought. *Compliance. Capitulation.*

"Then the distant Republic becomes the Duchy of Endland," the druin explained, almost cheerfully. "And perhaps, someday, an ally to the courts of Grandual—"

"You can't be serious!"

All eyes turned to Gabriel, but none quicker than Lastleaf's, whose gaze flooded with hateful recognition. *"You!"* he hissed, ears trembling with rage, his mask of civility shattering in an instant. He didn't reach for a sword—not yet—but Clay didn't need a druin's prescience to see violence brewing.

Even so, what happened next surprised him.

Sensing an opportunity, Obolon Han surged forward, bare sabre bloodied by the setting sun. Lastleaf, his focus nailed to Gabriel, didn't see the Cartean coming until it was too late, and even then he'd barely begun to turn when the Han's sword came chopping down—

Something dark eclipsed the sun; a sound like the sky tearing split the dusk.

The Han's blade went spinning away, missing Lastleaf by mere inches, and Obolon's feet scissored madly as the wyvern's jaws snapped shut over his head. For just a moment Clay could hear the Han's screams echo down the monster's throat, until, with a wet crunch, Obolon's torso was ripped free from his legs. The wyvern spread her wings and tipped her head back. Clay would have sworn he saw her throat bulge as the Cartean (well, half of him anyway) was forced down her gullet.

There was shouting—the din of general panic—among the gathered delegates, but no one actually moved. Even the Han's Ravenguard seemed rooted to the spot, too afraid to draw their bows lest the wyvern single them out next.

Lastleaf was on his rump, apparently dazed, likely grappling with the fact that all his careful schemes had, for the space of a heartbeat, seemed as fragile as a spider's web at the mercy of the wind. His long ears had gone limp. He raked red-gold hair from his eyes as he scrambled to his feet, then reached back and withdrew the topmost sword from its scabbard. The blade looked as though it were made of sun-baked stone laced with igneous cracks. The air around it shimmered with searing heat.

By now, however, most everyone on the hill had recovered from the shock of Obolon's death. The druin spared a snarl for Gabriel before he turned, coat whirling at his knees, and stalked beneath the wyvern's outstretched wing.

He shouted, *"Ashatan!"* and the creature stooped so Lastleaf could grasp hold of a spine and haul himself onto her back.

The wyvern's powerful legs propelled her upward. Her wings thrashed the air as she soared out of bowshot, and Clay could smell her stink in his nostrils, a scent like carrion bloating in still water.

The Isle, meanwhile, dissolved into pandemonium. Pike's warriors were scuffling with a number of Doshi's pirates. The Han's men scattered, racing toward their shrieking mounts. The Sultana's Kaskars ushered her palanquin away; the storm-wracked sails of her skyship crackled and the tidal engines whirred to life. Crossbow turrets along its rails were aimed at the darkening sky.

Clay looked to his friends. "We should probably... what?" he asked. "Moog, what is it?"

Gabe's eyes were skyward still, but the wizard was gawping downhill. Clay followed his gaze, and at first didn't know what exactly he was seeing. Lights like blue-white candles were flickering all across Lindmoor, coalescing into the shape of...

Men. Or the ghosts of men. There were hundreds of them, and hundreds more sparking to life among the shadowed eaves to the east.

Clay decided now was a good time to conclude his earlier thought. "We should go," he said.

"Matrick!" screeched Lilith, clinging tightly to her body-guard's arm.

The king, in a vain attempt to keep the peace, had wedged himself between a Kaskar twice his height and a Phantran with anchor-shaped tears tattooed on her cheek. "Yes, dear?" he asked, before catching sight of the wights glowing in the fen below. "Oh."

He managed to extricate himself and ordered his guards-men escort them, with haste, to the river. As their party rushed down the southern slope, Matrick fell in step with his bandmates. "I may be stabbing at spectres here, but I'd say the Council was a spectacular fucking failure."

"Speaking of spectres..." Clay cast a wary eye at the iri-descent figures plodding past them on either side, converging slowly on the Isle. "Should we be worried?"

"Nah," Matrick waved a hand. "They won't hurt us. Probably. Hopefully." He whistled at the captain of his guard. "Let's pick up the pace a bit, shall we?"

When Lilith swooned, overcome by exhaustion, Lokan hoisted her gallantly in his arms. When Matrick, wheezing, tripped over his own weary feet, Clay and Gabriel propped him up between them.

"Moog," whispered the king, "do me a favour?"

"Anything," said the wizard, drawing near.

"Kill me. Tonight."

Chapter Fourteen

Farewell to the King

Matrick was found dead the next morning. Two physicians were summoned to the scene. The first declared that the king had drunk himself to death, while the second insisted he'd been poisoned. Shortly after a breakfast prepared by Lilith's personal chefs, the second physician fell ill and died. The first physician wisely ruled his associate's death a complete and utter mystery.

Clay and the others were permitted to remain in the palace, though it was made clear the queen's hospitality would extend only until Matrick was buried. Lilith seemed eager to get the funeral under way, so the following morning they joined the royal procession as it moved in silence through the near-empty streets of Brycliffe.

A baker clapped her flour-dusted hands as the grave parade went by, and a pair of mummers paused their rehearsal to watch it pass. One of them had dyed his hair bright orange and donned a pair of ears that were likely meant to look druin but were obviously part of a rabbit costume. The other was draped in a black sheet and had rickety wings strapped to his arms.

"I thought there would be more people," muttered Gabriel. "I'd heard he made a pretty good king."

"Lilith didn't tell them," said Moog. "I heard she locked the servants up overnight and threatened to kill them if word got out the king was dead."

"Why?" Clay asked.

"She said the crowd would slow us down, and that people would throw flowers, and that it was hard to clean flowers off cobblestone."

"Seriously?" Clay glanced over his shoulder at the queen, sitting high and regal on her horse and laughing at something Lokan had said. "Gods, Matty sure can pick 'em, eh?"

They passed beneath a postern and followed a winding, switch-back trail through the steep forest behind Brycliffe Castle. At last the procession skirted the stony shore of the river until they came to a stretch of sandy beach. Clay's first clue that Moog's not-so-elaborate plan to fake Matrick's death and dig him up afterward was maybe not such a great idea after all was when the sombre march stopped at a pier and not, as was customary, in a graveyard.

A small cluster of nobility waited by the shore, and Clay sidled up to the nearest of them. "Isn't there a . . . royal tomb or something?" he asked.

The man, who was holding a pristine white kerchief but seemed reluctant to tarnish it by dabbing his dripping nose, nodded. "There is—in the catacombs below the castle—but Her Grace has recently been fascinated by all things—" his eyes darted to Lokan and back "—um, northern."

"And how do they bury kings up north?"

The nobleman looked out over the river. "I don't think they do."

A beautifully crafted boat was carried to the shore by a dozen strong men. Matrick's body was laid to rest inside, rendered deathlike by a potion Moog had cooked up in the palace kitchen after the Council. His skin had gone white as bone a perfectly natural side effect of something called shaderoot, the wizard assured them. The king's sparse hair had been oiled back. His clothes were immaculate, and he was draped in so much gold—rings, chains, torcs, and a great gaudy crown set with precious gemstones—that Clay feared the boat might sink the moment they set it adrift. *Roxy* and *Grace*, his beloved knives, were crossed over his breast.

A wreath of red nettles had been placed on Matrick's brow as an offering to the Autumn Son. Without it (or so Vail's priests alleged), the Heathen would betray the king's soul to the Frost Mother and so condemn it to eternity in the icy halls of hell.

The royal children were dressed all in black, their grief as varied as their parentage. The twins cried (which Clay was beginning to think was their natural emotional state) while Lillian stood with crossed arms, glaring with those fierce blue eyes at any who dared console her. Kerrick's fat face was a mess of tears and running snot. Whenever he thought no one was looking he stole a handful of what Clay hoped were raisins from his pocket and jammed them into his mouth. Only the oldest, Danigan, remained composed. He actually looked *bored* as the priest droned on, commending Matrick's achievements not only as a king, but as a doting father, and a loving, beloved husband.

Lilith, for her part, played the role of grieving widow so well that Clay half-expected the crowd to start tossing roses at her feet as she took her bows. The act was belied only by the way she clung to Lokan's arm, as though she were adrift at sea and he the last spar of a sunken ship. The broad-shouldered Kaskar had found some ornate black armour for the occasion, and he wore an expression of grim austerity that looked somehow fraudulent on the face of one so young.

Is he fool enough to believe she might make him a king? Clay could almost pity the boy if he actually thought so. Lilith would no more want for another husband than she'd want a rotting pumpkin for a head. It was likely she'd assumed upon marrying Matrick that he would drink himself into an eternal stupor and leave the governing to her. Instead he had risen to the task and become, by all accounts, a competent, compassionate king. Now she would rule alone, without the need to keep her rapacious desires in check.

Once again Clay had spent too long inside the maze of his own head. He found the exit in time to hear the priest invoke the gentler half of the Holy Tetrea, consigning Matrick's soul to the Summer Lord's eternal care and the Spring Maiden's everlasting ministrations. Matty, were he not actively engaged in the act of faking his own death, would no doubt have made a joke at precisely that moment. Finally the boat was shoved off from the shore, where the quickening current took hold and carried it east downriver.

"This is fine," said Moog, leaning in. "Better, actually. We don't even need to dig him up. Just follow the course of the river and collect him later. Did you see all that gold they sent off with him? We'll be rich!"

Gabriel didn't look as confident. "It doesn't make sense," he said. "What's to stop anyone else from doing the same? There could be brigands downriver just waiting to loot the king's boat. Why would..." He trailed off. "Oh."

Clay followed his gaze and saw Lokan holding a longbow. The northman had an arrow already nocked, and was holding its pitch-smeared tip over the flame of a small brazier.

The Kaskars did not, apparently, simply send their dead kings floating peacefully downriver. They also set them on fire.

Suddenly every eye in the assembly was upon him, and Clay realized he'd just screamed "NO!" at the top of his lungs.

Roll with it, Cooper, his mind goaded. *And fast—they're all looking at you.*

"No," he repeated. He took a step forward, still unsure of what to say or do next, and then found himself reaching for the bow in Lokan's hands. "Let me. He was my friend. I would send him to the gods myself. Please," he added, as the northman looked to his queen for confirmation. Lilith appeared skeptical for a moment, but then nodded, and Lokan handed the weapon over like a child forced by his mother to share his new toy with a sibling.

Clay claimed the bow, purposefully bringing the arrow's flaming tip close to Lokan's face as he squared himself to the river. The boat was little more than a hundred yards off—a shot even someone who'd never shot a bow in their life could make with careful aim and a bit of luck.

He drew. He fired. He missed. Badly.

Clay heard a few groans behind him; a couple snickers as well. "Sorry," he said lamely. "Blinded by grief. Let me try again." The Kaskar handed off another arrow, and Clay took his time setting the tip alight. Finally he took aim, and this time he missed by a much more narrow margin.

"Damn that wind," he muttered, beckoning Lokan to pass him another arrow. The northman regarded him skeptically, probably because there was no discernible breeze whatsoever.

His third shot splashed down just short of the boat, which was nearing a bend in the river that would take it out of sight. Already it was shrouded in a cloud of white fog rolling out from behind the distant tree line.

The queen sighed. "Lokan, will you please show this oaf how to properly set the body of my dear, departed husband on fire?"

The northman's smarmy smile returned. "Of course, My Queen."

"Your Highness—" Clay started to protest, but Lilith cut him short.

"Enough. You've made a mockery of this hallowed ritual. It is lucky for us that Lokan is a master of the bow—and of several other weapons besides," she added coyly.

It was all Clay could do not to roll his eyes at the innuendo. He relinquished the bow, and took a short step away, waiting as the young northman casually put another arrow to string and set it alight.

Cocky little bastard's making a show of it, Clay realized. He saw Gabriel shift nervously in his periphery.

Lokan planted his feet and set his sight on the king's boat, now barely visible for the fog. Difficult as the shot would be from so far off, Clay had little doubt the queen's champion was capable of making it, and so he waited until the man had drawn the bow to its full extent before he said, too quietly for anyone but the northman to hear, "Have you picked out a name for your son yet?"

"Wha—!?" The string snapped. The arrow went backward, spinning dangerously into the crowd. As the mourners scrambled from the missile's errant path, Lokan wheeled on Clay. His face went from pink to red to livid purple, coloured by anger, or shame, but probably anger.

"I've always thought 'Orag' had a noble ring to it. A good *northman's* name, that."

Lokan was obviously furious, but when the youth took a step toward him Clay matched his gaze. *"Fuckin' try it,"* he said, quiet and cold as an ice-mantled mountain. The Kaskar stopped dead in his tracks.

The gathering had gone quiet again, and after a few moments Lokan blinked as though released from a spell. "My Lady, I am sorry. I..." his eyes flitted to the crowd, to Clay, then back to his queen. He bowed his head. "I have failed you."

"No matter," Lilith said breezily. She straightened, pulling her black shawl up over slim white shoulders. "The fire is just a formality, after all. It is well that my husband's soul is gone, for his body will be broken on the Teeth of Adragos."

"The Teeth of who now?" asked Moog.

It was right about then Clay realized the fog on the river was not fog at all. It was mist. Which was sometimes a vastly different thing altogether.

* * *

In the end, it was being dead that saved Matrick's life.

They found him at dusk, sitting on a rock near the base of the falls. There was a nasty gash across the left half of his face that had sheared off the lobe of one ear, and he was covered head to toe with dark bruises. The eye above his injury was terribly swollen, so that when he saw them and smiled it shut completely.

"Glif be praised! I'm free!" he yelled, his voice almost lost to the roar and rush of water.

The others were gazing up at the towering waterfall, apparently known as the Teeth of Adragos, likely due to the spires of sharp black stone that jutted from the lake below.

"How . . . ?" Moog seemed unable to finish the question, and so Gabriel asked it himself.

"How did you survive?"

The self-exiled king of Agria shrugged. "Beats me," he said. "I woke up right before I went over, but the drug—that shaderoot, or whatever—hadn't quite worn off yet. I couldn't move, at least not until I'd taken a couple knocks on the way down, which loosened me up enough I could swim to shore when it was all over. Still, I think being a bit limp was what spared me getting all smashed up. Well, *more* smashed up. Anyway, I managed to keep these ladies safe." He patted the pair of daggers resting beside him on the rock.

The wizard moved to the edge and peered down into the churning water. "The boat? The treasure?"

"Lost, I'm afraid. Except what I've got on me." Matrick brandished his hands, glittering with golden rings. He was still wearing several chains as well, but the crown was gone. Nevertheless, they'd left the castle with full rations, and what remained on Matrick's person could be pawned for more than enough to keep them fed for however long the gods saw fit to let them live.

"Lucky," said Gabriel.

Clay glanced at him sidelong. "I'm not sure that word means what you think it means."

"We should keep moving," Moog declared. "There might be folk seeking a scrap of that treasure. Or Lilith might wise up and send someone out to look for us."

"True enough," Clay agreed. He scratched at his beard and looked to Gabriel. "You sure about Fivecourt?"

"What's in Fivecourt?" Matrick asked. He reached tentative fingers to his wounded ear and winced in pain.

"*Ganelon*," said Clay and Gabriel at once.

The king frowned at his bloody fingers. "Really? Fivecourt's backtracking a bit, though..."

"Even so," said Gabriel, glancing over at Clay. "We need him. If we're going to cross the Heartwyld. If we're to have any hope at all of getting Rose out of Castia. He is—"

"He's Ganelon," Clay said. "I know. And I know we need him. I just...don't think he'll be all that happy to see us."

"Yeah, well. We have to try."

Clay exhaled. "Okay. All right. Fivecourt it is."

"We can follow the river right to it," Matrick suggested. "Four, maybe five days through these woods? It's not as fast as the road, but we should keep a low profile anyway, right? If someone sees us and Lilith finds out I'm still alive she'll have my head on a platter. All our heads, in fact."

"And its likely Kallorek knows where we're going," added Gabriel. "He'll have men on the road, I should think."

Fantastic, Clay mused. *A spiteful queen and a vengeful booker to watch out for. As if heading into a monster-infested forest on our way to a hopelessly besieged city wasn't trouble enough. Whoever wants us dead should just sit back and let us kill ourselves.*

They set off east. Gabriel took the lead, with Moog and Matrick chatting excitedly behind, while Clay brought up the rear, still lost in thought.

Ah, but look on the bright side, Cooper: You have friends by your side, food to eat, and gold to spend.

He didn't know it then, of course, but by noon the next day he would lose two of the three.

Chapter Fifteen

Breakfast with Thieves

They stopped for a rest shortly before sunrise. Matrick offered to keep watch while the others snatched an hour or two of precious sleep, and so Clay set his back against the mossy corpse of a fallen tree and was out within minutes.

He dreamt of home, imagining his house filled with frogs of every shape and size as Tally pulled more and more from inside her pockets. Next he was swimming in Kallorek's so-called pool, when suddenly one of the tiled walls fell away and he plunged over the edge into black oblivion. Finally Clay dreamt of Jain, the woman who had robbed him and Gabriel on the road to Conthas. He saw her standing over him in those silly patchwork clothes, a bow in her hands and a great big smile on her dirt-smeared face.

"Mornin', Slowhand."

He blinked. Could you blink in your dreams?

"Rise and shine, man!" Jain kicked him gently with her boot, and he glimpsed one of his wife's knitted socks peeking out the top.

His voice was a hoarse croak. "I'm not dreaming."

The brigand snorted at that. "Course not. Or I wouldn't be wearing so many bleedin' clothes now, would I?"

Clay straightened and glanced around. Jain's gang—the

Silk Arrows—were scattered around the camp. They were all of them armed, but none looked particularly threatening. In fact it looked as though they'd been here for a while before Clay had finally stirred awake. They'd long since relieved Matrick of what valuables he'd managed to salvage from his funeral, jamming rings onto already ring-crowded fingers and adding chains of gold and silver to the numerous scarves and shawls around their necks. A few were sitting with Moog while the wizard regaled them with some story that required him to flail his arms like a pair of flapping wings. His audience laughed and clapped, and so Moog—an entertainer at heart—redoubled his efforts, which drew another bout of laughter from his crowd.

He spotted Gabriel sitting by a small fire, eating eggs out of a frying pan. When his friend saw that Clay was awake he swallowed and set down his fork. "We're being robbed," he said matter-of-factly.

"Evidently." Clay rubbed at his eyes to clear them. He looked at Matrick, who was leaning sullenly against a nearby tree. "Weren't you supposed to be keeping watch?"

"Sure was," said Matty. "I *watched* them appear out of nowhere with bows."

Clay frowned. "Fair enough."

Jain prodded him again with her foot. "Up and at 'em, Slowhand. There's eggs and bacon—maybe even a few sausages left, if your friends haven't gobbled them up already. Just cause we're taking your stuff don't mean we can't be civilized about it. We've had some fair good fortune since we saw you last. More than you anyway, from what I've heard."

Sure enough, the profusion of garments on Jain's person *did* seem to be of slightly higher quality than when he'd seen her last week. When she saw him eyeing her black silk gloves, the bandit raised her hand and pushed her sleeve up to the elbow to show it off.

"You like?" she asked. Jain had cut the tips off the thumb

and the first two fingers so she could draw an arrow without losing her grip. Clay had to admire the woman's pragmatism, if not her fashion sense. "Scooped these off some highborn lady on her way to the king's funeral," she said, before kissing the exposed fingers and touching her heart. "May the Summer Lord light his way."

She hasn't recognized Matrick, Clay realized. *They don't know who he is.* Better to keep it that way, he figured. Once Lilith discovered their deception—and she would, eventually, of that he had no doubt—she would come after them like a dragon who'd counted its hoard and found it a penny short. Which was to say: swiftly, and with terrible vengeance.

Clay climbed slowly to his feet. His back ached, and his knees popped when he straightened them. He was careful not to make any sudden move that Jain or one of her lady-thugs might perceive as aggression. Getting an arrow in the chest was a sure way to spoil a good breakfast, and if he was going to be robbed he might as well score some bacon in the deal.

Jain led him to the fire, where he settled down beside Gabe. She passed him a skillet and a crude wooden fork before claiming one for herself and squatting to eat. The eggs were cold, but there was a thick slab of salted pork belly and a few fat sausages that were still warm when he bit into them. All in all, a pretty square meal.

"The birds say there's a bounty out for the pair o' you," said Jain, nodding toward him and Gabe.

Clay froze with his mouth full. He glanced over at Gabriel, hoping to catch his friend's eye, but Saga's frontman was staring determinedly into his empty skillet.

Jain chuckled and waved her fork dismissively. "No need to piss your britches, Slowhand. I ain't no bounty hunter. There's a long shot between the occasional robbery and trading a man's life for a few lousy courtmarks. Heck, I'd bet the *Maiden's Virtue* there's a fair price on my head to boot." She snorted a laugh. "I'd be insulted otherwise."

"Do you think it was Lilith?" asked Matrick, before Clay could tell him to keep his stupid, stupid mouth shut.

Jain's brow furrowed. "You mean the Ice Queen of Agria? Why would..." She cocked her head at Matrick. The king's face was still mangled from his fall. The welt beneath his left eye had swollen to the size of a plum, sealing his eye shut. Clay held his breath, praying the brigand wouldn't identify the battered old rogue, but the light of awareness crept across her face, certain as a new day dawning. "Well fuck me with a Phantran's salty dick, you're Matty Skulldrummer!"

The king grinned sheepishly. "I used to be," he said.

Jain laughed and slapped her knee. "My daddy always said you were the fastest son'bitch with a knife there ever was. Said you could carve up a turkey 'fore the thing even knew it was dead!"

"And eat it, too," said Matrick, patting his prodigious gut.

Jain got another laugh at that. She wolfed down another sausage and licked grease from her bare fingers. When she'd finished she asked Clay, "So what's all this about, eh? Last we met I figured you and not-so-Golden Gabe here for a couple of old coots bound to get your rocks off in Conthas—and yet here you are: halfway to Fivecourt, with Magic Moog and Matty Skulldrummer in tow. Now your wizard's clearly a few arrows short of a full quiver"—as if to prove her point Moog was now jumping in circles and quacking like a duck—"but why would a summer-kissed king shirk his crown to slum it in the woods with you three? Unless..." She paused to swallow, and a wry grin tugged at the corner of her mouth. "Don't tell me you're getting the band back together?"

"We're getting the band back together," Clay admitted. Gods, but it sounded dumb when he said it out loud.

The brigand's next question was obvious. "What the hell for?"

Clay blew out a sigh. He shared a questing look with Gabriel, who offered a scant nod in response, and then he explained why they were trying to re-form Saga, and what they intended to do once they had.

By the time he'd finished the rest of Jain's girls had all stopped to listen. Jain herself simply stared at him for a bit, chewing salt pork like a cow working down a mouthful of cud. "Y'all are fucking crazy," she said finally.

When breakfast was done and the dishes rinsed clean in the river, Lady Jain and the Silk Arrows finished robbing them. Matrick was permitted to keep his knives, and Clay his shield, but the sword he'd managed to plunder from the palace armoury was confiscated. Moog's enchanted bag appeared empty, so they left him that. Everyone but Clay and Gabe had a good laugh when Gabriel dumped the same collection of dull rocks from his pack. They were permitted to keep the rations they'd brought from Agria, thankfully, but one of the girls took a shining to Matrick's good leather boots, which left the man who had ruled a kingdom just three days ago wearing naught but a pair of wool socks on his feet. The Silk Arrows left him those, at least; they had no need of socks, after all.

"Listen," said Clay, sidling as close as he dared to Jain and lowering his voice, "we went to some trouble faking Matty's death. If Lilith found out he were still alive—"

"No worries, Slowhand," Jain assured him. "We won't go spilling your secret. Me and mine have no love for the Ice Queen of Agria, I'll you tell that. Far as we're concerned, Old King Matrick is dead and gone." She threw a wink in Matty's direction. "Long live the king."

Matrick offered a stiff bow in return.

As her girls dissolved into the forest Jain turned to take them all in. "Keep well," she said, leaning on her unstrung bow. "With any luck we'll meet again before you fools hit the Heartwyld, but if not..." She squinted at Gabriel, and her eyes went hard above her bandit smile. "I hope you find your little girl. I truly do. She's lucky to have a da' what looks out for her." Jain looked as though she would say something further, but instead she stepped away, waving a silk-gloved hand in farewell before strolling off into the woods.

"What a nice bunch of girls," declared Matrick, watching her go.

"They certainly were," Gabe agreed.

"I mean, they made us breakfast and everything," said Moog, and the other two nodded.

Which left Clay to state the obvious. "Y'all are fucking crazy," he said.

Around noon the next day Gabriel asked to see Moog's crystal ball. Clay had actually been wondering why his friend hadn't done so already, which didn't make it any less distressing now that it finally happened. Moog, at least, did an admirable job of dissembling the matter.

"What? Oh, that old thing? Whatever for?"

"You know what for," said Gabriel.

They'd stopped for a brief rest, each of them scarfing a handful of berries and mushrooms the wizard had pointed out as they walked. Matrick, sensing the awkwardness at hand, wandered off to relieve himself in the woods.

"It probably won't even work, you know. Damn thing's been dropped a dozen times or more. It's as unreliable as a barbarian librarian!" Moog laughed at that, but when no one else did he looked genuinely shocked. "Really? Because barbarians... well, never mind."

Gabriel favoured the wizard with that broken smile of his. "Even still."

"All right. Okay. Once we get to Fivecourt I'll have a look for it. Sound good? Or maybe we can find a proper diviner who "

"Now. Please."

Moog tugged nervously at his beard. He looked to Clay for help, and Clay took a good hard look at a really quite fascinating knot in the tree he was standing next to. At last the wizard relented. With a sigh he rummaged in his bottomless bag until he found what Gabriel had asked for.

"She is very, very far away," Moog warned as he handed it over. "You might not be able to see that far, or very clearly, even if it does work."

Gabriel sat cross-legged on the loamy earth, nestling the crystal ball in his lap. Moog plunked himself down across from him. Clay remained where he was, unsure he wanted to see whatever the glassy orb revealed.

"So what do I do?" asked Gabe. "Say her name? Call out to her somehow?"

"You don't have to say anything, no. She can't hear you at all. You just sort of ... summon her to mind. Form a picture of her in your head, and then hold on to it for as long as it takes."

Gabriel did as he was told, squinting into his lap and biting anxiously at his bottom lip. The whirl of violet mist inside the ball was so sudden all three of them started.

"Concentrate," said Moog. "Once you have her in mind, try to make every detail as vivid as possible."

The smoke within the orb continued to roil, now and then coalescing long enough for Clay to pick out a small detail—the curve of an ear, the arch of an eyebrow—before it was lost to the swirl and eddy of purple vapours. At last the smoke began to clear, and they saw a vast black ocean heaving beneath a grey sky.

Not an ocean, Clay realized. *It's the black forest. The Heartwyld*.

The sea of desiccated wood went on and on, and Clay shuddered to think what horrid things lurked beneath those gnarled eaves. At last the trees gave way to stony foothills; then a wall of imposing mountains—the Emperor's Mantle—reared up like the battlements of some ghastly, snow-capped fortress. They were armoured in sheer ice, their hearts infested with monstrosities that thrived in the deepest, darkest places of the world. Clay caught a glimpse of something soaring among the mist-shrouded peaks. Long necked and leather winged, it dived behind a bluff and was gone.

A loud snap stole his gaze from the orb. Matrick had returned and was standing behind Gabriel, who was too intent upon the sphere to notice.

Beyond the mountains lay a plain of yellow grass, traced here and there by stone roads and dotted by small hamlets. Endland. Gabe's vision swept along the course of a frothing river. They saw a herd of wild horses splashing through, and then, after a few fleeting seconds, the image in the orb came to rest on a village bisecting the river.

Something was wrong. It was a moment before Clay's mind could reconcile what it was he was seeing. There were corpses in the water. *Thousands* of them. A mound of bloating bodies so huge it threatened to dam the river. He saw pale limbs and weeping red wounds, white-eyed faces frozen in horror and pain and madness.

"They're polluting the water," said Gabriel. "Poisoning the city with their own dead."

"Focus!" snapped Moog, as a haze of purple mist began to overtake the scene. "Keep going."

The view ambled on, but Gabriel's sight seemed transfixed on the river below, choked by an oily morass of bloody gore. At last he managed to wrest his eyes from the fouled water, and Clay, who had taken a few steps closer to the orb without realizing he'd done so, felt his breath catch and his heart go cold.

Castia was a mighty city, or so he'd been told. It was the farthest outpost of human civilization, a testament to the indomitable spirit of those who had built the city of their dreams in a place beyond nightmares. But Clay couldn't see it. Or rather, he couldn't *make himself look away* from what surrounded it, on all sides, to the limit of every horizon.

He'd seen a few armies in his day. He'd seen a number of levied militias, and too many mobs (angry and otherwise) to count. He'd seen what a crowd of a hundred thousand could look like, when every band in Grandual gathered for the War Fair in the ruins of Kaladar. But he had never seen a Horde until now. His mind reeled at the sight. His mouth went dry. The hope he'd nursed of bringing Rose home safe drew the shutters, blew out the candles, and curled up under its bed.

Gabriel cried out as though he'd been struck. The image in the orb winked out, and for a long while no one moved. Matrick stood rooted to the spot. Moog covered his mouth with his hands. He was watching Gabe as if he expected the other man to explode before his very eyes.

Which was exactly what happened next.

Gabriel seized the crystal ball and lunged toward a knob of exposed rock.

"Gabe, wait!" Moog reached out, but made no move to stop him. The wizard knew better than that, at least.

With a sound that was part anguished scream, part blood-curdling war cry, Gabriel raised the orb above his head and brought it violently down onto the stone. It *clinked* like silverware striking glass. Again, and again, he smashed it against the pitiless rock, until at last Clay heard it crack. With each successive blow the sound grew louder, until he feared the orb would shatter, and whatever magic it held would boil out and, well, he had no idea what to expect, really.

But now Gabriel was on his feet, running downhill through the trees, roaring like a Kaskar berserker toward the river below. A trail of purple smoke billowed behind him, issuing from within the fractured sphere. When he reached the riverbank Gabriel hurled the orb—which vanished with hardly a splash—and then, his fury spent, he sagged to his knees and wept by the water's edge.

Moog was on the verge of tears. "I'm sorry," he said to no one in particular. "I thought if maybe he could see her it might lift his spirits. Or if nothing happened . . . well, then at least we would know."

"So she's there, in Castia?" asked Clay. "She's alive?"

The wizard blinked. "Well, yes, she's alive, or we wouldn't have seen anything at all. But . . ." He didn't finish. He didn't need to. Rose was alive, but no more so than an insect struggling in a web, while an uncountable legion of spiders closed in for the kill.

But you knew that already, didn't you? Clay asked himself. *And so did Gabriel.* What they'd seen in the orb changed nothing. Going to Castia was a shitty idea, but no more so now than it had been the week before.

Shouldering his depleted pack, Clay called down to his friend. "Hey, Gabe, the boys and I are gonna go ahead and rescue your daughter. If you feel like doing that instead of crying down by the river, we'd love to have you along." Saying that, he turned and trudged off eastward without bothering to look if the others were following.

But they were, he knew. Of course they were.

Chapter Sixteen

Snakes and Lions

Gabriel lagged well behind for several hours after the episode with the crystal ball, and shortly before evening they lost track of him entirely. Clay bid the others to stop and rest while he retraced their path. He found Gabe curled up among the tangled roots of a toppled maple, shaking and sobbing into his hands.

"She's dead," he moaned. "She's dead, Clay. She's dead."

"No," said Clay, willing a certitude he didn't feel into his voice. He crouched, using one hand to steady himself when his knees protested. It had rained briefly this morning, and wet leaves plastered themselves to his knuckles. "Moog says she's alive, or else we wouldn't have seen..." His mind recoiled from the memory of what the orb had shown them. "She's alive, Gabe. Right now. Your daughter is alive."

Gabriel looked up, his eyes red-rimmed. "But you *saw*," he said. There was an edge of accusation in his tone, as though he resented Clay's persisting optimism. "You saw. Everyone in that city is dead. It's only a matter of time. Even if the courts sent an army—which they won't—it would be too late."

"Which is why we need to keep moving," Clay told him.

His friend began nodding, but his face crumpled as another wave of grief swept over the bulwark of his resolve.

"But what can we do? Moog is dying of the rot! Matty couldn't climb a flight of fucking stairs, and we expect him to walk a thousand miles? To cross the Heartwyld? To scale a mountain? Even if we *do* reach Castia . . . even if we somehow get there in time . . . what chance do we stand?"

The words *none at all* stood poised on Clay's tongue like an actor ready to stride onstage, but he kept the curtain closed. "I don't know," he said finally. "I really don't, Gabe. But then again, I don't know how we did half the stuff we've done."

Gabriel wiped at his nose with a mud-soiled sleeve. "What do you mean? What stuff?"

"Coldfire Pass," Clay said. "Hollow Hill. Castadar. How many hopeless battles have we fought?"

"A few . . ." Gabe admitted.

"And how many did we win?"

His friend considered that a moment. "All of them?"

"*All of them*," Clay confirmed. "And yeah, sure, we've just been robbed by a gang of girls—"

"Twice," said Gabriel.

"Twice, yes, well . . . we're a bit rusty. Of course we are. But we've beaten the odds before, is what I'm trying to say. Remember Turnstone Keep? Three bands against five hundred bloodthirsty cannibals, and still we survived. We've killed how many gods-forsaken murlogs? How many orcs, and ogres, and shit-spawned warlocks bent on destroying the world? Frozen Hells, we killed a *dragon* once."

Gabe frowned. "You mean Akatung? I thought—"

"Okay, we *almost* killed a dragon once. We definitely hurt him real bad. But he didn't kill us, did he? We're still here, still fighting. And Rose is fighting, too, but she's desperate, and she needs our help. She needs *you*, Gabe. If you don't save her from Lastleaf and his fucking Horde, no one will." He could see hope kindling inside Gabriel, and so offered the last log at his disposal to the flame. "We were giants once, remember? Kings of the Wyld."

Gabe's ghost had uttered those words to Clay on the night his old friend appeared on his doorstep, a prodding reminder of what they'd been. Of what they were daring to be again.

"Kings of the Wyld," whispered Gabriel, and Clay saw the words catch fire in his eyes. "We were giants. We still are." He exhaled a long, shuddering breath, and appeared to take in his surroundings for the first time: the wet earth, the fallen tree, the dripping eaves of the forest around them. When he spoke again there was a note of shame in his voice. "Thank you, Clay. Without you . . ."

"Don't worry about it," said Clay, and then shrugged, since it seemed the only appropriate thing to do.

What remained of their journey to Fivecourt passed *almost* without incident, at least until the clowns attacked.

Clay thought at first that they had come across a troupe of mummers rehearsing their act, but they were brandishing weapons and screaming bloody murder, which set off a few *it's an ambush* alarms right there. The face of the first man to reach him was painted white, with red stars over each eye and a broad, bloody grin smeared from ear to ear. Clay introduced that face to *Blackheart*'s with a sickening crunch, and the man dropped like a corpse cut loose from a tree.

He cast around, trying to number their assailants. *Three, four, five*, he counted. *Two swords, two clubs, one spear, and a bow.* An arrow zipped past his legs, whining like an iron-nosed mosquito. *Two bows*, he silently corrected himself. *Six clowns total. Or no, not clowns. Mercenaries. A band, maybe, or something like one.*

He recalled Gabriel mentioning the rising trend of face paint among would-be warriors these days. It had sounded ridiculous at the time, and was no less so now that this bunch of idiots had come howling between the trees.

Gabriel, weaponless, dodged a club's heavy swing and

retreated toward Clay, while Moog sidestepped a sword's thrust and ducked behind Matrick, whose attempt to reach his knives cross-handed was hampered by the bulge of his gut.

"To Hell with this, I'm the king of Agria!" Matty blurted, prompting Clay to wonder why they'd bothered to fake his death in the first place. "Surrender at once!"

The nearest merc sneered, revealing teeth the colour of rotted wood. "You don't say? Well I'm Vail, the Son of Autumn!" he said mockingly, then pointed out a scrawny woman with stringy wet hair and even worse dental hygiene. "And that there's my sister, the Spring Maiden. Say hi, Glif."

The woman, who was most definitely *not* Glif (and probably no maiden, either), growled like an animal and launched herself at Matrick, chopping at his head with a rusted sword. The king got a knife up just in time to deflect the blow, but she lashed out with a foot, striking his knee, driving him to the ground with an unkingly yelp.

Clay missed what happened next, as two more attackers closed on him. The first, a spearman, came in point first. Clay twisted, grasping the haft of the weapon and pulling hard. The spearman tripped, pitching onto his face.

"Got 'em," said Gabe, landing a boot on the back of the man's skull.

The second man's hair was spiked like a flail and dyed bright blue. He swung his sword at Clay's legs, but the blade bit harmlessly into *Blackheart*'s mottled flesh. The swordsman tried something similar to what had worked on Matty, throwing a punch over the rim of Clay's shield, but Clay was ready. He caught the man's fist on the meat of his palm and clenched. The swordsman blew a breath through gritted teeth, trying in vain to pull his hand free. Clay met his rictus grin with one of his own, and *wrenched*.

His foe's gasp became a squeal, then a curdling scream as the bones in his wrist gave way with a *click*. Clay released his shattered hand and the swordsman stumbled away.

"You f—" he started to say, until an arrow sprouted in the side of his head.

Somewhere deeper into the forest a bowman swore. Clay ignored him, since the shooter would need a moment to reload, and faced up to his next assailant. This one wielded a heavy club spiked with nails. His face was painted red, with a gold moon carving down the bridge of his broad nose. He was built like a Kaskar berserker, and hollered like one as he charged, broadcasting an overhead swing that Clay swiftly decided not to be on the receiving end of.

He rushed forward, bowling himself shoulder first into the big man's legs. It was a desperate move, and it half-worked: the giant came down, but he came down directly on top of Clay, crushing the breath out of him and pinning him to the forest floor.

Clay had a brief moment in which to assess how the rest of the battle was going. The so-called Spring Maiden was down, crying, clutching her stomach with blood-soaked fingers. The one who'd mockingly named himself Vail was still on his feet but retreating frantically now that Matrick had found his rhythm. *Roxy* and *Grace* took turns darting at the man's face, and finally one landed a kiss. The merc yelled in pain, raising both hands to protect himself, and Matty went in low, opening a slice behind the poor man's knee that left him sprawled and screaming in pain.

Gabe took off at a sprint toward the other bowman. Moog was on his knees, rooting around in his bag for the gods-knew-what.

A wand that shoots fireballs would be nice, Clay thought. *Or one of those chain-lightning bolts. Anything but another dose of Magic Moog's Magnificent Phallic Phylactery*...

Someone—the giant on his back, presumably—pushed Clay's face into the damp earth. He got a mouthful of dirt, and when he tried instinctively to breathe he got a lungful of it. He struggled to roll away, but the big man had him trapped like a fox in a snare. Or, more aptly, like a fox flat-tened beneath a huge fucking rock. Stars swirled across the black of his vision, and Clay felt the muscles in his legs start to spasm as he slipped toward shock.

And then suddenly, light. Blessedly, air.

The pressure on his back eased enough for Clay to lever himself up and drag his body free. He coughed once, and then vomited a short stream of mud onto the patchwork leaves below him. Rolling over, he saw Matrick standing behind the big man, whose expression had gone slack in death. The king's knives were buried to the hilt on either side of the giant's neck.

Clay spat out a mouthful of leaf and mud. "Thanks."

"That was...intense," said Matrick. He was smiling, but his voice quavered, and his hands were visibly trembling. How long had it been, Clay wondered, since the king of Agria had killed a man with those hands?

Clay was about to voice his agreement when movement behind the king drew his eye.

The archer, he realized, *angling for another shot.*

"Matty, *down!*" he shouted, and the king dropped to his belly. Clay scrambled to his feet as the bowman drew, surged forward behind *Blackheart* as the arrow left the string in a blur. He felt the iron tip jolt his shield and was already reaching for it, yanking it out, spinning it round in his fingers. He found a grip, saw the bowman's eyes widen as his arm whipped out and he hurled the arrow as hard as he could.

In almost every circumstance, Clay knew, throwing an arrow was an awful idea. He'd tried doing so only once before, years and years ago, but it hadn't gone well—and so no one was more surprised than Clay when it sank halfway to the fletching in the archer's throat.

Well, no one but the archer. The archer was *almost certainly* more surprised than Clay.

He tried giving voice to his disbelief, but blood flooded his mouth, and he slumped to the earth, dead.

Matrick whistled from where he lay from the ground. "Did you just—"

"Stop!" they heard Gabriel cry. He was still chasing the second bowman, who had circled back toward the site of the ambush. As the gap closed between them, the mercenary abandoned his bow and wheeled on Gabe, drawing a curved Phantran cutlass from a sash at his waist.

"Stay back!" he wailed, brandishing the sword with both hands. "Stay back, or I'll have your guts out!" He addressed the pair that had attacked Matrick earlier. "Get up, you feckless curs! I ain't paying you to lay around whinging!"

The merc hamstrung by Matrick rose unsteadily and limped over to his boss, but the woman remained where she was. "Go fuck yourself," she spat. "You ain't paying me to get knifed up neither!"

The clown-faced man Clay had knocked out earlier had come round as well. He lurched groggily to his leader's side, and the three men stood side by side, grunting and growling like cornered animals.

Gabe slowed, stopped, and raised his empty hands. "Listen, you don't . . ." he squinted. "Wait. I know you from somewhere."

The cutlass bearer flinched, averting his eyes. He was a round man—as round as Matrick—with a slick wisp of hair plastered across his otherwise bald head. Clay guessed that his features had originally been painted to resemble some sort of hunting cat, but sweat or rain had turned the black and orange stripes into a slick brown mess. Beneath that, however . . .

"Vail's Rotten Breath, *Raff Lackey*!? Is that you?" Clay took a step toward him, careful not to trip over the giant's out-flung arm. Startled, the merc whirled, waving his sword like a child swatting at stalks of grass. "Woah, hey, Raff! It's me, Clay Cooper."

The merc scowled. "I know who the fuck you are, Slowhand. You look just the same as you always did, 'cept older."

"And you look..." Clay found himself at a loss for words. It had been several decades since he'd laid eyes on Raff Lackey, who looked as though every one of those years had roughed him up something fierce. "You look older, too."

Raff snorted, but said nothing.

"Hold up," said Matrick. "If you knew who we were, why did you attack us?"

The old merc risked a quick glance at Gabriel. "Well...ya see..."

"The bounty," Clay said.

Moog leapt to his feet, holding what looked like a silver flute. "Finally! Wait, what bounty?"

Old Raff looked abashedly from Clay to Gabriel. "Kallorek put a price on the two of you. Ten marks apiece, twenty-five for the pair."

Ten lousy courtmarks, Clay thought dismally. He'd owned cloaks that had cost more than ten marks. "How did you find us?" he asked.

Raff shrugged. "Kal said you were headed to Fivecourt, but you can't claim a bounty inside the city, so we just sort of ranged around hoping to get lucky."

"Well, you got lucky," said Matrick. The woman on the ground moaned piteously and he frowned down at her. "In a manner of speaking."

Gabriel shifted, lowering his hands. "So you're hunting people now, Raff? What's wrong, monsters too scary for you? Surely there's a few rot-ridden goblins somewhere you could put out of their misery."

Clay winced. Goblins would be a sore spot for the weathered mercenary. Raff Lackey's old band, Viscera, had soared to fame when they'd managed to take down a firbolg within sight of Fivecourt's walls. They were the muse of many bards for a time, but their fall from grace happened almost as swiftly.

Compelled by their newfound celebrity to take on more dangerous contracts, Viscera, whose victory against the firbolg had been more luck than skill, found themselves hopelessly outmatched. Tragan, Raff's brother and bandmate, fell off a cliff while running from a direwolf, and their wizard was boiled alive by ogres. Rock bottom came shortly after, when Raff was taken prisoner by a clan of goblins he'd been hired to exterminate. The goblins stripped him, flayed him bloody, and marched him through the village of Rednettle in bizarre mockery of a tour parade.

"Go fuck yourself, Gabe." Raff made a show of summoning a mouthful of phlegm and lobbing it in Gabriel's general direction. "You're looking a little tarnished yourself these days, golden boy." An ugly smile crept onto his face. "Say, when you stopped in on Kallorek did you happen to meet his wife? She's a rare beauty, I'm told, though a bit old for my tastes. Heard she's got a real pretty daughter, though. And one with daddy issues, no less. Those are my favourite."

Gabriel went rigid. His jaw bunched and his eyes flared like a horse scared shitless. Raff was trying to goad him, and doing a damn fine job of it. Clay himself supressed an urge to throttle the old merc senseless, even as his mind scrabbled for a way to steer their course clear of further violence. He'd come on this fool's quest to rescue Rose, after all—not to murder men in the woods outside Fivecourt.

They outnumbered Raff and his remaining companions, but those three were armed, and if there was any lesson to be learned from Raff Lackey's rise and fall, it was that even a shit fighter got lucky from time to time.

"Leave off, Raff," said Clay. "You've got injured need seeing to. Dead to bury. Let us go our way, and we'll put this whole bloody business behind us."

"A brilliant idea!" said not-Glif from her place on the ground. The limping man looked hopeful as well. Whatever Clown-face was thinking was a mystery to Clay, since that crimson smile was a permanent fixture.

Their boss chuckled darkly. "An offer of mercy from Clay

Cooper? You'll forgive me if I doubt your sincerity, Slowhand. As my brother used to say: If it sounds like a sheep but looks like a lion, it's probably a lion."

"A real sage, your brother," quipped Matrick. "Ran himself off a cliff, didn't he?"

Raff sneered. "Laugh it up, Your Highness. I'm claiming that bounty, no doubt about it. You've spared me having to split it six ways, at least, so I'll thank you for that." He shifted his grip on the cutlass, and Clay could sense he was growing restless. "You lot aren't as soft as I'd hoped you'd be, but I still count three swords to none."

What Clay mistook for the mating cry of some forest creature turned out to be Moog's quiet cackle. "I think not," he said cryptically, and brought the silver flute to his lips. The instrument emitted an eerie hiss, a sound like a distant kettle boiling. Raff looked suddenly panicked, fearful of whatever magic the wizard had unleashed upon them. Gabriel took a careful step back, and Clay hefted *Blackheart*, bracing himself for whatever came next.

What came next was the sigh of the wind through the trees, the song of birds warbling to one another, the whisper of a snake gliding over fallen leaves, and the snap of a twig as Matrick shifted uneasily from foot to foot.

Essentially, nothing happened.

Moog tried again, but the result was the same. Raff shared a perplexed look with his two companions. The wizard turned the flute around and tried blowing on the other end. He blew until he was red in the face.

Still nothing.

"Uh, Moog?" Clay ventured.

"Gods of Goblinkind!" the wizard cursed, causing Raff to twitch compulsively. "I bought this off a peddler in Conthas who swore by the Summer Lord's beard it would turn swords into snakes. Or was it spears?" he wondered. "Shit, he might have said spears." Moog scratched his bare scalp with a spindly finger, which drew Clay's attention to the massive python descending from a branch just above the wizard's head.

"Moog—" Clay repeated, but then something brushed against his boot and Clay, looking down, saw that the forest floor had become a carpet of writhing snakes.

At which point several things happened at once: Not-Glif screamed as the jaws of a bright green viper clamped down on her leg, Moog squealed as the python sprang like a bolt of scaled lightning to envelop his torso, and Matty ran to the wizard's defense, hacking at the monstrous snake with both knives in an effort to free him.

Everyone else tried to kill one another.

Vail the limper went down first. Gabriel rushed him, caught his wrist when he tried to swing, grasped a handful of greasy hair, and pulled the man's face into a rising knee.

Clown-face, eager to revenge himself upon Clay, yelled and rushed forward. The ground between them was a hazard of coiling reptiles; every stick and fallen branch was now slithering underfoot. The merc stumbled over a rising cobra and went down. The offended serpent flared its hood, staring the prone man in the face, and if he'd remained still the merc might have emerged unscathed. Instead, Clown-face began shouting, triggering a series of rapid-fire attacks that left him bloody faced and gasping for air.

Clay moved gingerly around his fallen aggressor, careful to avoid stepping on serpentine backs. He scanned the ground for a weapon, but the giant had collapsed on his nail-studded club, and Clown-face's sword was still clutched in his flailing hand.

Sensing an opening, Raff raised his cutlass overhead and charged.

Clay acted on instinct. Afterward he would curse himself for a fool—and worse—but for the time being he stooped and snatched up the nearest weapon to hand. When his enemy's sword came down Clay brought his shield across to knock it aside, then lunged in and thrust his arm forward. The snake in his fist lashed out, sinking venomous fangs into Raff Lackey's exposed throat.

For a moment he and Raff were face-to-face. The reptile's sinuous body was coiled tightly around Clay's arm, and he could feel its jaws working, pumping deadly poison directly into Raff's neck, which was already swelling, darkening from pink, to red, to sickening purple. Clay's ears were filled with an awful clatter, produced, he realized numbly, by the rattle quivering on the serpent's tail.

Raff gasped for a final breath, and used it to utter words that floated across the abysmal inches between him and Clay. "I'll be waiting for ya, Cooper," he gurgled, "along with all the rest."

Chapter Seventeen

Fivecourt

Of Raff's motley crew there were but two survivors: not-Glif and the man with the wood-brown teeth whom Gabe had knocked out earlier. The woman was deathly pale and delirious; Clay figured it was an even wager on whether the venomous snakebite on her leg or the festering wound in her gut killed her first, though he'd have put his money (had Jain left him any) on the bite. The man was in slightly better shape, though half his teeth were missing and he would no doubt walk with a limp for the rest of his life. The two of them staggered off in the direction of Fivecourt while Clay and the others saw to the corpses of their companions.

They cleared away the snakes—an arduous task, since Moog had turned every stick suitable for doing so *into* a snake—and then set about burying the dead. Raff, despite having made himself their enemy, had been a good man once, and deserved a proper rest. Moog performed the Rites of Glif, sprinkling water over each of the graves and invoking the Spring Maiden's Mercy. Matrick spoke a few words as well, commending the souls of the fallen to the Summer Lord.

"Judge them for what they wished to be," he begged the Father of Gods, "not what the world made of them."

The afternoon sun had burned away the lingering clouds

by then, punching through the forest canopy in bright, shifting spears, but Matrick's words cast a cold shadow over Clay's thoughts.

He was remembering the man he'd been upon returning to Coverdale after Saga disbanded—a man not altogether different from the boy who'd struck out with Gabriel a decade earlier, except that he was moderately rich and much more famous.

The money went fast, but the fame lasted a fair bit longer.

Mostly it got him into fights. There were plenty of wannabe mercs eager to test their mettle against the notorious Slowhand, and Clay had been more than happy to show them just how meagre their mettle was by breaking a chair over their heads, or dragging them face-first down the length of the bar. After ten years of fighting he'd found himself restless, constantly seeking provocation to upend the stew of his simmering rage over some fool's head.

He'd done many a good deed during the years he'd toured with Saga, but he'd done bad things, too, and had seen too many bards die in too many ways to sleep well at night. He was tormented by his dreams, and even awake he was haunted by his violent past. He mistook every galloping horse for a charging centaur, every ring of a blacksmith's hammer for a distant clash of arms. Wherever there was smoke, Clay Cooper saw fire.

And then he'd met Ginny. She was the daughter of Giles Locke, chief groomsman of the stables behind the King's Head, and Clay fell for her like an anchor tossed overboard. It wasn't just that she'd been beautiful (though she was), or dauntingly intelligent (she was that, too), but because she perceived in him what few others did—the quiet kindness beneath the warrior's façade—and she evoked in Clay something he hadn't felt since quitting the band and parting ways with the only friends he'd ever known: the need, fierce and bone deep, to protect someone.

Clay Cooper had seen a dragon roused in anger. He'd faced down a legion of shrieking grimlocks and matched gazes with the cold fury of undead kings. Despite all this, asking Ginny to marry him had been the most harrowing moment of his life. She'd said yes, and soon after they moved into their place near the marsh. Things had been good for a time, but one evening, shortly before the wedding, he came limping through the tavern door after a skirmish with Whitewood poachers, and someone made the terrible mistake of remarking how much Clay resembled his father.

The man who'd said so was taken by wagon to the clinic in Oddsford, where he slept for three months before waking up unable to recognize his own children.

Ginny called off the wedding, and Clay began seriously contemplating a standing offer from Kallorek to embark on a solo career. He'd gone to the house to gather his things, but Ginny stopped him at the door and gave voice to the question he'd been asking himself ever since returning to Coverdale.

Which are you, the monster or the man?

It wasn't the words that had moved him. It was the look in her eyes, green as the sunlit sea. She was offering him absolution, the defining choice of a lifetime balanced on a blade's edge. The truth, he knew, was that the world needed his kind of monster. It was a brutal place. It was unfair. And Clay Cooper, such as he was, was quite simply the right kind of wrong.

But Ginny wanted the man. The man, Clay knew, that his mother had been trying to raise—not the monster her killer had made of him.

The man, he'd said.

Yeah? she'd asked, looking hopeful.

Yeah. The world has enough monsters, I think.

His answer had made her smile, and so he'd known it was right. But this morning, with the lives of his friends at stake, Clay had felt that old anger resurface inside him like blood fouling a clear spring. He'd seen, reflected in Raff's dying gaze, the monster staring back at him.

They cleared the forest shortly before nightfall. On the plain below, the uncountable lights of Grandual's greatest city glowed beneath the darkening sky like a bed of windblown embers.

Moog raised his arms in triumph. "Fivecourt at last! The beating heart of civilization! It's been far too long, gentlemen! Far too long!"

Gabriel, whose sullen mood had returned over the past few hours, gazed down at the immensity of the circle-shaped city, while Matrick raked a hand through his thinning hair and sighed.

"I sure could use a drink," he said. "And a hot meal. And a warm bath. And a soft bed." He rolled his shoulders, wincing at some nagging ache. "Gods, a woman might be nice. Do you think if I tell them I'm a king...?"

Clay ignored him, staring down upon Fivecourt's majesty with the same overwhelming awe he normally reserved for the sweep of stars overhead. Even at the height of Saga's celebrity, coming to Fivecourt had always made him feel small. How could it not, he wondered, when the lives of half a million souls were unfolding all around? In Coverdale he'd been a big fish in a small pond, but here...

You're still a big fish, he told himself. *But Fivecourt's an ocean.*

There was a commotion at the city gate. An eight-wheeled argosy with *The Screaming Eagles* painted on the side in sloppy blue letters was blocking the road. Clay could hear loud music within, poorly played. A stream of pipe smoke and women's laughter issued steadily from the open door. A young man was sitting on a set of fold-down steps that led into the massive wagon's dark interior. He was shirtless and scrawny, his pale torso marred by crude but colourful tattoos. His long hair was dyed platinum white, and he swept it from his face as Clay and the others passed by.

"The fuck you looking at?" he asked Clay.

"The fuck *you* looking at?" Clay countered, moving on before the younger man found the wit to respond.

A courtsman wearing the six-striped tabard of the city's urban militia was arguing with a sweating booker out front of the wagon. "I don't care who's inside it," said the guard, "that thing isn't going past this point. This road is for foot traffic and small wagons only, not for shit like this." He gestured at the shabby monstrosity parked before the gate. "Anyway, you'll have to back it up and go round to the Arena Gate. Or they could just get out and walk."

"Walk? *Walk!?*" The booker, red-faced, was strutting and spitting like a bird in heat. "The Screaming Eagles don't *walk* anywhere, son."

"You could send for a carriage," suggested the guard.

"I sent for one half an hour ago and it still ain't here! Listen, if I don't get these boys to the Riot House before dark it's my ass."

"Your ass'll be in a dungeon if you don't move this thing soon."

"Well *your* ass better hope you-know-who doesn't hear you kept her headlining band from entering the city."

"First of all, I *don't* know fucking who. And second, my ass'll be just fine," said the guard. He waved Clay and the others by without bothering to question them.

"Not if my ass goes, it won't. If *my* ass goes, *your* ass is next."

The two of them were still directing threats toward each other's asses when a carriage ambled out of the crowd. Two white-feathered akra were yoked to its traces, mewling like sheep as they drew to a stop. The long-necked birds were a rare sight outside cities, but on cobblestone streets their dry, pellet-sized stool made them preferable to horses. The driver shook his head at the argosy wedged in the gate, and was about to whistle his arrival when Clay flagged him down.

"You're late."

The driver gave them a once-over, his gaze lingering on Moog's sun-and-star pyjamas. "You're the Screaming Eagles?" he asked dubiously.

"We are," Clay answered without hesitation. He climbed aboard as if the carriage belonged to him. "We're in a hurry."

The driver looked toward the row going on at the gate. "Yeah, well, there's a fight in the Maxithon tomorrow, so the city's bursting like a brothel on two-for-one night, but I'll go fast as I can without getting blood on the streets. Where to?"

Clay opened his mouth before realizing he had no idea where they were headed.

"Two stops," said Gabriel. "Coinbarrow first, and then the Narmeeri Ward."

"Narmeeri Ward's a big place," said the driver. "Anywhere specific?"

"Pearling Heights."

The man looked over his shoulder, clearly surprised. "The gorgon's place?"

Gabe nodded, and the carriage lurched into motion.

"The gorgon?" Clay muttered. He looked over at Gabriel, but his friend was gazing out over the sprawl of the city and would not meet his eyes.

Fivecourt was often called "the city at the centre of the world," which was, as wine-addled cartographers had an annoying habit of pointing out, not even remotely true. It was, however, situated more or less in the middle of Grandual, governed by a council of representatives from all five kingdoms, and patrolled by a small army of dedicated courtsmen whose allegiance was to Fivecourt alone. The land for leagues in every direction was considered sovereign territory. Unlike the Free

City of Conthas, however, which existed beyond the jurisdiction of any of Grandual's monarchs, Fivecourt belonged to all of them. The city was, both geographically and metaphorically, the hub around which the wheel of Grandual turned.

The city itself was shaped like a shallow bowl. The homes of the wealthy ringed the circling heights, while the poorest lived in squalor at the bottom. It was divided like a pie into six wards, one for each of Grandual's kingdoms, while the sixth doubled as an administrative district (at the top) and a seedy criminal underworld (at the bottom), though Clay had heard many joke that the two were interchangeable. The river cut a broad stroke through the city's heart, spanned by half a dozen bridges and clotted with bustling boat traffic.

Floating improbably at the very centre was a colossal arena, bound against the river's current by four massive iron chains anchored to towers on either shore.

As they rattled down the slope toward Coinbarrow, the arena looked even more daunting. Matrick, following Clay's awestruck stare, cleared his throat. "The Maxithon, they call it. The largest man-made arena in all of Grandual," he declared.

"There are others like this?" Clay asked, incredulous.

"Well, not quite like this. Brycliffe's arena is a quarter the size, and the Ravine outside Ardburg is bigger, though it's more or less just a conveniently shaped canyon. There's one off the coast of Phantra called the Giant's Cradle."

"Good name," Clay was forced to admit.

Matrick grinned. "I know, right? It's shaped sort of long and narrow, like a boat, and it can actually cross the bay between Aldea and Eshere. It's impressive, but not quite as big as the Maxithon."

"If you say so," said Clay warily. He wondered to himself why someone would build something as unnecessarily excessive as a sailing arena. Or a floating one, even.

As if reading his thoughts, Matrick went on speaking. "The world's a changing place, Clay. Used to be there were monsters everywhere. Every cave, every forest, every swamp a lair for some awful thing or another. You couldn't turn over a rock without finding a bloody murlog underneath it. The Courts couldn't pay army regulars to fight monsters—not that they could handle that, anyway—and everyone figured the Heartwyld was someone else's problem, so things just got worse and worse, until—"

"—until we came along."

"Exactly," said Matrick. "The bands changed everything. We cleared the goblins out of every sewer, killed every giant this side of the Wyld."

"We turned over the rocks and killed all the murlogs," said Clay.

"Damn right we did." Matrick nudged him with an elbow. "So what was left? What glory remained for the bands of today?"

"They could still tour the Heartwyld," Clay ventured.

"Sure, but there's the rot to think of, and that's a risk few are willing to take. Instead they build arenas like that—" Matrick pointed to the Maxithon looming dead ahead "—and bring the Heartwyld to *them*. Most bands today never go anywhere near the forest. They just tour from city to city and fight whatever the local wranglers have on hand."

"And where do the wranglers get monsters from if not the Wyld?"

Moog poked his head up from the seat behind. "They breed them."

Clay scowled to hide the fact that Moog had just startled the shit out of him. "They breed what, the monsters?" The wizard nodded, and Clay's frown deepened. "Well, that's just...stupid," he said, peering up at the torch-lit Maxithon as the carriage reached the quay and turned sharply right.

He wondered what might be caged in the bowels of that place even now, stirring restlessly in the dark, waiting for its chance to kill or be killed as a crowd of thousands looked on.

And they call this civilization, he thought sourly.

Chapter Eighteen

All That Glitters

To most who lived in Fivecourt, Coinbarrow was considered the bad part of town. To those visiting from lands beyond, it was usually the first stop after they arrived.

While the north shore of the river was fronted by palatial manors with manicured lawns, elaborate hedge-mazes, and stone jetties where pleasure barges and white-sailed dhows bobbed on the drowsy current, the south side was more what Clay would have expected a harbourfront in Grandual's largest city to look like.

Here were the gambling holes, the scratch dens, the smokehouses; here the seedy taverns, the wild brothels, the raucous inns. Here were the pawnshops and fence stalls, the moneylenders and the rowdy, run-down theatres where the actors were twice as drunk as the standing crowd and half as entertaining.

Block for block, Coinbarrow was home to more fighting pits than anywhere west of Phantra. Fortunes were won and lost on contests pitting desperate men against vile monsters, vile monsters against vicious dogs, vicious dogs against strutting cocks, and the ever-popular (and wildly unpredictable) desperate men and vicious dogs against vile monsters and strutting cocks.

"Gods, but I've missed this place," said Matrick, hopping down from the carriage and stretching his arms.

"The prodigal son returns," quipped Moog, whose wild white fringe and soiled pyjamas helped him blend right in with the colourful denizens of Fivecourt's filthy dockside.

Even at night the streets were crowded. As he stepped clear of the carriage Clay recalled the very first time he'd ever set foot in Coinbarrow. He and Gabriel had come in search of cheap lodgings while Kallorek was trying to secure them gigs. It had been morning at the time, and the quay was simultaneously bustling with industry and teeming with those best described as orc-shit crazy. Gabriel, probably thinking he was doing a fine job of talking the place up, had assured Clay that come nightfall it was just as lively, except everyone was orc-shit crazy.

On the nearest corner, for instance, was a man in dirty green robes beseeching passersby to repent their sins at the shrine to the Spring Maiden, while on the opposite corner stood an immaculately dressed man proclaiming that two blocks over was a back-alley brothel in which Glif herself would spread her legs for a silver crown.

"Wait here," Gabriel told the driver. "We won't be gone very long."

The man narrowed his eyes and frowned below a bushy moustache. "I'll be needing some collateral from you, then," he said.

Gabriel looked momentarily defeated, but then Matrick offered the man one of his jewelled knives—either *Roxy* or *Grace*. Clay had never known which dagger was which.

"If you leave without giving this back," said Matrick, "I will hunt you to the curling edge of the fucking map and pull your tongue out through your ass. Are we clear?"

Good to see being king only softened his stomach, Clay thought amusedly.

A fight broke out on one of the merchant ships moored

nearby, and the birds out front of the carriage baulked at the sound of shouts and ringing steel. Akra instinctively changed colour when they were startled or distressed, and the feathers of one were already flushed pink.

The driver looked appraisingly at the knife Matrick had given him. "Clear as glass," he said. "But you pay double the fare from here to Pearling Heights. Unless you'd rather I go and see if the *real* Screaming Eagles need a lift," he added, when it looked as though Matty meant to throttle him.

"Fine," said Gabriel.

Clay hadn't the slightest idea how Gabe planned on paying a double fare—or any fare at all, for that matter—but decided to keep his mouth shut.

"And a word to the would-be wise," said the driver. "The next time you lot decide to masquerade as mercenaries, maybe don't choose one of the most famous bands in all of Grandual. The Eagles are headlining the Maxithon tomorrow. There may be a few cheap seats left if you've a mind to see real mercs at work."

Gabriel turned on his heel and set off toward the shadowed mouth of the nearest alley. Moog and Matrick hurried after, leaving Clay the choice between staying to ponder the staggering irony of the driver's words or to follow along.

"Hey, wait up," he said.

Gabriel led them up a set of rickety stairs set against the shabby tenement on their right. The boards creaked dangerously beneath Clay's heavy tread, and somehow the reek of stale piss got stronger the higher he climbed. They'd surprised a pair of trash imps upon entering the alley below. The critters had squealed piteously and scampered into the darkness farther down the way, but now they returned to continue a spirited tug-of-war over what looked to Clay like a broken latrine seat.

Gabriel knocked on the warped wooden door at the top of the stairs, and when the hovel's occupant failed to materialize he hammered it with his whole forearm, which set the sign above the door teetering on its rusting hook.

"*Fender's Cakes and Custards*," Moog read aloud.

"Seriously?" Matrick looked dubious. "We came to an alley in Coinbarrow for dessert?"

"Fender!" Gabe shouted, giving the trash imps below another scare. "Open up."

"Who's Fender?" Clay asked.

"A friend," Gabe answered. "He collects things, sells things, stores things..."

"So he's a fence?"

"He's a kobold."

Clay decided to stop asking questions, since Gabe's enigmatic answers only spawned more. Fivecourt was one of the very few cities that granted a form of limited citizenship to nonhumans, so long as they behaved themselves. He supposed a kobold was as capable as any creature of living among humans, though Clay had never seen one outside a cave or a sewer—or without several hundred others of its kind yapping angrily alongside it.

Half a minute passed. The discordant music of half a dozen taverns wafted over the rooftops above. A pair of Carteans staggered by the alley mouth, trading poorly sung snatches of song back and forth. Something dripped into Clay's hair, and when he looked up to discern whether or not it was raining (it wasn't), another drop found his open mouth.

"Vail's bloody fucking—"

The *thunk* of a bolt being thrown came from beyond the door, then another, and another. Clay heard the *slink* of several chains, followed by the scrape of a wooden plank being drawn from its brackets. At last a reedy voice called from within. "Is open!"

Pretty tight security for a custard joint, Clay might have joked, had he not been busy trying to figure out what the hell had trickled past his lips just now. His tongue tasted like he'd fished a copper coin out of a sewer drain and popped it in his mouth.

"Careful," Gabe whispered, before easing open the door. When nothing barreled out at him he crept over the threshold, and the others cautiously followed.

Inside it was dark. The smell of urine retreated as its cohorts mould, dust, and rusting metal advanced in its place. Clay could hear something scuttling in the shadows, and detected the faint sound of rasping breath from somewhere nearby. The roof was so low it grazed Clay's head if he didn't stoop a little.

"Something tells me the cake was a lie," grumbled Matrick.

Clay became aware of several pairs of lights floating like wisps in the darkness, faint as shuttered lamps.

"Whoosit?" came the shrill voice again. "Name you, now!"

"Fender—" Gabriel began.

"Fender is Fender."

"Yeah, I know that. I'm Gabe."

"Gabe? I know Gabe. Good Gabe Good."

"Good Gabe Good, that's me. Hey, can we maybe get some light in here?"

The speaker clapped its hand and barked, "Chittens! Lights!"

A series of scratches sounded all it once. The sour reek of sulfur barged in to rub shoulders with mould and rusted metal, and a trio of fish-oil lanterns sputtered to life. The band found themselves surrounded by scrawny kobold children— five of them, by Clay's count—each of them wearing a pair of soot-smeared goggles, which dimmed the glow of their bright yellow eyes. Two of them were holding knives.

Fender—presumably their father—crouched opposite the door. He was no taller than Matrick's waist, and looked like nothing so much as a scraggly rat standing on its hind legs. He was wearing goggles as well, and also, unbelievably, the *exact same pyjamas* as Moog, except he had a tasselled cap and pointed slippers to match. He was also hoisting a loaded crossbow with the safety sprung and three long bolts glinting in the dim light.

"Maiden's Mercy, Fender." Gabe raised his hands slowly. "Put that thing away."

"Is nice, yes?" The kobold gave the crossbow a loving pat, which rattled the bolts and set the trigger wire trembling. Clay went rigid, Gabriel flinched, while Moog and Matrick each tried to place themselves in front of the other and ended up in an awkward embrace.

"Fender!" shouted Gabriel.

"Sorry me, sorry me." The kobold set the weapon aside without resetting the safety, which prompted Clay to wonder if he even knew it existed. He pushed the goggles up onto his forehead, his yellow eyes glowing bright in the gloom. "Why come you now? Is late night. Fender and chittens were sleep-dreaming."

Clay squinted into the shadows, assessing the room. The place was a hovel, but not the cozy hovel of the sort inhabited by poets and scribes, crammed with bookshelves, candles, and antique curios. Nor was it the sparse kind of hovel, occupied by little more than a ragged blanket and a straw-stuffed mattress: It was a kobold's hovel, and that meant shithole.

He caught sight of several small nests in the far corner of the room, presumably what Fender and his children (or chittens, as the kobold called them) employed as beds. The rest of the cramped space was given over to what could best be described as entirely useless junk. Among the many pointless treasures was an old bronze helmet with the skull staved in, the tarnished silver frame of a broken mirror, a box of assorted cutlery, and dozens of jars and cans filled to spilling with copper pennies, brass buttons, and just about anything else that might catch a kobold's eye.

Gabe swiped a strand of dirty blond hair from his eyes. "I left some money with you a while back. A big bag of coins."

The kobold cocked its head, wrinkling its pink nose and twitching its mangled whiskers. "Shiny?"

"Yes, shiny. Lots of shiny, for you to keep safe while I was gone, remember?"

"Yes, yes. Fender remembers. Fender hope Good Gabe Good fall in hole and die. That way shiny keep to Fender." Despite the ugly sentiment, the kobold's words carried no animosity at all, just plain old wishful thinking.

Clay flashed Gabriel a skeptical glance. "A friend of yours, huh?"

"I didn't fall in a hole, Fender. Sorry."

The kobold sniffed. "Too bad."

"Yeah. Well, no, but——" Gabriel faltered. "Listen, I need the shiny, okay? All of it. Can you get it for me, please?"

"Yes, yes. You wait." He scurried away, bounding over the crossbow and scaling the hovel's crumbling plaster wall with alarming dexterity before disappearing through a hole in the ceiling.

While he was gone Clay took a moment to survey the kobolds' dingy quarters. He made his way toward the back, picking his way carefully around piles of rubbish. He saw a rusted brazier topped by a charred metal grille that served double duty as both a cooking appliance and a heat source. There were two tin buckets, one for discarded bones and offal, and a second whose contents made the first bucket look appetizing by comparison. A scrap of breeze-blown rag served as a curtain for what was either a window or a sizable hole in the wall.

He looked again at the nests crowding one corner. They were made primarily of straw and cloth scraps, but each had been decorated by its occupant according to their taste. Oddly, one of them was festooned with bent knives and broken arrow shafts. When Clay knelt to examine it, one of Fender's so-called chittens yelped and leapt inside it, then bared its teeth at Clay and hissed.

"His name is Shortknife," said Gabriel. "He's a bit...strange."

Clay stood and backed off slowly. "You know their names?" he asked.

Gabriel nodded. "That's Cowlick, Boneriddle, Sharptongue," he pointed each out as he named them, and then glanced down at the one nuzzling his leg. "And this is Shyeye."

"Since when are you on a first-name basis with bloody kobolds?" asked Matrick.

"And why trust one with your shin—" Clay caught himself before the word *shiny* left his mouth, but barely. "With holding on to coin?" he finished.

"You've seen kobold lairs," said Gabriel. "They hoard any- and everything that glitters, and they never spend it."

True enough, Clay had to admit. Kobolds might be filthy, but most were filthy rich. The concept of coins as currency was utterly lost on them. If something didn't shine, gleam, or sparkle, then it held little value outside of bartering for something that did. You could trade a brass ring to a kobold in exchange for a healthy horse and the kobold would think it came out on top.

"I met Fender a few years back," Gabriel explained. "I had a gig to drive a clan of urskin from part of the sewer, and there turned out to be more of them than my employer let on. A lot more. Fender and Oozilk hid me for a while. They even helped cure me of a poison the frogmen used on their arrows."

"Oozilk?" Moog asked.

"His wife," said Gabriel, and then cast around as if only now realizing she wasn't there.

Clay heard a thud overhead. Bits of plaster and chips of rotted wood rained down. Followed by the sound of something heavy being dragged across the floor above them.

"Anyway, I solved their urskin problem, and then vouched for them when they made the move from sewer to city, so I guess you could say we trust one another. Before heading out for Coverdale I left everything I'd earned these past few years with Fender."

Everything he'd earned came plummeting through the hole in the roof, thankfully contained in a tied-off sack that landed with a heavily clinking thump. Fender came down after it, dangling by his claws for a moment before dropping lightly onto the sack. He sprang off it, and dragged it with two hands across the grimy floor. The chitten named Short-knife watched it greedily, the way a human child might watch an elaborate dessert paraded out after supper.

"Shiny here," Fender grumbled, abandoning his burden at Gabriel's feet.

Gabe found half a smile somewhere. "Thank you, Fender. Hey, where is Oozilk?"

"Not here," the kobold said quickly. "Gone."

"Gone?" And there went the half smile. "Gone where?"

Fender made a groaning sound that reminded Clay of the one Griff made whenever Clay ordered the little dog off the bed. The kobold's torch-bright eyes seemed to gutter when he spoke next. "Oozilk get in fight-scrap at give-take."

"Give-take?" asked Moog.

"The market," said Gabriel distractedly. "She got in a fight at the market. Go on, Fender. When was this?"

"Ah, year back, year back. Oozilk tooth-bite merchant-man, merchant-man send club-goons, club-goons take Oozilk. Fender try and fight-scrap club-goons, but they make warning: Take Oozilk, or take chittens. So Oozilk gone."

"Gone where?" Gabriel asked. "Where did they take her? Back to the sewer?"

"No sewer," answered Fender, then pointed a crooked finger at the south wall, beyond which lay the sluggish river and the colossal arena floating upon it. "To noise-bowl."

Clay was only half-surprised to see the carriage still waiting for them when he and his bandmates emerged from the alley. The driver looked just as relieved to see them, since his akra were growing restless. Both of them were bright red now, and whining like chicks awaiting the worm.

The ship on which the fight had broken out was on fire. Those on both sides of the clash had gathered on the quay to watch it burn.

Matrick hauled his bulk into the carriage, nodding curtly as the driver returned his dagger. The king, somewhat creepily, kissed the blade before sheathing it. Moog climbed in after, and winced at some pain in the foot he was using for leverage.

The left one, Clay noted. *The infected one.*

"You all right?" asked Matrick.

Moog still hadn't worked up the courage to tell Matty about his affliction. "Fine!" said the wizard a little too loudly. "Just not as spry as I used to be."

Matrick chuckled and put a hand on his stomach. "Fucking tell me about it. Hey Gabe, maybe give me a few months' warning the next time you decide to drag my fat ass across the Heartwyld, eh? I'd have done a few laps around the castle, or maybe not eaten a pie every day."

Moog looked doubtful. "You ate pie every day?"

Matrick shrugged. "Damned right I did, or else what's the point of being king?"

Gabriel, meanwhile, was still standing at the alley mouth. At a glance, Clay assumed he was watching the ship in flames, but then realized he was looking past it, transfixed by the daunting immensity of the Maxithon.

"Gabe," Clay called, and after a moment his friend tore his gaze from the arena and joined them in the carriage. Gabriel sat with the sack cradled in his lap, saying nothing. The quiet sullenness that seemed the dominant part of his nature these days had returned, and not without reason. Gabriel had vouched for Fender and his wife to move from the sewers into the slightly less foul-smelling streets above. He no doubt felt responsible for Oozilk's capture. Her death (because Clay couldn't imagine a kobold lasting long in the arena) would join the many burdens camped like crows on the frontman's shoulders, from letting his band fall apart, to allowing his marriage to crumble, to driving his daughter to repeat the same reckless mistakes of her father.

The driver cracked the reins, urging his red-feathered akra on through the riotous streets of Coinbarrow, weaving through the press of drunks, scratch addicts, scratch dealers, off-duty courtsmen in six-striped tabards, and rowdy river men looking to exchange a few silver crowns for a strong drink, a keen woman, and an itchy red rash come morning.

The air itself was a wild brawl of smells and sounds: the punch of unwashed flesh, the scream of a scratching mandolin, the jab of tobacco smoke, the glee of a whistling pipe, the occasional head butt of sour urine, the aching sorrow of a moaning lute. All that, and voices singing, laughing, yelling, swearing, and groaning in myriad different ways.

Clay craned his neck as they rattled by one of the four square towers to which the Maxithon was anchored by the thickest chains he'd ever seen. Graffiti marred the tower's base, most of it illegible, although Clay's eyes picked out four words scrawled in bright white paint that stood out from all the rest: *Long live the Duke.*

They veered right, rumbling uphill, and soon left Coinbarrow behind. As their unease abated, the akra's feathers changed colour. One of them went white again, while the other turned a dusky blue. When Matrick ventured to ask the driver what the bird's blue feathers denoted the man glanced over his shoulder and growled, "I'll say this: Don't bend over near it."

They turned left onto the city's main thoroughfare, a broad avenue called Sintra's Ring that carved a circle through every ward in Fivecourt, and soon passed beneath a massive arch into the Narmeeri Ward. Carved in relief along the top of the ward gate were the words SUFFER NO TYRANTS, the origin of which Moog used to explain every single time Saga had been to the city. Clay had never been much for history lessons—he had trouble remembering the words to most songs—but it was hard to forget one that had been drilled into your head five times a year for ten years running.

In the wake of the Reclamation Wars, when the last of the Hordes had been scattered, the Company of Kings had envisioned a unified Grandual: a single, spanning empire to rival the lost Dominion of druinkind. They promoted one among them to the rank of Emperor, and named Fivecourt the Imperial capital.

But hardly a year had passed—and the foundations had only just been laid for the Emperor's grand palace—before the new Emperor issued two ill-fated edicts that historians unilaterally agree proved to be his undoing. The first of these was, as Moog colourfully phrased it whenever he told the story, "to tax the living shit out of his subjects." The next was to demand that the firstborn daughter of every noble household be sent as a hostage to Fivecourt. Upon their arrival the Emperor announced their great good fortune of being the founding members of his brand-new harem.

The noble daughters responded poorly to this decree, and the first Emperor of Grandual died due to what Moog dubbed "testicular asphyxiation," which is to say they stuffed his severed balls down his throat.

The daughters were executed, the nobles rebelled, and the Emperor's son and heir fled west, through the Heartwyld and over the mountains, to Endland.

"Hey," Moog blurted, startling everyone. "Have I ever told you guys why it says 'Suffer no Tyrants' above the ward gates?"

"Yes," said Gabriel.

"You have," said Clay.

"Like a hundred million times," said Matrick, and the wizard slumped back into his seat.

They'd entered the Narmeeri Ward, and but for the arena

floating on the river below, Clay could have imagined the carriage had ambled into the southern sultanate itself. The streets here were cramped and curving; bands of pale moonlight filtered between swathes of red and gold cloth draped overhead. The driver wisely avoided the night market, but Clay could hear the babble of voices from the grand bazaar near the heart of the ward. The mingling scents of spice and heady hookah smoke wafted on an unseasonably warm breeze that contained a startling amount of gritty sand.

They rolled by several temples to the Summer Lord, who the southerners called Vizan and worshipped with a sort of reverent fear, the way everyone else did the Winter Queen, and finally passed through another gate into the highest tier of the city. Here were the estates belonging to Narmeeri grandees, and even a small palace occupied by the Sultana herself whenever she deigned to visit Fivecourt. Her salvaged druin skyship, *The Second Sun*, was moored there now, its fanning sails crackling with static discharge.

Clay decided he'd let Gabriel sulk long enough. They were nearing their destination, he presumed, and yet he had no idea where exactly it was they were going, or why.

"What's the money for?" he asked.

Gabriel looked over, his blue eyes hooded, his jaw working as though he were chewing on something. Finally, he answered, "It's for Ganelon."

Matrick frowned, leaning forward. "When did he get out of prison? I was led to believe those sent to the Quarry were sent there to stay."

Clay, too, had been under that impression. He'd tried to ask Gabriel about it before Jain and the Silk Arrows had robbed them outside Coverdale.

Ganelon had killed a Narmeeri prince, after all—the eldest son of the Sultana—and neither Saga's celebrity status nor the fact that he'd committed murder for a very, very good reason could protect him from her wrath. The Sultana's magi had hunted him down, and for reasons each their own, Ganelon's bandmates had been conspicuously absent when he'd needed them most.

The warrior was eventually captured, confined to an inescapable prison known as the Quarry—inescapable because its inhabitants, which included a veritable who's who of Grandual's most dangerous criminals, were turned to stone. Clay had heard it said the Quarry was tended by Keepers, who were blinded at birth and raised to know every inch of the prison by touch alone, and guarded by basilisks, the gazes of which could turn exposed flesh to stone.

"He's out of the Quarry," said Gabriel.

"Is he a mercenary?" Moog wanted to know. "Did he go solo? I mean, I understand he may not like us much, but... Ganelon never really seemed that interested in getting paid, you know? It was always more about the...um..."

"Killing," said Matrick helpfully.

"Well, basically, yeah. It just seems odd he'd refuse to help save Rose unless you paid him."

"The money isn't to pay Ganelon," Gabriel said, his eyes still glued to the sack of coins on his lap. "It's to set him free."

Chapter Nineteen

Guests of the Gorgon

The money, Gabriel confessed, was for a woman named Din-antra, in whose anteroom Clay and his bandmates were left to wait by a half-naked male servant who had greeted them at the door. Like Kallorek, who was often referred to as the Orc behind his back, Dinantra was known by a similarly monstrous moniker: the Gorgon. Whereas Kallorek's nickname was a testament to his brutish manner and prodigious over-bite, however, Dinantra owed hers to the fact that she was, in truth, a gorgon.

Despite that, when she finally swept into the anteroom Clay found her strikingly beautiful for a woman with a head-ful of snakes. The scales of her serpentine tail were the green-ish gold of rain-washed copper, paling to cream at her throat and on the underside of her arms. She wore a tightly-cinched bodice that proffered her breasts like melons at a market stall, but it was all Clay could do not to drown in her eyes, which were the red of bruised apples in the fickle lamplight. The nest of serpents surrounding her face were the same colour. They hissed quietly whenever she spoke, underlying each word with a sibilant whisper.

"My dear Gabriel," she said, "how pleasant to see you again. I'll confess I didn't expect you to return so soon, if at all."

"I've brought your money," said Gabriel.

"And friends as well," she said, casting that smouldering gaze around what seemed to Clay to be a suddenly cramped room. There were plinths along each wall adorned with the sculpted heads of what, presumably, were the gorgon's vaunted ancestors. "I do enjoy company," purred Dinantra. "In fact, I already have some."

Gabriel swallowed. The sack in his arms clinked as he shifted uncomfortably. "We could come back tomorrow," he said, "but no later. I need—"

"Nonsense," she said, her voice seeming to tickle the inside of Clay's ear. "You've come all this way, and I think you'll find my guest as diverting as I."

Before Gabriel could muster a protest she turned and slithered deeper into the house. Gabe sighed, and started after her. Moog reached out to touch the snake-stone hair of one of the ancestral busts, while Matrick found his reflection in a nearby mirror and raked self-consciously at his tousled hair.

"I know the whole 'gorgons turning men to stone' thing is a myth," he said quietly, "but I'm hard as a rock right now."

Clay levelled a glare at the man who'd been his king less than a week ago. "Seriously?"

Matrick's reflection winked in reply.

There was a dull snap, and Clay turned to find Moog holding a broken stone snake in his hand, looking as guilty as a child caught with their hand in the cookie jar.

"Nothing," said the wizard. "What? Wasn't me." He pried open his bottomless bag and tossed the shard inside, then motioned to the hallway down which Gabe and the Gorgon had disappeared. "Shall we?"

Clay had encountered a few gorgons in his time, and so knew a little about what to expect beyond the anteroom. Such creatures were avid art collectors, prizing everything from tastefully framed paintings to elegant furniture. What they loved most, though, were statues, and there were several in the expansive room into which Dinantra led them. Broad ramps curved up to either side, prompting Clay to realize that he'd never considered the difficulty a gorgon might have with conventional stairs.

The opposite wall was an open portico hung with gauzy curtains adrift on the cooling breeze. The room was aglow with the soft light of tall candles, and Clay watched Dinantra's silhouette waver before them, marvelling that a woman whose lower half was a snake could manage an enthralling sway of her hips. The scent of cinnamon and roses wafted in her wake. There was music in the air, lilting Narmeeri twangs that reminded Clay of the desert, and of desert nights.

The gorgon's other guest stood near the opposite side of the room, facing whatever lay in the darkness beyond. He wore a tattered red longcoat, and there were three scabbards slung sideways—

Oh gods . . .

Clay froze. Gabriel froze. Moog and Matrick, who'd been chatting to each other as they entered, fell silent.

The Duke of Endland turned, grinning his jagged druin grin. "Hello, Gabriel," he said in a tone a cat might have used to greet a sleeping mouse stirring awake beneath its gaze. "And is that Old King Matrick I see behind you? I'd heard you were dead."

Matrick tried giving voice to some jibe or another, but instead he just stood there, gaping like a fish left to die on the bottom of a boat.

Lastleaf's mismatched eyes brushed over Moog, lingered a moment longer on Clay himself. "My apologies for not recognizing the rest of you at Lindmoor. I was rather preoccupied at the time, and in fairness you've aged considerably since last we met."

Clay belatedly noticed at least a dozen heavily muscled men positioned around the room. Each wore a mirrored buckler on one arm, a close-faced helmet, and a loincloth sewn with gold coins. They each stood at rigid attention, clasping a long spear in both hands before them. Clay hadn't decided yet whether or not to be reassured or worried by their presence.

Gabriel spoke to the gorgon without taking his eyes off Lastleaf. "What is he doing here?"

Dinantra slunk into a lowered seating area and began piling her coils onto a divan. "It has been my privilege to host the Duke during his visit to Grandual. He is an honored guest, as you are." She extended her arm and a young man wearing nothing but white trousers cinched at the knee hurried forward to place a delicate bowl in her hand. "Come and sit, Gabriel. Have wine."

Gabe shook his head, retreating a step. "We'll be back tomorrow," he said. "Clay, let's go."

"If you wish to leave, leave," said Dinantra. There was a new, impatient edge to her voice that had been previously absent. "But do not return. Ganelon can remain just as he is. In fact, I quite prefer him this way."

That brought Gabriel up short, and Clay saw Lastleaf's grin deepen into something decidedly more predatory before it disappeared behind the rim of his own wine bowl.

Clay and the others filtered down among the furniture. Gabriel, without taking his eyes off the druin, perched on the edge of a high-backed chair with the bag of gold at his feet. Matty and Moog squeezed into a small sofa. Matrick was stuck holding a silken, cylinder-shaped pillow that he was forced to wedge between his legs. Clay settled for something like a cushioned footstool that made his back ache the moment he sat down.

"There is room here," said the gorgon, patting the empty space behind her rump.

Clay offered a tight smile in reply. "I'm good," he said.

Wine was brought and poured into bowls for each of them. When the servants left, Dinantra made a show of raising hers and taking a sip, a custom among the Narmeeri (whose culture she seemed to have appropriated) to assure guests that the wine had not been poisoned. The snakes on her head seemed to strain forward as she did so.

"You two have a history, I understand." She glanced between Lastleaf and Gabriel with obvious relish, a blood-hungry spectator watching bitter rivals face off on an arena floor.

"We do," said Lastleaf.

"He ambushed us in the Heartwyld," said Gabriel.

"He gave me this." The druin touched the scar beneath his darkened eye.

"He tried to steal my sword."

"He killed my father."

A profoundly uncomfortable silence followed, during which Matrick drained his bowl of wine in several long, loud gulps. When he'd finished he made a show of smacking his lips, stifling a belch, and asking, "Is there...um...more?"

At a gesture from the gorgon, the king's wine was refilled. As the servant retreated Clay stole a glance at the trio of scabbards slung across the druin's back. All three swords were of various lengths and sizes. The topmost he'd seen drawn on the Isle at Lindmoor. The blade had been short and wedge shaped, radiating heat and riddled with cracks that glowed like a fire blazing behind a black iron grill. The middle scabbard was long and narrow, very slightly curved. The last was longer still, white as sun-bleached bone. The pommel of the sword it sheathed was wrapped in ragged black cloth.

Clay hoped—though not optimistically—that he'd never have occasion to see the weapon inside.

Gabriel opened his mouth to speak, but the Duke, informed by druin prescience, cut him off.

"I know Vespian asked you to kill him." Lastleaf's white-furred ears were flat against the top of his head. "And I know you used *Vellichor* to do it. My father did not deserve such a mercy."

Having your own sword pushed through your heart

hardly seemed like a mercy to Clay, but he decided to try his wine instead of saying so. It was delicious: a heady blend of pepper, spice, and smoke. Unsurprising, since he'd never met a villain (or villainess, in this case) without impeccable taste in wine. It was a prerequisite, he figured, to being rich and evil.

"Where is it, by the way?" The druin narrowed his mismatched eyes. "Where is the priceless relic my craven father entrusted to a *human*?"

Clay winced. Lastleaf said the word *human* the way a human might say *pile of shit*.

Gabriel straightened. "*Vellichor* is hidden, beyond your reach." A lie, of course, but telling the truth—that he'd traded the Archon's fabled weapon to a crooked booker to pay off debts and satisfy his drug-addled, pacifist wife—wouldn't have done Gabe any favours. The frontman made a point of transferring his attention from Lastleaf to the gorgon. "I came for Ganelon," he said to her. "You and I had an agreement. Six hundred courtmarks—"

Moog choked on his wine, coughing a mouthful of it back into his bowl. "Courtmarks?" he sputtered. "You mean that's *gold* in there? All of it?" He clasped Matrick's shoulder. "Have you ever seen that much money in your entire life?"

"I had an *actual* castle," Matrick reminded him.

Moog palmed his forehead. "Right, never mind." He cleared his throat quietly and nodded at Gabriel. "Pardon the interruption."

Clay, too, was stunned by Gabriel's declaration. He'd assumed the bag was full of silver crowns, with plenty of copper and the odd courtmark lurking in the mix. But six hundred gold coins was a sizable fortune, especially considering Gabe had shown up at his doorstep with rags for clothes and holes in his boots.

"Six hundred courtmarks," repeated Gabriel, leaning forward on his chair. "That's twice what you paid the keepers to have him out of the Quarry, and a hundred more than I promised you. Give us Ganelon, and it's all yours."

Dinantra eyed the bag rapturously. "How generous," she cooed, but then affected a crestfallen pout. "Alas, if you'd come just a few weeks sooner I'd have happily honored the bounds of our little arrangement. The good Duke, however, has suggested an amendment, and has made me an offer more tempting than gold."

Clay peered over at Lastleaf, who was smugly swirling the bowl of wine in one long-fingered hand.

"And what offer is that?" Gabe asked flatly.

The gorgon's ample chest swelled, forcing Clay to look at something, anything else, and he found himself examining her tail instead. There was a rattle on the end, each segment painted in fine detail with flowing Narmeeri script. He'd heard it said you could tell how often a snake had molted by the number of those segments, and so Clay found himself counting before the gorgon's reply startled him out of reverie.

"I'm to be an Exarch of the New Dominion," she said.

Moog blinked. "*New* Dominion? You mean the Old Dominion. There isn't . . . he doesn't . . . you can't just—" The wizard blinked several more times in rapid succession. "Wait, I'm confused. I've confused myself."

"You can't be serious," breathed Gabriel.

Lastleaf bared his teeth. "I can be. And I will soon have need of those used to wielding power." When he turned his jagged smile on the gorgon it grew a fraction warmer, a glimpse of sunshine on a bleak winter's day. "My Lady Dinantra, such as she is, will prove most suitable to the task, I think."

So would Kallorek, Clay found himself thinking. The thug turned booker turned magnate would no doubt leap at the chance to become an Exarch, regardless of the circumstances. *Although his ego will need a bigger pond to swim in*, Clay mused.

"A *New* Dominion?" Matrick scoffed. He gestured dramatically with the bowl in his hand, but there was no wine left to spill. "And where do you suppose this magical kingdom of yours will spring up, huh? There isn't..." He trailed off as the obvious occurred to him.

"Castia!" Moog exclaimed, having shrugged off his self-inflicted bewilderment.

"Castia," said the druin, and then looked to Gabriel as though expecting him to speak next.

Which he did. "Then why destroy it?"

"For several reasons," said Lastleaf. He stepped away from the curtains, his footfalls silent on the marble floor. As he crossed behind Dinantra the snakes on her head turned to track him, hissing softly.

When the druin drew near to Clay he felt his blood go hot and every hair on his body rise as if in warning. His nose was filled with the scent of crushed autumn leaves, of dry brush burning, and of something less pleasant, more sour, like rancid wine gone to vinegar. The silvered scale beneath Lastleaf's coat whispered metallically as he passed to stand before a vast painting framed in polished rosewood, which he examined while he spoke.

"As I believe I mentioned at Lindmoor, the Horde is hungry, and that hunger must be sated. They need a victory. *I* need one, to bind them to me."

"Didn't you trounce the Republic army already?" Matrick pointed out.

Lastleaf glanced over, arching a brow. "That was too easy." He said so without bravado, which Clay found unsettling. "I would hardly call it a battle at all. Oh, the Castians certainly made a show of coming out to face us. They formed up in their neat little squares. They waved their banners and blew their horns, and then they broke the moment the Horde hit them. Your vaunted mercenaries put up a better fight, at least, though they were far too few to matter. If not for them we might have swept the battlefield clean that day, and Castia would already be mine. Which is why, again, those who took refuge in the city cannot be spared."

Gabriel wrung his hands. He looked as though he was about to be sick—or rather, like he'd already swallowed a mouthful of his own bile and was struggling to keep it down. "So this 'Duchy of Endland' you spoke of at the council..."

"Nonsense, obviously." Lastleaf returned his gaze to the artwork before him, which Clay only now realized depicted the fall of Kaladar, the great and glorious capital of the Old Dominion. The city—a mountain of fine arches and reaching white spires—was on fire, shrouded in smoke, surrounded on all sides by a shadowy sea of clambering beasts. "If the courts suspected I had plans to revive the Dominion, they would have no choice but to unite against me. Instead, they believe I aspire to *join* them." He chuckled into his bowl as he raised it, drinking deep.

Matrick sighed and rubbed at his whiskered jowls. "And you don't think wiping Castia off the map will cast any doubt on your credibility with the courts? If I were—"

"But you're not," said Lastleaf, turning on him. "You are no longer a king. You are *no one*."

"Well that's a bit mean," Moog grumbled beneath a furrowed brow.

"Though you raise a valid point," the druin admitted. "The courts may decide I am a threat after all, in which case the destruction of Castia can serve my purpose just as well. Those who survive the city's fall—" he bared his teeth in a mirthless grin "—and I will ensure there are one or two who *do* survive—will return to Grandual as stricken souls, bearing word of atrocities you could scarcely imagine. If my offer of friendship, or the threats I made to the council, does not lull the courts to inaction, then let the Republic's fate serve as an example to those who make of me an enemy."

Matrick bristled, his back rigid with righteous pride. He might even have pulled off "regal" but for the wine stains on his shirt and the vaguely phallic-shaped pillow he'd wedged between his legs. "And just what did the innocent people of

Castia do to *make of you an enemy*?" he asked, mimicking the druin's archaic manner of speaking. "I assume you just flipped a coin, no? Heads for east, tails for west. Or did you fear the kingdoms of Grandual would prove too worthy a foe, and so decided to pick on the Republic first?"

Lastleaf looked genuinely bewildered. "The *innocent people of Castia*?" he sneered. "Do you know how the *innocent people of Castia* went about building their glorious Republic?" He took a threatening step toward Matrick, who involuntarily clenched his legs, which in turn forced the pillow between them to spring upright—incongruous, but easy enough to ignore as the druin went on, incensed.

"Four centuries ago, when your ousted Emperor and the exiled remnants of the Imperial court arrived in Endland, they found it already inhabited by what you humans so broadly refer to as *monsters*. They fought with the cathiil over lands they wished to settle, and when the cathiil elected to migrate further west the *innocent people of Castia* hunted them to extinction."

In his periphery Clay saw Moog just *dying* to ask what a cathiil was, but the druin's burgeoning rage stifled even the wizard's curiosity.

"They traded food and fur with the mountain folk for the ore with which to build their vaunted walls, but before long the *innocent people of Castia* decided to claim the mines for themselves. Whole clans were enslaved, worked to death in the very mines they'd once called home. The *innocent people of Castia* bribed urskin chieftains with precious gemstones and then drained the swampland to power their ravenous mills. They massacred ixil villagers who refused to relocate at their whim. They culled the great herds of the Orgone Plain and drove the centaurs from their ancestral lands into the forest. They poisoned the wells of gnoll settlements, and those hearty enough to survive the plague that followed were taken to Castia and made to fight in the Crucible."

Lastleaf's long ears quivered. He'd turned his back on the painting now, the death throes of ancient Kaladar providing an eerily suitable backdrop for his mounting anger.

"Or did you think all these grand arenas of yours were a novelty?" he asked. "The Crucible precedes them all, and in the warrens below that place entire generations of fell creatures have been born and bred in darkness, suffered to live only until they are deemed fit to die in sunlight, and shame, while the *innocent people of Castia* look on and cheer."

Matrick scowled down at his empty bowl, doubtless wishing it would suddenly, magically, refill itself so he could at least enjoy a drink while he suffered the druin's tirade.

Clay, meanwhile, shifted uncomfortably on his stool. If Lastleaf despised the Republic for the way they'd treated monsters in the past, then the druin would surely take issue with the decades-long rise to prominence of Grandual's mercenary bands, who made a living killing creatures of every kind and were celebrated for it. Even Clay found himself wary of the latest trend—arenas springing up in every city, monsters held in captivity, waiting to be killed for nothing more than a crowd's diversion. He remembered the expression on Gabriel's face as he'd gazed at the Maxithon after learning that Fender's wife had been taken there to die—a mix of fearful awe and wary bemusement, like a plainsman stepping out of his yurt to find a sixty-oar galleon stranded on the grass.

There was something about the arenas that didn't sit well with Clay. He lacked the capacity, even in his own mind, to frame it. Moog could have done so, and probably Matrick after a cup or two of wine (but not after three). It wasn't as if mercenary tradition was especially wholesome—far from it, in fact. Often you hunted monsters to their lairs and killed everything inside, even the young. If you were lucky, whatever you intended to kill was sound asleep, or eating, or drunk. Hells, Clay had once put a single spear through two rutting trolls. Pressed to describe the difference between slaying a creature in the wild versus doing so on an arena floor, he might have said that the former seemed, to his mind at least, more *honest*.

Not better, since killing was killing. But yeah . . . honest.

"For more than seven centuries I skulked and hid in the Heartwyld," Lastleaf was saying now, "side by side with what your fledgling civilization calls monsters. After my father's death I was free to roam at will, and so I went myself to Castia, where I hoped to intercede on behalf of those who had suffered for so long beneath the Republic's heel. And do you know what the 'noble' senate did? They called *me* a monster. They put me in chains and confined me to the dungeon beneath the Crucible. For three years I was held prisoner, forced to fight in the arena, with no choice but to kill at the whim of my captors. Until the day I found Ashatan."

Ashatan? Clay racked his brain to recollect where he'd heard that name before now, but Moog—clever Moog—beat him to it.

"The wyvern matriarch."

The druin wet his lips. His odd-coloured eyes narrowed as he continued, as though he were squinting at the now-distant memory of that day. "She was locked in a room so small she could barely spread her wings. She was heavily sedated, of course. Her neck was shackled to the floor. They'd been breeding her for years, using her offspring as fodder in the arena above. I could sense the rage in her. I could feel it like heat rolling off a fire, and so I set her free. I set them *all* free—every wretched thing imprisoned there—and together we drowned the Crucible in the blood of ten thousand Castians."

"The Red Sands," Matrick said, shuddering visibly. "I heard about that."

Clay had heard no such thing, but grim tidings (like modern plumbing and court couriers) had a way of getting lost on the way to Coverdale. Come to think of it, he was surprised word of the Heartwyld Horde had reached him before Gabriel did.

"The Red Sands was just the beginning," said Lastleaf. His anger had changed, somehow—like a molten blade drawn from the forge, it had cooled into something sharp, dark and deadly. "What happens to Castia when I breach its walls will be far worse. It will be a massacre, the scale of which has not been seen since . . ."

Lastleaf glanced over his shoulder at the painting of Kaladar besieged, falling, fallen, and for a surreal moment Clay wondered if the druin, this forsaken prince of the Dominion, had long ago stood witness while his city—his entire civilization—was devoured by a monstrous Horde.

Time is a circle, he remembered Lastleaf saying at Lindmoor, in twilight. *History a turning wheel.*

And here it is, Clay thought wryly, *turning and turning, grinding us all to dust.*

Chapter Twenty

The Soul in the Stone

"I don't care about Castia," lied Gabriel. "I came here for Ganelon."

Lastleaf's long ears perked inquisitively.

Moog looked from Lastleaf, to Gabriel, to Dinantra. "I don't understand. Is he a prisoner still?"

Dinantra's hair hissed at the wizard. "Not a prisoner," she clarified. "A possession. By releasing him I risk making an enemy of the Sultana—something I was prepared to do even before ... recent developments made doing so inevitable. Nevertheless, I am altering the terms of our agreement, as per My Lord's request."

Gabe looked suspiciously at Lastleaf, but it was Clay who asked what they'd both been wondering. "You knew we were coming?"

The druin wore a wry smile, but said nothing.

"He mentioned having seen you at Lindmoor," Dinantra answered, "and expressed interest in meeting you again, face-to-face. Since I assumed you were coming here for Ganelon, I invited him to extend his stay in Fivecourt awhile longer."

"Well, that was thoughtful," said Matrick flatly.

Lastleaf sighed airily. "Wasn't it? She will make a wonderful Exarch, I am sure."

Gabriel's jaw worked furiously. His hopes of rescuing Rose depended on securing Ganelon's freedom, because without the warrior's help they stood little chance of surviving the Heartwyld. Having the rest of Saga by his side meant (hopefully) that Ganelon was less likely to kill him when Gabriel proposed that he come to Castia.

Whatever "alteration" the druin and Dinantra had cooked up, Clay and his bandmates had little choice but to swallow it.

"So what is this request?" Gabriel managed through gritted teeth.

The druin seem to relish the taste of his next words before giving them voice. "I would have you know how it feels to risk death for the amusement of a mob, to hear a crowd of thousands howling for your blood. It would also, I confess, please me to watch you die. Dinantra, fortunately, is well positioned to arrange both."

"Holy Tetrea," whispered Matrick, who'd gone pale despite the flush of having consumed two bowls of wine in a very short span of time. "You want us to fight in the Maxithon?"

Lastleaf's grin spread like a plague across his face. "I do," he replied to Matrick, though his mismatched eyes were nailed to Gabriel. "After all, you've gone to such extraordinary lengths to reunite your little band. You must be planning something—a farewell tour of Grandual's grand arenas, perhaps?" His ears skewed forward, curious. "You wouldn't dare enter the forest, of course. Not at your age."

"So what is it you want us to fight?" Moog asked, changing the subject before the druin could make another guess at their objective. He pointed at Lastleaf. "Not you? You? Don't say you."

Dinantra's laugh was soft and sibilant. She shared a conspiratorial sneer with the druin before answering. "We have something special in mind. A thing this city has never seen before. If you win, Ganelon goes free."

She left the alternative unspoken, Clay noted.

"What if we say no?" asked Matrick. "If we refuse to fight, what happens to Ganelon?"

A ripple of irritation passed over Dinantra's ruthlessly beautiful features. The snakes in her hair hissed reprovingly. "Do you imagine it is easy for me to live in Fivecourt? There are laws that grant me the right to do so, and my wealth, of course, makes things a great deal easier. And yet the people of this city barely tolerate my presence here. There are lewd murals of my likeness to be found throughout every ward. I must send servants to the market for fear of being attacked, or refused service. I am told there is even a whore in Coinbarrow who shares my name. She wears a wig of painted ropes and pretends—or allows *men* to pretend—that it is me to whom they are making love, as if a mortal man could survive such exquisite pleasure."

Clay saw the pillow between Matrick's legs twitch slightly.

"I have lived among these people for years," said the gorgon, "and yet I must work tirelessly to maintain their goodwill. To my shame, that often means staging fights in the arena—something Lastleaf has assured me will be barred once our New Dominion takes root in Castia. Nevertheless, I have promised this city a spectacle, and I shall grant them one, with or without your assistance. Should you refuse to fight, Ganelon will face his death alone. And he *will* die, I promise you that. The Maxithon will have its blood, one way or another. Now choose."

Gabriel opened his mouth to protest.

"We'll do it," said Clay.

The others all looked to him. Moog smiled tightly. Matrick shrugged. Gabriel nodded, regret and relief plain in his eyes.

"Excellent," hissed Dinantra. "You will fight tomorrow. I have another band headlining, but I'm sure the arena master will make an exception for Saga—the Kings of the Wyld, reunited at last."

"Tomorrow's fine," Clay said, before anyone could object.

Moog knocked his bony shoulder into the king beside him. "The sooner we finish this, the sooner we head west, right?"

Clay saw Lastleaf's ears cant, but the druin gave no other indication he'd caught the obvious implication in the wizard's words.

Gabriel spoke up before the silence provoked further inquiry. "Can we see Ganelon now?" he asked.

The gorgon's tail shivered, its rattle summoning the servants from the edge of the room. She handed off her bowl, slithered from her seat, and fixed Gabriel with her ruby glare. "Leave the gold," she ordered. "Come with me."

Gabriel raised no objection. He stood and made to follow, leaving the sack where it lay.

Lastleaf returned his attention to the painting behind him. "I'd wish you good luck tomorrow," he called over his shoulder, "except, well, you know."

Dinantra led them past the curtained portico into the private yard beyond. They followed her down a pathway lit by small clusters of squat candles and set with coloured stones, pink and green and white. There was a manicured garden on their right. A servant wearing nothing but his standard-issue coin-sewn loincloth was trimming a hedge by torchlight into the shape of two men wrestling. At least Clay *thought* they were wrestling—it was hard to make out in the gloom. The man knelt as Dinantra went by, pressing his forehead to the grass. On their left was a pond similar to the one they'd seen in Kallorek's home. Clay wondered briefly if gorgons could swim. He thought they probably could.

"Why purchase him from the Quarry in the first place?" asked Matrick.

"Because he is dangerous"—Dinantra's voice drifted back to them—"and I collect dangerous things."

There was a small stone building at the rear of the garden. Dinantra moved to one side of the entrance and piled her green-gold coils beneath her. "Ganelon is yours for the evening. I will arrange rooms for you in the city. Something suitable, I assure you. I will also provide guards to make certain you honour our agreement. Now go on," she said. "He is inside."

Gabriel went first, pushing open the heavy door and stepping into the shadowed interior. Moog and Matrick disappeared after him. Clay stood outside for a few heartbeats more. There was a cold spear of dread in his gut. He imagined Ganelon's resentment at having been abandoned by his so-called friends when he'd needed them most, the bitterness he no doubt felt at being released from the Quarry only to become the slave of a mercantile gorgon. As much as anything, he feared to find the warrior a shadow of his former self, broken by prison, cowed by a decade of indentured servitude. Would they find him on his knees, with nothing but a cloth of tarnished coins to hide his shame? Or had Dinantra kept him in chains, caged like a beast in this shadowed place?

The gorgon was watching him, the hint of a simper on her lips.

He stepped through the door. The room beyond was dark. Bands of pale starlight streamed through the close-set bars of a west-facing window. The air inside was stale. The dust kicked up by their arrival took to the air, swirling like snowflakes around the room's petrified occupant.

"It's him," said Moog, reaching to graze his fingers across the basalt face. His voice was reverent and softened by sorrow. "It's Ganelon."

They had a saying up north: *the coin that broke the dragon's back*. It was derived from the idea that a dragon hoarding one trinket too many might drown beneath the weight of its own avarice, and it meant—or at least Clay *thought* it meant—that even the mightiest of things (dragons, for example) had a point at which even the smallest detail could signify their doom.

They had a similar saying down south: *the straw that broke the camel's back*—though why you'd put a piece of straw on a camel's back was, to Clay, an utter mystery. They were a curious people, southerners.

Although Ganelon murdering the Sultana's son wasn't solely responsible for Saga's disbanding, it was, in hindsight, the coin that broke the dragon's back.

Not that Clay could fault him for doing so, of course. The Narmeeri prince, while visiting the town of Mazala, had forced himself on a woman Ganelon was exceptionally fond of, and Ganelon responded by killing the entire Narmeeri garrison. As a consequence, the prince ordered the woman burned to death in the town square, prompting Ganelon to visit a similar fate upon the prince himself, though not before hurting him so badly that death by fire was an act of mercy.

The Sultana was justifiably furious, and Ganelon's bandmates, for one reason or another, were unwilling to bear the brunt of her wrath.

Months earlier, Valery had confessed to Gabriel that she was carrying his child. The augurs told her it would be a girl, and Gabriel had blithely remarked that she would grow up to be a big-time hero, like her father. Which was, everything considered, devastatingly ironic.

Moog's husband, Fredrick, who was a renowned mercenary in his own right, had contracted the rot a year before, having forayed one too many times beneath the poisoned eaves of the black forest. The wizard was determined to find a cure, and had already requested a leave of absence from the band. By the time he heard of Ganelon's arrest, Moog was too concerned with saving Freddie to lend his aid. Freddie, despite this, died a few months later.

In those days Matrick was receiving letters almost daily from Lilith, who hadn't yet evolved into the merciless, sex-crazed harpy-queen she eventually became. The young princess was besotted with Saga's rogue. She wrote to him that her father was gravely ill, and that Matrick should remain in Agria, marry her, and rule as king once the old fucker (as she so lovingly put it) was dead.

And as for Clay Cooper? He'd never dreamt of being in

a band, nor wanted any part of the notoriety that came along with it. He loved the boys like brothers—even Ganelon—but although Clay was awfully good at killing things, the thought of doing so for another ten years while avoiding the ire of a vengeful monarch didn't sit with him at all. He'd wanted to go home, to leave violence in his past, and, more than anything, to try and live up to the words he'd scratched onto the birch that marked his mother's grave all those blood-soaked years ago.

So Ganelon took the fall alone. It wasn't a betrayal—not really, since he was in fact guilty of murdering a prince, and several "innocent" men besides—but it certainly felt like one to Clay, who had borne the burden of that choice like a cloak of cast iron ever since. He wondered now if freeing Ganelon only because they needed his help might not be, as far as Ganelon's forbearance was concerned, the straw that broke the camel's—

Ah, Clay thought, as the meaning behind the metaphor became suddenly obvious, *I get it now.*

Gabriel's desperate plan had come, at last, to fruition. Against all odds, the band was back together.

It would be just like old times, except that Moog was dying of an incurable ailment, Matrick was hideously out of shape, Gabriel—their proud and fearless leader—had gone meek as a newborn kitten, and Clay wanted nothing more than to go home, hug his wife, and tell his darling daughter stories of grand exploits that were all, thankfully, far behind him.

Ganelon, at least, would be virtually unchanged, as hale and healthy as the day the Sultana's magi had turned him to stone nearly twenty years before.

As Moog searched his bag for a means to undo the southerner's petrifaction, Clay found himself envisioning how the moments following Ganelon's release might unfold. In almost every scenario Clay and his bandmates ended up dead at the warrior's feet. Ganelon had always been Saga's most skilled fighter; for him to end them now would be a simple thing, easy as an eagle killing its offspring.

Ganelon had been conceived, born, and bred to violence. He'd been an orphan by the age of eleven, a mercenary since fourteen. The southern warrior had no doubt undergone as many wild adventures before joining Saga as the five of them had in the ten years after. He claimed there'd been a bard around for most of them, but Clay had yet to hear a song or story about Ganelon's youth that did not come from the warrior himself.

More so than most—Clay included—Ganelon was a man defined by his origins. His mother had been sold as a child to a brothel in Xanses. His father had been one of the Sultana's prized Kaskar bodyguards, and the union of these two disparate souls had been in no way romantic, or loving, or even consensual, Clay presumed, since the Narmeeri whore had killed the Kaskar giant in his sleep immediately afterward.

From his father, Ganelon had inherited a northman's green eyes and imposing height, an explosive temper, and an innate capacity for bloodshed. From his mother: ferocity, fortitude of mind, and a small voice in the back of his mind that served, when he was wise enough to listen, as his conscience.

"Ah, here." Moog carefully withdrew a potted cactus from the void within his bag. "Hold this," he said, handing the sack off to Matrick. He knelt and set the cactus on the floor before, very cautiously, plucking one of its spines and clamping it between his teeth. Then he motioned for his bag and swiped it over the cactus like it was a feral cat he feared might scratch him. Finally he took the spine from his mouth and used its tip to prick the hulking stone statue in the foot.

Standing, Moog flicked the spine away. "This should just take a minute," he told them.

Clay wondered as the seconds ticked by how exactly one emerged from a state of petrifaction. Would the warrior rage and flail, his mind still trapped in the instant the spell of stone had taken hold? He took a cautious step back, flexing his right hand, ready to catch *Blackheart*'s grip should he need to shrug it free.

He examined the southerner's statue as he waited. Ganelon wasn't quite so tall as Clay. His arms weren't as bulky, his shoulders not as broad. And yet Ganelon, to Clay's mind, had always cut a more imposing figure. Whereas Clay Cooper was built like a great big bear—as adept at fighting as he would be at sleeping through a harsh winter in a cozy cave—Ganelon was lean as a wolf, sleek as a panther: His whole physique seemed formed by the brutal economy of nature for a deadly and singular purpose.

Clay watched, fascinated, as the spell began to fade. The dull stone became braided black hair strung with ivory beads. It became dark brown flesh and corded muscle laced with pale scars. Deep browed, broad nosed, black whiskered... Ganelon blinked dust from his lashes, and after a disoriented moment he seemed to realize he wasn't alone. The warrior levelled his green-eyed glare at each of them in turn. His nostrils flared, and Clay started counting down the seconds until the bloodbath—their blood, his bath—kicked off.

Those seconds stretched on and on, until finally Ganelon cleared his throat, turned to Gabriel, and asked in a voice that cracked like old parchment, "How long?"

"Nineteen years," said Gabriel.

The warrior closed his eyes. His jaw worked furiously. His chest heaved as the breath of empty decades flooded his lungs. At last he loosed a long sigh. He rolled a kink from his shoulders and pressed his neck to one side—it *cracked* so loud Moog jumped like a startled rabbit. Ganelon glanced at the wizard and chuckled. Slowly, his eyes moved to Matrick, then to Gabriel, then to Clay. Another silence took hold, leadened by the weight of settling dust.

"You all look like shit," he said at last.

Chapter Twenty-one

The Riot House

The Riot House was Fivecourt's most infamous tavern. There was a sign above the door that depicted a man riding a sheep. The words WYATT'S REST were carved out beneath, but whoever Wyatt was, he'd ridden his sheep out of town long before Clay had ever set eyes on the place. It was an inn, an alehouse, a brothel, and a gambling den. It was a place for fences to fence and whores to whore, a haven for drunks, a sanctuary for addicts, a seven-storey circus that Clay hadn't known how much he'd missed until he walked through the door with his band at his back.

It looked much the same as he remembered it: the bar, the booths, the dicing tables scattered in the centre of the room. There was a skirted stage backed by a double-wide fireplace, currently occupied by a troupe of four women, three of whom were playing instruments while the fourth wailed like a banshee falling off a cliff. The warped wooden floor was stained with spilled beer and dried blood. Shattered bottles and the splintered remains of broken chairs told the story of epic brawls (the Riot House was good for one a night, at least), and the smoke-clouded air was filled with the babble of several hundred patrons shouting and laughing and cursing all at once.

Clay was gazing up at the stacked tiers of the inn's hollow

interior. He spotted the fourth-floor balcony from which Matrick had thrown a burning mattress onto the commons below, and there: the third-floor balcony from which Clay himself had fallen during a brawl with a Kaskar whose sister he'd refused to take to bed. Kaskars were funny that way.

To be back in the Riot House, to find it unchanged after all these years, felt to Clay like a dream, as though he'd taken a step twenty years into the past. He half-expected to see his old self swagger by, young and dumb, unmindful of anything but the drink in his hand, the woman on his arm, the coins burning a hole in his pocket.

Gabriel clapped him on the shoulder. "I'll go see about the rooms."

"I'll be at the bar," said Matrick.

And then someone, somewhere, shouted, "There they are!" and things pretty much went downhill from there.

The whole place had been waiting for them. Dinantra had sent word ahead, and every newcomer through the door (beside which the gorgon's thugs stood to make sure Ganelon and the others remained inside) assured them that word of their fight the following day was spreading like fire through the city. Mercenaries formed a queue for handshakes and high fives. A bard took the stage to sing their exploits, and the balconies teemed with patrons eager for a look at what had once been the greatest band in all the world.

Clay recognized plenty of faces he hadn't seen since his touring days. Here was Deckart Clearwater with his double-hafted hammer strapped to his back. And there was Merciless May Drummond, who had slain more giants than anyone Clay knew and had once borne an orc's child just to settle a bet. Her kid was a merc, too, in fact, and ugly as the night was dark.

He saw Jorma Mulekicker fighting three men at once, and Aric Slake losing badly at cards. All five of the Skulk brothers were sharing a pitcher at one table, while the six members of the ironically named Seven Swords were arguing heatedly at another. He saw Beckett "Greensleeves" Fisher embroiled in a game of Contha's Keep, in which you took turns removing and restacking blocks from a tottering tower until it fell, at which point you finished what remained of your drink and started all over again.

"Slowhand Clay Cooper!" Nick Blood—the lesser half of the husband-and-wife mercenary duo known as Blood and Gloria—took Clay by the shoulders and shook him fiercely. "Heathen's Bloody Cock, man, it's really you!"

"It's really me," Clay verified. "How's Gloria?"

"Dead," Nick stated matter-of-factly. "Rot took her about ten years back."

Clay swallowed the foot in his mouth before speaking again. "I'm sorry to hear it."

The old mercenary shrugged. "Happens," he said. "Anyway, I'm back in the game! I was supposed to be opening the Maxithon for the Screaming Eagles tomorrow, but I hear the gorgon found herself a new headliner." He nudged Clay with his elbow and winked. "You're a lucky bastard, Cooper. One day out of retirement and you're the biggest show in town. That's Saga for you, I guess. No one did it like you guys, man."

Clay smiled like a man who'd won first place in a "Whose Life Sucks the Most" contest. "Good to see you, Nick," he said, brushing by and making a straight line for the bar.

Matrick was there. Some idiot had given him a bottle and was letting him pour his own drinks. Consequently, the bottle was almost empty.

"Look who's here!" the old rogue yelled over the noise, gesturing toward someone beside him at the bar.

Clay blinked in disbelief.

"Pete?"

"Slowhand, hey. Ain't seen you round in a bit."

A bit? "It's been a while, yeah. You look ... exactly the

same," said Clay, and boy was *that* true. Pete was a lifetime regular at the Riot House. He kept a room on the first floor and was a permanent fixture at the wood. He helped pick the place up in the morning, and in turn was fed three times a day and afforded an ostensibly bottomless tab. His hair was drawn into a queue at the nape of his neck, still as black as the plain short-sleeved jerkin Clay had long suspected was the only shirt the man owned.

"Matrick here tells me he was a king," said Pete, who seemed thoroughly unimpressed by the fact. "Seems like a lotta hassle, and for what? A man needs food, beer, and a pot to piss in. Name one thing a king's got that I don't!"

Clay was about to start with *an entire country* when the bartender arrived—another relic from the days of old. Uric was a minotaur, a pit fighter who'd won his freedom in the days before arenas like the Maxithon had sprung up in every city. His once-lustrous beard had gone ratty and grey, his horns yellowed by smoke, and his voice scratched like a suit of shoddy chain mail.

"Drinks?" he asked.

"Beer," said Pete.

"Whiskey," said Matrick.

Clay raised a hand. "I'm fine, thanks."

"Three beers," growled Uric, shuffling off.

"You run into Raff Lackey out there?" asked Pete, examining the dregs of his current drink.

Clay shared a hesitant glance with Matrick. "We did, yeah."

Pete only nodded. "I'll say a prayer for him tonight, then. Told him ain't no bounty worth picking a fight with Clay Cooper."

"I didn't mean to..." Clay started to explain, but what could he say? *Sure, I put a venomous snake to his throat, but how was I supposed to know it would kill him?* "Things just got out of hand," he finished lamely.

"As they do, Slowhand. As they do."

When Uric returned with the beers, Clay seized the

opportunity to excuse himself. Matrick followed as far as the gaming tables, where he spotted a game of tiles in need of a fourth and was warmly welcomed to the empty seat.

Gabe and Ganelon were seated in a booth along one wall. The most fervent admirers had said their pieces by then, and the southerner's glare managed to stave off those who weren't quite drunk enough to dare his presence just yet. Clay settled onto the bench beside Gabriel.

Maybe because of Ganelon's uncannily youthful appearance, or because they'd been sitting in a booth just like this, Clay was reminded of the day they'd first met Ganelon. Gabe had lured Clay to Conthas under false pretences, with the undisclosed aim of introducing him to a street thug turned booker named Kallorek. In a tavern called the Loose Moose, the Orc (as Kal was more commonly called back then) had in turn introduced them to a young pickpocket named Matty and a bard whose name Clay couldn't have recalled now for all the icicles in Hell.

As chance would have it (Clay liked to believe the gods had better things to do than get a band going) Ganelon had also been in the Moose that evening. A few hapless drunks had taken one look at the southerner's brown skin and vivid green eyes before giving voice to some disparaging remarks about his mother's taste in men.

Ganelon put a knife in one, and when half the crowd jumped him Gabriel insisted he and Clay leap to the southerner's defense, if only to make it a fair fight. Matrick joined in as well, and before the night was over Saga had won its first battle and lost—by accident, of course—the first of its many bards.

Clay smiled to think of it, which earned him a curious look from Gabriel as he glanced over. "What?"

"Nothing."

"I was just filling Ganelon in," Gabe told him. "About Last-leaf, and Castia, and Rose. He said he'll help."

Clay looked across the table. It was so strange to see

Ganelon sitting there, twenty years younger than he ought to have been. The warrior scratched at the scar below his left eye. "What?" he asked defensively, "you thought I wouldn't?"

"No," Clay started, "I just figured..."

"That I'd be a little bit pissed?" suggested Ganelon. "That I'd wonder where my friends were when the Sultana's men came to take me down? That I might resent having been turned to stone, sent to the Quarry, and then sold to a gorgon who plans on killing me in the arena?"

Clay took a sip of his beer. "Yeah, that," he said.

Ganelon made a face and shrugged. "Well, I ain't pissed. I don't resent you...much. Way I see it, justice was served. Those who needed killing got killed, and I missed out on twenty years of sweet dick-all."

"Well, I wouldn't say—"

"You know what I mean, Slowhand," Ganelon cut him off. "Wives. Children. *Settling down.* It ain't really my scene." He took a pull from his mug and wiped froth from his lips. "But here I am, and here we are, and Gabe's little girl needs rescuing, so let's get it done. Wouldn't mind seeing Lastleaf, either. Sounds like he needs his ass kicked again."

So that was that, then. No bitterness. No animosity whatsoever. As far as Ganelon was concerned, things were business as usual. He wouldn't have called the southerner a simple man—far from it, in fact—but his pragmatism was astounding, even to Clay, for whom it was practically a religion.

Having concluded matters with Clay, Ganelon turned his attention to someone seated at the nearest table. "Somethin' the matter?"

Glancing over, Clay recognized the platinum-haired youth he'd seen earlier that evening, sitting on the steps of the argosy that was blocking the gate.

"Naw." The lad's voice was an affected parody of the southerner's drawl. "I was just trying to figure out what the big deal is with you guys."

Gabriel slunk into the corner, and Ganelon stared without speaking, so Clay took it upon himself to respond. "We're just a band," he said.

"Just a band?" The youth sneered and shared a mocking laugh with the others at his table. There were two petulant-looking young men and a woman sporting a diamond-studded eye patch. "Well then, why the fuck are you headlining the Maxithon tomorrow instead of us?"

"We supposed to know you?" asked Ganelon.

The white-haired merc looked genuinely shocked. "You mean you don't?" Ganelon shook his head. "We're the Screaming Eagles, man. We're the biggest band east of the Heartwyld."

"Which means anywhere," one of the others put in.

"I got that," Clay said.

The scrawny frontman leaned forward on his seat. "You been under a rock or something?"

Ganelon didn't quite smile. "Something like that, yeah."

"*We* were supposed to fight for the gorgon tomorrow," said the one with the glittery eye patch, who wasn't actually a woman, Clay realized. "We came all the way from Drumskeep, and now we're to sit with our dicks in our hands while some washed-up old-timers bleed on the sand?"

"Now hold on, Parys," said the other. "Didn't these guys kill a dragon in its sleep, like, a hundred years ago? Show some bloody respect!"

Derisive laughter followed.

Clay glanced over, afraid Ganelon's temper would boil over, but the warrior was still holding his beer, so that was a good sign. *When he sets it down, I'll panic,* Clay figured. He tacked on an easy smile, hoping to smooth things over before they escalated further.

"Well, if it makes you feel any better, I think Dinantra has something pretty nasty in mind for us tomorrow."

White Hair crossed his tattooed arms, looking emphatically unimpressed. "What could she have planned for a bunch of washed-up heroes? A few crippled kobolds? A blind cyclops? Or maybe she intends to make you all just stand around and see how long before one of you dies of old age."

More laughter. Clay hid his faltering grin behind a sip of beer. "Maybe," he said.

White Hair wasn't finished yet, though. "Kings of the Wyld—isn't that what they used to call you? Where did the gorgon even find you guys? Last I heard you were scattered to the wind."

"I heard one of you died," said Eye Patch.

"I heard one of you fancied boys!" crowed another. "Which one prefers the sword to the sheath, eh? The blond one, I'll bet. He's the prettiest."

Clay rubbed at his beard, in danger of misplacing his smile altogether. "Listen, fellas, I'm sorry we stole your show. I really am. I'm sure the Screeching Eagles are a—"

"Screaming," White Hair snarled.

"Screaming what?"

"It's the *Screaming* Eagles. Not the 'Screeching Eagles.'"

Clay frowned. "Are you sure? Because the sound an eagle makes—"

And quite suddenly the boy was on his feet, sword in hand. "I know what a fucking eagle sounds like!" he screamed, which drew the attention of every table nearby, and in the ensuing silence Clay heard the quiet but ominous thud of Ganelon setting his beer down on the table.

The story of how the Riot House burned to the ground was chronicled by several bards, a few of which were actually present on the night in question. Even those privileged few, however, were accused of distorting the truth, embellishing facts in an attempt to promote their account as the "definitive" version of the events that inevitably led to the all-consuming fire. What is known for certain is that the fight between the

Screaming Eagles and the reunited members of Saga, which in turn gave rise to a full-scale brawl, was only the beginning.

In her ballad *House in Flames*, Tanis Two-fingers suggests that several members of the City Watch, initially dispatched to quell the barroom battle, acquitted themselves with such prowess and ferocity that they were recruited by a booker and went on to become the band known by the admittedly uninspired name The City Watch. *Fire and Feathers*, written by the renowned poet Jamidor, provides a detailed account of the pillow fight that raged between the fifth and sixth floors of the ill-fated inn sometime after midnight.

Is it true that Matrick Skulldrummer, the renegade king of Agria, was responsible for the fire? The song *Drinking and Dragons* proposes that after consuming a quantity of liquor sufficient to render a small giant impotent, he vomited onto a candle and set an entire table ablaze. Others maintain that Arcandius Moog was at fault. The wizard and celebrated alchemist allegedly summoned an elemental ifrit to resolve an argument about whether demons are hatched or naturally born—a futile gesture, since everyone knows they are hatched.

Regardless of its origin, the resulting fire brought about the end of an era. The Riot House was never rebuilt, and among its ashes there remains but a single testament to its decades of debauched existence: a small, innocuous tombstone to mark the grave of what (remarkably) was the night's single unfortunate casualty, a man known simply as Pete.

The inscription reads as follows: WHEN WE SEEK TO RULE ONLY OURSELVES, WE ARE EACH OF US KINGS.

Chapter Twenty-two

The Maxithon

In retrospect, getting blind drunk the night before fighting for his life in the arena had been a terrible idea. Clay's stomach gurgled like a cauldron left to boil. His head was pounding, and the not-so-distant thunder of thirty thousand people screaming beyond the shadowed corridor in which they stood wasn't helping. Nor was the fact that the Maxithon, despite being fastened by four mighty chains against the river's current, was *floating*. The effect was subtle, but unnerving, like standing in the hold of some colossal ship.

Clay decided to add *vomit everywhere* to the long list of things he'd rather not do today, right beneath *get killed*.

He could hear Dinantra addressing the crowd. Her voice, altered by magic to carry across the arena, was promising a show unlike any they had seen before. The gorgon hadn't yet revealed what Clay and his bandmates would be fighting, only that it had been brought "with considerable danger and great expense" from the "darkest depths of the Heartwyld," which could have meant pretty much anything.

"Maybe it'll be an owlbear," said Moog excitedly. The wizard seemed unfazed by the exploits of the previous night. "Can you imagine if it was? Be a shame to have to kill it, though. Terrible shame."

Clay didn't bother asserting that owlbears didn't exist. They'd been through it before, many times. The wizard had once offered "proof" that such creatures were real by showing them a crude drawing in an old book of what looked to everyone but Moog like a bear with comically large eyes.

The gorgon had fallen silent. There was a brief fanfare, followed by a resounding cheer, and from that noise emerged a single word booming over and over again, ceaseless as the ocean surf, echoing like a deep drumbeat down the long stone corridor, so loud it shook the dust from the ceiling and set the ground trembling beneath their feet.

Saga, Saga, Saga.

Clay caught Moog and Matrick sharing an eager grin. *These two idiots are actually enjoying this*, he thought, while trying to suppress his own... well, he certainly wouldn't have called it *excitement*, since excitement implied an optimism he didn't particularly feel about what awaited them in the arena, but there was, admittedly, something undeniably thrilling about hearing their name on the lips of so many thousands of people.

Ganelon cracked his knuckles and rolled his neck from side to side.

Gabriel sat ahead of them in the tunnel, slouched against the wall with his head between his knees. When the crowd began chanting he stiffened, and his head rose like an animal catching wind of its prey. After a moment he stood, his shadow slender against the bright tunnel mouth.

"It's time," he said, and then, "Are we ready for this?"

"Ready," Matrick confirmed.

"Yessir," said Moog cheerily.

Ganelon grunted, "Sure."

Clay sighed and shrugged. "Guess so."

Gabe nodded, turned, and led the four of them up the gently sloping corridor. Clay listened in a hangover-induced daze as the crowd's incessant chant grew louder, as the tunnel mouth grew wider, brighter.

And then Gabriel stepped into the sun's partitioning light and the chant dissolved into a wordless, furious roar.

Like each of them, Saga's frontman had been suitably equipped for the occasion. The armour provided for him was lacquered white and gold, impressive looking but too ornate for Clay's taste. The sword he carried was a poor imitation of *Vellichor*, huge and heavy, hideously grey. Gabe's hair had been washed and brushed out by one of the gorgon's slaves, so that except for the slump of his shoulders and the haunted look in his eyes he somewhat resembled the "Golden Gabe" this crowd was expecting to see.

Moog went out after him. The wizard had been given proper robes to replace his soiled one-piece pyjamas. He bore nothing but the bag slung over his shoulder, and he waved with both hands at the circling thousands.

Matrick was next. The king wore a black leather vest studded with iron rivets, which he couldn't quite fasten over the bulge of his stomach. The jewel-encrusted hilts of *Roxy* and *Grace* gleamed at his waist, and as he stepped into the arena some of the more patriotic Agrians in the stands began singing his name as well.

Clay grimaced. *If Lilith doesn't know yet that Matrick is alive,* he thought, *then she will very soon.*

Ganelon walked out ahead of Clay. Dinantra had given the southerner back his axe, which she'd purchased from the Quarry along with Ganelon himself and had kept in her personal treasury these past nine years. Clay couldn't help but stare at it as he followed along: twinned black blades swept like a wyvern's wings down either side of the haft. Each wicked edge was traced by a filigree of druic script that pulsed blue-white only when the weapon was hefted by the warrior himself. Whenever he did so, the axe itself began whispering quietly, urgently, in a language even Moog didn't recognize. If used by anyone else, the weapon was as deadly as any other razor-sharp length of metal, but in Ganelon's hands it was a

thing of awesome lethality. It was called *Syrinx*, and asking
the stoic southerner how he came to possess such an artifact
was as likely to garner an answer as asking a goat for directions to the nearest library.

Clay went out last, raising an arm and squinting against
the sun's punishing glare. He'd chosen a jerkin of boiled
leather from the arena's armoury that fit him surprisingly
well. He had *Blackheart* strapped to his right arm, and he'd
found a reasonably sharp sword that looked as though it
might not snap the first time he hit something with it, so that
was promising.

The five of them stalked to the wide-open centre of the
Maxithon and stood there as wave after wave of deafening
adulation washed over them.

This, Clay thought to himself, *is why the bands of today
don't bother touring. This is the reason they avoid the Heartwyld.
Why risk being ambushed by monsters when you can pick and
choose which to fight? Why put yourself in danger of getting lost,
or contracting the rot, when you can simply visit your local arena?*

He turned a slow circle where he stood, eyes climbing
ring after ring of seething multitudes. Uncountable screaming faces. Innumerable waving hands. Why kill in obscurity
when you could do so here, and bask in the glory granted by
thirty thousand adoring witnesses?

Dinantra was watching from the patron's box on the lowest tier, which was backed by a tiled wall and shaded by a
roof of fluttering silk awnings. The Duke of Endland sat in
silence among her gaggle of courtiers, arms crossed and ears
flattened against the autumnal sweep of his slicked-back hair.
His eyes were fixed firmly on Gabriel, who in turn was staring across the sand-strewn expanse at the huge wrought-iron
gate that stood opposite the corridor they'd emerged from a
few minutes earlier.

"It's opening," he called over his shoulder.

Clay's tongue had gone dry as cured beef, and it tasted like someone had ashed a whisky-drenched cigarette in his mouth. Sure enough, the heavy portcullis was grinding slowly up. Whatever Dinantra and Lastleaf hoped might spell the end of Saga was about to come roaring out at them.

Clay shifted his weight from one foot to the other. His back had been aching since this morning, and he leaned back to stretch it. Considering the draw that he and his bandmates seemed to be, he was unsurprised to find several skyships skimming lazy circles above the arena, from which those fortunate enough to have unearthed the airborne relics could peer down into the Maxithon like bloodthirsty gods.

There was a *clang* as the gate reached its apex, then a hush as the circling sea of spectators fell suddenly becalmed. And then the thing that might indeed spell the end of Saga *actually did* come roaring out at them.

At which point Clay vomited onto the sand at his feet, and so crossed off the list the first of the two things he hadn't wanted to do today.

It was a chimera—likely the very same one he and Gabriel had seen during the parade in Conthas. The thing was a monster in every sense of the word. It had the paws of a lion, the hind legs of a goat, a sweeping reptilian tail, and three heads: a dragon sheathed in deep crimson scales, a black-maned lion, and a white ram with unsettling pink eyes. It had been caged when he'd seen it last, heavily sedated. But now it was free, and very much alert, and pounding across the sand like a dog racing toward its long-absent master, only Clay very much doubted it wanted only to knock them down and give their faces a lick.

The Maxithon made a sound that was half cheer, half horrified gasp. They had come to see an old band reunite for one last clash of arms. Some had dragged their children along so the young ones could see what a *real* band looked like. Others had brought their mothers or fathers, who no doubt waxed nostalgic about how kids today wouldn't know a true mercenary if one kicked down their door and ate their supper. Instead, they would stand witness as four old men and one pissed-off southerner were savagely mutilated before their eyes.

Startled by the noise, the monster skidded to a halt. The ram bared its teeth, the lion roared, and the dragon loosed a spout of red-orange flame into the sky. The crowd cheered wildly, having apparently deciding to make the best of things.

At least they'll have a good story to tell, Clay mused darkly. *Oh, you saw some no-name band fight a clutch of half-starved bugbears? I watched Saga get torn apart by a fucking chimera!*

The monster made an effort to open its wings, which were tightly bound, and the heads snarled in mutual frustration at its thwarted efforts. Having no better option, they decided as one to descend on the prey Dinantra had so kindly made available.

"What do we do?" Moog's voice was shrill with fear. Beside him, Matrick looked as if he were about to follow Clay's example and empty the contents of his stomach on the ground.

"We survive," said Ganelon. He tightened his grip on *Syrinx* and took a step forward, as though he meant to protect them from what was coming. As if he possibly could.

Gabriel wasn't even looking at the thing. His eyes were nailed to the patron's box, where Lastleaf and the gorgon lounged beneath the shade of a silk awning. His expression was grave, but Clay could see what smouldered beneath that ashen gaze. It went without saying that if they died here today, there would come a tomorrow when Rose would perish as well—if it hadn't already come. And worse, she would die without knowing that her father had cared enough to come for her, that he'd been willing to risk anything to see her safe. Gabriel knew this fight for what it was: a death sentence. Not only for himself, and for the men who stood at his side, but for his daughter as well.

Gabe was no longer the hero he'd once been. The young lion had grown into a meek old lamb. But even a coward found his courage in a corner, and there were things even a craven heart could not allow.

The beast came on, and Gabriel charged out to meet it. He raised his sword. The dull iron gleamed like druin steel in the bright afternoon sun. His hair streamed behind him like a pennant of pure gold, and the sound in the Maxithon rose to a frenzied pitch. *Here* was the glory they'd come to witness, the spectacle they could brag about for years to come.

The chimera hit Gabe like a charging bull. The ram's head lowered—the sword clanging uselessly off one horn—and then Gabriel was soaring through the air over Ganelon's head. The dragon attacked next. Its jaws snapped shut in the space where the warrior had been an instant earlier. Ganelon was rolling to his left and came up swinging. *Syrinx* bit into the scales alongside the dragon's head and it recoiled, hissing in pain.

Clay plodded forward as fast as his legs would carry him. Matrick was just behind, Moog slowing to help a stunned Gabriel to his feet. The chimera turned on Ganelon, and twice more the dragon lunged. Ganelon's axe whirled before him, both attempts leaving the dragon bloodied. At last it drew itself up, like a snake preparing to strike. Ganelon dropped to a crouch, realizing too late he should have started running. A spark flashed inside the dragon's maw and a torrent of fire streamed out.

Clay's skid brought him between his friend and the flame, which battered harmlessly against *Blackheart's* weathered face. The force of it knocked him back into Ganelon, and the two of them sprawled helplessly as the chimera advanced.

But then Matrick arrived, shouting at the monster. The ram's head twisted to look at him, drawing the others, and Matrick launched himself at it. His first swipe fell short, and he was forced to dance back clumsily as the ram's yellowed teeth bit at him, missing by inches. Matrick responded by stabbing his right-hand dagger sideways into its eye. The beast screamed—a disturbingly *human* sound—and tried again to bite him. Reacting without thinking, Matrick offered his entire left arm to the creature's maw, twisting at the last second so that as its jaw clamped shut the knife in his hand plunged up through the roof of its mouth and (allegedly) into its brain, since it died immediately.

One head down, Clay thought, *two to go.*

The crowd was deafening. Matrick was on his knees, clutching his arm. He looked both exultant and terrified, but mostly terrified. The chimera wheeled on him, and Clay was too busy fretting over that to see the tail swipe that took him in the head.

From his side, several feet away from where he'd been standing a moment earlier, Clay saw Moog unleash a handful of small pellets at the beast. The wizard shouted some arcane command, and all but one of the pellets puffed into smoke. The last bloomed into a fitful fireball that smote the lion's head as it descended toward Matrick.

"Fucking things," Moog cursed, rummaging through his bag for what Clay hoped was something more effective than whatever he'd just employed.

Gabriel took advantage of the distraction, dragging Matrick away by the collar and putting himself between the injured man and the monster. The chimera stalked toward them. The ram's head hung limp to one side, blood drooling from its mouth. Ganelon was trying to get at the thing from behind, but the tail was lashing like a viper, keeping him at bay.

The lion loosed a roar in Gabriel's face, and Gabriel roared back, stepping cautiously to his right in an effort to draw it away from Matrick, who looked to have passed out from shock. The chimera lunged, and Gabe leapt clear of the lion's jaws, then slashed at the dragon's head when it came close. His sword, too dull to be effective, glanced harmlessly off the armouring scales.

Clay could see that the effort required to swing the weapon was already taking its toll. Gabriel managed to ward off another thrust of the dragon's head, but one of the beast's huge paws took him by surprise and sent him tumbling face-first onto the sand. He rolled onto his back, but before he could rise it pinned him down. The armour kept him from being crushed, but its wicked talons punched through. Gabriel cried out once, but then suddenly his limbs went stiff. His sword fell from fingers that could no longer grasp the hilt.

Paralyzed, Clay realized. As if this monster didn't have enough methods of murder at its disposal, it could also leave you helpless in case it would rather murder you later.

"Aha!" Moog pulled a wand from his bag, or rather a gnarled twig wrapped in bronze wire that Clay sure as hell hoped was a wand. The chimera, having decided that Gabriel was no longer a threat, turned on the wizard. It roared and flexed its wings again. The thick cords of rope that bound them groaned, but held. By then Moog was pointing the wand, and as the beast sprang at him he shouted something incomprehensible. There was a *crack* that drew a silent breath from thirty-thousand people, and an arc of white lightning leapt from the bronze-wire wand. It hit the lion between the eyes, dissipating instantly. The beast shuddered, dazed but not dead. Its front legs went out from beneath it even as Clay climbed groggily to his own and stumbled toward the wizard.

Ganelon might have killed it then, but the dragon head was still alert. It belched another stream of fire, and the warrior was forced to leap away.

"Ha!" Moog made a flourish with the wand, basking for a moment in the adulation of the crowd. He *did* look pretty impressive, Clay supposed—resplendent in borrowed robes, his wispy white hair shimmering like sun-warmed silk. As Clay drew near, the wizard glanced over, grinning. "Watch this!" he said, and what happened next might have been extraordinarily funny were their lives not at stake.

But they were, so it wasn't.

Chapter Twenty-three

Born to Kill

Moog levelled the wand like a knight marking a foe with the point of his sword. He spoke the words that invoked his spell, and a bolt of lightning bridged the space between the bronze-wire wand and the dragon's head. This time the lightning crackled harmlessly over the creature's metallic scales. The bridge remained intact, a buzzing filament linking Moog to a powerful current of conjured electricity. The wizard's body jolted once—his fringe of long white hair blew out like the crown of a dandelion gone to seed—and then he collapsed in a heap, unconscious.

Clay slowed, then stopped. He stood dumbstruck as the absurdity of what he'd just witnessed washed over him. *Three down,* he thought morbidly. *Two to go.*

He heard Ganelon shout his name, glanced over his shoulder to see the chimera bearing down on him. With his left hand Clay slashed out, scoring the dragon's snout with the point of his sword. He brought *Blackheart* to bear as the lion rushed in after. Its teeth gnashed against the face of his shield, pushing him backward. Out of instinct alone Clay turned his momentum into a roll, narrowly avoiding the swipe of a taloned paw. On his knees, he deflected another claw, then another attack by the lion. When the dragon struck he was ready, angling *Blackheart* so that the shield wedged itself in the serpent's mouth. Before it could wrench itself free he jammed his sword to the hilt in the side of its neck.

The scales split with an echoing ring. Blood frothed warm over his hand. The dragon shrieked and his shield came free, but Clay lost his grip on his sword as the head retreated. Hopelessly off balance, he stumbled almost out of the chimera's reach. But only almost.

He felt its razor claws slash through the back of his leather cuirass. There was pain for a moment, replaced quickly by an ice-cold numbness. The muscles in his legs spasmed, and Clay pitched forward onto the sand. Like Gabriel, he managed to roll onto his back, but the shadow of the beast fell upon him as he did. He saw teeth as long as his arm, a pebbled pink tongue, and beyond both, the black oblivion of the lion's gaping maw. Its breath gusted over him, rank as a rotting carcass, and Clay kept his eyes open as death's door yawned in welcome.

All at once the crowd went berserk; the chimera's two remaining heads howled in anguish, and death's door slammed shut in Clay's face.

Ganelon had cut its tail off, or so Clay discovered as the creature spun to face the warrior and he saw the severed stalk thrashing behind it. The chimera's claws hadn't cut him deep, but even still his limbs felt sluggish. He could open and close his fingers, but bending his elbow, or commanding his legs to help him stand, was out of the question. It would be several minutes before he could wrest control of his extremities from the toxin's grip, and by then it would be too late.

So he could only watch, as much a spectator as those looking on from the stands, or from the skyships wheeling like vultures in the blue sky, as Ganelon faced down the chimera alone. *As is fitting,* Clay supposed, since the two of them shared a similar, singular quality: They had both been born to kill.

The dragon's head appeared unfazed by the sword in its throat. It darted in and Ganelon sidestepped, bashing it senseless with the flat of his axe, then hammered it twice more before the lion came to its rescue. The warrior ducked under the jaws and rolled beneath it, punching the pointed tip of *Syrinx* up into the creature's belly. The chimera staggered away before he could do any serious damage. Ganelon pressed the attack, and the monster retreated, roaring defiantly, buying time for the dragon's head to recover.

It did so suddenly, lunging at the warrior's left side even as a barbed paw swatted at his right. Ganelon turned his weapon sideways, jamming the haft into the creature's palm, while the sweeping blades kept the dragon at bay. When the lion came at him he kicked it hard in the snout, stunning it, then launched himself at the dragon's head. He grasped one of the jutting spines at its collar and hauled himself up as if mounting a horse. From his perch the claws couldn't reach him, nor could the lion's teeth.

He has it, thought Clay. *Ganelon's going to kill it, and we'll be free. Free to go and die far, far to the west. But not here. Not today.*

The chimera knew it, too. The dragon screamed, the lion bellowed bloody fury—the desperate cry of a predator overcome by its prey. Its claws raked furrows in the sand as Ganelon raised his axe. Its wings strained against the ropes that bound them...

...and the ropes snapped.

Spring Maiden's Mercy. Clay's toxin-addled mind was having trouble reconciling what he saw. Wings like black sails unfurled against the sky, billowing once before stretching taut. There was a muted silence as the crowd grappled with the terrible implications of a chimera in flight, and an instant later their terror took shape. The flap of draconic wings sent dust swirling across the arena floor. Cloven hooves kicked free of the earth, and the beast was airborne.

Up, up it went, rising with each sweep of it wings. Ganelon abandoned his axe, clinging with both hands to the spines on the dragon's head. Hampered by the corpse of the

ram's head, unbalanced by the loss of its tail, and trying desperately to shake the murderous parasite from its back, the
chimera lurched crazily. One of the larger skyships, a lumbering caravel that looked to be some sort of festival barge, was
banking to turn when the chimera crashed into it. One of its
orbs—or tidal engines, as Moog had called them—tore loose
and went plummeting toward the river below. The ship listed
as though caught by a cresting wave, and Clay saw several
revellers clinging by their fingers to the rail.

Nearby, Moog bolted suddenly upright. His hair was in
wild disarray, his eyes bloodshot. He coughed a gust of smoke
and looked dazedly at Clay. "Is it over? Did we kill it?" With
some effort, Clay managed to extend the index finger on his
left hand and point skyward. The wizard looked up. The
bulky caravel was quickly losing altitude, careening dangerously toward one of the support towers. The chimera swept
low overhead. Ganelon had torn a spine from its skull and was
trying without success to stab it through the scales.

"Oh," Moog said, looking mightily depressed.

Another skyship—a frigate with sleek webbed sails and
whirling engines at fore and stern—opened fire on the monster. Rail-mounted crossbows launched a trio of bolts as long
as Clay was tall. The first sailed out over the river. The second
dropped to impale some luckless man in the arena crowd. The
third took the chimera in the side, and for a moment it faltered, wings flailing like a bat confounded by a pane of glass.
Another bolt leapt from the attacking ship, but the beast
veered as those on board hurried to rearm the weapons.

Dragon fire washed across the deck. The ship sagged forward as the front engine began to steam. The crossbow turrets were abandoned by men and women rushing to keep the
flames from spreading. The chimera turned sharply and came
on again. When it struck, Clay knew, the ship was doomed. It
would crash into the Maxithon and very probably kill a great
many people.

He wondered briefly if Dinantra and Lastleaf were still watching. *The gorgon will be halfway to the city gates already if she's got any wits,* he figured. She'd wanted to give Fivecourt something they would talk about for months to come. *Well,* he thought sourly, *mission accomplished.*

Clay didn't look to see if they were there or not. He couldn't take his eyes off the catastrophe unfolding in the sky above. He saw the chimera descend on the floundering warship, saw the dragon head surge forward, preparing to unleash its fiery breath. Ganelon was straining at something—another spine, maybe?—and whatever it was came loose with a spray of blood.

Flame erupted from the side of the dragon's neck.

My sword, Clay realized. *He tore it out, and now the fire . . .*

He watched in disbelief as Ganelon leapt from the dragon's head to the lion's, clutching its mane with one hand while punching the sword in and out of the creature's throat. Behind him, the dragon sagged as the tear in its side ruptured. An instant later the entire head burst in a wash of blood and gushing fire.

Man and monster plunged into the Maxithon, causing mayhem as they crashed into the uppermost tier and then tumbled down the sloping stands in a thrashing ball of gory fur and blood-slick scales. Spectators scrambled to clear a path, and most of them managed to do so. Those on the lowest tier, however, had no notion of the impending danger. Clay's eyes preceded the chimera's destructive path, and so he saw that both the Duke and Dinantra remained inside the patron's box.

"Please," he prayed to whichever of Grandual's gods was in charge of killing people at random with the corpses of chimeras, "grant me this one . . . fucking . . . thing."

Lastleaf turned to find him staring. The druin's white-furred ears perked straight up, as though he'd somehow heard Clay whispering. Too late, he seemed to comprehend what was about to happen. At the last moment Clay saw Lastleaf duck and Dinantra rise, her head crowned by a halo of hissing serpents, and then the chimera exploded through the awning, crushing the gorgon and her entourage of half-clad servants before sliding to rest on the arena floor.

Remarkably, Clay found he could bend his joints. He clambered onto his stomach, pushed himself to his knees. Moog was standing, swiping dust from his new robe. When he finished he straightened and looked to Clay.

"You okay?" he asked.

"I think—"

There was a sound like a mountainside crumbling. The ground shuddered, throwing Clay down. He rolled to his side, looking skyward. Had the frigate come down in the chimera's wake? Had one of the seating tiers collapsed? He could hardly see for the dust in the air, but as it cleared he saw that the wallowing caravel had crashed into the northwest chain-tower.

The tower crumbled. The Maxithon heaved against its chains, and a heartbeat later the one fixed to the southwest tower tore free in a shower of stone and mortar, because that's just the sort of day Clay was having.

The arena was *moving*, carried east on the river's current. The great chains went slack as the two remaining towers loomed closer. The Maxithon dissolved into pandemonium, the roar of the crowd now a chorus of panicked terror as spectators fled toward the exits. Not that there was anywhere to escape to; the tremulous bridges connecting the arena to either bank would have broken away as soon as the arena began moving.

Clay staggered to his feet. His knees trembled, and his balance nearly failed him again. He saw Moog helping Gabriel to sit. Matrick was up on one elbow, blinking at the chaos like a sleeper who'd awoken in the midst of a battlefield.

There was no sign at all of Ganelon. Clay was wondering if he'd been crushed in the fall when one of the chimera's wings began to twitch. Clay fumbled at his hip for a sword that wasn't there. He glanced toward Moog, but the wizard was busy knocking on various parts of Gabe's armour and asking if he could feel anything. Matrick, at least, had seen the monster move as well. He made no move to help, only brandished his bloody arm and shouted over the din, "You got this."

Clay swallowed, turned, drew *Blackheart* up beneath his chin, and stepped tentatively forward. He'd taken three steps when the body heaved again, and Ganelon rolled out from beneath the corpse, gasping for air and choking on a lungful of dust.

Clay sighed in relief. The respite was short-lived, however, as the Maxithon reached the length of its shore-bound tethers.

The north tower went first. Its chain popped loose, whipping dangerously across the sky. Miraculously, the south tower withstood the first hard pull. The Maxithon swung toward the southern bank and began a slow, spinning circle, but at last the arena's momentum dragged the tower into the river behind it. Clay felt the ground quake, and could only imagine the destruction ensuing outside: piers breaking like brittle fingers, boats capsizing, crushed by the mammoth bowl of wood and stone as it hurtled downriver with thirty thousand screaming passengers aboard.

Clay made it to Ganelon's side. "Are you okay?"

The warrior brushed off his concern. "I'm fine. Where's my axe?"

"It fell over there," he said, but before he could turn to point out where Clay saw a figure rise from the wreckage of the patron's box.

Lastleaf was sheathed in dust, spattered with blood. His hair was in disarray and his ears skewed to crazed angles, neither of which made him look any less frightening as he bared his serrated teeth at Clay and withdrew the long, slender sword from the middle scabbard on his back. It sang as it came free—a sound like the last, lingering echo of a ringing bell—and again as he brought it scything crossways and took hold of its hilt with both hands.

Before he could use it, however, a shadow bloomed on the sand between them.

Looking up, Clay saw a skyship dropping toward the arena floor. At first he assumed it was crashing; he opened his mouth to scream a warning to Gabe and Moog, but then he saw the wizard waving.

When he turned back Lastleaf had vanished into the maelstrom of dust kicked up by the descending ship.

The vessel slowed as it attempted to land on a surface that pitched like the deck of a ship in a storm. It was small, hardly bigger than a dhow, with a single engine spinning on its stern. The name *Old Glory* was painted on the side, which meant nothing to Clay until he saw the faces peering down over the rail.

"Vanguard," he breathed, quiet as a prayer that had already been answered.

Chapter Twenty-four

Flying by Night

"Motherfucking *Saga*. I'll be a troll's new testicle, I still can't believe it. Tiamax, are you seeing this?"

"With all six eyes," said Tiamax.

"Unbelievable." Barret reclined in his seat, long legs stretched out before him. Vanguard's frontman was as tall as Ganelon and as broad as Clay himself. His shaggy hair and beard were shot through with grey, but his thick arms were still corded with muscle, and he seemed as fit and full of vigour now as when Clay had seen him last.

Vanguard's skyship, which the band had found half submerged in a swamp during their last tour of the Heartwyld, was small but remarkably comfortable. The hull was flat bottomed, roofed by a sail that peaked like a tent overhead. Now and again currents of blue electricity would arc across the sail's metal ribs, but since no one else seemed concerned about that Clay kept his misgivings to himself. There were sofas set against either wale, and an exceptionally well-stocked bar toward the stern. Candles in clouded glass jars were suspended above, bathing the deck in soft, swaying light.

Barret was shaking his shaggy head. "Holy Tetrea, but I never thought to see the five of you in one place again. I'd have bet on watching a parade of owlbears through the streets of Ardburg first."

"You still might see those owlbears," Moog grumbled.

Barret turned his big grin on Clay. "How long has it been, Slowhand?"

"Uh..."

"Ten years, maybe? Twelve? We passed through on our way west and had drinks in that shithole dive Coverdale calls a tavern. The King's Head, was it?"

"That's the one," said Clay, and couldn't help a wistful smile sliding onto his face.

"You had a girl with you, I remember. Pretty young lass with tits like the Spring Maiden's."

"Ginny," Clay replied. "My wife."

Barret whistled. "Good on ya, lad. Good fucking on ya. Worth settling down for, tits like those..." He fell silent, gazing out at the red-gold sky as if he'd said something profound and needed time to contemplate the wisdom in his words.

Vanguard's bard, Edwick, was slouched at the helm, keeping half an eye on a pair of polished onyx steering orbs and strumming quietly on a weathered mandolin. The old man had been with the band since their inception, which Clay found nigh incredible, since Saga had gone through more bards in their ten touring years than Clay could hope to remember.

The rest of the band was mostly intact. Barret was still Barret, big and coarse and immanently affable. Ashe was still hard, still pretty, and still pretty mean. Her hair was shaved close on the sides, braided down her back, and dyed a shade of bright purple Clay hadn't known existed until he'd seen her a few hours ago. Tiamax, the arachnian, looked as unsettlingly alien as he always had, though the bristly whiskers around his mouth had turned grey. He'd lost the lower half of one mandible and wore criss-crossed patches over two of his eight faceted eyes.

Only Hog was missing, replaced by a man Barret had introduced as Hog's oldest son. The lad had inherited his father's shocking obesity, his hesitant nature, and the unfortunate nickname of Piglet. The boy, sweating despite the cool wind wafting across the deck, was plundering a plate of honey-glazed donuts as though it were the first meal he'd eaten all day. Clay very much doubted that was the case.

"It's a real honour," Piglet said between mouthfuls, "to meet you guys in person. My father always talked about you. Barret talks about you too. Best band there ever was, he says. Besides Vanguard, I mean."

"We're not really a band anymore," said Clay.

"Well you certainly looked like one on the sands today," said Tiamax. He was standing behind the bar, a glass or a pestle or a bottle in every hand, making drinks as fast as the others could hammer them down. "We came across a chimera once, you know, out in the Wyld."

"You kill it?" asked Ganelon, stretched out on a sofa by himself.

The arachnian's laugh was a series of staccato clicks. "Kill it? Gods, no."

"We ran as fast as we bloody well could," said Ashe, who was perched on a stool beside Matrick. She was a southerner, like Ganelon, and her voice affected the same lazy drawl. "The hatcher here won that particular race, if I recall."

Tiamax clicked again—admonishingly this time, which left Clay wondering how it was he could tell the difference. "Now now, Ashe, no need to be slanderous. Is that why you haven't slept with me yet? Are you afraid of giving birth to eggs? It's easier than pushing out a baby, or so I'm told. No arms or legs to poke and prod you on the way out, just...plop, an adorable little egg."

"I won't sleep with you because you're a fucking *bug*, is why."

"A bug with *six* hands, my dear. Think on it." Tiamax cracked a polished wooden shaker into halves and poured a cherry-coloured drink into Matrick's empty glass.

Matty smiled appreciatively. He was nursing his wounded arm, still, but the arachnian had given him something for the pain. "I'm just glad you all showed up when you did," he said. "Things were getting dicey back there."

Dicey struck Clay as a bit of an understatement. He'd been looking overboard as the Maxithon smashed itself to splinters against the arch of the eastern water gate, spilling panicked multitudes like a beehive dashed against the ground.

Barret sat up suddenly, planting both feet on the deck. The expression he fixed on Clay was serious. "Listen, are you sure about this Castia business? I mean, you'll be months in the Wyld, and even if you do make it..." He spread his hands, daring a quick glance at Gabriel, who sat staring into nowhere and had said nothing since coming aboard. "Assuming you *do* make it, all right? You're just one band."

What could Clay do but shrug? With Gabe in the state he was, it had been left to him to explain the reason behind Saga's improbable reunion. "Even still," he said.

Ashe set her mug on the bar with a *clack*. "We almost went, you know, to Castia. When the Republic put out the call for bands. Barret was all for it, of course, and Piggy's too young and dumb to know better. Even Edwick was in favour." She snorted. "I think the old fucker has our eulogy half composed already."

"It'll be beautiful," called the bard over his shoulder.

"Anyway, the hatcher and I actually agreed on something for once. We both saw the stormclouds gathering o'er that one. We had a contract with a temple in Hamshire at the time— gargoyles running amok or some shit—and so we ended up sticking around. Gods be praised, too, or we'd be—" her eyes flickered toward Gabriel "—well, we wouldn't be here."

"So no chance of us hitching a ride all the way to Castia then?" asked Matrick wryly.

Barret sighed. "I'm sorry, no. Even if I wanted to—which I don't—I have my family to think of. My boys are barely grown, and Avery's been on me to retire for years now. She wouldn't go for this one bit. Flying over the Heartwyld is near as bad walking through it. There's lightstorms and sparkwyrms..."

"Plague hawks," said Tiamax.

"Manticores," Ashe chimed in.

"Lamias," Barret added, "and blood locusts..."

"Wyverns," said Matrick, unhelpfully.

"Wyverns everywhere," said Barret. "And what are those things that look like dragons and sound like dragons?" he asked facetiously.

"I believe they're called dragons, boss."

"Thank you, Ashe." He sighed heavily and dragged his fingers through his shaggy hair. "I'm sorry, guys, I really am. I mean, flirting with the Frost Mother is one thing, but putting your cock in her mouth is just plain stupid."

"That's really pretty," said Edwick, pausing to tune his instrument. "Would you mind if I use it in a song?"

"Be my guest," said Barret.

"It's a shame you're so pressed for time." Tiamax reached up to scratch beneath a leather eye patch. "The War Fair is hardly a month away. Every band in Grandual will be there. Plenty of young mercs as well, eager to make a name for themselves. Maybe an army's worth."

"Bah, the War Fair ain't what it was," grumbled Ashe. "Used to be only real fighters showed their faces in Kaladar. Nowadays every snot-nosed whelp with a hair on his chin and a sword in his hand thinks he's got what it takes to be a merc. All they care about is getting paid and getting laid."

"Hear, hear!" said Tiamax, raising four glasses at once.

Clay hadn't found much to like about mercenary life, but he had to admit the War Fair was—or had been, anyway—a hell of a good time. He'd been to Kaladar three times. It was, essentially, a three-day orgy of booze, drugs, and rampant violence, with a few *actual orgies* thrown in for good measure. There was even a popular saying: *What happens in Kaladar . . .*

"I'm serious," said Ashe, pressing her point. "The world used to be a scary place, remember? We were trying to make it better. Well, most of us, anyway."

"We *did* make it better," said Moog, who'd been uncharacteristically silent until now.

Matrick drained his cup. "Damn right we did."

From his couch, with his eyes closed and his hands tucked behind his head, Ganelon said, "Seems just the same to me."

They were quiet for a bit after that. The sun set at last, and it wasn't the wisest idea to stay airborne at night, but Edwick insisted he was good to fly for a while yet. Piglet finished his donuts and ambled over to the bar for a beer. Ashe volunteered her spot, moving to sit beside Gabriel. He flinched when she put a hand on his shoulder, but she spoke to him in gentle tones, like a groom attempting to placate a skittish horse.

"Piglet," said Moog, "forgive me, but can I ask about your father?"

The boy slurped at his mug. "Like how he died, you mean?"

"Yes, please. If you don't mind..."

Piglet shrugged. "It was the rot."

The wizard closed his eyes, nodding as if he'd already guessed the answer. "Damn," he said.

"He actually lasted longer than we figured he would," Piglet elaborated. "He was a big man—well, you know that. But he was strong, too. Really strong. Until, well... It started in his toes, and his fingers, so he couldn't get around very well. We had to feed him after that. And when they cracked and broke off we thought maybe..." He said nothing for a moment, turning and turning his mug on the spot. "But it started up again on his arm, then his face. His nose and ears just sort of...dried up, you know? By then he was tired all the time. He didn't speak much, and didn't make much sense when he did. And he was so *scared*. He—"

"I know!" Moog snapped, and it was obvious straightaway

he'd spoken more harshly than he'd meant to. "I'm sorry," he said, reaching out to pat the boy's arm. "I...that is...I know what it's like to lose someone that way. To watch them waste away before your eyes, wishing there was some way to make them better, or to make them suffer less. Except you *can't* make them better. And they *do* suffer..." The wizard's voice quavered and broke off. He looked out over the rail, pretending to scratch his head while swiping at one eye with the sleeve of his robe. "They suffer..."

"But not alone," said Clay.

Moog glanced his way, and Clay saw, for perhaps the first time in all the years they had known each other, a naked, bottomless fear in the wizard's face.

"You're not alone," he repeated, and then watched, without knowing what more he could say, as pure terror writhed behind the wizard's eyes. Until finally Moog closed them, biting his bottom lip as a pair of perfidious tears streamed over his cheeks.

The silence around the ship changed perceptibly. Tiamax froze in the midst of shaking Matrick's next drink. Barret sat up on his sofa, sharing a concerned glance with Ashe. Even Ganelon craned his neck to look over, dark eyes gleaming in the swaying lamplight.

"I don't..." Matrick glanced around, visibly perplexed. "What? What does that mean, 'You're not alone'? Who's not alone?"

Slowly, Piglet reached out and placed a pudgy hand on the wizard's knee. "Where is it?" he asked, almost a whisper.

And because Clay was looking for it, he saw Matty's face go granite hard. The king and Moog were close—as close as he and Gabe, perhaps, though they hadn't known each other for quite so long. The two of them shared a deep kinship, a bond of unflagging (and sometimes ill-advised) cheer under even the most dire circumstance. As distraught as Clay and

Gabriel had been to hear of Moog's infection, Matty would be utterly devastated, which was probably why the wizard had put off telling him.

"Where is what?" asked Matrick in a voice gone cold and sluggish as a river in winter.

He knows, thought Clay. *Of course he knows. He just doesn't want to believe it.*

Moog blew out a long breath before opening his eyes. He tried on a smile that vanished the moment he opened his mouth to explain. "My foot," he said quietly. "It's on my foot."

Another silence followed, but this time it was loaded, the ominous hush of an axed tree falling earthward.

Matrick exploded from his chair, charged the wizard, grasped the collar of his robe in one hand and pinned him, squirming, against the side of the ship. "It's on your fucking *foot*? The rot, you mean? The Heathen's fucking Touch, right? It's on your *godsdamned foot*!?"

"Urk," said Moog.

"When were you planning on telling me, huh? When?"

"Grgh," the wizard replied.

"Why are you even here right now?" The king's voice skirled higher with every word, strained near to breaking by rage and grief and disbelief. "You should be locked in that shitty little tower of yours day and night—day and fucking night—until you find a cure."

"There is..." Moog managed to gurgle "...no cure."

"*THERE'S A FUCKING CURE!*" Matty screamed. "Do you hear me, you shit-brained sorcerer? *There is. A fucking. Cure.*"

All at once the fight went out of him, and Matrick sagged to his knees, dragging Moog down with him as he went. The wizard hesitated just a moment before gently wreathing his arms around Matrick's head and holding the crumpled king while wave after wave of soul-racking sorrow rose and broke, rose and broke, rose and broke within him.

*   *   *

They landed shortly after outside a dimly lit hamlet that Barret claimed was Downeston but Matrick, who'd doubled his efforts to get shit-faced drunk since Moog broke the news, insisted was Tagglemoor.

"I was the fucking king here," he slurred from his seat at the bar. "I know this land like the hand of my back. Er, the hand of . . . hey, Doc, my glass is empty."

"Help yourself," said Tiamax, who had since retired to a couch of his own.

Matrick reached over the bar, and Clay shook his head at the arachnian. "You've doomed us all," he said.

Piglet snorted at that. He'd found an apple somewhere and was crunching happily away. "Let's play a game," he suggested. "We each take a turn and say the first thing we ever killed. I'll go first, okay? Mine was a trash imp who attacked me in Fivecourt."

Clay slunk into his seat and sipped his beer. He wasn't a fan of this game.

"A trash imp?" Ashe scoffed. "They usually run from anything bigger than a rat. Never heard of one attacking a human."

Piglet looked abashed. "Yeah, well, someone threw out a whole box of oranges . . ."

Ashe was still cackling at that when Moog chimed in. "I was eleven when my dog died. I tried to resurrect him—"

"Oh, wow," said Barret.

"I know—it was stupid. Anyhow, I lit the candles, scribbled the runes . . . I did everything by the book, or so I thought. But whatever came back . . . well, it wasn't Sir Fluffy, I'll tell you that."

"I don't know what disturbs me more," said Edwick, who was curled up in the pilot's chair. "That you dabbled in necromancy or that you named your dog Sir Fluffy."

Tiamax chittered gleefully. "Mine was . . . I don't even know what it's called. It was sort of this giant lizard-frog thing covered in spikes, and its tongue was made of fire."

"That sounds horrible," said Matrick. "My first was a gnoll shaman."

"Are gnolls the one with horse heads?" asked Piglet.

"Those are ixil," said Ashe. "Gnolls are like jackals that stand on two legs."

"So this fucker blinded me," Matrick went on. "Thought I was done for, but then he started laughing when I tripped and fell. Hard to hide with a laugh like that, even from a blind man."

"Mine was a harpy," said Barret. "She actually managed to pick up my little sister and carry her halfway up a mountainside. I climbed up after her, broke her neck, and made harpy egg omelettes for breakfast the whole week after. How about you, Ganelon? Yours was something vicious, I'll wager."

The southerner only shook his head. "Slavers," he said, but offered nothing further.

"Mine was a spider," Ashe said. "A big one." She smirked across the cabin at Tiamax. "Nasty things, spiders."

The arachnian's mandibles clacked in amusement. "So that's why my daddy went out for milk and never came home. And here I thought I was just a terrible son."

Ashe cackled and turned to Clay. "What about you, Slowhand? Wait, let me guess: Some poor sap spilled beer on your boot and you slaughtered his entire family while he watched."

Clay took a breath, and was about to confess that the first life he'd taken had belonged to his father, except Gabriel (the only one among them who already knew) finally spoke up and saved him the trouble of explaining why.

"How far will you take us?" he asked, directing the question toward Barret.

The frontman cleared his throat and shared brief, meaningful glances with Ashe and Tiamax. "Turnstone Keep," he said finally. "It's farther than I'd like, but what are friends for if not risking death by sparkwyrm, or wyvern, or whatever the hell else might kill us out there."

More than fair, thought Clay. *Hell, we owe them plenty already for getting us out of the city in one piece.* From Fivecourt to the forest's edge alone was a week's hard ride, and the *Old Glory* would have them there sometime tomorrow. It wasn't as far as they could have hoped for, but it was more than they could have expected.

Gabriel swiped hair from his eyes. "What about Conthas? Could you drop us there instead?"

Barret furrowed his brow. "Of course we can. I suppose you'll be needing to gear up for the journey, eh?

"That, yeah," said Gabriel. "But first I need to see a man about a sword."

Chapter Twenty-five

Treasures of Varying Usefulness

They walk five abreast up the eastern slope of the hill upon which Kallorek has constructed his lavish citadel. The morning sun hurls their shadows out before them, hulking spectres of the men to whom they belong, or rather—as the guards who watch them approach will later reflect—harbingers of their dark intent, reaching like fingers that would soon become a fist.

Among them is a renegade king, he who sired five royal heirs without ever unzipping his pants. A man to whom time has imparted great wisdom and an even greater waistline, whose thoughtless courage is rivalled only by his unquenchable thirst.

At his shoulder walks a sorcerer, a cosmic conversationalist. Enemy of the incurable rot, absent chairman of combustive sciences at the university in Oddsford, and the only living soul above the age of eight to believe in owlbears.

Look here at a warrior born, a scion of power and poverty whose purpose is manifold: to shatter shackles, to murder monarchs, and to demonstrate that even the forces of good must sometimes enlist the service of big, bad motherfuckers. His is an ancient soul destined to die young.

And now comes the quiet one, the gentle giant, he who

fights his battles with a shield. Stout as the tree that counts its age in aeons, constant as the star that marks true north and shines most brightly on the darkest nights.

A step ahead of these four: our hero. He is the candle burnt down to the stump, the cutting blade grown dull with overuse. But see now the spark in his stride. Behold the glint of steel in his gaze. Who dares to stand between a man such as this and that which he holds dear? He will kill, if he must, to protect it. He will die, if that is what it takes.

"Go get the boss," says one guardsman to another. "This bunch looks like trouble."

And they do. They *do* look like trouble, at least until the wizard trips on the hem of his robe. He stumbles, cursing, and fouls the steps of the others as he falls face-first onto the mud-slick hillside.

They broke a great deal of furniture and several arms as they fought their way through Kallorek's compound. Moog lobbed what looked like avocados stuffed with wicker fuses into adjacent rooms. The volatile fruit burst into clouds of yellow smoke that stung the eyes and burnt the throat, flushing out cowering servants and guards they might have missed along the way. Clay weathered a few blows with his shield, and Ganelon hit a man so hard with the flat of his axe the poor fellow sailed ten yards before crashing through a glass window. Gabe prowled ahead with an anxious single-mindedness, like a man wandering a brothel in search of his missing daughter.

They came across Kallorek lounging in the shallow end of his pond. Two naked girls scampered out the opposite door. The booker had barely pulled a robe over his bulk before Gabriel's mailed fist hit him squarely in the nose and sent him sprawling on the water-slick tiles.

"Bring him," Gabe said without slowing. Ganelon snatched the dazed booker by the collar and dragged him along.

In the chapel hall where Kallorek hoarded his assortment of illustrious artifacts, Gabriel made straight for the
sword-bearing statue of the Autumn Son. He stopped short of
it by fifteen yards and held his waiting palm toward Moog. The
wizard rummaged briefly in his bottomless bag before drawing out what looked like a short length of rope dipped in tar.

"Is that—" Clay began.

"Firewire, yes," confirmed Moog. He offered it to Gabriel
as though he were handling a live viper. "Be very careful," he
warned.

Moog advising someone else on the cautious use of alchemy,
thought Clay. *Gods of Grandual, we have gotten old.*

Gabe approached the statue. Lamplight gleamed on the plates
of his armour, so that he seemed to radiate softly as he climbed
the steps of the dais. He knelt at its feet, and with slow care he
looped the corrosive strand around one of the statue's legs.

"Stand back," he said over his shoulder, and then touched
the frayed ends of the firewire together. They fused with a hiss
and the cord turned molten red, constricting as the fibres hardened into something like steel. The statue's leg buckled, and an
instant later the whole thing toppled forward, smashing itself
to pieces. The statue's head, which had been altered to resemble Kallorek's orcish features, rolled to a stop at Ganelon's feet.

Gabriel stepped lightly down the dais steps, picking his
way through the rubble until he found what he was looking
for. He pried *Vellichor* from the shattered stone grip, and when
he stood he was grinning like a boy.

The sword was double-edged, near as long as Gabe was
tall. It had belonged to Vespian, the druin Archon, and was
widely considered the most sacred (and second most dangerous) relic of the Old Dominion. The blade was silver-green,
and in its surface one could sometimes glimpse a swathe of
twilit sky, or the colossal trees of some primordial forest, as
though the sword itself were a window to another, older age.

Perhaps the most unusual aspect of *Vellichor*, however,

was its smell. Most swords smelled like iron, or oil, or else they didn't smell at all, but *Vellichor* wafted like a spring breeze, rife with the scent of flowering lilacs and fresh green grass.

Gabriel stood with his eyes closed amidst a veil of rising dust. He whispered something too quiet to hear, and then opened his eyes and looked to Kallorek. "The scabbard. Where is it?"

The booker coughed and spat at his feet in answer.

Gabe spared a glance for Ganelon, and the warrior introduced the booker's face to his steel-shod boot.

"Over there!" Kallorek blurted, pointing toward one corner of the chapel hall. "There's a chest over there somewhere. Take the scabbard and get the fuck out of my house."

Gabriel still wore his wide smile. "Oh, I'll take the scabbard. And we'll be out of your—" his eyes flitted to Kallorek's greasy comb-over "—hair soon enough. Thing is, though, Kal—the Wyld's a dangerous place. I think it's probably best we grab a few more things while we're here, don't you?"

The booker looked as if he would spit again, or scream, or lunge at Gabriel and wring his throat, but then he flinched as his limited imagination reminded him what Ganelon's boot tasted like. He nodded grudgingly and growled, "Sure. Of course. Take whatever you'd like."

Gabe gave Kallorek's jowls a friendly slap. He straightened, took a breath, and looked around at his bandmates like a man awakened from a restful sleep. "Gear up, boys. If we're gonna play heroes we might as well dress the part."

Moog went to pick through the wreckage of the broken bookcase, while Matrick snatched a pair of luxurious leather boots off a nearby table. Ganelon crossed to where a set of wrought-iron bracers glimmered beneath a glass casement. He used his bare hand to smash the glass and lift them clear.

Clay wandered idly, perusing a wicked-looking scimitar that he could have sworn whispered his name as he drew close, and a hammer whose ivory-bound haft was startlingly cold to the touch. He saw the imposing helm of Liac the Arachnian that Kallorek had shown them during their previous visit, and beneath it the suit of crimson mail called the *Warskin*, through which, the booker had alleged, no sword or spear could pass.

A fine quality in any piece of armour, Clay reckoned, and so he took it.

It fit as though it were made for him. There was a silk undercoat so the links wouldn't chafe, and segmented steel bands above and below each elbow to allow ease of movement. There were pauldrons on either shoulder that flared into a high-collared guard to protect his throat. The coat itself draped almost to his knees, and it was belted at the waist by a metal band whose opposing ends seemed drawn together by some intangible magic.

"Oooh, magnets," said Moog, who noticed Clay clasping and unclasping the belt in obvious wonder.

"Magnets?"

The wizard got that look in his eye, a teacher relishing in the ignorance of a student. "It's actually quite fascinating . . ." he began.

"I'm sure it is," murmured Clay, already walking away. He picked up the frigid hammer as he went, deciding on a whim to call it *Wraith*.

On his way back toward Gabriel he saw the sarcophagus over which Gabe and Kallorek had tripped during their previous visit. It was empty, its heavy lid ajar, and Clay wondered briefly what manner of ghastly horror they'd unleashed upon the world.

The rest of the band were busy equipping themselves as well. Ganelon found a suit of black dragonscale to match his shiny new gauntlets, while Matrick bore a gnarled horn at his hip. When he saw Clay looking he said, "Watch this," and blew briefly in the mouthpiece. There was no discernible sound, but as he did so a small flurry of winged insects swarmed out the other end.

Clay brushed a wasp away from his eyes. "So...it's a horn that vomits bees?"

"Isn't it great?" asked Matrick.

Clay frowned, thoroughly disgusted. "Not really, no."

"I win! I win!" Moog hurried between two armour-draped mannequins. He knocked one over in his haste and had actually turned to apologize before thinking better of it and moving on. He was wearing the sort of wide-brimmed, pointy hat that wizards wore all the time in storybooks and practically never in real life, probably because it looked ridiculous.

"Yep, you win," Matrick agreed. "You look the stupidest."

"That's not a word," Moog informed him. "But watch!" He pulled off the hat and plunged his arm in to the elbow. "It's like my bag, but different. There's an enchantment inside! You can't put things in it, only take them out. But not just anything—oh, yes, here we are."

Clay looked on in disbelief as the wizard withdrew a chicken from the confines of the hat—not alive, but plucked and roasted, glazed until the skin was brown and crisp. The smell alone set his mouth watering. "How...?"

Moog tossed the chicken aside and Matrick lunged for it, using his uninjured arm to brace it against his chest. "What the..." he started, but then Moog reached into his hat again and pulled out another, which he tossed to Clay, and then another. He threw this one to Ganelon, but the warrior sidestepped it, eyeing it warily where it lay on the ground.

"Chicken from a hat," he muttered in distaste.

"It's perfectly fine," Moog assured him. "But anyway, there's more." He continued plucking foodstuffs out of thin air: loaves of bread, ears of corn, ripened tomatoes, pastries stuffed with fruit and topped with sweet-smelling icing.

By now Matrick's arms were overflowing. "Now *this*," he told Clay, "is better than a horn that vomits bees."

Clay shrugged. On that, at least, they could agree.

Chapter Twenty-six

The Revenant in the Room

They were on their way out of the compound—Ganelon prodding a shambling and hugely uncooperative Kallorek ahead of them—when Valery emerged from a bedroom and called weakly to Gabriel. Clay saw her voice snag his friend like a hook, slowing him, dragging him round to face her. The air of confidence Gabe had radiated since reclaiming *Vellichor* slipped for an instant, and there was the coward again, the beaten dog slinking back into its master's shadow.

"Valery," he croaked.

She took a feeble step toward him. She looked wasted and pale. There were dark hollows beneath her eyes. Her hair was in disarray, and she wore a long white nightgown, as if she'd only just now roused herself from bed. Clay found himself staring at the angry red scars on her bare arms.

"I'm sorry. I've been...I'm trying to get clean. I've been sleeping." She looked around in bewilderment at the empty house. "What's happened? Why are you here?"

Gabe said nothing, but put his hand on *Vellichor*'s ornate pommel. Her tired eyes tracked his movement. "Ah, of course," she said. A hint of bitterness soured her tone. "Did you know, Kal used to say that if he offered to give you back either *Vellichor* or me, that you would choose the sword? I think maybe he was right."

Of course he was right, Clay thought, but opted to stay silent.

Gabriel didn't bother responding, but Valery didn't press the matter. She looked wearily around at all of them, lingering longest on Ganelon, but at last her eyes settled on Clay.

"You were here before," she said. "I . . . remember." And now her face crumpled, the dread of revelation darkening her gaze. When she spoke again her voice was thick with panic. "Oh. Oh no. Rosie? Is she—"

"She's alive," said Gabriel. "She's in Castia." He took a step closer, drawn to her by the hook in his heart.

"Castia." She said it first without inflection, and then again, with a dawning horror that drew Gabe another step nearer.

"I'll find her, Val," he promised. "I *will* find her. And I'll bring her home."

Kallorek scoffed, which earned him a back-handed slap from one of Ganelon's new gauntlets and a hateful glare from Valery, who looked as though she was torn between screaming and sobbing.

"Okay," she said, wringing her hands. "Okay. You'll bring her home? Good, yes. Please, Gabriel. Please . . . bring our little girl home." She reached out with trembling fingers to stroke his cheek. Gabe flinched as though her touch were a burning brand, but he endured it.

Clay tried to imagine such a rift existing between himself and Ginny. There had been a time when Gabe and Valery had been inseparable, as blissfully happy as two people could be. They'd been lovers, yes, and they'd been friends as well. But now the two of them seemed like strangers, or animals of separate species, neither of whom knew how to act or react around the other.

"We should go," said Gabriel. "We're taking Kal with us so he doesn't try and stop us from reaching the forest, but we'll leave him a day or so south at the Heartwyld's edge."

Her expression lapsed deeper into confusion. "The forest? You're not going to *walk* all the way to Castia? There's a skyship—"

"Bitch!" snarled Kallorek. "Shut your godsdamned mouth!"

This time it was Matrick who struck, so hard the booker went sprawling. "Shut *your* mouth," he said, and then added, "bitch."

Gabriel took his ex-wife's hand in his. "Valery, tell me about the skyship."

Valery scratched absently at the scars on one arm. "They found it in the Underground, when they dug for the renovations," she said. "There's a brook on the south side of the hill. A cave. It's in there," she insisted. "You can take it. You can fly."

"We can fly," said Gabriel, and his face lit up like parchment kissed by a candle's flame.

They found the brook, and the cave mouth from which it issued. It was guarded by sentries who they relieved of both duty and consciousness. Inside they discovered a vast cavern housing a massive skyship that was as much a brothel as it was a boat.

It was huge—near as big as the Sultana's flagship they'd seen at Lindmoor, and again in Fivecourt—with three ribbed sails slanted to shield the deck from sun and rain. The deck had been restored with darkly varnished wood, and the rails were capped with white moonstone. Leaping from the bowsprit was a solid gold siren with arms outstretched, her bare breasts gleaming in the ruddy light from outside.

The vessel's name was carved in florid letters beneath the prow: *The Carnal Court.*

Inside was a galley stocked like a palace kitchen, a lavish dining hall, several bathrooms, and no less than eight bedchambers, each so gaudily furnished as to make even a spoiled princess cringe.

A master suite at the stern, likely reserved for the booker himself, was the most garish of all, hung with a series of lurid paintings that ranged from distastefully erotic to disconcertingly vulgar. The worst of these portrayed a shamelessly nude Kallorek and a wild-maned female centaur engaged in what could most safely be termed as "horse play." The bed was draped in red silk curtains and looked as though it had recently been slept in. The bottom sheet was missing, and Clay shuddered to imagine what depravity this room had borne witness to.

Near the bow was a commons, complete with plush couches, gaming tables, and a bar that put the *Old Glory*'s to shame. It was here they found a zombie sitting on a stool, tuning what Clay assumed was a bizarre-looking instrument and nursing a glass of red wine.

"Oh! Well, this is awkward." The corpse set aside the instrument—which looked like nothing so much as a spiderweb encased by an eight-sided wooden frame—and stood. "I'm afraid I wasn't expecting company, or I'd have made the bed. And probably hidden underneath it until you left," he added.

"Who are you?" asked Gabriel, his hand straying toward *Vellichor*'s hilt.

"Not your enemy," the zombie cautioned. He had a strangely prim accent, at odds with his ghastly appearance. He was dressed in what looked at first glance like a robe, but was in fact the missing sheet from Kallorek's bed. He sketched a formal bow, which revealed a savage-looking dent in the back of his skull. "I am Kitagra the Bold," he introduced himself. "Also known as Kitagra the Reckless, and sometimes as Kitagra the Willfully Suicidal. I am a roving revenant, itinerant poet, and was once, briefly, Court Musician to Exarch Firaga of Teragoth, though I am currently seeking employment. You may call me—"

"Kit!?"

The zombie blinked. Well, it didn't so much blink as one

of its withered eyelids twitched in apparent surprise. "Arcandius Moog? Is that you, you incorrigible scallywag?"

The wizard rushed past Gabriel and threw his arms around the creature. "Kit, you old ghoul! I thought you'd gone west! What the heck are you doing here?"

Clay's mind had just now pieced together the fractious puzzle of who this was: "Kit the Unkillable," who had formerly been trapped inside the sarcophagus in Kallorek's treasury.

The zombie pried himself from Moog's grasp. "Well, I'm hiding out," he said. "I've been daydreaming, and playing cards against myself, and drumming up a few new songs. And also drinking like a Phantran fish. But before all *that* I was locked in a very dark box for a very long time, courtesy of that piggish-looking man in your company." He cast a disdainful glance at Kallorek, bound and gagged behind them. "Not a friend of yours, I assume?"

"Not currently, no," said Moog.

The zombie scratched a partially exposed rib with grey fingers. "Glad to hear it. But how about you? Have you discovered your miraculous cure yet?"

Moog looked down at his feet—or foot, maybe. "For the rot? No. But that potion I made for your, um, condition? It's been very successful, actually."

"The phylactery? As well it should be!" stated Kit. "I had that erection for two weeks, you know. The whores of Conthas thought I was Lusty Lucian back from the dead. Well, to be fair, that's who I told them I was, and then I paid them a king's fortune to believe it. Ah, but don't worry, my friend—you've got the cure in that maze somewhere." He pointed at the wizard's head. "Just keep wandering till you find it." He glanced past Moog at the others. "Am I to assume you are commandeering this skyship?"

"We are," said Gabriel.

"Very well then. If you gentlemen will but give me a few moments to finish my drink and collect my things, I'll be out of your way."

Moog waved dismissively. "Nonsense! Why don't you come with us? We could use a bard!"

Clay smirked, finding it somewhat ironic that, after all these years, Saga might actually enlist the services of a bard that was already dead.

Kit looked intrigued. "Oh? Where is it you're going?"

"Uh, well, Castia."

"Castia!" the zombie actually sounded pleased. "Jewel of the Republic! A shining bastion of human civilization. I used to sing in a chorus at one of its theatres, oh, sixty years ago? Lovely, lovely city."

"Not anymore," said Ganelon.

Kit's eyelid twitched again, but before Moog could explain Gabriel broke in. "We're wasting time. If the zombie wants to come, he can come. We should go now and hit up Conthas for supplies."

"I'll come," Clay said, already anxious to be off this eyesore of a ship.

"Me too!" said Moog. "I could use some things in town as well. Kit, you wanna tag along?"

"I suppose I wouldn't mind stretching my legs," said Kit, then favoured Gabriel with a grisly smile. "Also, I feel it necessary to point out that I am what is known as a *revenant*—or a ghoul, if you'd prefer. Either will suffice. But I am most certainly *not* a zombie."

"Ghoul, zombie . . . what's the difference?" asked Matrick.

"There are several, in fact. Most notable, however, is that zombies eat people."

"And what do you eat?"

Kit sipped his wine, looking thoughtful. "Anything but people," he said.

Chapter Twenty-seven

Bounty

Matrick volunteered to stay behind and watch over Kallorek while the others hit the mud-slick streets of Conthas. Moog and Kit set out to acquire what the wizard referred to as "indispensables," while Gabriel, despite Moog's assurance that his magic hat could feed them all the way to Endland, went in search of rations. Clay and Ganelon were tasked with seeking news of Castia, so they picked a tavern on the strip called the Back Door, where Clay hoped they could ask after gossip in relative anonymity.

The plan went up in smoke the moment they stepped inside. Clay was still blinking in the shadows when a familiar voice piped up.

"Frost Mother fuck me, it's Clay Cooper!"

He saw a hand waving, two pink fingers and a black silk glove. Jain and her gang of overdressed outlaws were seated at a long table littered with empty pitchers and the leftover scraps of a meal. "Have a seat, Slowhand! I owe you a beer, I'd say."

You owe me a week's worth of sandwiches, a dozen pair of socks, a small fortune in jewellery, and two swords, Clay thought ruefully. "I suppose you do," he told her.

Ganelon looked dubious. "She a friend of yours?" he asked.

"We've met twice and she robbed me both times," said Clay, scratching his beard. "But sure."

The warrior said nothing, though something like amusement glittered in his green eyes.

The two of them were given a wide berth as they made their way across the tavern floor, possibly because Jain had said his name so loud, but probably because Ganelon had the look of a killer and a giant axe strapped to his back. The Silk Arrows shuffled to make room on the bench, and by the time Clay and Ganelon settled themselves across from Jain there were full tankards and heaping plates on the table before them.

Jain was dressed even finer now than she'd been in the forest east of Brycliffe. There were a few more bangles tinkling on her wrists, a few more rings twinkling on her fingers, and a familiar-looking silk scarf piled around her neck.

"You like?" she asked, mistaking his assessment of her neckwear as keen interest. "I nabbed it off some fancy Phantran lass 'bout a week back. Nice girl, actually."

And then Clay knew where he'd seen that scarf before. "Was her name Doshi?"

Jain fingered the scarf. "You know, I believe it was. Said she was some admiral's daughter, but she cussed like any old sailor when I relieved her of this." She jutted her chin at Ganelon. "Who's this now, eh? You get tired of being robbed by girls and hire some real muscle?"

Clay shook his head, using a wooden fork to scrape the peas on his plate well wide of a pile of mashed yam. Couldn't have those two things *consorting*, now, could he? "Ganelon," he said, before filling his mouth.

Jain threw a skeptic look at Ganelon and back. "Try again, Slowhand. I may be a babe compared to you, but I wasn't born yesterday."

"It's true," said Ganelon.

Jain remained unconvinced. "Then why aren't you . . . ya know?"

"Old?" Clay suggested.

"Yeah, that."

"It's a long story," he told her, reaching for his cup.

"Got turned to stone," said Ganelon. "They turned me back."

"Okay, it's a short story," Clay admitted.

"It's fucking suspect, is what it is," said Jain. "That said, they say Ganelon's a dark-skinned southerner with a north-man's eyes, mean as a manticore with its tail up its ass—so you damn sure look the part."

Ganelon seemed to be weighing the merits of pressing his claim versus laying into a saucy leg of lamb. He chose the lamb, and so Clay took it upon himself to steer the conversation along. "We're looking for news out of Castia. Have you heard anything recently?"

Jain scoffed. "The only news I expect outta Castia is that there ain't no more Castia," she said. "I take it you're headed that way now? Got the whole band back together?"

"We do. And yeah, we are."

The brigand shook her head, smiling sadly. "A proper epic end it will be, then. Here's to Saga." She raised her mug, prompting her girls to do the same. "The second best band there ever was." Laughter and cries of "hear, hear" followed. Jain tapped her cup once on the table and then guzzled it down.

Clay drained his cup as well, because it would have been rude not to. "Second best?" he enquired. "Don't tell me you're a fan of the Screeching Eagles?"

"It's the *Screaming* Eagles, Grandpa. And no—I'm referring to the latest, greatest band in the land: Lady Jain and the Silk Arrows!"

"Never heard of 'em," said Ganelon.

Jain thumbed her chest. "*I'm* Jain, and these lovely ladies sitting around you are the Silk Arrows. Not long ago we were merely bandits, but Clay Cooper here inspired us to make something more of ourselves."

Clay nearly spat out a mouthful of mashed yam. "I did?"

"Well you put the seed in my head, anyway, back on the day we first met. We've booked our first gig, even. Seems there's a herd of centaurs causing trouble up near Coverdale, and the good people there have hired us to drive 'em out."

Clay remembered Pip telling him about the centaur spotted near Tassel's farm, what seemed an age ago now. He swallowed a surge of concern for his daughter's safety. Centaurs had a nasty habit of kidnapping children and roasting them on spits. But then again, small-town folk had a nasty habit of making a big deal out of nothing at all.

Forget about it, Clay told himself. *Might just be a clutch of wild deer, or some sickly old scout who got left behind by his hunting party. Tally is fine. Ginny is safe. Rose is not, and she's the one you're out to save...*

"After that we're headed to Kaladar," Jain was saying. "Kal says the War Fair's a good place to get our name out there and rub shoulders with other bands. He—"

"Wait, Kal?" Clay interrupted. "Tell me you don't mean Kallorek. Big fat booker? Lives up the hill?"

Jain looked annoyed. "Listen, I don't like him, either. Reminds me a bit o' my daddy, actually, except he's a long shot uglier and has more 'n two coins to rub together. Still, he's the only game in town, and..."

The brigand (or *ex*-brigand, Clay supposed) trailed off. She was staring over his shoulder with a look of naked awe on her face. Turning in his seat, Clay saw a pair of new arrivals. The first was a bald monk in a sleeveless red robe. Standing beside him was the most beautiful woman Clay had ever seen.

No, she's not, a part of his mind amended. *Ginny's the most beautiful woman you've ever seen. This woman is...is...*

She was tall, her pale limbs hard with lean muscle. She wore a formfitting black breastplate that seemed to drink in the light, heavy greaves, and a pair of taloned gauntlets that reminded Clay of a falcon's claws. The collar of her cloak was lined with sleek plumage, and a pair of swords were strapped to her back. Her hair had the blue-black sheen of a raven's feather; it fell straight to her waist but for her bangs, which cut a razor-sharp line above her finely arched brows and large, long-lashed eyes.

Okay, Clay's mind conceded, *she's the most beautiful woman you've ever seen. Except for . . . except for . . .* There was someone he was forgetting. Ah, yes. His wife.

Clay nearly jumped out of his seat when Jain clamped hold of his wrist. "You should go," she hissed. "Get out of here, now. Out the back, preferably."

"Why?"

"*Why?*" Jain's eyes bulged out of her sockets. "Don't you know who that is?"

He didn't, of course. Unless this woman had stormed the north wall of Coverdale in the last ten years (and she hadn't, Clay was certain), then how would he? "A mercenary?" he guessed.

"A bounty hunter," Jain informed him.

Ganelon, intrigued, looked over his shoulder. "She's pretty," he grumbled.

"So what?" Clay asked.

"So you've got a bounty on your head, remember?"

"Sure, but you can't—" He'd been about to say that you couldn't claim a bounty inside city limits, but that was the law of the Courts. *You're in the Free City of Conthas, you idiot. The law of the Courts is worth less here than a copper penny dropped down a shithole.*

As if to drive that point home the woman at the door spoke into the lull created by her arrival. "I'm looking for a man," she announced.

More than half the men in the room bolted to their feet. Clay, irrationally, felt his own legs urging him to follow suit.

Ginny, he thought to himself, using his wife's name as a mantra to clear his addled head. *Ginny, Ginny, Ginny . . .*

"A very specific man," the woman clarified, and the men

who'd stood sat down, abashed. "His name is Matrick Skull-drummer, formerly the king of Agria."

Clay spared Jain a quick glance. Whatever spell the new-comer had cast over the denizens of the Back Door—and Clay was certain that was the case—the brigand had managed to shrug it off. In fact she looked positively terrified, and mouthed something to Clay that might have been *lock spoor*, or maybe *look spry*—Clay had no idea which.

If this woman was looking explicitly for Matrick, how-ever, it meant the bounty belonged to Lilith. But if the queen thought a single hunter—even one fearsome enough to unset-tle Jain—was capable of reclaiming Matrick from Saga's grasp then she was seriously underestimating . . . well, Ganelon. She was underestimating Ganelon.

The woman at the door went on speaking. "The king was kidnapped by his old bandmates. There is a reward offered to any who provide information on Skulldrummer's where-abouts, or any other member of the band called Saga."

"What sort of reward?" someone asked.

The bounty hunter fixed her gaze on the speaker, a blond-bearded fellow with swirling tattoos across his fore-head. She advanced slowly toward him. Her heavy boots *clanked* on the wooden floorboards with every step. Reaching out, she placed the tip of one black-taloned finger beneath his chin, lifting his face as she lowered her own, until they were so close it looked as though they might kiss. Absurdly, Clay felt a stab of jealousy at the thought.

"My eternal gratitude," she purred, and the man whim-pered like a dog. "And, in case that's not incentive enough, Queen Lilith of Agria has offered the sum of one hundred courtmarks to whosoever helps facilitate his . . . safe return. My little birds tell me that he and his friends have been spot-ted here in Conthas."

There was a moment of brief chatter, during which Jain whispered across the table at Clay. "*Run*, you fool."

Clay would have loved nothing more than to slip out unnoticed, but he and Ganelon weren't exactly an unremarkable pair. The moment they stood, they'd be spotted.

The bounty hunter was listing off the names of Saga's members as she stalked toward the bar. "Golden Gabe. Ganelon. Clay Cooper, better known as Slowhand..." She was standing with her back to the room, and so didn't see a dozen men raise their hands, every one of them looking at Clay and salivating at the prospect of whatever they imagined her "eternal gratitude" might entail.

The bench beneath him creaked as Ganelon shifted his weight, preparing to fight. Or run. But probably fight—this *was* Ganelon, after all.

The woman went on. "Arcandius Moog..."

"Here!"

Clay looked to the door—everyone did—and there was the wizard, hat in hand, ghoul in tow, smiling and waving at the woman who'd said his name.

Chapter Twenty-eight

Larkspur

The red-robed monk reacted first. He withdrew a small knife from somewhere and flicked it toward the wizard in the doorway. Kit, who'd drawn his sheet over his head to serve as a hood, lurched into its path.

The blade punched through the pallid flesh of his chest, and the ghoul glanced down, frowning as though he'd found a stain on his favourite sweater. "Oh, dear. That's going to leave a hole."

Clay and Ganelon launched themselves from the bench. Clay barrelled down the aisle, intent on tackling the monk, who was staring curiously at Kit. Ganelon mounted the table, scattering bowls and spilling cups as he pounded down its length. He ducked under a slanting beam and then leapt at the woman standing by the bar.

She grinned, turned a half step to her right, and spread her wings.

They were beautiful, black feathered, and powerful enough to knock Ganelon on his ass. Clay had a moment in which to feel exceptionally stupid for mistaking folded wings for a feathered cloak before he reached the monk, who turned and got a faceful of *Blackheart*. He sailed backward, unconscious before he hit the floorboards.

At the door, Kit plucked the knife from his chest and examined it. "Tipped with poison," he announced. "A paralytic, actually. This wasn't intended to kill."

"I don't care about its *intent*." Moog was frantic. "That thing could have put my eye out!"

Ganelon, meanwhile, was only halfway to his feet when the woman's metal boot crunched into his face. She kicked him again in the gut as he lay sprawling. His hand moved mechanically toward the haft of *Syrinx*, but the woman stamped his arm to the floor and pinned it there.

"You must be Ganelon," she said. "I thought you'd be... older."

"Who the fuck are you?" he asked through bloodied teeth.

She drew a sword from her back and lowered its tip to his throat. "My name is Larkspur," she told him, "and I'm the last woman you'll ever love."

An arrow skimmed past the long feathers at the end of one wing, *thudding* harmlessly into a keg behind the bar. She and Clay both looked to Jain, who had another arrow already to string.

Larkspur *tsk*ed and shook her head. "You're a terrible shot, my dear."

"Am I?" Jain snarled. "Care to find out?"

"Jain—" Clay started, but she cut him off.

"Get out of here, Slowhand. Leave the manhunter to us." To their credit, the Silk Arrows looked prepared to back Jain up on that. Every one of them had a weapon to hand, even if they looked a little in awe of their opponent.

"Manhunter..." Larkspur looked as though she was savouring the word. "I've always loved that name." She turned her eyes on Clay and he felt his blood rise. "I only need Matrick. The rest of you are none of my concern."

"He's not here," Clay said. "And he's not going back to Agria in any case. Tell Lilith she can choose a new king."

Larkspur laughed softly; the sound set butterflies to flight in

Clay's gut. "Oh, she already has. Pretty as Glif, he is. Strong as an ox and just as smart. Matrick's return is merely a formality. I imagine she'll charge him with treason and have him killed."

Clay didn't bother pointing out the injustice in that. This woman hardly seemed the sort to concern herself with moral trivialities. "Well, that sure as fuck ain't happening, so how about we go our way and you go yours. You're outnumbered anyway."

"Am I?" she asked, echoing Jain's earlier query with the same dangerous implication. "Care to find out?"

Clay remembered the raised hands when she'd called his name before. A quick look around told him all he needed to know, and the news wasn't good: smitten grins and mooning eyes adorned the face of every man in the room.

You know what would come in real handy right now? asked a voice in his head that sounded an awful lot like Matrick. *A horn that vomits bees.*

Luckily, Moog came up with something else instead. He produced a glass alchemical globe from his bag and hurled it over Clay's head. Larkspur ducked aside without letting her foot off Ganelon, and the globe smashed against the bar behind her.

There was no explosion. No puff of colourful smoke. Clay looked from Moog to the bar and back again. "Uh . . . thanks?" he murmured.

The wizard winked slyly. "You're welcome."

Larkspur chuckled. "Tell you what," she said. "Ganelon and I will stay here and get to know each other while you run and find the king." She giggled again, then frowned.

Ganelon gave a throaty laugh. "I'd rather get to know the ass end of an owlbear."

"What's an owlbear?" asked Larkspur, evidently amused, because she was grinning from ear to ear.

Clay heard a snort, and looked to see Jain trying to keep her bow steady. A few titters escaped the girls behind her, and some of the men on the opposite side of the room laughed as well, for no apparent reason whatsoever.

Another fit of mirth overcame Larkspur. She managed a bemused glare at the wizard before it consumed her. She threw her head back, cackling wildly. Ganelon rolled free of her boot, but even he was chuckling as he crawled away.

The broken globe. Clay now understood. *This is Moog's doing.* He could smell it now, a scent like raw sugar left to burn on an iron skillet. Clay couldn't recall the concoction's name, but he could remember the wizard using it at least twice before: once so the band could escape a Phantran prison, and again to liven up what turned out to be the most hilarious funeral he'd ever attended.

"Wait by the door," said Kit, brushing past him. "I'll grab your friend."

Clay nodded. "Jain, get your girls out of here."

The ex-brigand was too overcome by glee to heed his words, but a pair of Silk Arrows braced her between them and escorted her out.

By now everyone sitting or standing near the bar was laughing uproariously. Kit, who was unaffected by the gaseous content of the broken globe, groaned as he hefted Ganelon to his feet. "Grooms of Tamarat! You're as heavy as a stone!"

Ganelon, who had been a statue these last nineteen years, found that remark positively hilarious. He giggled maniacally—a sound as incongruous to Clay as a troll reciting poetry—and slapped the ghoul on the back, which nearly toppled them both.

Clay stole a last glance at Larkspur before he bolted out the door. The woman was doubled over, bracing herself against the bar as fits of laughter racked her body. Her wings shuddered, loosing a storm of black feathers over the chaos of the common room. Her eyes locked onto him as she raised one arm, leveling the point of her sword at his chest. Despite the absurdity of her condition Clay felt his soul shrink away from the malevolence in her glare.

Jain was on her knees in the street. "Who ever heard of a fucking *owlbear*!?" she howled. "What even *is* that?"

Moog looked harried. "It's a real thing," he muttered, and Kit patted him consolingly on the shoulder.

It took a few seconds for Clay to notice Gabriel standing among them, a heavy pack over each shoulder. He was gaping at Ganelon as though the man had grown horns.

"What's the matter with him?" Gabe asked.

"I'll tell you on the way," said Clay. Glancing up the street he spotted a cluster of men wearing the same red robes as Larkspur's pet monk. He knelt by Jain and touched her shoulder. The woman who'd robbed him twice and who'd probably just saved his life wiped tears from her eyes. "Thank you," he told her.

She snorted and laughed in his face, but she managed a nod.

Clay stood, wincing at the ache in his lower back. The Silk Arrows were watching him, a few of them beset by snickers of their own. "Get her out of here," he said. "And good luck with the centaurs up in Coverdale. You girls are gonna make one hell of a band."

A few of them accosted Clay for handshakes and brief hugs before melting away, as deft at hiding in city streets as they were in a wooded forest—even better, perhaps, considering their garish attire. When they'd vanished Clay relieved Gabriel of one pack and prodded him toward the western gate. "We need to run," he insisted.

Moog, who was already scampering ahead, called back over his shoulder. "Forget running," he shouted, "it's time to fly!"

Kallorek was in a mood when they got back. Matrick had him tied to a chair and was seated opposite, sipping something that wasn't wine from a wineglass and smiling placidly as the booker raged.

"I'll pop your fucking eyes out and eat them with cheese! I'll have you flayed and salted! I'll turn your skin to jerky and feed it to dogs. I'll feed it to rotters and feed *them* to dogs!"

Matrick raised his glass as the others entered. "Welcome

back. Kal and I were just catching up." He took one look at Ganelon, still beset by an irrepressible fit of high-pitched giggles, and his jaw dropped. He immediately looked to Moog. "What did you do to him?"

"He got a lungful of Jackal's Jest," the wizard explained. "Things got a little hairy in Conthas."

"You're a wanted man, by the way," Clay said to Matrick.

The king paled a shade or two. "Lilith knows I'm alive?"

"If she didn't *before* we wrecked the Maxithon, she does now," Clay told him. "She's hired a bounty hunter. A woman named—"

"Larkspur."

Clay blinked. "Yeah, that's her. She's...bad news," he concluded.

Matrick nodded. "Oh, she's bad news, all right. I was afraid Lilith might resort to this. We hired Larkspur a few years back to track down a servant who'd stolen some of Lilith's jewellery. She found him right quick, cut his hands off, and carved *thief* onto his forehead with a knife. It was almost a mercy when Lilith had him executed."

Ganelon sniggered as if Matrick had told a bawdy joke.

"Moog." Gabe tilted his head at the warrior. "Would you mind...?"

"Ah, sure." The wizard took Ganelon by the shoulder and steered him toward the hallway. "Come on, big guy. Let's go up top and get some air."

When they'd left Clay turned to Matrick. "So what is she, exactly?"

The old rogue shrugged, perplexed.

"She's a daeva," said Kit.

"Which is...?" Gabe prompted.

The revenant shrugged, which set something—a rib, perhaps—rattling inside him. "Just that. Daevas are daevas. I have no idea where they come from, but aside from their wings—"

"Wait, she has *wings*?" asked Gabriel, but then raised his hand. "Never mind. You were saying?"

"Yes, well, aside from their wings, the daeva also possess a certain...charisma. *Compulsion*, I think, would be a better term for it."

"You mean they can control people?" Clay inquired, relieved to know there'd been a justifiable reason behind his curious infatuation with the woman in the bar.

"Essentially, yes," said Kit. "Their mere presence, or so I've heard, is enough to induce a mild fascination. Should one of them make a real effort to charm you...I suppose a strong mind might resist, of course, but a weak one..." He scratched at a bloodless gash across his throat. "I've heard of daevas commanding small armies of besotted thralls, ready and willing to carry out their bidding."

"So what about our daeva?" Gabe wanted to know. "Larkspur, was it?"

Kallorek grunted a laugh, but a glare from Matrick settled him quick.

"Larkspur, yes. Although she once went by the name of Sabbatha," Kit told them. "There are a number of songs about her. Most of them quite dark, as you can imagine. I'd be more than happy to sing a few, if you'd like?"

"Just tell us," said Gabe, impatience clouding his tone.

The ghoul did something that might have been a sigh had there been breath in his body. "Most recount a troubled birth, a tumultuous childhood. A bloody one, even."

Reasonable enough, thought Clay. Considering kids would tease one another for something so trivial as a haircut, or a simple stutter, he could only imagine that having a pair of black-feathered wings might draw the ire of other children—and the ire of children could be cruel indeed.

"At any rate," said Kit, "she ended up at Taliskard, which was once a fortress and was then a secluded monastery renowned for breaking the spirits of troubled young girls."

"Great job, guys," Matrick scoffed.

The ghoul adjusted the drape of his bedsheet garment. "Indeed, Larkspur—or Sabbatha, as she was called at that time—proved too tough a nut to crack. There was an incident with the headmaster—something about him castrating himself in the bathtub—and before long she staged a revolt, took control of the fortress, and used it as a staging ground when she became a mercenary."

"She was a merc?" asked Clay.

"Briefly, yes," Kit affirmed. "And it was around this time she cast off her old name and became Larkspur. But it's said she grew tired of fighting monsters, and had no desire to enter the arena, so she turned her sights upon a more unpredictable quarry."

"People," said Gabriel.

"Exactly."

"And now she's hunting us," Clay muttered.

Kit grimaced. "I'm afraid so."

"Do you think she'll follow us into the Wyld?"

Kallorek laughed harshly. "Oh, she'll follow you. I'd bet my teeth on it. You're all dead men," he sneered. "Might as well tip the hourglass and start counting sand. Twenty years ago you guys might have been a match for Larkspur. But now? She's gonna tear you apart. Maybe Ganelon could take her down—*maybe*—if she fought him fair. But I've heard a couple o' them songs myself—enough to know she don't fight fair, oh no. She'll come at you sideways, rip your fucking heart out, and lick it clean. Frigid bloody hell I wish I could be there to see it."

Clay shrugged. "Yeah, well, you can't always get what you want, eh?"

The booker's grin was an ugly thing. "You'd be surprised," he said.

Chapter Twenty-nine

Flight

The pilot's cabin was high on the stern, fronted by shuttered glass windows and furnished with a plush chair equipped with mug holders on either arm. Matrick offered to fly, but he'd been drinking since noon and was slurring his words, so Gabe delegated the job to Moog instead.

The wizard pulled three levers, one after another. The trio of sails fanned open, accompanied by a loud *crack* as lightning leapt across their metal ribs. The tidal engines—there were two at either end of the ship—whirred into motion. From so close Clay could see the four concentric rings within each spinning faster and faster as *The Carnal Court* came to life.

Moog was beaming. "I'll say one thing for the druins, they sure left us some wonderful toys to play with."

Clay flinched as the air spun into a fine mist around him. "Is there water inside?" he asked over the rushing noise.

Moog brushed his fingers over the steering orbs and nodded enthusiastically. "Of course!" He began to explain about *hydro-gyres* and something called *cyclic pitch*, but Clay had already stopped listening. They had drifted clear of the cave mouth and were climbing skyward. It was a few moments before Clay's stomach reluctantly decided to join him in the air.

He glanced over at Gabriel, who was standing at the rail and staring westward.

Hang on, Rose, Clay thought. *For whatever it's worth, we're on our way.*

"Let's say you find Gabe's brat," supposed Kallorek, who was slouched on the steps leading up to the foredeck. "Say you make it across the Heartwyld—which you won't—and somehow get past the Horde into Castia—which doesn't seem likely—and Rose is still alive—which she probably ain't. What then? What's your plan, Slowhand?"

The booker had been ranting all afternoon. Moog and the revenant were in quiet conversation near the prow. Gabriel was taking a turn as pilot, which basically involved not touching anything at all, and Ganelon had long since laughed himself to sleep in the master suite below. Matrick was below as well, probably drinking, and so Clay, who was watching the sun set from the starboard rail, was the only one within earshot.

He weighed a few responses to the booker's question and finally settled on one among many in his vast repertoire of shrugs.

Kallorek scoffed. "You don't have one, do you? Well let me save you the trouble: Rose is fucked, you hear me? And when you find her you'll be just as fucked as she."

Clay said nothing. They passed through a wisp of cloud and the sail crackled with silver light.

"There's still time, Slowhand. Time to wise up and turn this boat around. Give Gabe a little bump on the head, convince Moog it's for the best. That old bugger hangs on your every word, you know. And put that bloody zombie back in a box where he belongs. The other two are out till morning—we could be back in Conthas before sunrise, and you a rich man."

Kallorek's a snake, Clay reminded himself. *He'll hiss and hiss in your ear until what was once incomprehensible suddenly seems like a damn fine idea.*

"I'm not the type to hold a grudge," the booker lied. "And I *like* you guys. I really do. You practically *made* me. I was a small-time hustler before Saga. Take me home, Clay, and what's done is done. Water under the bridge. Whaddaya say?"

"You'll be home soon enough," Clay said. "We'll leave you just outside the forest. You'll have a two-day walk, maybe three, then you'll be back in Conthas, safe and sound."

"The edge of the Wyld is barely safer than the Wyld itself," Kallorek complained. "Something kicked the centaur tribes into a frenzy—they're bloody everywhere these days. I'll be lucky not to end up on a horseman's spit with a fucking apple in my mouth. And besides, you know how much it cost me to make this thing skyworthy?" He waved a hand at the ship around them. "Too damned much to have you ass-rats take it sightseeing into wyvern territory. Do you see a ballista on board? A lob tosser? Any weapons at all? This boat ain't cut out for crossing the Wyld! You'll be a duck in a shark pond out there!"

"Don't you mean pool?"

Kal's face went the colour of a plum gone rotten. "Ha ha fucking ha," he grated. "We'll see who's laughing when you and yours are buried in a pile of slag."

Clay employed another shrug, subtly different from the one preceding it.

The booker shook his head, shifting uncomfortably in his restraints. After a while he started up again, but with a different tack.

"I wasn't kidding about Larkspur, you know. I've met her a few times. Even tried to lure her back into the mercenary game, but I'd might as well have asked a wolf to eat a head of lettuce. She's a killer, that one. She has a taste for blood, and the faster you run the hungrier she gets. I could manage that for you. I could buy her off, or at least pay her enough to say Matrick was dead and gone. Think about it, Slowhand. I'm the only chance you've got."

Clay just stared out over the rail, squinting his eyes

against the sun's molten glare. *The Carnal Court*, due to its size and in spite of its four tidal engines, was a great deal slower than Vanguard's *Old Glory*. They were flying due south for the time being, skirting the Wyld's edge. Come morning they would veer west and make a straight line for Castia.

Kallorek kept on, relentless. "Okay, best-case scenario: You find the girl and you somehow manage to rescue her. You'd might as well stay in Castia and become faithful citizens of the gods-forsaken Republic then, cause there'll be nothin' left for you here. I'll destroy everything you leave behind."

He pitched his voice so the wizard could hear him. "Hey Moog, you know what's left of your shitty little tower? Nothing! Just rubble and ruin. I burnt all your books, and I killed all your stupid animals. I even ate one of the bastards. You know what's delicious? Tiny elephant! That's right, I ate your tiny fucking elephant, Moog! Do you hear me? You've got nothing but the clothes on your back, you pillow-biting little rat."

"Careful," Clay warned, but Kallorek went on anyway.

"Tell you what: I'll *double* the price on Matty's head. I'll drag him to Brycliffe myself and slit his fucking throat on the castle steps. And Ganelon? He's headed straight back to the Quarry, but this time I'll bury him so deep the basilisks won't even find him for fear of the dark. Oh, and I've got special plans for Valery. She's trying to get clean, you know, but I'll put an end to that. I'll ply her with so much scratch she'll look like a whore's bedpost! She'll be a mindless junkie until the day it kills her."

"Kal..." Clay broke in.

"And *you*, Slowhand—"

"...don't."

"—I'll burn your whole world away. You think Coverdale has a centaur problem? It'll have a *razed to the fucking ground* problem. I'll trash whatever hovel you call home and give your wife to my guards for sport."

Clay left the rail, started toward him.

"And that little daughter of yours...what did you say her name was? Tally? I think I'll keep her for myself. Teach her a few things you never could."

Kallorek chortled wickedly. He was peering down at his own fat stomach, and so yelped in surprise when Clay's shadow fell over him. The booker closed his eyes and raised his chin, ready for the punch he assumed was coming.

But Clay Cooper didn't punch men who threatened his wife—or his little girl, for that matter.

What he *did* do was grab them by the collar, haul them to their feet, take three long strides to gain momentum, and then hurl them headlong over the skyship's rail. Kallorek, too surprised to even scream, disappeared into dark oblivion.

Afterward Clay just stood there, chest heaving, blood pounding in his head like a slavemaster's drum. His hands were trembling, so he gripped the moonstone railing to keep them still. Even the greenest branch could only bend so far, and when Kallorek started into his family something in him had just...snapped.

The monster, he knew. *Not gone. Never gone, it would seem. Just...dormant.*

His senses returned at the sound of clapping. Moog and Kit were applauding him. The wizard was smiling broadly, while the ghoul wore a grimace likely meant as a grin.

Gabriel appeared at his side, peering overboard into the empty dark. "What the hell just happened?" he asked.

Clay opened his mouth to explain, but closed it, for fear that rage would hoarsen his voice. Instead, he shrugged.

There was a pall above the forest each morning, a grimy black mist that reeked of decay and tasted like ash on the tongue. Most days it dissolved by noon, and Clay would gaze out over the grey ocean of sullen, sinister trees that stretched to every horizon. Come evening the sun burned like a pyre in the west, and soon after the stars would gather to mourn its passing, glistening like tearful eyes, sometimes falling.

On the second day they passed through a patch of violet cloud that reeked of decay and left their flesh cold and wet. Matrick went down with a fever and insisted that copious amounts of Kaskar whiskey were the only cure. Kit, who claimed he'd once done a stint as a battlefield physician, corroborated this. The others were justly skeptical, but Matty awoke the next morning with nothing but his usual hangover.

Twice in the first few days they caught sight of something trailing them, but whatever it was vanished before it could be identified. Clay found himself weighing whether he'd rather Lastleaf or Larkspur attack them up here. His preference varied by the hour, at least until he remembered what that wyvern matriarch had done to Obolon Han.

Despite the extravagant apartments below, the band spent the majority of their time on deck. Gabe's eyes were fixed ahead, always ahead, while those who had crossed paths with Larkspur back in Conthas cast wary glances behind.

They pointed out landmarks to one another as they passed overhead. There were the ruins of Turnstone Keep, where bands had met to trade news and tell stories, and where Saga, along with Vanguard and the Night Roosters, had turned back a small army of Ferals after a three-night siege. The only casualty had been their bard, whose name Clay couldn't remember, who was killed by an arrow as he urinated through a gap in the crenellations.

Ganelon nodded down at the remains of Brookstrider, a walking tree even more massive than Blackheart (from whom Clay had carved the wood for his beloved shield). No one knew who or what had killed Brookstrider, but his moss-shrouded corpse was surrounded by the remains of several dozen smaller treants, prompting some to wonder if he'd been the victim of, as Moog had dubbed it, *arboreacide*: the murder of trees by other trees.

And there was the crater in which they'd happened upon

the body of something none of them recognized, a gelatinous mass of throbbing sacks and tentacled limbs that looked as though it belonged in the ocean depths rather than the middle of a poison forest. They'd assumed it was dead, and Matrick had set about poking it with a stick. It wasn't dead after all, and they'd had to cut Matrick out of its stomach when it finally was.

By the third evening, as the six of them lay sprawled on couches they'd hauled up from the apartments below, Clay discovered his mood perceptively lightening. The sense of dread he'd been harbouring since...well, since the night Gabriel showed up on his doorstep, was slowly starting to ebb. After all, they'd managed to reunite Saga, reclaim *Vellichor*, elude their bounty hunters, survive a chimera, and escape the destruction of the Maxithon. And to top it all off, they'd lucked into their very own skyship.

To have traversed the Heartwyld on foot would have taken months, if they'd made it at all, and it would have been a terrible, treacherous slog through a nightmare landscape teeming with horrors hell-bent on killing them. It would have meant spending night after sleepless night on the hard ground, fearing the snap of every twig, the whisper of every falling, fetid leaf, listening as the dark itself breathed and hissed around them.

And from what Clay had heard the Heartwyld was as dangerous now as it had ever been. Too many bands were taking the easy way out: mopping up on the arena floor and sleeping in taverns every night. Too few mercs were willing to explore this dank cave or check out that haunted ruin, and only the bravest among them were willing to risk the Wyld.

But no matter: They were flying. And despite the legitimate concerns of Barret and his bandmates, the journey so far had proven mercifully uneventful. Perhaps they'd get really lucky, Clay imagined, and skip the forest, soar over the mountains, catch the Horde unawares and dip into Castia long enough to find and rescue Rose, then return home to find all this bounty business blown over.

Hell, thought Clay, *I solved half our problems by tossing Kal overboard.* Maybe they could invite Lilith on a "friendly cruise" and do the same to her when they got back.

A soft strumming drew Clay out of his head. Kit had retrieved that bizarre-looking instrument of his and was using his grey-green fingers to pluck a soft, stirring music from its web of silver strings.

"What is that thing anyway?" asked Moog. The wizard had discovered a small library below and was currently leafing his way through a book called *Unicorns: Beware the Horn.* "I've never seen anything like it."

"Nor will you again, my friend," said Kit. There was a note of melancholy in his reedy voice. "Batingtings are so rare as to make skyships seem as common as copper coins."

It occurred to Clay that, if given several hours with which to mull it over, he would be hard-pressed to think of a dumber name for anything than *batingting.*

"A batingting?" Moog closed his book, leaning to examine the cumbersome octagonal instrument resting in Kit's lap. "I thought they'd all been destroyed when the Dominion fell."

"Here we go," sighed Ganelon, drawing a laugh from everyone except the wizard and Kit.

"As did I," said the ghoul. "I found this beauty among Kallorek's many artifacts and decided to relieve him of it."

"Fascinating!" said Moog.

"Is it, though?" Clay loaded his voice with as much sarcasm as it could bear.

The wizard, unfazed, pressed on. "How many strings does it have?"

"Twenty-six to a side, one hundred and four in total." Kit pulled a few scintillating notes from it as he said so. "It's unlikely anyone alive today knows the secret of their making, and I daresay I may be the only ghoul in the world capable of playing one."

"Let's have a song," said Matrick, who Clay thought had been the one flying the ship. It turned out nobody was, though that didn't seem to matter much anyway, since the thing essentially flew itself. "You're supposed to be our bard, ain't ya?"

"A song it is, then," said Kit. He looked from face to face, and then closed his eyes, swaying like a riverside reed. "Let me see, let me see. Ah." His eyes snapped open. His fingers fluttered and the bones in his wrists popped as he flexed them. He strummed a few disparate notes, hands dancing like spiders upon that eight-sided web, before a melody emerged, flitting like a bird into the warm evening air.

And then, in a scratchy, lilting, remarkably pleasant-sounding voice, he sang.

Moog bobbed his head to the tune. Matrick's fingers drummed along on his belly, while Ganelon watched the revenant's roving hands as though mesmerized. Gabriel, as he did so often of late, turned his gaze to the west, toward Castia. And Clay, as was his habit, looked behind them, toward home.

Kit's song, as the best songs did, told a familiar story in a simple, striking way. He sang of Grandual's gods, the Holy Tetrea, and of the Summer Lord's battle against a spirit of utter darkness. Victorious, he banished it to the heavens, where it watches and waits for time to unravel, its million eyes twinkling in the unfathomable dark.

He sang of the Summer Lord's wife, a goddess of compassion and surpassing beauty, who bore him two children. The first of these was Vail, the Autumn Son, but the boy's spirit was spiteful and sickly, and his Father shunned him. Next the Mother gave birth to Glif, the Spring Maiden, though in doing so she perished.

Clay realized partway through the song that Kit was now singing in an altogether different tongue. He knew enough druic to recognize the language, but the words themselves were shapeless, formless, as delicate and deliciously random as the petals of flowers grazed in the dark.

Still, he knew how the story ended.

Vail, who men now called the Heathen for the hatred he bore his father, gave his own life so that his mother might be reborn. Death, however, had changed her. The fruit of her compassion withered to harsh austerity. Her beauty grew cold and terrible, if no less lovely.

And so went the cycle, turning and turning upon itself until the end of days, as autumn's death gave rise to winter, and winter gave birth to spring.

The last, lingering notes of Kit's song shivered into the evening air. Ganelon, Clay saw, was snoring softly. Moog and Matrick wore wistful grins; the wizard's eyes were shimmering with unwept tears.

"Beautiful," he said. "Just beautiful."

And it was, of course—even more so for having been rendered in a lost tongue and given music by an instrument that was, very likely, the only one of its kind remaining in the world. Even so, Clay had long suspected the story was just that: a story. A means of making sense of an all too senseless world. It couldn't be true—not all of it, anyway. It was simply too incredible to believe.

But then again, he supposed, a little embellishment was so often the difference between a good story and a great one.

The following morning they spotted something in the sky ahead. Clay's first thought was that Lastleaf had discovered their plan to rescue Rose and had flown to intercept them. He squinted, fearing to see the flap of draconic wings, but whatever it was moved far too slow to be the druin's fearsome matriarch.

"It's a skyship," announced Gabriel. "It's changing course, coming toward us."

Ganelon slipped his axe off his back. The weapon's whispers filled the air around him. "Might be pirates," he said.

Clay chuckled. "Right. Sky pirates?"

The warrior shrugged. "Why not?"

Clay could think of several reasons why not, but he gripped the cool haft of the hammer at his waist, just in case.

His fears were unfounded. The ship, which appeared to belong to another band, was just passing by for a look. She was bigger than the *Old Glory*, but not by much. The words *Lucky Seven* had been painted on her belly, but the *seven* had been crossed out, as had the *six* below it. The word *five* was scrawled underneath, but Clay only spotted four people at the rail and wondered silently if the ship was due for another paint job.

They'd been attacked, it looked like. Their skyship's front sail was mangled, though it looked like they'd rigged it to remain functional. One of its two tidal engines was inoperable. Its rings, Clay recalled Moog mentioning, were made of pure duramantium, and so could not be broken, but they'd been knocked askew somehow.

Matrick waved. "They must think we're crazy, flying a boat like this over the Wyld."

"No more so than they," said Kit. "They are but one faulty engine away from a long fall."

One of the "Lucky Five" waved back, then pointed behind past the stern of her ship. Squinting, Clay could see a pile of ominous clouds spanning the western sky. The woman began gesturing emphatically in the opposite direction.

Moog stated the obvious. "She thinks we should turn back."

Clay glanced over at Gabriel. "Looks like some kind of storm up ahead. We could land," he suggested. "Wait for it to blow over?"

"Land?" Matrick sounded skeptical. "In the Heartwyld? I vote no. And I'm *technically* still your king, remember."

"We're not landing," said Gabriel. "And we aren't turning back. Unless you think a few black clouds are worse than this Larkspur you say might be following us?"

They both looked to Clay, who was busy weighing the threat of the darkness ahead against the darkness behind. At last he sighed. "Into the storm, then."

Chapter Thirty

The Dark Star

So going into the storm turned out to be an orc-shit idea.

Plague winds rocked *The Carnal Court*. Black rain washed the deck. The triple sails hummed with barely harnessed electricity. All this, however, unnerved Clay a fair bit less than the lightning wrought by the storm itself.

It couldn't just be normal lightning—the kind that killed men and set whole forests ablaze. Oh no, not here in the Wyld, which had an evil reputation to live up to. *This* lightning was blue. It announced its arrival with a crack like a giant's spine snapping in half, and then roared into crackling pillars that seemed to buttress the roiling clouds above.

Moog was back in the pilot's chair, though in fact he was standing. His fingers danced on the steering orbs as he manoeuvred between columns of blistering light, doing his best to see through the rain-scoured windows fronting the cabin.

Matrick was drunk and clinging to the siren on the prow, one hand cupping a golden breast. He screamed wordlessly into the face of the storm. Clay watched him finish off half a bottle of wine before lobbing it toward a pillar they'd very narrowly avoided. The bottle blew apart, and Matrick whooped like a child watching summer fireworks.

That's my king, Clay thought miserably.

As if wind and rain and lightning weren't hazard enough, there were sparkwyrms to worry about. The serpents were each as long as *The Carnal Court*, near invisible until they approached one another and their bodies glowed a brilliant blue-white. Crackling strands of electricity linked pairs together, and Clay couldn't help but imagine two of them passing on either side of the ship, dragging a current across the deck that would kill them all in an instant.

We should have landed, he told himself. *Or turned back until this storm broke.*

The ship rocked beneath him as Moog veered away from the crack and boom that signalled another blast of lightning, which struck so close Clay felt his heart jolt and the hair on his arms stand on end. The shuttered windows of the pilot's cabin thrashed and were torn from their casements. Rain and wind battered the wizard, hurling him backward. He toppled over the arm of the chair and disappeared from sight.

The Carnal Court ploughed aimlessly through the storm, beset by high-voltage cyclones and snakes of coiled lightning. Clay took hold of the rail to steady himself, and made the terrible mistake of thinking things couldn't get any worse.

Kallorek was wrong: Larkspur didn't come at them sideways. She came at them head-on.

Her skyship (because *everyone* had a fucking skyship, Clay was starting to think) cleaved like a blade through the clouds ahead. The thing was enormous: as vast as a Phantran dreadnought, sails upon sails splayed like the webbed claws of a sea hag. Clay counted her engines—two, four, six—and he saw crossbow turrets bristling along either rail, each manned by a monk in whipping crimson robes.

For a moment he feared the dreadnought would smash right through them, but suddenly *The Carnal Court* was diving. Moog was back at the helm, frantically spinning the orbs.

Larkspur's ship snarled overhead, her black hull lit by the static glow of the *Court*'s own sails, and Clay saw the bold white letters stamped along its considerable length.

DARK STAR.

Larkspur's skyship banked steeply, and the thralls on their turrets took aim. The first few bolts punched harmlessly into the deck. The monk behind one rail-mounted crossbow lost his footing and sailed into the sky. He was attached to his turret by a leather harness, but the skyship was dropping so fast the momentum snapped his back in the air.

"It's gonna hit us!" Clay yelled, but Gabriel pointed over his shoulder.

"No it's not."

A pair of sparkwyrms passed overhead, dragging a net of radiant electricity between them. The *Dark Star* altered course, pulling sharply upward, and Clay lost sight of it in the clouds.

"We should land," he told Gabriel, but his friend said nothing for a long while. "Gabe, we—"

The oceanic roar of tidal engines cut him short. Larkspur's skyship was above them again, careening between shafts of blue lightning. Clay looked up in time to see a dozen red-robed monks come spilling over the side. They dropped like stones at first, but then clutched their robes so that the wind billowed inside them, turning their free-falls into plunging glides. One of them lost his grip on the side of his garment and fell shrieking into the dark. Another came in high, his scream cut short as he collided with a static sail. The current set his robes aflame an instant before it reduced his bones to ash.

The rest of Larkspur's thralls managed to land with varying degrees of success. They bore no weapons that Clay could see, but Matrick staggered toward one and took a roundhouse kick to the chin that knocked him flat. Another tried something similar with Ganelon, but the warrior took hold of the poor fool's leg and flung him overboard.

Clay hadn't noticed the dark shape in the midst of the

monks, but suddenly Larkspur was among them. She settled
gracefully on the rain-slick deck, a hunting falcon in the company of lesser birds. The daeva's black armour gleamed like
polished obsidian in the rain. The wind whipped her hair
across the pale beauty of her face, and Clay felt a wave of compulsion crash over him. His heart stuttered even as his mind
shrieked at him to do anything but stand there like a bloody
mooning idiot.

She folded her wings and withdrew the paired swords on
her back, sharp enough to cut raindrops as she gave each an
exploratory slash. The monks formed a defensive ring around
her and struck poses that suggested they considered themselves dangerous regardless of whether or not they were
armed. Clay, for lack of evidence to the contrary, felt inclined
to believe them.

"Matrick Skulldrummer!" yelled Larkspur, casting her
gaze around the deck.

The king staggered to his feet. He gave his head a shake
and yanked the knives from his belt. The daeva used a blade
to point him out to the circle of red-robed thralls. "Take him
alive. Kill the rest."

So much for prebattle banter, thought Clay as the monks
exploded outward. Two rushed Matrick, another two set out
for the helm, and four of them leapt to intercept Ganelon, who
was standing with Kit near the opposite rail. The warrior had
Syrinx in hand and was glaring at Larkspur's back. The final
pair came for Clay and Gabriel, flanked by the daeva herself.

"Go help Moog," Gabe urged him.

"But—"

"He can't fight while he's flying the ship!"

Clay nodded at Larkspur. "But she's—" was as far as he
got before Gabriel pulled *Vellichor* from its scabbard. The flat
face of the blade was the bright blue of an alien sky, and as
Gabriel lifted it to his shoulder Clay saw a wisp of cloud, a
flock of birds in flight, and then a light so bright he turned his

face away. When he looked back it was merely a sword, albeit one whose blue-green blade gave off the scent of wet earth and clean summer rain.

"She's nothing I can't handle," said Gabe, with enough confidence that Clay decided to obey.

Moog was weaponless but not entirely helpless. He'd doffed his magic hat and was hurling honeyed hams and bricks of hard cheese at his assailants. Clay took the first one by surprise, bowling him over and pinning him to the ground. The monk swiped clumsily at his head, so Clay pinned down the offending hand and hit it with his hammer. The bones cracked under the blow. "Sorry," he muttered pointlessly. The man screamed and nearly bucked him off, so Clay brought *Wraith* down on one of his knees.

The second man punched Clay square in the face. He felt his nose crack like eggshell as his head snapped back. The monk went for his exposed throat, but Clay brought his shield up in time to deflect the fist into his nose again, which hurt like hell, but likely saved his life.

Blackheart weathered a flurry of blows as Clay reeled backward. His attacker gave him no space at all, and when he brandished *Wraith* the monk kicked his arm so that Clay struck his own face with the butt end of his hammer.

"Aaaaoooow!" he whined. The monk let slip a self-satisfied smirk.

Tendrils of cold snaked through Clay's head, chilling his ears and sheathing his brain in what felt like ice. He had the bright idea to block his attacker's next strike shortly after the next strike—another blow to his face, *surprise!*—had already landed. Clay fell on his ass, dazed, and before he could recover the monk kicked him in the chest. His head hit the deck hard, which might have hurt a lot more had his skull not been numbed by cold, and the man's bare foot pressed down on his throat.

There was blood in his mouth, rain in his eyes, but no air in his lungs, which was about to be a serious problem.

Suddenly the pressure on his neck let off. Clay gasped and blinked the swirl of black stars from his vision. He saw Moog holding his hat like a loaded crossbow. The monk was screaming; his eyes were squeezed shut, his face drenched in a steaming red liquid that Clay might have mistaken for blood were it not for the smell, which was awful.

Seizing the advantage, Clay swung his hammer at the monk's crotch. There was a wet-sounding crunch, and the man crumpled in a mewling heap. Clay pushed his body off him and mumbled another apology—because, enemy or not, when you hit a man in the nuts with a magic hammer the least you could say was *sorry*.

The wizard helped him stand. "That was cruel," Moog said.

"So was tossing hot soup in his face," said Clay. "Was that—"

"Infernal's Breath, yes. Bad enough when it gets in your mouth, let alone your eyes." The wizard actually looked guilty. "But he was trying to kill you!"

"Exactly, so fuck him." Clay pointed Moog back toward the helm. "Go. Keep us in the sky. I need to..." He scanned the deck: Matrick had downed one of his attackers and had the other on his heels. Ganelon, surprisingly, was still facing off against three opponents. The monks seemed content to engage him without committing to an attack that might get them killed, likely hoping to keep him distracted until their mistress finished dealing with the others.

Larkspur, meanwhile, had her hands full with Gabriel. The monks she'd sent ahead of her were facedown on the deck, and now the manhunter herself was being slowly pushed back, her swords whirling to keep *Vellichor* at bay. Gabe wore something between a smile and a snarl on his face. Larkspur, he saw, bore the same expression. The rain slicked their hair and hummed from the steel plates of their armour, bone white and deathly black.

"Clay?" said the wizard beside him.

"Mm?"

"You need to *what*?"

"What?"

"You said 'I need to . . .' and then you just sort of trailed off."

Clay gestured frantically at the empty cockpit and yelled, *"FLY. THE FUCKING. SHIP!"*

The wizard clucked under his breath and yanked his hat back onto his head. "Fine," he said petulantly and stalked off.

Clay's nose was throbbing. He could feel his right eye swelling where he'd smacked himself with his own hammer. He wiped blood from his mouth with the back of his hand, and set off to help Ganelon.

The monks were too preoccupied to see him coming. He pushed one within Ganelon's reach and the warrior took care of the rest, impaling the poor man on the tip of his axe. Clay leapt at the other, fending off a kick with *Blackheart* and striking back with *Wraith*. The monk evaded him once, but Clay caught him on the backswing. The hammer clipped the side of his head and the man stumbled, off balance. Clay pinned him against the rail and pummelled him until he stopped flailing.

Ganelon chased his remaining adversary to the bow, where the monk, his eyes fastened on the hulking southerner, backed accidentally into Kit, who'd been standing innocuously by while the battle played out. Now the man spun, one hand raised to strike, and screamed when he saw the revenant grinning back at him.

"Good evening," said Kit.

To be fair, that smile was a dreadful thing, but even still the monk reacted badly. Between what he likely mistook for a ravenous zombie and certain death at the hands of Ganelon, he decided to take his chances overboard. He climbed onto the rail and fanned out his garment, preparing to glide toward the dubious safety of the forest below. As he leapt, however, Ganelon managed to grasp a fistful of red robe. The monk slipped out the other end, naked as an infant, and fell screaming into the storm.

Matrick was pulling a knife from his opponent's sternum. He managed to wipe his blades clean on the dying man's clothes before the monk dropped dead. When he saw Clay watching he gave his daggers a theatrical twirl.

"I've still got it," he said smugly, before fumbling the weapon in his injured hand and chasing it awkwardly across the deck.

A growl from Larkspur drew Clay's attention. The daeva was growing frustrated. She'd doubtless hoped to deal quickly with Gabriel, but instead found herself on the defensive. Her allies were dead, or unconscious, or too busy lamenting their hopelessly crushed testicles to be of use, and now Clay and the others closed a wary circle around her.

"Larkspur!" said Matrick, but she ignored him, slashing viciously at *Vellichor*, ignoring everyone but Gabe as if they were nothing more than spectators. "Larkspur, it's over! You've lost!"

The daeva bared her teeth, dancing back and crossing her swords protectively. Gabriel relented, but kept his blade ready. He was breathing hard. If the fight had gone on much longer, Clay knew, he would have faltered, and Larkspur would have killed him.

Then again, that was the point of being in a band, wasn't it? A tiger, however fearsome, could be hunted into a corner. It fought alone, so it died alone. But to hunt a wolf was to constantly look over your shoulder, wondering if others were behind you in the dark.

"Lost?" Larkspur's laugh was mirthless. "Know what happened to the last man who told me I'd lost? I put his cock in his mouth and his head on a pike."

"No way my cock would fit in my mouth," said Matrick, as though it were an obvious fact. Kit barked a short, incongruous laugh.

Larkspur wasn't amused. She returned her focus to Gabriel. "Is it true you're headed for Castia?"

Gabriel seemed reluctant to answer, but finally nodded. "That's right."

"Why?" she asked.

"My daughter is trapped inside."

For just a moment Clay could have sworn he saw something change in the daeva's expression, as though the ice in her eyes were melting into merely frigid pools. Whatever it was, it passed quickly. The ice returned, harder than before.

"Then she's dead," Larkspur told him. "And you're a bloody fool for going after her."

"You're half right," said Gabriel. "Anyway, like Matty said: You've lost. Go back to Lilith and tell her...actually, I don't care what you tell her, but kindly get the hell off my ship."

As if on cue the *Dark Star* appeared off the portside rail, a behemoth roaring in the rain.

"With pleasure," said the daeva. She made as if to stab at Gabriel and he slipped into a guard. Then she lashed at Ganelon, who parried with the haft of his axe. Clay brought his shield to bear, but Larkspur was already lunging at Matrick. She was inside his reach before he could react, tackling him against the rail. He cried out in pain and once again lost his grip on the knife in his damaged hand. His bandmates dashed to his rescue, but Larkspur unfurled her wings, forcing them back.

The daeva launched herself into the air, dragging Matrick with her. Her wings swept down once, lifting them both out of reach, and then again, propelling them toward the open sky.

"Matrick!" Gabriel raced to the rail, but Clay pulled him back by the shoulder as the air around them cracked with static charge.

"Wait—" he managed, before thunder made a whisper of his voice, and light, impossibly bright, blinded them both.

Against the red glow of his eyelids Clay's mind played out the last thing it had seen: the shadow of wings against the searing glare of a lightning column...

...Larkspur and Matrick entangled and falling, like birds shot dead from a tree.

Chapter Thirty-one

A Walk in the Wyld

When his vision returned and the ringing in his ears abated, Clay saw Gabriel slumped against the side of the ship, one hand still clasped on the moonstone rail. Only minutes ago, as he warred with Larkspur across the storm-wracked deck of *The Carnal Court*, he had seemed formidable: a legend come alive, a champion sprung from the pages of a storybook. Now he looked decidedly mortal again, old and wet and weary.

Gabe glanced over, and Clay saw the struggle warring across his friend's face: to delay their journey and risk landing in order to look for Matrick (who was probably dead), or to press on without him and be left to wonder ever after if you'd condemned a friend to certain death. To Gabriel's credit, it was not a decision he weighed for very long.

"Tell Moog to land," he said hoarsely. "We're going down."

Clay had heard it said that once you'd walked in the Wyld, you could never really leave it behind. The adage was particularly true of those who contracted the rot, since the forest had literally infected them, but for Clay it carried a lesser, if nevertheless tormenting, connotation.

He dreamt of it. Not often, thankfully, but now and then

his slumbering mind would find itself lost on its labyrinthine paths, mired in its boiling swamps, or running terrified from one of its many deadly denizens. He would awake panting, sometimes screaming, occasionally sobbing, and Ginny would kiss his sweat-soaked forehead. She would whisper soothingly and stroke his face until the dreams receded. She never asked about them, and he never spoke of them out loud. It wasn't the sort of thing you shared with someone you loved.

But now the nightmare was real, the dream made manifest in the burnt-parchment leaves and the open sores weeping on the face of leprous trees. The air was thick with gloom, and every so often the dread silence was pierced by the screeches of hunters and their prey, killing and dying in the dark beyond.

They split into pairs. Kit agreed to stay behind and watch over the ship, which they'd landed in a broad ravine to help hide it from eyes above. Gabriel, brooding like a child forced to go walking with his parents, stood with Moog. The wizard withdrew a tall wooden staff from his bag, the head of which was capped by a crystal globe clutched by silver serpentine fingers.

"It's a scrying device, like that old crystal ball of mine that Gabe..." He faltered. "Uh...that Gabe disposed of for me. Kindly. In the river."

Gabriel, agitated, waved him on.

"It only works at close range," he explained, then tipped his hat back and set his face so close to the orb his nose grazed its surface. His bushy brow furrowed, and Clay saw a wisp of purple smoke swirl inside the globe. After several long moments, however, the mist dissolved, and Moog stamped the base of the staff on the ground in frustration. "Blast this gods-forsaken forest," he swore. "I never could get any bloody reception in here. Anyway, Matrick is that way." He pointed east.

"How do you know?" asked Gabriel, brightening somewhat.

"Because that's where he fell," said Moog. He set off briskly, and Gabe skulked after him.

Clay and Ganelon set out south and east, close enough to the others that a shout could alert them if need be. Clay spotted few living creatures as they went, but the ones he did see were deeply unsettling. There were fleshless owls crouched in hollowed-out trunks, tracking their steps with eyes that glowed like embers. Birds the size of crows with long, hooked beaks perched in rows upon twisted boughs. He saw something disappear down a hole in the ground that looked distressingly like a grubby child with a long, ratlike tail.

They trod carefully through a stand of trees with writhing white snakes for branches. The serpents stretched toward them as they passed, and more than once tried lunging and hissing loudly, hoping to catch them off guard, or to startle them into stepping within reach of another tree. Clay had seen that trick work before, and so had died yet another of Saga's countless bards.

Once, Clay heard the snap of a twig behind him and turned to find a huge black warg an arm's reach away, so close he could feel the hot gust of its breath on his face. The monstrous wolf was the size of a Kaskar plough horse, and Clay had just begun composing his death scream (he was thinking something high-pitched, sort of a *falling from a great height* meets *I've just shat my pants*, with a touch of *petulant little girl doesn't get her way* thrown in to spice things up) when he heard a deep growling behind him.

Two wargs, his mind told him. *You're gonna need a new scream, Cooper.*

But then Ganelon brushed by his shoulder. The warrior's teeth were bared, his face a frozen snarl, and the growl was his, growing louder, until he and the warg were nose to broad, wet snout. Ganelon's growl became a throaty yell, and then a wild, bloodcurdling scream. The beast's ears went flat against its skull, and a moment later it slunk back a step, then another, before turning and fleeing with its tail between its legs.

Clay stood openmouthed as Ganelon turned and walked back past him without any commentary whatsoever.

Strangely, they heard nothing from Gabe and Moog after that, which meant either they hadn't heard it happen or were in no position to respond. In any case, that was probably bad.

The smothering forest gave way to marshland and they were forced to tread carefully. Pools of miasmic slime gurgled and steamed; one misstep and he'd soon be short a boot—or a foot, if he didn't pull it out fast enough. Clay couldn't help but remember the sort of things they'd usually found in places like this: quivering oozes that devoured flesh and turned metal to rusted scrap, scuttling beetles that exploded if you mistakenly stepped on their shells. He had heard it said by an exceptionally clever bard that if you tried to number the ways you could die in the Heartwyld you'd be dead before you finished counting.

His least favorite was a carnivorous plant with a grasping black tongue that mimicked the terrified shrieks of its past victims.

"Helpmegodspleasehelpme!" it howled as they went by, and then pleaded with the voice of a frightened young woman: *"Pleasestopithurtsithurtshelp."*

And just when Clay thought he couldn't be any more freaked-out, a skeleton in a soiled white wedding dress came shambling through the knee-deep muck. It clutched a wreath of dead flowers to its bony breast, and its empty sockets gazed mournfully at Clay as it waded past.

He suppressed a shiver. He really, really hated this forest.

"Oh, it's not so bad," said Ganelon, indicating to Clay that he'd spoken out loud without meaning to do so.

"Not so bad?" he scoffed. "It's like the...baddest place ever. Name one place that's even remotely as bad as this."

"The Quarry," Ganelon replied instantly.

Clay said nothing, mostly because he had nothing at all worth saying. The two of them plodded along in uncomfortable silence for a while. They plunged back into a thickly wooded forest. The trees here were bent and gnarled, squatting like a colony of rotters beneath ashen cloaks. Something that looked identical to blood wept through fissures in their knotted trunks, and Clay could have sworn he heard a few of them weeping in the gathering dusk.

"You can *see* here," said Ganelon eventually. "You can hear and smell, even if it smells awful. And you can feel." He reached to snag a leaf from a tree overhead. It crumbled in his hand and he tossed it to the putrid wind. "You can't feel anything in the Quarry."

Clay ducked beneath a spanning spiderweb, careful not to graze it, lest its occupant come scurrying down from the darkness above. "I guess so," he said. "But you were just a statue, right? So at least you didn't know what you were missing."

"Is that what you think?" asked Ganelon.

Something about the other man's tone stopped Clay in his tracks. If he didn't know better he might have thought the southerner sounded hurt. "What do you mean 'Is that what I think?' You were stone. I saw you."

Ganelon slowed, then stopped. He rubbed the back of his neck and looked discomfited, like he wished he hadn't brought up the Quarry in the first place. "Stone is stone," he said, cryptically. "But when you're petrified . . . I don't know. I can't explain it. I mean, it's magic, so maybe Moog would know more about it than I do."

Clay felt a premonition of dread flower in his gut. "So what are you saying? You were a statue . . . but you weren't stone?"

"Not really, no. I couldn't see. I didn't feel. I wasn't hungry or thirsty. But I was still there, inside."

Inside?

Clay shook his head. "That's . . . no . . ."

Ganelon's laugh was a bitter thing. "I ain't lyin', Slowhand." He wheeled and resumed walking.

Clay stood dumbfounded for so long that he was forced to

jog to catch up. "Are you telling me you were *alive* in there? That you were *awake*? For nineteen years?"

"Pretty much." Ganelon didn't look back. "Well, I guess I sort of slept sometimes, or at least my mind just shut itself down. But mostly I was awake, yeah."

Clay couldn't believe what he was hearing. He'd assumed, like anyone would, that when you turned someone to stone they were simply that: a stone. Accordingly, he had thought the prisoners of the Quarry to be, in a way, fortunate, since the entirety of their sentence, whether it was ten years or a thousand, would pass in the blink of an eye. But now Ganelon was telling him that all those statues, those *people* standing silent in the dark warren of that terrible place, were still conscious.

What became of a mind left to languish for a thousand years? Or ten, even?

Or nineteen? Clay felt ill, suddenly.

"Ganelon," he said, but the southerner marched on without slowing. "Ganelon, wait!"

The warrior glanced over his shoulder. "What is it, Slowhand?"

Clay fumbled for words. "I . . . I'm—"

"Sorry?" Ganelon turned on him. "Well, don't be. Being sorry don't change anything."

"You must have hated us," Clay reasoned. *You must hate us still,* he left unsaid.

Ganelon shrugged. "Yeah, maybe. For a while."

"A while?"

Finally Ganelon stopped. "Yeah, like, ten years or so. I hated Matrick for wanting to settle down with that brat princess. I hated Moog for wasting time trying to cure the rot instead of *spending* time with the one person he was trying to save. You know what the cure for the rot is, by the way? Don't fucking come *here*. Ever. I hated Gabe for buying into that *monster-love* bullshit Valery was spouting all the time, and I—actually, you know what? I never hated you, Slowhand."

Clay swallowed. "No?"

"No. But I *did* wonder where you'd gotten to, why you weren't there when the Sultana's men came for me. I've had less friends in this world than I have fingers, but I counted you among them. You're honest, and brave, and too damn loyal for your own good. Hell, you're just about the best man I've ever known, and so I thought: What kind of monster must I be, that even Clay Cooper gave up on me?"

Clay gaped, speechless. He cast his eyes to the blackened earth, overcome by shame and sweeping guilt. *I was tired,* he might have said. *Tired of fighting, of killing. Tired of Kallorek's greed, and Matty's drinking, and Moog's antics, and Gabriel's insufferable pride. I wanted to wash my hands clean of it all. And also: I thought you deserved it. You killed a prince, and a lot of innocent men besides. And after ten years of trying to make the world a safer place, I thought it would be safer without you.*

He might have said all of this, but instead he said nothing.

"Never mind." Ganelon stalked off, with Clay plodding sullenly behind. Before long they heard a dull roar overhead and concealed themselves beneath the eaves of hoary trees as the *Dark Star* sailed past.

Larkspur's thralls were peering over the rail in hope of spotting their fallen mistress. Clay caught himself thinking they were looking in vain. He'd seen her fall, struck by lightning—but he'd seen Matrick fall, too, and yet here he was traipsing through the Heartwyld in search of his friend's corpse.

He had a vague memory of sitting at his kitchen table not so very long ago, telling Gabriel there was no way he was going to Castia and no chance he would set foot in this awful forest ever again. But then a half-asleep nine-year-old girl had asked him a single question and convinced him otherwise...

Moments later they heard a woman cry out in pain. The sound had come from a thick copse of trees up ahead, and by the time Clay took three steps Ganelon had crashed through the brush and disappeared altogether. When Clay finally fought through the tangled branches and stumbled into the clearing beyond, he saw the southerner facing down a scrawny troll in a lumpy hat who'd been crouching over Matrick and Larkspur—both of whom, he noted, were very much alive.

"Wait!" cried Matrick.

The troll raised a hand in what Clay belatedly realized was a friendly greeting. Ganelon, however, realized no such thing, and so hacked the creature's arm off at the shoulder. The troll toppled backward. Matrick threw himself between it and Ganelon, who was already hefting his axe for another swing.

"Wait! Stop! He's with us!"

Ganelon froze. "He's . . . wait, what?"

Matrick had scarcely opened his mouth to explain when Moog exploded into the clearing brandishing an alchemical globe and howling, *Kill it with fire!*"

"No!" Matrick shouted, once again putting himself in harm's way. "Don't kill him with anything! Guys, this is Taino. He's helping us. He's a doctor."

"Wheechdoktor," corrected the troll, seemingly unconcerned that Ganelon had just dismembered him. The wound hardly bled at all, and thanks to the regenerative nature of trolls the limb would likely grow back within the hour. He stood, brushing dirt from his behind with his remaining hand, then straightened his lumpy hat and clapped Matrick on the shoulder as if the two were old friends. "Me was jus makin sure your frens here were irie. He an she took a long bad fall, ya know."

Gabriel, who had trailed the wizard into the clearing, motioned for Ganelon to stow his axe. "We know," he said. "Matty, are you okay?"

Aside from a few scratches on the side of his face, Matrick

looked better now than when they'd found him sitting on the rocks below the Teeth of Adragos after his bogus funeral. He spread his hands and chuckled. "Somehow, yeah." He jabbed a thumb toward the daeva. "She sort of flew most of the way down. I just hung on for dear life."

The troll flashed a brown-toothed grin. "Ay, dis one's proper fine. He's an ironmon, no doubt!" He waved his hand at Larkspur, who was sitting with her legs splayed and her head lolling on her chest. "Dis one ain't so lucky. She done took a fierce knock to da head, an she's gotta busted wing, see?"

Clay *did* see. Larkspur's right wing was folded behind her, but the other jutted crookedly beyond her left shoulder. He looked around for her swords and was grateful when he didn't spot them anywhere nearby.

Matrick cleared his throat. "Oh, yeah, regarding that knock to the head . . ."

He fell quiet as Larkspur stirred, blinking groggily. She looked around at each of them before her gaze settled on Ganelon. "Hi," she said brightly, and to Clay's amazement her smile bore no trace of malevolence whatsoever. "I'm Sabbatha."

Chapter Thirty-two

Drums and Drugs and Dreams

"Who the frigid hell is *Sabbatha*?" Clay asked it quietly enough that Larkspur, walking behind them with Ganelon, Gabriel, and Moog, wouldn't hear him. The witchdoctor Taino, who had offered his home as a refuge to wait out the perilous night, loped a few steps ahead, humming quietly to himself.

Matrick glanced over his shoulder before leaning in to whisper, "Kit said it used to be her name, remember? Before she became a bounty hunter and all that. She came to for a bit earlier, and she was...well, she wasn't...Listen, I have no idea what happened to her. She broke more than just her wing, I think." He rapped on his skull. "She's crazy."

"Yeah, well, let's hope she stays that way." Clay glanced over his shoulder. Despite her injuries the daeva was smiling and chatting amicably with Moog. She laughed at something the wizard said and Clay felt his gut turn a somersault, which meant her powers of attraction remained intact.

For the meantime, they'd sated her curiosity by telling her *The Carnal Court* was her ship, and that they'd hired her in Conthas to take them over the Heartwyld, to Castia. Thankfully, she'd believed it.

"Clay?"

"What?"

"Do you think?"

Better than I listen, apparently. "Do I think what?" he asked.

"That maybe she's like this for good? Maybe that bump on the head sort of . . . I don't know . . . knocked the evil out of her."

"I wouldn't count on it," said Clay.

Matrick rubbed at his jowls. "Okay, yeah. Wishful thinking, I guess. So, what do we do with her?"

Break her other wing and run for it was his first instinct, but Clay only sighed. "I don't know. Wait and see, I guess. And hope our new friend 'Sabbatha' sticks around for a while."

The troll made his home beneath the curtaining shroud of a mighty willow. It was dark beyond the draping eaves, though there were hanging clusters of pear-shaped fruit that gave off a queer violet glow. The troll led them on a meandering stone path between rows of tall, fragrant plants. When Matrick slipped and stumbled into one, Taino chuckled to himself. "Is dark ere, ya? Lemme getcha some shiny, fren." He reached up to a low branch and plucked one of the glowing pods, at which point Clay realized it wasn't any sort of fruit at all.

It was a bat. Taino curled its talons around one of his long fingers and set off again, holding the sleeping creature aloft like a lamp.

"Fascinating!" said Moog, and Clay recalled with a shiver the luminescent spiders scattered like stars across the roof of the wizard's tower.

The tree itself was decked with vibrant fungal shelves, beneath which were beds of what appeared to be perfectly harmless moss. The troll bade them sit while he shuffled about, pulling dry mushrooms from the pointed barbs of low-hanging vines and replacing them with fresh ones from an old leather bag slung over his shoulder. Once pierced, the mushrooms gave off a soft light, so that within minutes the lower reaches of the tree were festooned in colourful strands of phosphorescent fungi.

When he finished Taino trotted over, grinning. "Sorry to wait. Is plenty more easy wid two arms."

Ganelon looked away and mumbled something that might have been *sorry.*

"No worries," their host assured him. "Everyting cool. Be gud as new soon, see?" He proffered the stump where his new left arm was already half-formed, growing like a dry sponge soaked in water. He then ambled over to where a big iron cauldron burbled above a bed of smouldering embers and withdrew a brace of fleshy lizards from his satchel. "You lot ungry?" he asked.

Moog leapt to the rescue, removing his hat and taking orders: mildly spiced lamb for Clay, pie for Matrick, a fillet of pink trout for Gabriel, and steak for Ganelon, who had apparently decided that eating from a hat was preferable to whatever inhabited the witchdoctor's master stock. Larkspur asked for a pickled banana sandwich and clapped delightedly when Moog produced it with a flourish. Lastly, the wizard presented Taino with a heaping plate of butter-string pasta, which the troll ate with his hand, slurping down noodles and very obviously enjoying himself.

Clay was immensely grateful they'd found somewhere safe to spend the night. *As safe as anyplace in this gods-forsaken forest, anyway.* He'd seen enough horrors in a single day to last him another nineteen years. He couldn't wait to get back to *The Carnal Court*, but for now he contented himself with the fact that they'd found Matrick alive and relatively unscathed.

When they'd finished dinner Taino shuffled over to a hollowed trunk and scooped them each a bowl of what turned out to be beer. Matrick was the first to taste it. "Delicious!" he declared, and when he didn't keel over and die shortly afterward, the rest of them drank up as well. As they did so, Taino entertained them by showing off the many treasures he'd managed to accrue over the years.

First was an ancient druin helmet complete with chain-mail sleeves to protect a pair of tall, pointed ears. Next was the skull of a cyclopean bull, which Clay wouldn't have believed existed were it not for the single empty cavity at the top of its snout. There was a Tetrea board made of onyx and pearl (though Taino confessed to having eaten all of the pieces years ago), and a moonstone bust of some long-forgotten Dominion Exarch that actually blinked if you stared at it long enough. There was plenty of jewellery as well: rings and trinkets, including a medallion that looked similar to the one Kallorek had used to control his golems.

The troll possessed two leather-bound canvas picture books, both of which he insisted on reading aloud in his near-indecipherable accent. The first was *Trent the Treant*, a popular children's story that had been one of Tally's favour-ites four or five years ago. The second was an illustrated guide to lovemaking among trolls, and the half hour it took for Taino to guide them through his favourite pages was among the most awkward experiences of Clay's life.

At last the witchdoctor produced an elaborate wooden pipe carved into the shape of a brumal mammoth with its trunk in the air. He foraged briefly among the plants in his yard, then returned and packed the hollow in the mammoth's back with a sticky brown flower. He used a glowing brand to set the flower ablaze before inhaling the vapour it gave off through the end of the trunk. After a long moment he exhaled a puff of smoke and his wizened face split into a great wide grin.

"Magic mudweed," he cooed. "Dis ere is de cure for many tings: busted heads, broken wings, de sick what eats the eaters. It'll mend ya inside and out, tru and tru." He gave the pipe to Larkspur, who took two long pulls from the trunk. When she finished she offered it to Moog.

"Yes, please!" said the wizard. He gulped a lungful of smoke and then coughed noisily as he passed the pipe around the circle. "Mudweed?" he asked when his fit subsided. "I've never heard of it. It is psychotropic? Hallucinogenic? It smells a bit like Shepherd's Secret, doesn't it? A bit earthier, though, like Dreamer's Leaf. How long does it usually take to oooooh shit there it is." He slumped back into his bed of moss and fell silent.

Matrick took a hit, but Ganelon passed, as did Gabriel. When his friend handed it to Clay he waved it off. "I'm good, thanks."

Gabe was insistent. "Go for it. Your face looks like someone hit it with a hammer."

Clay smiled crookedly, though doing so made his nose ache. "Someone did."

"Go on, then."

The match had burned out by then, so Clay knelt to light it. Putting his mouth to the trunk he found Taino smiling at him with big yellow teeth and gleaming brown gums. "Smoke up, smoke up," urged the troll, so he did.

It kicked in almost immediately. The ache in his nose vanished; the pain around his eye disappeared. The throbbing in his back ebbed away. Even his knees and feet stopped hurting as the mudweed took hold. Clay settled into the moss behind him and tried to put the sensation into words, but the words slipped beyond reach, darting like fish in a shallow pond.

Taino had reserved his favourite treasure for last: a trio of hide drums leashed together by leather bindings. He sat cross-legged with the drums in his lap, and only then did Clay realize the troll's missing arm had regenerated completely. Taino admired his new hand with evident delight. He tested it a few times on the lip of the drum, adjusted the floppy hat on his head, and began to play.

What followed was, for Clay, a journey.

It began with slow, tentative steps. His mind wandered

back through the events of the past several weeks. First was the clash with Larkspur and her thralls aboard *The Carnal Court*, and then the surprised terror in Kallorek's eyes as he hurled the booker overboard. He watched Gabriel draw *Vellichor* from a sheath of stone rubble. He remembered Tiamax the Arachnian chittering as he poured Matrick a drink.

Clay found himself alone on the Maxithon floor, turning in place, witnessed by the empty sockets of innumerable skeletal spectators. A turn too far, and the three heads of the chimera roared in his face.

He was dimly aware that Taino had hastened the rhythm of his music, and his mind quickened to keep up. The Riot House went up in flames. A kobold kid with lamp-bright eyes growled in a nest of blades. Raff Lackey promised vengeance above a swollen, snake-bit throat. Clay loosed a flaming arrow over grey waters, watched Lastleaf slip from the wyvern's back, saw Jain saunter onto the road, stood with Ginny on a hill at dawn. Her eyes that were sometimes green and sometimes gold looked into his.

Come home to me, Clay Cooper.

His daughter laughed from her perch on his shoulders, then cried in his arms as a babe. He felt his calloused fingers caress the taught skin of his wife's swollen belly, felt her lips against his on the bright day they were wed. And now her voice again, hot as the fire in her eyes when she'd asked him on a night long ago: *Which are you, the monster or the man?*

The drumbeat grew faster still. Time galloped like a running horse, and from its back Clay watched as the golden years with Saga blurred past—the memories so numerous they flashed by only in glimpses. He saw a host of living trees laying siege to city walls, a fortress of black glass buried by earth and time. He heard the laughter of friends, the sighs of lost lovers, the screams of those he'd killed, and killed, and killed.

And here was Kallorek, slick and fat, while Gabriel stood behind him with a smirk on his face.

Our friend here says you can fight.

All at once the drumming slowed. The silence between every beat stretched into eternity. When they came at last they fell in pairs, resounding in his head like the languid breaths of an exhausted heart.

Ba-dum.

A knife scratching at the skin of a white tree.

Ba-dum.

Wait, please. His mother, begging for her life while Clay cowered in the dark.

Ba-dum.

The whisper of rain on the roof above his bed. Raised voices in another room.

Ba-dum.

The glimmer of sunlight through the sway of green leaves.

Ba-dum.

A blond boy points to the field of wind-blown grass behind their home. *Why can't I go there?*

Because, he is told by a voice he can barely remember, *there are wolves.*

Ba-dum.

Ba-dum.

Ba-dum.

Chapter Thirty-three

The Flesheater

When Clay woke it was still dark. All but a few of the coloured mushrooms had lost their uncanny light. The bats had left to hunt whatever it was glow-in-the-dark bats hunted. Glow-in-the-dark mice, he supposed. Matrick and Taino were engaged in a clamorous snoring contest. Ganelon and Moog were sound asleep, and even Gabriel, who barely slept most nights, had managed to drift off.

Larkspur—or Sabbatha, as she'd called herself earlier—was sitting with her arms around her knees, one wing folded over her shoulder like a blanket. The other, the broken one, loomed crookedly behind her. She was near enough to what remained of the fire that Clay could see her face: the strong jaw, the arched brows, the large dark eyes that gleamed like starlit pools by the light of dying embers. She didn't notice he'd awoken until Clay quietly cleared his throat.

It seemed an effort to pull her gaze away from whatever it was she'd been watching with her mind's eye. When she did she smiled, and Clay felt his heart skip a beat.

"I had dreams," she said.

"Me too."

"Good ones?"

Clay had heard his mother whimpering in the dark. "Not really, no."

"Me neither," she said. "Though I remembered a part of my past."

Clay's mouth went dry. His mind started running scenarios that began with Larkspur lunging across the fire and mostly ended with him dying at her steel-shod hands. He considered going for his hammer, which lay just out of reach, or maybe diving for Ganelon instead, since waking the warrior was probably his best hope of survival. Finally he swallowed his fear and asked, as evenly as he could, "Like what?"

The daeva chewed her lip for a moment. "Do you know how my kind are born?" she asked.

Eggs? he almost guessed, but instead just shook his head no.

"Immaculate conception."

"What? That's impossible," he blurted, before considering whether or not it was polite to do so.

She laughed quietly. "My father's reaction was much the same, I'm told. He was away in Phantra when I was conceived, and when he came back north to find my mother pregnant he nearly killed her. He nearly killed me, too. When I was born he left me in the snow overnight as an offering to the Frost Mother."

"But you lived," said Clay.

"I lived," she confirmed. "My father found me the next morning wrapped up in my wings—hungry, but otherwise hale. He left me alone after that. He must have assumed I was blessed by the gods."

What was it about fathers, Clay wondered, that compelled so many of them to test their children? To insist that a daughter, or a son, prove themselves worthy of a love their mother offered without condition?

"But as I grew older," Sabbatha told him, "the other children in my village were afraid of me. They thought me a freak, a monster. They called me 'harpy.'" Her grin turned savage. "I didn't mind. I even found myself a nest—a cave on a steep hill where I went to be alone. But eventually, when they realized their words had no power to hurt me, they used fists instead, or stones, and neither the gods nor all the feathers in the world could protect me then."

Clay couldn't say for sure whether the sympathy he felt for her was real or artificial, but at some point while she was speaking he had ceased suspecting she was about to attack him. "Is that what you dreamt of?" he asked. "Being tortured by those kids?"

The shake of her head was almost imperceptible. "I dreamt of killing them, of hunting them down one by one." She appeared to take no pleasure in saying this—insofar as Clay could tell—but nor did she seem aghast at this shadow of herself revealed by Taino's drug. Her voice was strangely even, as though she were still half immersed in the dream, dictating out loud what she was seeing with her mind's eye.

"The first was a boy named Borys, the village headsman's son. He had a knife, which he held against my throat while he groped me. He would have done worse, I think, but I took his knife and used it to kill him."

Clay shifted where he sat. The mudweed had alleviated the gnawing pain in his back, but the daeva's confession made it hard to get comfortable, even on the bed of plush moss. "Borys had it coming, sounds like."

Sabbatha's eyes flickered briefly to his. "Of course he did. And so did the next girl, Sakra. She'd thrown me down a flight of stairs once, so I pushed her off a cliff. And after that was Crystof, who was especially cruel. He beat me worse than any of them, and so I tied him to a tree, and I used a rock to break him, little by little, until he died."

One of the mushrooms above them lost its lustrous blue glow, leaving the daeva's face bathed in ruddy red light. "Misha used to cut me. She was younger than me, and smaller, but she'd have one of the others hold me down. Once she pricked my eyes with the point of a nail and threatened to blind me, so I . . ." Sabbatha trailed off, unwilling or unable to divulge the gruesome details of whatever revenge she had taken upon the girl. "She screamed and screamed, and in the end she begged for mercy. I don't know why . . . but I let her go. I might have made her promise not to tell the others who it was that hurt her, but I didn't. I think I wanted them to find out . . . to know what I was capable of."

Clay had a fair idea as to how this story ended. He wondered if all of this had been a part of Sabbatha's dream, or whether, like himself, she had glimpsed her past in a succession of broken shards and was only now piecing them together.

The daeva blinked several times in rapid succession. Her tongue slipped out to wet her lips and Clay felt his breath catch. "I spent the following night in my nest. By the time I returned to the village my parents were dead, our home burned to the ground. They had cut my father's head off, left his body in the yard for the dogs. My mother was hung by her feet from a tree and pelted to death with stones."

"And yet they spared you," Clay observed.

"Apparently so. Though I can't recall why, or what happened next. It's like . . . a veil, or a fog I just can't see through."

The last of the fungal lamps went out, so that only the seething embers remained by which to see. Somewhere beyond the shroud a wild thing howled in the dark as it killed, or was killed. It was hard to tell one way or another with bloodcurdling howls.

"Maybe it's for the best if I don't remember who I was before," she said. In the dark her voice sounded closer than before, more intimate.

"Why is that?" Clay asked.

"Because I can't have been a very good person. After what happened to my parents, and what I did to those children, what could I have become but a monster?"

What else indeed? Clay knew a few things about trying to escape your past. He was remembering the look on Raff Lackey's face as the snake in his fist had pumped poison into his veins.

I'll be waiting for ya, Cooper, the old merc had told him, *along with all the rest.* Whatever vengeance Raff's ghost had planned, it would be standing at the rear of a very long and disgruntled line. Just now, though, he was imagining Sabbatha being greeted in death by her own host of accusing wraiths, the first of which would be three ruthless, empty-eyed children...

"You seem nice enough to me," he said after a while.

Larkspur twitched her broken wing in what Clay recognised as a shrug. "Yeah, well, I suppose that's what matters now. Taino said my memories might never fully return, or they might come back little by little, or else suddenly, all at once."

Broadly ambiguous prognoses were exactly the reason Clay didn't put much faith in doctors—witchdoctors in particular. In this case he hoped the former supposition was accurate: that the woman who had glared so hatefully at him in Conthas and then dive-bombed them during a lightning storm was gone for good. He couldn't exactly tell *her* that, however, and so was about to offer something clichéd and conciliatory when he heard the sound of a footfall behind him.

Glancing over his shoulder, Clay was dismayed to find the tip of a sharpened stone spear hovering scant inches from his nose. A face floated in the gloom behind it, skeleton-pale, and a word wriggled into his mind like a worm in an apple's rotted core.

The word was *cannibal.*

The cannibal's name, it turned out, was Jeremy. His grasp of the common tongue was limited, but he and Moog were able to communicate through a combination of frantic gestures and words repeated very loudly and very slowly.

"He's actually quite a nice fellow," the wizard told them, as Jeremy and Taino wandered off among the tall plants in the yard. The troll could understand the tribesman's guttural pidgin, and they had evidently met each other before. "He's a forager from the Boneface Clan. Hence the skull painted on his face, I guess. Their village is very close to here, he says."

Matrick whistled quietly. "Good thing we didn't land there. You'd have been lucky to find our bones. And maybe L—" he caught himself before uttering the name *Larkspur* "—maybe Sabbatha's wings."

"I didn't even know cannibals were a real thing," she admitted. "Do they actually eat people?"

"They do, yes," Moog told her. "Though they aren't fussy about it. They'll eat chicken, beef, pork—anything that bleeds, really. Often they'll just skirmish with neighbouring clans and eat whoever is unlucky enough to die."

"That's mad," said Larkspur.

Moog shrugged. "Perhaps, but in Grandual we kill each other all the time, for all sorts of stupid reasons. The Ferals, as we call them, use the bones of the dead for tools, the teeth and ears for jewellery, the skin for tents and clothing, and eat pretty much everything else, including the eyeballs. It's all very efficient, if you ask me."

Matrick put his arm around the wizard's slim shoulders. "See, now *that's* mad."

"They don't eat vegetables, or fruit," the wizard continued. "They deem plucking your food off a tree as cowardly. Consequently, a great many of them have scurvy."

Larkspur looked bewildered. "Scurvy? Is it contagious?"

"Gods, no," said Moog. "But I wouldn't go kissing one if I were you. Eating people gives you bloody rotten breath, as you might imagine."

She did imagine, and made a disgusted face that Clay, despite himself, found utterly adorable.

"So what is he doing here?" asked Gabriel.

Moog smoothed the silky length of his beard against the front of his robe. "Their chieftain is very sick, apparently. Jeremy was sent to ask Taino for a cure."

"Well, he's the man to see," said Matrick. "That mudweed

of his is magic, like he said. All my bruises disappeared, all my cuts scabbed up, and my arm feels good as new."

"My wing feels better," Larkspur mentioned. "Not great, but better. Can someone remind me why I was flying in a thunderstorm again?"

"We should get moving," said Gabriel, ignoring her question. "We've wasted enough time already. I still think we should have walked through the night. We'd be back in the sky by now."

Jeremy and Taino returned from their stroll. Besides the skull painted on his face, the cannibal's whole body was riddled with scars and covered with a chalky green powder that served both as camouflage and to make his flesh taste terrible if he fell in battle with the enemy. He used his spear like a walking stick and carried a bundle of mudweed stalks in a sling on his back.

Taino gave them each a gangly hug farewell. "Walk gud, y'ear?"

"We hear," said Matrick.

Jeremy, who was staring at Larkspur with what Clay hoped was lustful (as opposed to literal) hunger, nearly jumped out of his skin when Moog began yelling in his face. "US GOING," the wizard told him, accompanying the words with elaborate hand-motions. "BACK TO SHIP. NICE MEETING YOU. GOOD LUCK CURING CHIEF."

The Feral responded in his own incomprehensible language. "KI TOBARA. IK OOKIBAN DONO GARUK."

"He said he will come with us part of the way," Moog translated—unnecessarily, since Jeremy had pointed at them and used his fingers to indicate *walking*.

"IKKI DOOKA PUBARU. KOO PASSA PIKAPA."

"Also, we're invited to the Boneface village for lunch."

"Lunch with cannibals?" scoffed Matrick. "Over my dead body."

Clay clapped him on the shoulder as they headed out. "I think that's the general idea," he said.

Chapter Thirty-four

Hope in Flames

They parted ways with Jeremy an hour later. If the cannibal was worried about being in the forest by himself, he showed no sign of it whatsoever and waved merrily as he set off southward.

The five members of Saga, with Larkspur in tow, backtracked the way Gabriel and Moog had come yesterday, so that Clay was treated to a whole new host of the Heartwyld's numberless horrors. The first of these was a maze of winding gullies spanned by webs inhabited by spiders the size of dogs.

They ran into an ettercap at a fork in the path. The creature, which looked something like a scrawny old man with bulbous black eyes, snapping mandibles, a distended belly, and a forest of long, quivering spines on his bent back, had chased something into a hollowed log and was desperately trying to ferret it out one side or the other.

It froze in a crouch at their approach, and appeared ready to attack or flee should the opportunity for either arise.

"Do you understand me?" Gabriel asked it.

The ettercap nodded, regarding him warily with those glossy black eyes. Its fingers and toes were unnaturally long, Clay noted, and very sharply pointed.

"Which of these paths will take us west?"

The creature tilted its head, then slowly raised one of its wiry arms and pointed to the way behind it.

"Thanks," said Gabriel, and took off at a stride in the opposite direction.

Ettercaps had a reputation for lying, and a habit of hissing right before they attacked, which this one did as it lunged at Gabriel, grasping with those long, sharp, spindly fingers.

Clay had been waiting for it; the fingers scrabbled harmlessly against *Blackheart*'s face, and Ganelon, who had also been expecting treachery, chopped the wretched thing in half with his axe.

Once the ettercap stopped thrashing, its quarry scurried out of the log. It was white-furred and red-eyed, and it looked to Clay like a weasel with eight legs and heads on either end of its body. He'd seen one just like it in a cage in Moog's tower, Clay remembered. Both its heads squealed angrily at them before the thing ran off at a lope.

They pressed on, exiting the ravine-maze to find themselves in a forest of tall, leafless trees. A mist rolled in, curling around their ankles as though it were a living thing. Clay could have sworn he felt it snag his foot, and found himself taking slow, deliberate steps, like a man treading through murky water. After a while the mist seemed to grow restless and prowled off.

At last the forest began to look familiar. They'd seen that fungus-decked tree before, they'd stepped over that acidic streamlet going the other way.

The skyship's just ahead, Clay thought, relieved. *We're almost there.*

A short while later they spotted a green-skinned, white-faced tribesman prowling through the forest alongside them. When they caught sight of another, this one carrying a crude shortbow, Matrick started to get nervous.

"Do you think he sent them after us?" he asked.

Moog frowned. "Who, Jeremy? Not at all. The Ferals are

a very territorial people, you know. They're probably just tracking us to make sure we stay well clear of the village." He gestured to a painted warrior slipping between the trees nearby. "Consider this an escort. An honour guard, if you will." Hardly a breath had passed when a stone-tipped arrow shattered the crystal orb on the top of his staff. The wizard's face went pale. "Fuck me, they're hunting us!"

"Run!" yelled Gabriel, as if it hadn't occurred to each of them already. He had *Vellichor* in hand—the vibrant majesty of an ancient forest visible in the broad face of the blade. Ganelon slipped *Syrinx* from his back with a sinister grin, as if he'd been hoping the cannibals would attack and was gratified they'd given him provocation to start killing them. Clay could hear the axe muttering quietly to itself, or to Ganelon, or perhaps to those whose blood it was about to drink.

The southerner motioned for Clay to follow the others with a nod of his head. "Move it, Slowhand. I've got the rear."

The savages came at them from everywhere at once, yipping like jackals and hurling a volley of shoddy spears as they stormed in. Gabriel blocked one missile with the flat of his blade and cut another in half before it impaled Matrick. A stone tip struck Clay square in the chest and splintered against the red links of the *Warskin*.

I like this armour, he thought, then shrugged his shield free as Ferals began dropping from the trees.

The first to do so landed near Matrick and got a dagger through the eye. The next fell on top of Moog. The wizard went down with a yelp, and his assailant lost hold of his spear. As he reached for it Larkspur stomped on the shaft, snapping it in half with her heavy black boot. She hit the cannibal with the serrated flare on the back side of one gauntlet, and with the other hand took up the pointed end of the broken spear and rammed it through the throat of another rushing Feral.

One hurled himself at Clay from the right and got batted aside by *Blackheart*. His head struck a tree and made a sound like a ceramic pot dropped on the floor. A second swung at Clay with a crude hammer. He met the weapon with his own and broke it apart, and another swing did the same to the poor man's skull.

Gabriel was too far ahead to see, and Ganelon was lagging, beset from all sides by shrieking cannibals. Ferals had a funny (if ill-advised) habit of attacking the strong before the weak, likely an attempt to exhibit their valour on the battlefield. In this case it was costing them dearly, as the southerner was killing them by the score. The path behind him was littered with limbless dead.

Clay lingered until the warrior caught up, and together they waded through the Feral swarm. Ganelon's axe, *Syrinx*, was a red mess, hacking off arms and slicing fatal gashes in guts, groins, necks—pretty much anywhere that bled a man out in a matter of seconds. *Blackheart* bore the bite of spear and arrow with the stoic fortitude of a seaward cliff. Occasionally Clay seized the opportunity to crack a skull or break a limb with his frigid hammer.

All at once the cannibals ceased their attack. They didn't flee, and they kept their spears trained on Clay and Ganelon, but they no longer flung themselves at the warrior with reckless abandon. One of them began to chant, "DOOK, DOOK, DOOK" and the rest took it up, stamping their feet and weaving like flute-charmed serpents. "DOOK, DOOK, DOOK! DOOK, DOOK, DOOK!"

The southerner muttered over his shoulder at Clay. "Are they saying *duke*?"

Clay sure as hell hoped not. He searched the forest around them, half-expecting to see Lastleaf in his ravaged red long-coat striding through the trees like some smug, sylvan prince. Thankfully, what came crashing through the woods was not a druin at all—only the biggest, most fearsome-looking Feral Clay had ever seen.

Dook, I presume.

The new arrival wasn't as broad shouldered as Clay, or as powerfully built as Ganelon, but what he gave up in bulk he made up for in height and reach. Each of his hands was the size of a small shield, and his loincloth, no doubt designed to fit a more modestly sized man, left little to the imagination. His bald head bobbed on a long neck and seemed altogether too small for his gargantuan body, which was curiously void of the green paint worn by others of his kind.

A sign of prowess, Clay guessed, since the green was a precaution against being eaten, and Dook didn't strike him as a man who planned on being eaten today.

Weapon-wise, Dook was a simple man: He carried a very large bone, obviously taken from a very large monster, which the huge savage had probably killed with relative ease.

"DOOK, DOOK, DOOK, DOOK!"

The massive Feral paused to bask in the adoration of his peers, roaring and pummeling the earth with his ivory club.

Ganelon hefted his axe. "You mind if I take this one?"

Be my guest, Clay almost told him, except he'd been thinking since yesterday about what the warrior had said regarding the Quarry, and the resentment he'd fostered for everyone but Clay.

What kind of monster must I be, Ganelon had asked himself, *that even Clay Cooper gave up on me?*

What kind of monster . . .

"It wasn't you."

The warrior cocked an eyebrow at him. "Huh?"

"When they came for you. When they turned you to stone. We should have been there, but we were selfish. *I* was selfish. I thought you deserved it," he admitted, and saw Ganelon's face spasm in what might have been hurt and must have been anger. Clay spoke quickly, afraid the warrior would cut him off. "But I was wrong. I was scared. Any one of us could have done what you did."

Ganelon sighed. "Slowhand . . ."

"Never again," Clay said. "Where you stand, I stand." He wanted to say more, to say how sorry he was for every solitary second his friend had spent down there in the dark, but Dook, as it turned out, wasn't one for sentimental moments, and he chose this one to raise his club and charge.

Clay and Ganelon leapt in opposite directions as the bone came down like a felled tree between them. In keeping with cannibal tradition, Dook went after Ganelon first, using his absurd reach to snag the warrior's ankle and then hurling him into a nearby trunk. Ganelon crashed into a heap at the bottom, dazed, and the Feral prepared another epic swing, tipping his grisly club behind his head so as to bring all his strength to bear.

Before he could, however, Clay rushed in from behind and brought *Wraith* chopping sideways, cracking against the club and throwing Dook off balance. The cannibal turned his flailing momentum into a spinning swing, and Clay barely had time to register that he—and not Ganelon—was its target before the breath blew out of his chest and Dook began shrinking rapidly.

Nope, he realized. *I'm flying backward.*

He crashed into a cluster of cheering Ferals, and they all went down in a tangle of thrashing limbs.

"DOOOOOOOK!" screamed the crowd of cannibals.

That blow should have snapped him like a reed, Clay knew, and he once again offered silent praise for the durability of Jack the Reaver's impenetrable armour. He tried getting to his feet, but his legs had other ideas. A glance told him that Ganelon was on his feet, pressing the attack, sweeping left and right with *Syrinx* while his adversary leapt back and sought an opening.

The Ferals he'd crashed into were recovering as well, and they had no intention of letting him reenter the fray. One of them drove a spear into his stomach, and Clay returned the favour by smashing *Wraith* up into his groin.

"Not even sorry," he muttered, rolling sideways as another Feral aimed an arrow point-blank at his face. The shot missed and struck the ground just inches away—the arrow's shaft broke and a shard of spinning wood opened a gash beneath his left eye. The man cast his bow aside and dived toward Clay, who managed to put a fair bit of strength into a backhanded swing with *Wraith* that did terrible things to the bones in the cannibal's neck.

The last of the three he'd landed on grabbed at Clay's shield arm, and as they both finally rose, the straps binding *Blackheart* to his wrist tugged loose and the unthinkable happened.

The Feral took his shield.

Forgetting the fact that Ganelon and Dook were fighting nearby on his left, and doing his best to ignore how suddenly light his right arm felt, Clay locked eyes with the man holding *Blackheart* and said, as calmly as he could, "*Give it back.*"

The Feral looked down at his prize and then back to Clay. He wavered. Clay could see him wavering.

"*Now.*" The word seethed through Clay's teeth, sizzled in the air between them.

Slowly, slowly, the man lifted the shield and offered it to Clay, whose trembling hands reached for that slab of mottled wood like a mother for her newborn child. The moment Clay took hold of it, the Feral turned and bolted into the forest.

"DOOOOOOOOOK!"

Clay wheeled, wriggling his arm back into *Blackheart's* straps and cinching them tight as he assessed how Ganelon was doing.

The Feral champion had landed another blow, it seemed, and Ganelon was slumped against the same tree as before, which was now pitched to a dangerous angle. Dook was tiring, at least, and advanced on the warrior much slower than before.

Clay took three running steps before his legs turned back to jelly and he staggered to a knee. Desperate to at least prove a distraction, he lobbed his hammer overhand. It sailed through the air and, miraculously, struck the lanky cannibal in the back of the skull. Unfortunately, Dook's round little skull was exactly as hard as it looked, and any elation Clay felt at having landed his throw evaporated as Dook turned, took him in with those beady, close-set eyes, and laughed.

Clay saw Ganelon rise. And Dook, though not especially bright, *saw* Clay see Ganelon rise, and so turned in time to see Ganelon swing his lethal, legendary axe—not at Dook, since he was too far away for that, but at the tree against which he'd been lying.

Syrinx sheared right through the half-shattered trunk, and the tree came down like a ten-ton drunk, crushing Dook (and several other tribesman standing farther behind him) to pulp beneath it.

"...Dook, Dook..." a single Feral's voice trailed into stunned silence, in which Clay picked out a low hum growing steadily louder, until it became a roar that rattled the trees and shook dead leaves from dying branches.

The *Dark Star* cruised overhead, so low Clay could feel the mist of its tidal engines filtering through the canopy above. The tribesmen, fearful of the lumbering dreadnought, scattered like mice beneath a falcon's shadow.

The ground began to shudder, rocked by a succession of rumbling quakes, one after another. Clay and Ganelon shared an uneasy glance, and once Clay had retrieved his hammer the two of them shambled along in the direction the others had fled.

"That was awesome, by the way," Clay rasped as they went.

Something like mirth tugged at the corner of Ganelon's lips. "I know."

They emerged behind Gabriel and the others into the wide, rock-strewn ravine in which they'd landed their skyship the day before. The ground beneath their feet was scorched black, littered by small fires and shards of broken wood. Clay was wondering how that had happened when he saw half a dozen pitch-smeared barrels come spilling over the *Dark Star*'s rail.

Oh, he thought. *Oh, no.*

He watched with a rapidly sinking heart as they tumbled down onto *The Carnal Court*, bursting in a spray of liquid fire that ate the sails like parchment and burned the hull to slag in a matter of minutes.

Against the glare of alchemical flame Clay saw Gabriel stagger, using *Vellichor* like a crutch to keep despair from driving him to his knees. Matrick crouched to one side, stoop shouldered, while Moog removed his hat and bowed the bald crown of his head. Clay and Ganelon staggered to where Larkspur stood, neck craned, watching as the *Dark Star* vanished over the forest to the west.

Clay stole a glimpse at her face, fearing to see the spark of recognition in her eyes. But there was only confusion, and a trace of sorrow in her voice when she spoke at last. "I assume that was my ship?" she asked, nodding toward the burning wreck of *The Carnal Court*.

Clay sighed. *Don't think about it*, he urged himself. *Don't think about the fact that your fastest way to Castia and back again is gone, burned, destroyed. Don't think about how much longer it will be before you see your wife, or hear your daughter's laughter, because then you'll start crying and nobody wants to see that.*

"It was," he said.

The daeva's dark eyes flitted back to the sky. "Who are they?"

Besides being a bunch of fucking assholes? "They're bounty hunters," he said, deciding to risk some part of the truth.

Larkspur's arched brows furrowed. "Why are they after you? Are you criminals?"

That depends on who you ask. "They're after Matrick," Clay told her. "His wife is the queen of Agria. He left her, so now she wants him dead."

"Dead? Why?"

"Because she and Matrick had five kids and none of them are his. I think she's afraid he'll put the only legitimate heir of Agria into the belly of whichever woman takes pity on him first."

She snorted her amusement, and Gabriel wheeled at the sound.

"Is something funny?" he asked. There was raw fury in his face, and it occurred to Clay that Gabe very probably blamed Larkspur for the destruction of *The Carnal Court*. And of course Larkspur *was* to blame, but the woman who'd emerged in the wake of her fall seemed a different person altogether.

"I . . . no." The daeva looked abashed. "I'm sorry," she said.

Gabriel's gaze darkened. He took a step toward them, and Clay's eyes were drawn to the sword he dragged behind him. He saw rushing water through the window of *Vellichor*'s blade, and a writhing fish so real he thought for a moment it might come splashing out into a world in which it didn't belong.

Gabriel's eyes had moved past her now, and his expression hardened.

Ganelon nudged Clay's shoulder and they both turned slowly around.

There was a small host of cannibals arrayed along the forest's edge. They stood with spears ready and bows drawn, bolas whistling and blowguns raised to puckered lips. They didn't attack, though, and two of them broke from the others, coming tentatively nearer to the band and its crippled daeva.

One of them was Jeremy, who slowly and loudly introduced his father, Teresa.

"Teresa?" Even mumbling, Larkspur sounded dubious.

"The Ferals remain nameless until after their first kill," Moog explained hurriedly. "They must consume the entire body themselves, after which they adopt that person's name, regardless of gender. It's not unusual to meet women with names like William or Todd. A man with a woman's name is quite rare, actually. Probably because women are rarely stupid enough to get killed by cannibals in the first place."

"ME TERESA," Jeremy's father announced redundantly. Clay wondered if Ferals ever spoke in tones quieter than a shout. "BONEFACE ELDER. WANT FOR PEACE." He made a placating gesture with empty hands. His eyes lingered on Ganelon—or more aptly, on the bloodied axe in the southerner's grip. "NO MORE KILLING, YES?"

"That depends," said Ganelon.

"THAT DEPENDS," Teresa repeated, clearly having no idea what the words meant. "YOU COME TO VILLAGE. SPEAK WITH CHIEF. HAVE TRADE."

Trade for what? Clay wondered as Gabriel sidled up beside him.

"We're not going to your village," Gabe said. "If your chief wants to speak with us he can come here. But he'd better come soon, or we're leaving."

The elder shook his head. "CHIEF NO COME. CHIEF SICK. YOU CHOOSE NOW: FOLLOW OR FIGHT. MAYBE US DIE. MAYBE YOU. THAT DEPENDS," he added, and Clay realized he'd sort of grasped the meaning of those words after all.

A smart cookie, Teresa.

"Fuck 'em," said Ganelon. "A few dozen of these bone bags against the six of us?" He spat on the barren ground. "Ain't nothin'."

"Ain't nothin'?" Matrick scoffed. "I count at least fifteen bows aimed at you, big guy. You aren't made of stone still, you know."

Ganelon opened his mouth to reply, but Gabe raised a stifling hand and turned to Clay. "What do you think?" he asked.

Clay eyed the wall of wicker shields, white faces, and bristling weapons, wondering how many of those spear tips and arrowheads might be poisoned. The blow darts certainly would be, or else what the hell was the point?

Fighting here or in the village made little difference, since it was likely this was most of what remained of the Boneface warriors, which would explain their sudden willingness to negotiate rather than risk the few fighting men they had left. There were clan wars to think of, and with Dook dead under a tree they could use every spear come springtime.

"We'd might as well go with them," he said finally. "We're screwed anyway."

Chapter Thirty-five

The Cannibal Court

They followed the Ferals back into the tangled forest, striking south until they came to a bluff of chalky white stone. There was a small camp here in which they spent the night. The band was offered shelter in a tall skin tent that had apparently belonged to the Feral champion, Dook. Teresa came to offer them supper, which was in fact just an assortment of severed hands, but Gabriel refused on their behalf, and for a second night running Clay was happy to gobble down whatever Moog's hat was serving up.

Come morning they followed the cliff face west, and as the afternoon waxed the air grew damp and sticky with heat. The trees here were enormous, with trunks that would have taken Clay a full minute to jog around. A troop of orange-furred monkeys tracked them from the canopy above, and upon some unknown signal began screaming and pelting the party with dung.

What Clay assumed was harmless mischief, however, was anything but. One of the sloppy pellets landed on Jeremy's bald head, and the cannibal wailed as the flesh beneath it sizzled and sloughed away. Other tribesmen cowered beneath wicker shields that caught fire when struck. Finally Teresa ordered a return volley of arrows and darts, which scattered the primates and brought one shrieking down with a feathered shaft in its chest.

Moog, naturally, took special interest in its corpse. "Holy Tetrea, they're spark monkeys!" He glanced excitedly at the others, but his enthusiasm was met by his bandmates with underwhelmed stares. "Half my colleagues at Oddsford didn't believe they were real. This might mean the entire pyromate genus exists as well. Scorch apes! Ember chimps! My gods, the ramifications..."

Teresa's Ferals were moving on, eager to be away before their assailants regrouped, and Gabriel led the others after them. Clay, the last to leave the site besides Moog, pretended he didn't see the wizard take a furtive look around before sneaking the dead monkey into his bag.

The sky was beginning to take on a darker shade of purple when the elder informed them they were nearing their destination. Craning his neck, Clay could see a palisade wall on the summit upon which headless corpses were impaled and left to bloat in the sun. Teresa pointed out a narrow switchback trail, and as they climbed the band was treated to the sight of yet more stakes, these ones adorned with severed heads in various states of desiccation. The elder stopped beside one to shoo a crow from pecking at a gory eye socket.

The Boneface village was like most other tribal settlements Clay had visited throughout his years of adventuring, except there were no animals in sight and considerably more body parts lying around. Arms and legs were stacked like kindling beside guttering cook fires; sheets of flayed skin had been left to dry on slatted racks. There were cages occupied by desultory-looking prisoners awaiting their turn in the pot. Most of these appeared to be Ferals from rival tribes, but Clay and the others were asked to wait near to where a massive ettin had been chained by both of its necks to a slab of jutting stone.

Clay had encountered a few ettins in his day. He knew that despite their huge size and monstrous appearance they weren't particularly inclined toward violence. Sure, if you pissed one off they were real bastards, but like any savage thing it helped if you approached them with kindness instead of open aggression.

That being said, the first instinct of anyone confronted by a hulking man-giant with two heads was usually to either run from it or kill it dead.

One of the monster's heads caught Clay staring and smiled toothily. "Good afternoon!"

"Urg . . ." Clay's first attempt at a reply was a hoarse croak. "Hi," he managed eventually.

"Fine weather we're having today, aren't we?" the ettin asked.

Clay looked up. Cobalt clouds of acidic rain crowded the rapidly darkening sky. "Could be worse," he replied with a shrug.

The creature nodded, rattling the collar at its throat. "Indeed it could be. My sentiments exactly."

The other head, which had been sleeping until now, roused itself groggily. When it turned toward Clay it was all he could do not to recoil in horror. It was hideously deformed: its nose a bruised smear, its mouth a gaping hole of shattered teeth. What few wisps of hair it possessed hung limply across a bulbous skull. Its eyes were the yellow-white of curdled milk, and when it spoke it confirmed Clay's suspicion that the creature was blind.

"Is someone there, brother?"

"Yes, Dane," said the first head. "We have illustrious guests! A band, by the looks of them. I'm sorry, I didn't catch your name . . ."

"Clay. Cooper," he said, doing his best not to gawk at the ruinous face. He introduced the others, careful to call Larkspur by her newly assumed name. Gabriel mumbled a greeting, but his eyes were glued to the mountains bordering the western horizon. Ganelon nodded but said nothing, Matrick waved a curt hello, and Moog, ever the amiable one, marched over to shake the ettin's hand.

"Arcandius Moog," the wizard introduced himself. "Archmagus and alchemy enthusiast."

"A pleasure to make your acquaintance, Arcandius," said the first head. "My name is Gregor, and this handsome gentleman is my brother, Dane. Say hello, Dane."

"Hello," said Dane.

Clay was still trying to reconcile the word *handsome* with the abomination before him, and was grateful when Moog took the reins of conversation from his hands.

"Nice to meet you both," the wizard said. He paused to watch two grubby children run past. One was chasing the other, wielding a severed arm like a club. "I only wish it was under better circumstances."

The first head, Gregor, shrugged the shoulder that belonged to him. "The circumstances could hardly be better," he declared. "My brother and I have been honoured guests of the Boneface tribe for several months now. They've gifted us these beautiful golden torcs you see around our necks. They feast us nightly on roast pheasant and warm wine, and in return we've helped them build a proud and glorious wall around their lovely village."

Proud and glorious wall? Clay scowled at the crude palisade encompassing the so-called *lovely* cannibal village. The Ferals had skewered bodies on the pointed tips and used blood to paint vulgar murals on its surface.

Moog was confused as well. "Torcs? Those are—"

"Beautiful, are they not?" Gregor shot the wizard a conspiratorial wink. "I only wish Dane could see how they shine. Alas, my poor brother was born blind, and so it is left to me to describe in detail the splendour of our surroundings."

Dane smiled his awful smile, lifting one hand to the iron slave collar at his throat. "It *feels* beautiful," he said.

"It is!" his brother agreed. "I wouldn't be surprised if it was crafted by the druins themselves."

Clay wouldn't have been surprised if it was stolen from the neck of a dead ox. He didn't say so, though. And neither did Moog.

"You might be right," said the wizard. He wore a crooked smile, and Clay caught the glint of moisture in the old man's eyes. "Indeed, I think you are. Druin forged, no doubt."

Dane's smile widened even further, and Gregor offered Moog a gracious nod.

They waited, and while they did a trio of Ferals went by, each dragging a net crammed with the bodies of those Ganelon and the others (but mostly Ganelon) had slain in the forest earlier. For a brief moment Clay assumed the fallen hunters were to be given a proper burial, but then he remembered where he was. A few nearby villagers looked on hungrily, apparently fine with the idea of eating tomorrow those whom they had called friends today. He practically saw them salivate when the corpse of Dook was hauled into the village.

Gregor described the morbid procession to his brother as it went by. "The brave hunters have returned!" he said. "And oh, what bounty! Dane, I wish you could see. There are spotted deer, and a great white stag whose antlers are so big they scrape furrows in the earth beneath him. They have five—no, six—braces of grouse, and a few fat turkeys. Oh, and here come the pheasants! I hope you're not sick of pheasant, Dane!"

"Never!" cried Dane.

Gregor went on long after the hunters were gone, recounting a pageant so detailed and exotic that Clay almost closed his eyes himself so that he could listen without being betrayed by his sight. Instead, he watched Dane's broken face light up with wonder, and felt a warmth in his heart, the kind that crept up on you during the first stirring notes of a song and then nestled in your lap like a purring cat.

That Gregor put such effort into describing for his brother a world that was so much more appealing than the one in which they actually lived...It was a gift, Clay decided. A profound and extraordinary blessing bestowed upon one whom the world had effectively cursed.

It was damned *noble* was what it was.

A short time later Teresa emerged from the chieftain's tent and scuffed his way over. "CHIEF SEE YOU NOW," he declared, holding up three fingers. "ONLY TWO INSIDE."

Gabriel cocked his head. "Two? Or three?"

"TWO," said Teresa, brandishing the same three fingers.

"I don't..." Gabe shook his head. "Never mind. Clay, Moog, with me."

The elder raised no objections at all when the three of them followed him across the track.

The chieftain's tent was shaped like a cone, the skin of gods-knew-what stretched over a frame of tall wooden poles. There was a steady stream of smoke issuing from a hole at its peak, and when they stepped inside the dim interior it was thick with a haze that smelled oddly familiar.

Glancing down, Clay found himself standing on a fleshy mat with the word *Welcome* etched out in the common tongue. "I..." he began, before a cry from Moog cut him short.

"Kit!"

The ghoul, whom Clay had forgot about entirely until this moment, was standing just inside the door, flanked by a pair of Feral guardsmen. He was still dressed in that bedsheet robe, and had accessorised with a red silk scarf to conceal the grisly wound in his throat.

"Gentleman, hello. I apologise for leaving the ship unattended, but our hosts were rather insistent I accompany them here."

"The ship is gone," Gabe told him. "Burned."

Kit frowned, but before he could respond the wizard stepped up and embraced him. "I thought you were dead!"

"I *am* dead," muttered the ghoul as Teresa offered them each a bowl. The contents looked deceptively like wine. Clay looked warily at his while Kit took a tentative sip.

"It's blood," he warned them.

"Human?" Moog asked.

Clay fixed him with an incredulous glare. "Does it matter?"

The wizard frowned into his bowl without answering.

"COME!" shouted Teresa, beckoning them farther inside the tent. There was a fire pit in the centre; several skulls stuffed with what smelled like Taino's curative weed were nestled among the smouldering coals. Smoke poured from their empty sockets, clouding the tent. Across the pit, Clay saw the Boneface chieftain lying on a bed of black furs. He wasn't sure what he'd been expecting, but a huge naked woman had definitely not been it.

Clay shuddered to imagine how much flesh a person had to consume to grow so large. Her entire body was painted white, so that her massive limbs looked like pale sausages drawn to bursting at her wrists and ankles. Her breasts were sagging pillows on her chest, and her flabby chin rested on a shelf of other, flabbier chins. She wore a headdress that looked like a scaffolding of tiny bones; her black hair coiled through it like vines on a garden trellis. One of her beefy arms cradled a painted red skull, lacquered to a gleam, while the other rested in the lap of a servant, who was kneading the palm of the chieftain's hand.

"Gods of Grandual," Moog gasped. "Her fingers."

Looking closer, Clay saw that her fingers were black and shriveled, like wood reduced to char after a fire. His mind recoiled in horror, and it was an effort not to give voice to the word that echoed like a curse in his head.

Rot.

She wasn't sick, then, as the others had claimed. She was dead. It was only a matter of time. Moog, Clay saw, was transfixed by the infected fingers, like a man matching the gaze of an ancient nemesis.

The elder knelt and murmured quiet words in the chieftain's ear. She said nothing in reply, but handed him the lacquered skull. Teresa scuttled closer to the fire. He pried open the crown and packed it with sticky brown clumps of mudweed before placing the skull among the others on the bed of glowing coals. When it started to smoke he snatched it up and returned to the chieftain. She palmed it with a pudgy hand and held the skull's face to hers, inhaling the vapour trickling from its grinning mouth.

Afterward she sagged into her furs, exhaling smoke in a long, languid stream before saying something too quiet to hear.

Teresa addressed the three of them from his knees. "CHIEF GLAD YOU COME. HAS WANT TO TRADE."

"Trade what?" asked Gabriel.

"THIS ONE," said the elder, pointing at Kit. "IS DEAD MAN. BAD FLESH. NO CAN EAT."

The ghoul self-consciously fingered the red silk scarf at his throat. "That's true. I would taste dreadful."

"WANT TRADE FOR ANOTHER," Teresa announced. "ONE FOR ONE."

Gabe scowled. "You want to trade us Kit in exchange for ... someone else?"

Teresa nodded. "TRADE FOR WING WOMAN, YES."

"They want Sabbatha," Clay said.

"Larkspur," Gabe corrected. "Fine by me." Teresa beamed and began relating the good news to the chieftain.

Moog tore his gaze from the chieftain's afflicted fingers. "What? We can't just *give* them Sabbatha!"

"Who is Sabbatha?" Kit inquired.

"Why not?" Gabriel turned on the wizard. "She's not one of us. She tried to kill us, remember?"

"Yeah, but—"

"But she's changed? Well what if she changes back?"

"I feel like I'm missing something," muttered Kit.

"She might not change back." Moog sounded as though he were trying to convince himself as much as Gabriel. "Taino said she might stay this way forever."

"Or she could snap back tomorrow," Gabe countered. "Anyway, I don't see what choice we have, Moog. It's her or the zombie."

"Revenant," Kit pointed out, though neither Gabe nor the wizard paid heed.

"So what?" Moog spluttered. "We just hand her over? They'll *eat* her, Gabriel."

"NO EAT!" Teresa interjected. "NO EAT WING WOMAN." Some of the fight went out of Moog then, and Gabe actually looked relieved, until the elder smiled excitedly. "USE FOR MAKE BABIES."

Moog threw up his hands, exasperated. "Babies! They're going to *breed* with her, Gabriel. Are you still okay with this?"

"She's dangerous," Gabe murmured, but without his earlier conviction.

Moog jabbed a finger on Gabriel's plate armour. "*You're* dangerous. Heathen's bloody balls, *I'm* dangerous. Ganelon's a natural fucking disaster! Excuse my language," he said to the chieftain, though if she understood him she gave no indication. "So Sabbatha has a sordid past! Don't we all? We've all done plenty of things we're not proud of."

Clay thought of Ganelon trapped in the Quarry, a prisoner in his own flesh. "We can't give them Larkspur," he said. "Or Sabbatha, whichever she is. We just . . . can't."

Gabriel sighed in resignation. "Okay, fine. So Kit stays?"

"I feel like that should be off the table by now," Kit said. "Also, I am lamentably ill equipped for making babies."

"No one stays," Clay uttered.

Gabriel set his jaw. "We fight, then." He glanced around, trying to number the guards within the smoke-shrouded interior of the tent.

There were six, Clay knew, since he'd already counted,

though one was an old man and was holding his spear upside down.

"You and I can handle these," he told Gabriel. "Moog, you get outside and warn the others. Light some fires, maybe open a few of those cages we saw. Gabe and I will be right behind you. Got it?"

Moog closed his eyes. "No."

"Good. Now when . . . wait, *no*?"

"There's another way," said the wizard. "A better way. We don't need to kill anyone, or leave one of us behind."

Clay glanced over Gabriel's shoulder. The chieftain was watching them with the appraising regard of something waiting for you to die so it could peck at your corpse.

"Moog, if it involves faking our deaths I don't think it's gonna work this time."

"No, I know," said Moog. He reached up and pulled the pointed hat off his head. "But this will."

Chapter Thirty-six

Rambling On

Moog was right: They settled it without blood, though the wizard looked close to tears when negotiations ended and he handed the enchanted hat to Teresa, who in turn offered it to the chieftain, who reached her hand inside and drew out a slab of raw red beef.

"She's not even using it right," he complained.

The massive woman wolfed it down almost without chewing, and afterward loosed a tremendous belch, which Teresa took the liberty of translating.

"CHIEFTAIN IS PLEASED," he announced.

"She ought to be," Moog grumbled. "This . . . *walrus* gets free steak for life, and we get stuck with a . . . stuck with a . . ." He trailed off, absently smoothing his beard against the front of his robe.

Clay placed a consoling hand on his shoulder. "Moog, you did—"

"*Her fingers,*" he hissed.

"I saw them."

"No, you didn't. You didn't, Clay. You didn't see them." The wizard's voice skirled higher with every word. He took hold of Clay's arm, his fingers trembling like a child hauled from the waters of a winter lake. "Clay, *they're healed.*"

Clay shook his head. What the wizard said didn't make sense. The rot didn't *heal*. The rot *spread*. The rot withered your flesh and made husks of your organs. The rot killed you. Always.

Moog was starting to bounce on the soles of his feet. A smile that threatened to tear his face in half spread from one ear to another. "They're healed! Clay, look! She's *licking* them!"

And so she was. Scant minutes ago those fingers had been useless, diseased beyond hope of reclamation.

Except apparently not.

Moog slipped around Clay and leapt toward the chieftain's bedside. The guards made to intercept him, but Teresa settled them with a wave. Shooing the servant girl away, the wizard knelt beside the gargantuan woman and flexed his hands like a thief preparing to tackle an especially complex lock. "May I?" he asked.

The woman rolled her big shoulders and offered her right arm to Moog, while the other plunged back into the magic hat and withdrew an uncooked chicken leg.

The wizard marvelled over the pudgy pink fingers. "I can't believe it," he breathed. "They're still a bit stiff, actually, but otherwise . . . I just can't even believe it."

Teresa cleared his throat and pointed toward the chieftain's feet. "SAME HERE. STONE SKIN. IS BETTER NOW."

Sure enough, the woman's right foot was sheathed in a black crust that flaked off as she wriggled her toes. Moog laughed and clapped his hands. "Brilliant! Beautiful!" He looked to his friends. "It's the mudweed. It must be. I mean, it fixed Matrick's arm almost overnight. It set the bones in Sabbatha's wing. Your nose, Clay—it was broken, right? Does it even hurt?"

Clay blinked. "Actually, no." He hadn't thought of it since waking up this morning. He touched it now, cautiously, and found there was no pain at all. It was still crooked, but since he'd had as many broken noses as he'd had birthdays, crooked was the best he could hope for. "But you—" he broke off, because what if it hadn't been the mudweed that cured the rot? Moog might very well have built up his hopes only to see them dashed to pieces again.

"Yes, I smoked it, too," said the wizard, and his eyes drifted to the tip of his left foot. "With everything that's happened, I suppose I haven't...I mean, I can't feel it, but..." He went very still, and Clay could see his dear old friend steeling himself against the possibility of disappointment. With the trepidation of a frightened child kneeling to peek under its bed, Moog reached down and used both hands to remove his soft leather boot, and then slowly, cautiously, pulled off the sock he was wearing underneath.

His face crumpled, and just as quickly reformed—like a mask shattering in reverse. He tried opening his mouth to speak, but couldn't seem to.

And so Clay spoke for him. "It's gone."

"It's gone," Moog gasped, as though he'd been holding his breath. He closed his eyes and exhaled a long, shuddering sigh.

The wizard sat for a while with his boot in his lap. His expression, bathed in the orange glow of smouldering embers, was torn between relief, disbelief, and utter misery. "All those years," he moaned eventually. "So much wasted effort. So many dead ends. But I *knew*. I knew there had to be a way, and now there is. *A cure for the rot*," he said with a mystified chuckle. "No more waiting for death. No more watching it happen. Now we can save them."

He laughed again, but there was a bitter edge to the sound. He grinned, but the grin was a broken thing, and breaking still, until Moog was only baring his teeth below eyes that brimmed over with tears. "I could have saved him," he whimpered, then brought his slender hands to his face and began sobbing.

Clay had no doubt who *he* was. Although Fredrick had been gone for nineteen years, his death was a wound the wizard had cauterized but never, ever allowed to heal.

They stood in silence as the wizard wept, unburdening himself of years and years of unexpressed grief. Only the chieftain seemed indifferent, noisily sucking meat from her chicken leg.

And so it goes, thought Clay. Life was funny, and fickle, and often cruel. Sometimes the unworthy went on living, while those who deserved better were lost.

Or not lost, he considered, since they lingered on in the hearts of those who loved them, who love them still, their memory nurtured like a sprig of green in an otherwise desolate soul. Which was, he supposed, a kind of immortality, after all.

The Boneface Clan held a feast that night in Saga's honour, which Clay thought was tremendously gracious considering Ganelon had killed their greatest champion—not to mention a few dozen other hunters—the day before.

The chieftain remained confined to her tent, but Teresa presented Moog's miraculous hat to the villagers, who had no reservations whatsoever about eating the food it produced. Cannibals were a notoriously adventurous people, culinarily speaking.

Moog had cheered considerably since his breakdown earlier, stowing whatever grief remained to him wherever it was wizards kept such things. In their heads, Clay suspected, and not their hearts. He demonstrated to a crowd of awestruck Ferals the full range of the hat's capabilities.

Out came slabs of roast venison, salted steaks, chicken spiced with subtle herbs, pork tenderloin wrapped in bacon and stuffed with mushrooms. He dazzled the children with bananas, sweet strawberries, clusters of fat purple grapes, and an enormous watermelon, which they took an unsettling delight in smashing open as if it were an enemy's head. For dessert there were custards, cakes, and pies. There was even flavoured ice, a treat favoured by the Narmeeri, and also by Ganelon, who ate three bowls by himself.

Bowls, of course, being a loose term for hollowed-out human skulls.

Matrick was in especially high spirits after learning of Moog's recovery, and Kit had even more good news for Agria's exiled king. When the Ferals demanded the ghoul leave *The Carnal Court*, he had smuggled with him two things besides his precious batintjng. The first was a bottle of sixty-year-old Tarindian Rum, and the second was *Grace*, the dagger Matrick had fumbled back on the ship. The king of Agria kissed the ghoul on the mouth for his trouble.

A long line of suitors formed a queue beside Larkspur, bearing gifts they hoped might persuade the daeva to forswear her companions and breed cannibal babies instead. Among the more interesting offerings was a necklace strung with clattering rat skulls and a shawl made of coarse human hair. One fellow handed her a small pouch from which she withdrew a scrap of old leather.

"What is it?" she asked through a polite smile.

Beside her, Moog spoke around a mouthful of cake. "His foreskin."

Her smile vanished like a snowball lobbed into the mouth of a volcano. Visibly furious, she returned the flesh to the pouch, then tossed the pouch into a nearby fire. The cannibal looked on sullenly as it burned, no doubt wishing he'd bestowed such a princely gift upon someone more appreciative.

Gabriel sat apart from the others, barely eating, distracted by his concern for Rose and gazing west as the sun set beyond the smudge of distant mountains.

*   *   *

The entire village woke to see them off at dawn. The magic hat was still being passed from hand to hand; everywhere Clay looked Ferals were gnawing happily on duck wings, biting into loaves of warm bread, eating salt and sugar by the handful. An old woman was cradling a fish as long as her arm, occasionally hoisting it up so she could lick its scales.

Clay almost said something but decided not to bother. *They'll figure it out*, he decided, watching another man consume an entire banana without peeling it first. *Eventually. Maybe.*

Moog was in a mood again. He was watching the ettin beside which they'd been left to wait the day before. Despite being chained by his throat to a rock, Gregor smiled and waved. After a whispered word in his brother's ear, so did Dane. The wizard waved back, then levelled a gloomy look at Gabriel.

Gabe stirred and looked over. "What?"

The wizard said nothing.

"What?"

Still nothing. But Moog's bottom lip edged out just a little.

Gabriel looked over at Clay, who shrugged. "Fine," he sighed, turning back to Moog. "Go tell Teresa we're altering the deal. The ettin is coming with us."

The Boneface Clan had yet another gift in store for the band, and it was a doozy. Having survived (if not *thrived*) in the Heartwyld for who-knew-how-many generations, they had a comprehensive grasp of local geography. The elder's son, Jeremy, offered to escort them for several days on their journey west, and the young cannibal—his head still pink from where the spark monkey's dung had landed—showed them the secret paths known only to his kind. When the way allowed they moved at a brisk jog, and, thanks to Jeremy's guile, managed to avoid the more treacherous parts of the forest.

Gabriel's mood, which had been dark upon departing the village, grew steadily more optimistic as the days wore on and the low ridge of the Emperor's Mantle became a white-capped wall and then resolved into distant, individual peaks. Clay found himself coming to grips with the skyship's loss as well. Though the first leg of their flight had been relatively benign, the storm had served to show them how quickly things could go south—or straight down, for that matter. On the ground, at least, they weren't so obvious a target, and if something *did* want to kill them it would have to do it the old-fashioned way.

At last Jeremy called a stop at the summit of a hill that sloped away westward, disappearing into a sea of murky trees.

"TIKOO PADA PA KA!" said the cannibal, gesturing first at the forest below and then back the way they had come.

"This is as far as he goes?" Clay assumed out loud.

Moog blinked at him. "I see you've picked up a little of the language."

Clay shrugged. "Here and there," he lied, and saw Matrick cover a smirk with his hand.

After Jeremy departed, Gabriel led them down into woods, though the forest they entered was very different from the one Dane experienced, enthralled as he was by his brother's wildly inaccurate narrative. While they stepped around puddles of toxic sludge, Gregor described sparkling pools of crystalline water. When they ducked below gnarled branches whose leaves dripped poison, Dane strolled beneath the eaves of majestic oaks. According to Gregor, and therefore Dane, the charcoal sky was blue, the ashen grass was green, and the reek of a mangled carcass they came upon was in fact the scent of vividly detailed flowers.

Even the insects received a kind word. One dusk, as the rest of the party plodded through a swarm of orcflies (so-called because they were *hideous* if you looked at them up close), Dane marvelled at a cloud of brilliant moonbugs.

"Wow!" he said, beaming. "I wish I could see them!"

"I wish *I* could see them," Clay muttered, slapping at something on the back of his neck.

They came to a bog, and Gabe led them straight on through. It was waist deep, and the footing was treacherous. More than once Clay stumbled over what he hoped was a submerged log but was probably a rotting carcass. Sabbatha (as he'd finally begun calling her in his own head) looked positively disgusted as she waded through, careful to keep her wings above the sludge. Kit, as well, kept his sacred batingting clear of the muck.

Poor Matrick tripped and went right under. He came up sputtering and groaned, "Oh dear gods, it's in my mouth."

In the heavy mist Clay mistook every jutting branch for the tentacle of some hidden horror, so that when something finally did come boiling up at Ganelon he was almost relieved. The warrior made short work of whatever it was. Once *Syrinx* had cut a few writhing limbs from its body the thing fled and did not return.

Onward they slogged, and for Clay it started to feel like old times again: Gabriel leading the way; Moog and Matrick laughing, or bickering, often both at once. Ganelon stalked with his axe in hand, spoiling for a fight, while Clay brought up the rear, desperate to avoid conflict of any sort. Following the bout of nostalgia, however, he was overcome by a pang of excruciating homesickness. He missed his wife, and his daughter, and his dog. He missed the way his home smelled, the way his bed felt. He even missed standing on the wall all day, looking north at mountains he never planned on crossing.

There was an Old Dominion road leading up out of the bog. It was straight and wide, and despite the filth that covered it the fitted stones were still intact. After wading through waist-deep water for several hours it was a welcome blessing.

"Gotta hand it to the rabbits," said Ganelon, "they sure knew how to make a road."

Sabbatha, walking behind him, tested the span of her wounded wing and winced in pain. "Ouch. Wait, *rabbits?*" she asked.

"A slang term for the druin," Kit informed her. "And not an especially clever one if you ask me. Ah, but you should hear what the druins used to call southerners!" He looked about to expound on this before catching a sidelong glare from Ganelon. "Alas, I . . . seem to have forgotten what it was."

The daeva folded her crooked wing back over her shoulder. "Cool story," she said. "So this road is, what, hundreds of years old?"

"Try a thousand!" crowed Moog. "It's likely this road was in disrepair long before the Dominion fell, and when the Emperor-in-exile came this way four hundred years ago he and his followers found the ruins of a once-mighty city on the other side."

"You mean Castia?" she asked.

The wizard chuckled. "I mean Teragoth—a druin city, much older than Castia, my dear. In fact, it was the son of Grandual's first Emperor who founded the Republic. He and his ancestors built Castia from the ground up, and I've heard you can see the ruins of ancient Teragoth from the city walls."

"You can," said Kit.

"You've never been there?" the daeva asked Moog, who shook his head.

"The mountains were as far west as we ever went. We were hunting monsters, after all, and in Endland, well . . . the Republic took care of its monster problems long ago."

"How so?"

Moog shrugged. "Genocide. Slavery. Second-class citizenship. The usual suspects."

"Nevertheless," said Kit, "the city is quite unlike any you'll see back east. Few of Grandual's strongholds could withstand a siege like the one Castia now endures. Its walls are a miracle of engineering, as are its bridges. And its arena, the Crucible, while not so ostentatious as the Maxithon or the Giant's Cradle, is an undeniably beautiful building, despite its vulgar purpose. But believe me when I say that however beautiful Castia is—or was, rather—Teragoth was more splendid still."

"Or so you've read," said Sabbatha.

The ghoul's laugh was a sound like parchment tearing. "So I've *seen*," he told her. "It's where I was born."

"What? How old *are* you?"

Kit looked mildly offended. "Excuse me? How old are you?"

Sabbatha shrugged. "I stopped counting at sixteen."

"Yes, well, I stopped counting at *six hundred* and sixteen."

"Really?" she asked.

"Really."

They trudged a little farther on before Sabbatha's curiosity caught spark again. "So how did you become a zom—" She closed her mouth before the word *zombie* could trickle out, but Kit huffed as though she'd said it anyway.

"Dead, she means," said Matrick.

"*Un*-dead," clarified Moog.

"Revenant," said Ganelon, and when everyone looked his way the warrior shrugged. "It's really not that hard to remember."

"Exactly," said Kit, fussing with the scarf around his neck. "Thank you. Anyway, it's a long story."

"So what?" asked the daeva. "It's a long road."

"Very well." Kit coughed once to clear his throat, and then began. "I was born in Teragoth, which was ruled by a druin Exarch named—"

"What's an Exarch?" asked Sabbatha.

"Uh . . . like a duke, or a governor . . . except, well, druin."

"Got it."

The ghoul scratched at the wound in the back of his skull. "Where was I? Oh, yes: Firaga, our Mighty Exarch, Scion of Tamarat—"

"Who?"

"Tamarat," Kit repeated, and when Sabbatha shrugged he heaved a ragged sigh. "The druin goddess? Did they teach you nothing in whatever backwater village you hail from?"

The feathers across her shoulders shivered in irritation. "They taught me enough," she grated, and Clay, who had never heard of Tamarat, either, offered a desperate prayer to whichever of Grandual's gods was charged with protecting foppish ghouls from the wrath of angry daevas.

Thankfully, Kit pressed on without further comment. "Anyhow, my parents were slaves—"

"Slaves!?"

Now it was the ghoul's turn to bristle with anger. "Do you want to hear the story or not?"

"I do," said Sabbatha. "Sorry. No more interruptions, I promise."

Kit's eyelids fluttered in what Clay took for skepticism. "We shall see," he said warily. "I should clarify, evidently, that in those days both humans and monsters were slaves to the druins. Humans, my parents included, were generally servants, while our beastly brethren undertook more laborious tasks like quarrying and construction. Despite our bondage, however, we were granted exceptional freedoms—at least until the war broke out and the Exarchs began hurling armies of angry monsters at one another. And don't you dare ask, 'What war?'" he said, preempting the daeva. "I can see it right there on the tip of your tongue! I'll tell you what war in a moment."

"Or you could just skip to the part where you became immortal," she suggested.

"But you'll miss out on the *context*," Kit whinged.

"I don't think it's *that* long of a road," Clay pointed out.

"Very well," sighed the ghoul. "In the interest of brevity I shall abridge the scintillating tale of my wayward youth, omit my discovery and subsequent mastery of the batintjing, ignore my musical heroics during the war against Contha and his implacable golem legions—"

"Musical heroics?" Clay heard Ganelon grumble under his breath.

"—and resume the story after my assignment as Court Musician to none other than Firaga himself. Now, before you go imagining some wild scenario in which I attain immortality by selling my soul to a necromancer, or eating the snow off a mountain peak, I should warn you that the cause itself is actually quite mundane. Embarrassing, even. I was bitten by a peacock."

At this point even Gabriel cocked his head in interest. Dane giggled and whispered something into his brother's ear that sounded a lot like "What an idiot."

"You see? I told you it was dumb. Of course it wasn't *really* a peacock, but the keeper of the Exarch's personal menagerie mistook it for one, and so did I. You see, I used to sneak into the palace at night and . . . entertain Firaga's lovely wife. I would sing to her, or play sweet music on my batingting, and quite often amuse her with a more . . . personal instrument, if you catch my meaning."

"Now we're getting somewhere," piped Matrick, which Clay found odd coming from a man who'd been cuckolded on at least five occasions that they knew of, and probably countless more.

Kit went on. "When her husband came calling she would hurry me out a secret door that led to a private garden, and on one such occasion, while skulking through the artificial trees of the Exarch's fraudulent forest, I crossed paths with the 'peacock' in question. Now I should confess that I'd consumed a vast quantity of wine earlier that evening and was, by this point in time, shit-faced drunk. And in what turned out to be the first of two very bad ideas, I attempted to pet it, and it bit me."

"What was the second bad idea?" asked Sabbatha.

"Killing it," stated Kit. "I bashed that fucking bird to death with my favorite batingting, which just so happened to have been a gift from the Exarch himself. My satisfaction at doing so was short-lived, however, since the bird was not, after all, a peacock. It was a phoenix."

Matrick snorted. "What?"

"A very, *very* old phoenix. I swear upon every eye of Tamarat it looked nothing like you'd expect."

"Unbelievable," said Moog.

"Is a phoenix the one that rises out of ashes?" asked Sabbatha.

"Technically, yes," said the ghoul. "Although *explode* out of the ashes would be a more accurate description of this one's method of rebirth. She set the entire garden on fire and then soared off like a comet. I was forced to flee back through the secret door and into Firaga's bedroom."

"Wow," said Matrick.

"Now *that's* a story," Moog chirped.

"And what did Firaga say when you told him?" asked Sabbatha.

"The Exarch?" Kit lifted grey-green fingers to the gash at his throat, concealed by his red silk scarf. "He killed me, naturally."

Chapter Thirty-seven

The Claw-broker

The old druin road led, unsurprisingly, to an old druin fort. The place was in shambles, though you wouldn't know it to hear Gregor describe the setting to Dane.

"Soaring battlements!" he said of walls that were little more than knee-high rubble. "A pristine tower so tall its heights are lost in cloud" was how he rendered a two-storey ruin cloaked in a mantle of hoary brown lichen. The remains of a statue stood at the centre of a dry fountain. Its head was missing, both arms were broken off, and no detail remained but pitted stone. "You should see it, Dane! The fountain is teeming with schools of little goldfish. They look like coins until they start zipping all over the place. And the statue is magnificent! Smooth white moonstone, with a face so stern and noble I think it must have been an Exarch of the Dominion."

"Or a great warrior!" Dane suggested.

Gregor laughed. "Oh, you're exactly right! There's a sword there on his hip."

"Can I touch it, Gregor?"

"And soil the clean water with our dusty feet? Come, brother, let's explore a bit, shall we?" Dane agreed heartily, and the ettin stalked off beneath a shattered arch.

Moog was shaking his head as he watched them go. "Those two..." he muttered.

The band spread out around the decrepit courtyard. Matrick settled himself on the ground and pulled off his boots, each of which spewed a torrent of bog water and muddy stones when upended. Ganelon leaned against a wall and closed his eyes. Moog and Kit began an animated discussion on druin architecture, while Sabbatha excused herself, stepped through a gap in the wall, and disappeared into the forest. Gabriel watched her go, distrust plain on his face.

Clay shrugged *Blackheart* off his back, kneading the bunched muscles in his shoulder. His back hurt terribly, and there was a knifing pain in his left hip that was worming its way down his leg with every step. His boots were soaked through, and he'd been unconsciously curling his toes as he walked, so they pained him as well.

You're getting old, Cooper, he thought to himself. *And if you think wet boots and a cracked old road are the worst of your problems, just wait till you reach those mountains...*

Gabriel was looking at him with concern. "Your back hurt?" he asked.

Clay realized he'd been grimacing and did his best to convert it into a smile. "My everything hurts," he said.

Gabe chuckled. "I sure do miss beds," he mused.

Clay made the awful mistake of imagining himself in bed, the warm press of Ginny snug against him. He could almost feel the curve of her hip beneath his hand, the tickle of her hair as it grazed his nose. He remembered how that used to bother him, but he'd give anything now to feel that tickling hair, to breathe her in and breathe out pure contentment. He remembered the shape of her back, a harp upon which his fingers had traced a music meant for her alone.

"I miss my tower," said Moog, glancing upward. "And my spiders. And having a roof."

Matrick sighed. "I miss my kids," he said, sounding

mildly surprised. "I didn't think I would. I mean, I love them and everything, and I certainly had my hand in raising them, but they weren't really..."

"Yours?" Moog said.

"Yes, exactly." Matrick laid his boots aside to dry and yanked off his socks, wringing brown water out of each. "But it's not like *they* know their mother was, well..."

"A whore?" said the wizard.

Matrick actually looked affronted. "Trying to kill me. And she's still my wife, remember. Besides, Lilith isn't a..." He swallowed and smoothed back his thinning hair. "She was just...unsatisfied. She thought I was this big-time hero, right? Daring and dashing and all that. But instead I just got..."

"Fat?" Moog supplied.

"Drunk?" said Ganelon.

Matrick glared at them both until the wizard guessed again. "Old! It's old, isn't it?"

"May the Heathen rot your balls," Matrick said politely. "And yes, I got old. And fat. And I was drunk almost every day of our marriage. Is it any wonder she resents me?"

Gabriel snorted at that. "She tried to kill you, Matty. She's *still* trying, remember?" He glanced in the direction Sabbatha had gone.

"Yes, well, it's all a bit extreme, sure," Matrick admitted. "But still. I should have done better. I should have drunk less, eaten less, screwed around less. I was a half-assed king, a shit husband, and now..." His eyes flitted around his circle of friends and then back to his bare feet, as though he were surrounded by mirrors of self-recrimination. "What will my children think of me?" he asked quietly.

Before anyone could offer consolation they heard a scream, then another. The first was Sabbatha, crying out in surprise. The second belonged to a man who stumbled into the courtyard, desperate to escape the daeva's evidently violent response to being caught off guard.

He was wearing a hooded robe that seemed to shift from green to grey as he entered the fort. His torso was criss-crossed with packs and sacks and satchels, and there was a whitewood staff slung across his shoulders and tied with brass pots and glazed decanters that clanged and clattered as he fled from Sabbatha, who came soaring through the gap in the outer wall. Her broken wing wasn't fully extended, but worked well enough to achieve a menacing glide. Her face was livid. She was holding a scrap of her leg armour in one hand, and Clay wondered what she'd been doing when the poor man had interrupted her.

The newcomer retreated from her as fast as he could. He tripped over Matrick's boots but recovered in time to slip deftly between Moog and Kit. He might have dodged Ganelon, too, except the warrior threw out an arm and the man ran directly into it. He landed on his back in a disastrous heap, cracking his head against the moss-carpeted stone.

"*Solusutholon! Usutholosulo!*" cried the man on the ground.

Clay froze with his hand on the haft of his weapon. *That language* . . .

Gabriel stepped between the hooded man and Sabbatha. The daeva reigned herself in with a snarl. Her taloned gaunt-lets curled as she glared at Gabriel, and for a moment Clay wondered if surprise and sudden anger had somehow brought back the memories she'd lost to the storm, but then a black feather floated between them, drawing her gaze, and the fury in her eyes went out.

"He startled me," she said sheepishly. "I thought he was . . ." She paused, taking a closer look. "Wait, what is he?"

Gabriel turned his back to her. "He's a druin."

"Not *that* druin?" asked Ganelon, glancing down.

"No," Gabe said.

The druin looked between them curiously.

Clay stepped forward to offer him a hand. The druin shrugged the whitewood staff from his shoulders before reaching to take it. His grip was strong, but the bones of his hand seemed delicate, like the skeleton of an animal Clay feared he might crush.

"*Dosulon*, friend."

Clay nodded. "*Noluso*," he answered, which he was pretty sure translated to "You're welcome" but might also have meant "cheesy bread." Druic was a tricky language, and it had been decades since he'd had occasion to use it.

The druin favoured Clay with a sharp-toothed smile as he drew back his hood. His hair was long and fine, draped like silver cloth over slim shoulders. A pair of tufted, blue-grey ears sprouted from the top of his head. They were nicked and weathered, but still firm. Some of the older druins Clay had met—Vespian included—had sported ears that drooped like a hound's. This one's eyes were almond shaped, with crescent-moon pupils against orange irises. They were the eyes of a predator, though this fellow didn't come off as particularly threatening.

"You startled me as well," the druin told Sabbatha in common courtspeak. His eyes lingered a moment on the feathers cresting her shoulders before he addressed the others. "I don't see many humans around these parts, as you might imagine."

"What should we call you?" Clay asked him. Since the Dominion's fall, the druins had become a largely nomadic people. They wore names like cloaks, oft-times casting them off in favour of something new.

The druin brightened. "I call myself Shadow."

"What are you doing here?" Gabriel probed.

"I am a scavenger," he answered. "Or a claw-broker, as I believe you call us. I collect whatever I find out here—old weapons, scraps of armour, skins, horn, bone—and I sell it in Conthas or Castia, whichever is like to offer the greater profit."

Moog ran a hand over the bald spot on his head. "Well, I wouldn't visit the Republic anytime soon. There's a Horde besieging Castia." He shot Gabriel a pitying look before adding, "It doesn't look good."

The claw-broker's ears wilted like a flower dead of thirst. "Ah. He's done it, then."

"He?" Gabriel looked suspicious. "You know Lastleaf?"

Shadow nodded. "Of course. He and I were as brothers once, before..." he shook his head as if to dispel some troubling thought. "But he has changed, and is no longer a friend to our kind. He has spent years inciting rebellion in Endland, forging alliances and treating with dark powers, goading the Heartwyld's inhabitants into a frenzy."

"He certainly hates the Republic," said Matrick.

"Not just the Republic," said the druin. "Lastleaf despises any who mistreat the fey, and these days Grandual is as guilty of that as Castia ever was. I fear what is happening in Endland is only the beginning. I suspect he plans on opening the Threshold."

Moog shook his head. "Impossible."

"What's a Threshold?" asked Sabbatha.

"The Thresholds were portals that allowed the Dominion to cross vast distances with a single step," Moog explained. "Druin magic, extremely cunning. There were three of them, or so I've read. Great big arches wide enough to drive an argosy through. One was out west near Teragoth, another in Grandual—Kaladar, to be exact—and the last was somewhere to the east, though I'm not exactly sure where."

"Antica," said Kit.

Matrick scoffed. "Antica?" He looked to Moog. "As in the island old Doshi was always going on about? Is Antica real?"

"Antica was real," Kit assured them. "In fact, its Threshold is still intact. Both are at the bottom of the ocean, however, and the city is infested with mermen."

"Mer...*men*?" Matrick asked.

"What, you didn't think they were all women?"

"*Of course* I thought that. *Everybody* thinks that."

"Excuse me," Shadow cut in. He gestured toward the sword strapped to Gabriel's back. "Is that... *Vellichor*?"

"It is," Gabe confirmed.

The druin's reverence for the weapon was evident. "The blade used by Vespian himself to carve a path between worlds..."

"So they say," murmured Gabriel.

"I'll confess I was...disappointed upon hearing the Archon had given it to a human, but you seem a worthy sort. It would have been a shame for such a treasure to have been lost, or to have fallen into the hands of someone undeserving of its legacy."

Kit's throat made a gurgling sound when he cleared it. "A scavenger, for instance."

Shadow paid the ghoul no mind at all. "May I see it?" he asked.

Gabriel smiled warily. "Maybe later," he said.

His answer seemed to satisfy the claw-broker. "Will you be spending the night, then? I visit this fort whenever I pass through the Bone Marsh. It is as safe a haven as one is likely to find in the Wyld."

Gabriel looked up, peering beyond the crumbling battlements at the darkening sky above. "Looks like," he said.

Chapter Thirty-eight

Tamarat

"So these Thresholds," wondered Sabbatha, "they're broken, right? Or else why not use the one in Kaladar to reach Castia instead of walking all the way there?"

They had built a fire in the courtyard and shared out the meagre supply of rations Gabriel had wisely procured in Conthas before they left. As he had during every meal since departing the Boneface village, Moog grew sulky, lamenting the loss of his enchanted hat. The daeva's question lifted the spell of melancholy in an instant.

"Well, they're not actually *broken*," he informed her. "They just...don't work."

"So they're broken," said Ganelon, which earned him a scowl from Moog and a sly smile from Sabbatha.

It had been days, Clay realized, since he'd felt the pull of the daeva's uncanny allure. So far as he could tell, none of the others were affected by it, either. Gabriel, he supposed, was too focused on Rose to give a damn. Matrick was afraid of her, and the daeva wasn't exactly Moog's cup of tea. And Ganelon...well, the warrior wasn't especially susceptible to enchantment. He could turn down a naked succubus if he had to—Clay had seen him do so, in fact.

"Well." The wizard looked to Kit. "Correct me if I'm wrong,

but I believe each Threshold requires a keystone without which it will not open."

"And let me guess: The keystones are lost?"

"Indeed they are," said Moog, "or we'd have been to Castia and back by now."

"And we'd have a Heartwyld Horde pouring out of the Threshold in Kaladar," said Ganelon.

The wizard bobbed his head. "Well, yes, that too. So it's probably for the best."

Gabriel, who was sitting cross-legged by the fire with *Vellichor* across his lap, looked over his shoulder at Shadow. "You mentioned Lastleaf might try and open the Threshold near Teragoth. How?"

"Technically speaking," said the druin, "not all of the keystones are lost."

The claw-broker was kneeling near a breach in one wall of the fortress, striking flint over a charm made of broken twigs. He'd set a number of them around gaps in the perimeter, claiming the smoke (and no doubt a dose of druin magic) would ward off predators. When he looked toward the fire his eyes flashed like an animal's in the dark.

Moog craned his neck to look at him. "They aren't?"

Shadow finished lighting the last of his charms and trotted back into camp. He gave Gregor and Dane a wide berth as he did so, and Clay wondered if it was because the ettin was a monster or because Dane, having listened to his brother describe the druin's ears earlier, had giggled and asked, *Like a bunny rabbit?* To which Gregor had replied, *Exactly!*

Shadow settled himself on the ground between Sabbatha and Matrick. His robes were changing colour as he moved, Clay was sure of it now. This close to the fire they were the pale grey of day-old ashes, mottled with shades of blue and pale orange.

He rifled through one of his dozen satchels as he spoke. "Well, Antica's keystone was lost when the city was claimed by the sea, and the key to Kaladar's Threshold was in the hand of that city's Exarch when a slag drake swallowed him, so we can assume that it, too, was destroyed."

A safe assessment, Clay mused. He had seen a slag drake only once, and if asked to describe it he might have said it was something between a giant lizard and a small volcano: skin like fire-glazed stone, and a mouth that opened onto an inferno and belched out globs of magma that could disintegrate steel. So yeah, it was safe to say that particular keystone was (like the Exarch who'd been holding it) long gone.

Moog leaned forward like a kid at a hearth-fire story. "And the last?" he prompted.

The druin sighed. He drew forth a handful of what looked like small black seeds, sorting through them with a pale finger. "Teragoth's keystone is rumoured to be still intact, though setting hands upon it would prove somewhat...troublesome."

"How so?" asked Ganelon.

"Because it is still *in* Teragoth," said Shadow, showing his jagged teeth. "But so is Akatung."

Matrick blinked. "Did you say Akatung? As in the *dragon* Akatung?"

"The very same," said Shadow. He leaned forward and scattered the seeds on the fire. They popped quietly and gave off a sweet-smelling smoke.

Moog frowned at that, but his thoughts were elsewhere. "I thought we killed him."

"We only injured him," Clay murmured. He remembered telling the same thing to Pip and his friends in the King's Head what seemed like an age ago.

"I put *Vellichor* through his jaw," said Gabriel.

"I cut him open pretty bad," added Ganelon. "He was holding his guts in when he flew off."

Shadow looked suitably impressed. "Well, his...guts, as you say...remained within, I'm afraid. He retreated to Teragoth, where he lairs in the bowels of the shrine to Tamarat."

Sabbatha frowned. "But isn't Teragoth within sight of Castia? Why haven't they just killed him and taken back the keystone?"

"Because Akatung is immensely powerful," said the claw-broker. "And they dare not risk his ire. Castia's walls are high and strong and well defended—which is why neither the dragon, nor Lastleaf's Horde, have breached them. But if provoked, Akatung would wreak havoc on their lesser settlements, and so they have an uneasy truce."

Both of the ettin's heads yawned at once. Clay caught a whiff of Dane's fetid breath and pretended to scratch at something just under his nose. "Good night, Gregor," Dane muttered.

"Night, Dane," said his brother. They promptly fell asleep on their back, snoring into one another's faces.

Gabriel looked off into the surrounding darkness. Shadows pooled in the hollows around his eyes. "So the keystone is part of Akatung's hoard?"

The druin spread his hands. "Presumably. Few have seen a dragon's hoard and lived to speak of it."

Few indeed, thought Clay. He'd known someone who had. One of their old bards had signed on without telling them she'd stolen something precious from Akatung's hoard. They found that part out the hard way, when the dragon came at them out of nowhere like a typhoon with scales. They'd managed to drive it off, mortally wounding it in the process. Or so they'd thought.

The bard had died, of course. As bards tended to do.

"It is evident, I suppose," Shadow went on to say, "that if Lastleaf should manage to coerce the dragon into relinquishing Teragoth's keystone..."

"He could put a Horde in the heart of Grandual before anyone could stop him," finished Matrick. The ruins of Kaladar were within a day's hard ride from Brycliffe Castle; Agria's capital city would very probably be their first target.

"Tell me about Lastleaf," said Gabriel to the druin. "When I met Vespian he was hunting his son. He said Lastleaf stole something from him. Something dangerous."

Shadow pursed his lips. *"Tamarat."*

Gabe paused. "The goddess?"

"The sword," said the druin. "Named for the lost goddess of druinkind. And yes, Lastleaf took it from his father. He carries it still, in a bone-white scabbard upon his back."

Clay remembered seeing the sword at Lindmoor, and again in the gorgon's manse. Of the three blades borne by the druin, it was the only one Lastleaf had not yet drawn.

"What's so special about this sword?" Clay asked, sharing a pointed look with Gabriel. "The Archon seemed pretty desperate to find it."

Shadow was watching the fire. Its light wavered in his eyes, gleamed on his teeth as he spoke. "Vespian was, among other things, a powerful sorcerer, and an unparalleled craftsman. He created weapons of formidable power, most of them swords. You have met Lastleaf, I assume? You've seen the other blades on his back?"

"We have," said Clay, who'd been curious about the druin's trio of scabbards since the Council of Courts.

"One is called *Scorn*," said the druin, "which the Archon fashioned for Lastleaf when he came of age. It is a . . . volatile weapon, capable of great destruction. The other is *Madrigal*, the singing sword, a gift from Vespian to the Exarch of Askatar."

"And the Exarch of Askatar . . . gave it to him?" Matrick asked, though his tone suggested he knew better already.

"Her name was Nyro, though after the Dominion fell she was called Sourbrook. She was one of Vespian's most capable scouts, and one day—this was several hundred years ago, mind you—she found what the Archon had sent her to look for. She tried to capture Lastleaf, but instead he killed her, and took her weapon for himself."

Clay remembered that second blade, *Madrigal*, ringing

like a bell when Lastleaf had drawn it in the Maxithon. He wondered how many other of the Archon's weapons had survived the Dominion's fall, and whether Ganelon's axe wasn't one of them.

Shadow reached up to scratch the back of one tall ear. "*Vellichor*, of course, remains his most remarkable creation. It was used, as you are no doubt aware, to shape a door through which the druins, my ancestors, escaped the ruin of their own realm."

Clay had never known whether or not to believe that was true, though he could think of no better explanation for the world he so often glimpsed through the flat of *Vellichor*'s blade. He found himself unable to doubt it any longer.

"In this new world, however, we found ourselves afflicted by a most paradoxical curse: We were immortal, insofar as we could not die except by violence, and yet our mothers could give birth to but a single child. Our numbers began to dwindle. One by one we burned out, or were snuffed like candles in the wind, our entire race destined one day to flicker into smoke and disappear forever. But such, alas, is the fate of every fire." The druin smiled sadly. "Consequently, druin children are especially precious, and so Vespian was overjoyed when his wife, Astra, announced she was with child. In time she gave birth to a daughter."

"Hold up," Sabbatha said. "Is Lastleaf not Vespian's son? How could he have two children? Did he have two wives?"

Kit threw up his hands, exasperated. "Good luck telling a story around this one," he said to Shadow. "Constant interruptions! No patience at all for dramatic exposition."

The druin's ears slanted sideways, thoughtful. "To be fair: She is mortal, while we are not. Her candle is burning down much quicker than ours."

The ghoul put a finger to his bloodless lips, pondering. "Fair point," he said.

"Go on," urged the daeva, and when Kit shot her a glare

she raised her hands. "What? You heard him! My candle's burning and all that."

Shadow went on. "Sadly, Astra perished shortly after giving birth to her daughter. It is rare among our kind, but not unheard-of. The Archon was beside himself, driven mad by grief, despairing of an eternity without his beloved wife by his side. And so in despair he did a thing—a terrible thing— that has shaped this realm forever after and may yet see it destroyed. He forged a final sword."

Gabriel's eyes narrowed. "*Tamarat*."

"Not since *Vellichor* had Vespian invested such power into a weapon, and I believe he paid a dearer price in the making, for he was...changed afterward. Darker, as you will see. For this new blade's purpose was singular, and singularly evil: If used to take the life of a druin—and *only* a druin—it could resurrect the woman for whom it had been made."

"Bugger me beardless," Moog hissed. *"Necromancy!"*

"Indeed," said Shadow. "And in the grip of madness, resentful of what the child's life had cost him—and perhaps, it must be said, to keep the nature of this abhorrent new weapon a secret—the Archon used the sword upon his infant daughter—"

"Liar!" Gabriel's hand leapt instinctively to *Vellichor*'s hilt.

"Let him finish!" barked Ganelon.

Gabriel looked beseechingly toward Clay, who wished to hell he could unhear what he'd just heard about a druin he'd thought a noble man, could do nothing but shrug. "We should hear him out, Gabe."

For a long, charged moment it looked as though Gabriel might actually draw his sword, but at last he took a calming breath and withdrew his hand, clasping it firmly with the other. "Go on," he told the druin.

"Astra, needless to say, was also changed. She despised Vespian for having sacrificed their daughter. She grew despondent, and within months of her resurrection she could no longer suffer the burden of grief, and so took her own life. But Vespian...Vespian brought her back. And when she killed herself once more, he used his cursed blade to revive her. Again and again she was revived, until..." He broke off.

"Until?" prompted Sabbatha.

"What came back was not Astra. Not anymore. The woman who wore her flesh was colder now, indifferent to beauty, or sorrow, or love. She became preoccupied with necromancy, and began to practice it without compunction. At first she revived only trivial things: flowers, birds, insects. The druins themselves are typically immune to such magic, which is why *Tamarat* exists in the first place, but before long she was bringing beloved servants back from the grave, or raising a slave who had collapsed dead from exhaustion.

"By now, Astra's erratic behaviour and the Archon's willingness to sacrifice his people was causing unrest throughout the Dominion. Soon after, Vespian lost his hold on the Exarchs. They rebelled against him, against one another, and so began the war that would spell the end of druinkind. But in the meantime, miraculously, Astra announced she was expecting a second child."

Sabbatha, of course, cut in. "But you said—"

"One child *per life*." Shadow raised an admonishing finger. "And it would seem undeath counted as her second. She gave birth to a son."

"Dear fucking gods..." Moog was holding his head as though he feared it might crack apart.

The claw-broker nodded. "The boy grew up sickly and strange, an outcast from the moment he was born. Who both loved and feared his mother, yet despised his father for the evil he had wrought. Who stole *Tamarat* from Vespian and fled into the Heartwyld, that the cycle of his mother's horrid half life might finally be broken."

Gabriel's eyes were downcast, fixed upon the sword he'd inherited, the blade itself a shard of a shattered world.

"This story..." Matrick was rubbing the grey-shot whiskers on his chin. "It's familiar, isn't it? Like I've heard it before somewhere, only told in a different way."

"Or sung," said Kit enigmatically, as if he'd already reached the conclusion Matrick was grasping for.

Shadow's smile was that of a benevolent father, or a kindly priest, which made what he said next all the more ironic. "I imagine you have. Indeed, you already know the names of Vespian's ill-fated children. The daughter, Glif. The son, Vail."

Glif...Vail

Clay felt his mouth go dry. A hollow he hadn't known was inside him yawned open, wide as an abyss, deep as the fathomless dark between stars, as his mind, reeling, gave names—*druic* names—to Grandual's so-called gods.

Vespian, the Summer Lord. Astra, the Winter Queen. Glif, the Spring Maiden. Vail, the Autumn Son, known also as the Heathen.

The Heathen...Lastleaf.

"No," he heard himself groan, as something in the fire snapped and gave off a puff of drifting smoke.

Clay had never been a particularly religious man. He offered prayers infrequently, and to no one in particular. But to learn that the gods of your people were not only a myth, but a myth derived from the sordid lives of an elder race that had once kept them as slaves...Even the most pragmatic mind would baulk at reconciling such a thing.

A long silence descended on the camp, as each of them digested—or tried to, anyway—the implications of Shadow's story.

Moog sniffed, sat up, and peered into the dark outside the circle. "Does anyone else smell that?"

"Smell what?" Gabe asked, stirring from a stupor of his own.

Sabbatha stifled a yawn. "The ettin farted, I think."

Moog shook his head. "No, it's something I...I can't put my finger on it..."

Gabriel laid his hands flat upon *Vellichor's* scabbard. "Even so," he said finally. "Lastleaf has gone too far. We can't allow him to destroy Castia. And if he opens that Threshold he could threaten all of Grandual."

Shadow nodded. The druin appeared to be deep in thought as well. "As you say."

Something else cracked in the fire, and another plume of smoke went up, blue-green against the black of night. Matrick, Clay saw, was asleep where he sat, chin-to-chest and already drooling.

Suddenly, Moog stood up. "WINKFLOWER!" he shouted. "UP! WAKE UP!" He snatched up a spoon and a copper pot and started banging them together, striding in a circle around the camp.

Matrick jolted awake, knives spinning into his hands. Sabbatha, too, had drifted off, and now looked around wild-eyed. Gregor and Dane slept on, unperturbed by the sudden clamour.

Gabriel sat up, blinking. "Moog, what the—"

"It's him!" Moog pointed at Shadow. "The seeds he threw on the fire! Winkflower! I knew it! I knew I knew that I knew it! He's trying to kill us!"

Shadow spread his hands. "The seeds are harmless," he declared. "I only thought you could use a restful sleep."

Ganelon stood like a dark tower rising. He had *Syrinx* in hand—glowing now, whispering unfathomable words to the forest night—and shook his head to clear it of the druin's spell. "Like hell you did."

The claw-broker remained seated, though Matrick and Sabbatha both edged away from him. And then Shadow grinned, sharp teeth painted red by the fire.

"Very well," he said. "But you should know I had not planned on killing you. I only sought to take what was rightfully mine." The druin's nature was changing rapidly, like spring turning to winter without all the fun stuff in between.

His eyes had settled on Gabriel, who was first among them to comprehend the druin's intent.

"You mean *Vellichor*?"

"It should not belong to you, human. That sword was never meant for mortal hands. The Archon made a grave mistake when he placed it in yours. You have *no idea* what it is you are holding."

"Why don't you tell me then?" said Gabriel. He wore a sneer that Clay recognized from way back—the one he used to put on whenever some villain waxed poetic about their plan to destroy this town, or assassinate that queen, or summon some unholy demon from the icy depths of hell.

"It is a key," said Shadow, and Clay saw Gabriel's sneer wilt just a fraction. "Lastleaf said that *Vellichor* is our only means of going home, to return at last to *our own world*."

"A world your people left for a reason," said Kit soothingly. "If you—"

The claw-broker spat on the fire. "*Kaksara!*"

Clay didn't know many druic curse words, but he knew that one, and he took insult on behalf of Kit's long-departed mother. Clay's heart started to pound. The blood in his veins ran hot, and his right hand flexed, itching to feel the familiar weight of *Blackheart*'s grip. There was violence coming. He could feel it in the air, foreboding as clouds before a summer storm.

The druin was still seated, but he seemed menacing nonetheless. The light from the fire seemed to throw his shadow in every direction. One of his hands, Clay saw, had curled around the haft of his whitewood staff.

"Give up the sword," said Shadow, "or I will take it, and do Lastleaf the favour of killing you besides. It may be that his vision exceeds our own. The Dominion had its time, and now the Courts. Perhaps the age of fey and fell things is at hand."

"Here we go," said Matrick, groaning as he got to his feet.

Moog was already rifling through his pack. "Friggin rabbits," he muttered. "So friggin dramatic all the time..."

Sabbatha's gauntlets curled into fists. Ganelon remained where he was, patient as a mountain in the breath before an avalanche. Clay dipped his shoulder, and *Blackheart* fell into his right hand, while his left grazed the ice-cold haft of his hammer.

Gabriel, finally, climbed wearily to his feet. "Listen, we don't have to—"

"Yes," said Shadow, "we do." He bolted upright, staff in hand, and Clay watched as a swirl of inky blue smoke revealed the wicked white blade at its head, concealed until now by what he could only assume was subtle druin sorcery.

It wasn't a staff, after all. It was a scythe.

Chapter Thirty-nine

The Spirit Beneath the Skin

So the scythe was worrying. It appeared to be made of bone, possibly the wing of something the size of a horse. But more troublesome still was Shadow's other, more unconventional weapon.

He loosed a breath that tore like a gale through the smoke above the fire. It blew past Gabriel and took on a form of its own, the same shape and size as Gabe himself, also bearing a massive sword that looked solid enough as it arced toward Gabriel's head.

Vellichor came free of its sheath in a blur of starlit night, dispelling the shade-figure the moment the two blades met, but already the druin was gesturing toward one of the smoking wards he'd set up around the perimeter of the camp. It raked through Ganelon and coalesced into a murky double of the deadly southerner.

Clay heard Matrick groan, "Oh *hell* no."

"He's mine," growled Ganelon, springing toward the shade of himself. It flew to meet him, and when their axes met the phantom not only remained intact, it chopped a grey hand into Ganelon's throat and sent him staggering.

Sabbatha dared a leap toward Shadow, ducking the scythe's first swing and dancing wide of the second. Matrick lunged from the opposite side, but the druin turned and lobbed a plume of smoke straight into his face. Momentarily blinded, Matrick sketched a defensive skein between him and Shadow, which did nothing to protect him from the apparition behind him. One dark knife opened a gash in his shoulder, while the other barely missed his ribs as he twisted in pain.

Clay saw the druin glance in his direction. Too late, he turned to see the smoke from another ward sweep toward him. Like an idiot, he braced behind his shield, and so managed to avoid being rendered blind by the gust. When he turned it was slowly, with a kind of shame, to face off against the spectre of himself.

"Hi," he said lamely. His shade said nothing as it unslung the hammer at its hip. Clay sighed. "It's gonna be like that, is it?"

Gabe, meanwhile, was fighting off phantoms as fast as Shadow could make them. *Vellichor* alone seemed able to dispel them with a single stroke. Ganelon was locked in a fierce melee with his own, while Moog, yelping and springing this way and that, had managed to elude the druin's attempts to double him.

But really, Clay had time to wonder as his spectre sized him up, *what harm could a phantom-Moog do?*

Matrick was scrambling from his own doppelganger, entirely on the defensive, which left Sabbatha alone to deal with the druin.

Or not entirely alone.

Kit staggered toward Shadow, wielding the only weapon he had to hand: his precious batingting, the scourge of phoenixkind. The druin, whose innate ability to glimpse the immediate future would be infallible against something so slow as a lurching ghoul, dodged fluidly and lashed out with the scythe, severing all one hundred and four strings of the world's only batingting at once with a sound like glass chimes shattering.

"This is *exactly* why I don't get involved in this sort of thing," Kit grumbled before a kick from Shadow sent him sprawling.

"*Umbra,*" said Shadow, tipping the scythe's blade so it gleamed like pearl in the moonlight. "A less elegant weapon than *Vellichor*, perhaps." He kicked one half of the destroyed batingting toward Sabbatha's feet. "But it gets the job done."

Clay's shadow-self finally summoned its courage and charged, leading with its shield. Clay met it with his own, swinging his hammer at the phantom's left side. The phantom, unsurprisingly, did exactly the same thing, and Clay winced as he felt the blow land. The chain links of his armour soaked up most of the damage, but his ribs warned him not to let it happen again. He and his double each launched another strike—hammers bounced from the faces of black shields—and then stepped back to assess one another.

"This might take all day," Clay muttered.

He saw Moog leap on the back of Matrick's shade, buying time for Matrick to swipe the dust from his eyes. By the time he did the wizard had suffered an elbow to the face and a nasty cut on his forearm, which spurred Matrick into a rage. He attacked in a frenzy, and as Moog stumbled away Matrick and his phantom exchanged a flurry of swipes and stabs so fast Clay could see nothing but a blur of steel and shade between them.

Ganelon grunted in pain as his shade opened a gash on his cheek. Sharp as *Syrinx* was, he was lucky to have kept his jaw at all. Beyond belief, however, he was grinning, and his expression only brightened as he and the illusory Ganelon hurled themselves at each other.

Shade-Clay came on again, this time leading with the hammer. Clay's first instinct was to offer up his shield, weather the blow, then try to counter with one of his own. It was what his double—being the pragmatic sort of doppelganger—would no doubt expect.

So instead Clay swung his own hammer, striking the phantom's weapon with a shrill ring that pierced his ears and sent a tremor up his arm. It was an awkward move, leaving them both unbalanced, but Clay, at least, had been expecting it. He recovered first, ramming *Blackheart*'s rim up beneath the phantom's chin. Its head snapped backward, and Clay murmured an apology as he brought *Wraith* arcing down into the thing's face.

It broke like a log turned to char, and was gone.

A yelp drew him round in time to see Moog trip over the ettin's out-flung arm. Dane came awake with a snort, and Gregor mumbled groggily as they sat up. "Is it morning already?"

Clay looked from the ettin to Shadow, who was already in motion. The druin tore open one of the sacks at his waist and lobbed a handful of grainy dust into the air. Thankfully, Moog had gained his feet and was standing between Shadow and the ettin, but when he saw Shadow take a breath he sprang out of the way.

"Moog, *wait*!" Clay called, too late.

Shadow exhaled. The dust-cloud enveloped the bewildered ettin, and Clay's heart sank. It took an effort to keep his knees from buckling, to not simply close his eyes and wait for the world to bash his brain open—because it was oh-so-obvious that it *wanted* to, or else why in the Frost Mother's unspeakable name did this sort of shit keep happening to him?

The phantom that took shape behind Gregor and Dane was monstrous. The first thing it did was reach down and knock the two heads of the ettin together, rendering them unconscious.

Of course that happened, thought Clay sourly. He shook his head, trying to comprehend how a single druin had got the better of five men, one woman, a ghoul, and half a giant.

"Clay." Gabriel's hand was on his shoulder. "I've got this."

Clay scoffed. "You've got *that*?"

"Go help Lark—" Gabe stopped himself. "Go stop Shadow. Knock him out, pin him down—but try not to kill him."

"Why not?"

"Because once we kill Lastleaf he might be the only druin left alive," said Gabriel. He took off running, leapt over what remained of the fire, and rolled beneath the massive phantom's swiping hand. *Vellichor* hewed into the creature's leg. It stumbled, but even the fabled blade couldn't hope to dispel a shade so huge with a single slash.

Clay spared a glance for Ganelon (forced by his shade through a gap in the outer wall) and Matrick (sweating and sparring furiously against his own double) before rushing to Sabbatha's aid. The daeva was backed against the ruined fort, ducking as the bone scythe struck shards from the brick above her head.

Shadow was turning just as Clay hit him from behind. The druin weighed so little Clay found he'd misjudged his momentum. They both pitched forward—which was fortunate, since Shadow hit the wall, spun, and brought the scythe across where Clay's head might have been were he not face-down on the ground with a mouthful of dirt. Sabbatha seized the opening, stepping in to deliver a steel-shod punch that Shadow somehow managed to dodge. Her fist cracked stone as if it were dry plaster.

"*Fuck*," she swore, but before she could try again Shadow darted past her, shifting his hold on the scythe and levelling it for another swing.

Clay surged to his feet just as the druin attacked. He thrust *Blackheart* toward the tip of the scythe and was relieved when it didn't split the shield down the middle. It *did* pierce through, however: he could see the pale glint of its tip just inches from his grip. Clay tilted *Blackheart* abruptly, wrenching the scythe from Shadow's grip.

"No!" The druin dove frantically for his weapon, but Clay stamped down on the haft, grinning like a village bully as his enemy tried in vain to retrieve it.

"Hey," he said, prompting Shadow to look up at him. When he did Clay swung his hammer backhanded, catching the druin alongside the head and laying him out cold. Clay turned to Sabbatha. "You okay?"

The daeva was leaning against the wall. Her eyes were

wide with fear and fury. "Thanks to you," she replied through gritted teeth.

Clay nodded once, his feet already taking him toward the open courtyard, where Gabriel was giving ground against the ettin's hulking shade. The thing was moving terribly fast, and Gabe couldn't hope to keep up with it for long.

Just then a heavy punch clipped Gabe and sent him stumbling into the rim of the ancient fountain. He inadvertently avoided the phantom's next swing as he went spilling over the ledge. The statue shattered overhead, raining stones and dust.

Clay raced past Matrick and his double just as Moog hurled a chunk of old masonry at the king's shade. The shade used a pommel to smash the piece in half, leaving itself open to Matrick's attack. The daggers darted in, staggering it, and then Matrick unleashed what remained of his energy, his hands a blur as he savaged the thing with a barrage of killing slices. It dropped a moment before Matrick did, and neither of them were getting up anytime soon.

Gabe was on his feet, but barely. He managed to fend off one of the phantom-ettin's attacks, but was grievously out of position as its other fist rose to pummel him.

Clay decided to yell, but then realized he was already yelling. The phantom half-turned in alarm, so when he hurled himself into the side of its knee it toppled awkwardly, pinning him to the ground beneath one of its legs. He craned his neck in time to see Gabriel launch himself from the fountain's edge.

Vellichor was clasped in two hands, the stars of an ancient world visible beyond the blade. It came chopping down, and Clay felt the body above him jolt as both the phantom-ettin's heads were sheared away at once. The hulking shade crumbled into an astonishingly small pile of dust, and for a few breaths Clay simply lay on his back without worrying whether or not something or someone was still trying to kill him. He heard a distant clang, then another, and suddenly remembered seeing Ganelon and his doppelganger spilling out through a breach in the wall. He forced himself to rise. Nearby, Gabriel was doing the same.

His friend flashed him a jaded grin. "How's your back feeling now?"

"Broken, I think," Clay replied, but still he staggered toward the sound of fighting. He heard Gabriel follow, clearly exhausted, his sword scraping on the ruined flagstones behind him.

If Matrick and his double had looked like a pair of sparring cats, Ganelon and his phantom were tigers, prowling in circles, conserving their energy for brief, brutal attacks that left one bloody and the other oozing wisps of black smoke.

Clay and Gabriel drew up short, neither in a hurry to enter the fray. You didn't stand between the surf and the sheer cliff, did you? Or step between two charging bulls and pick a side. You simply stood and watched, because to intervene was pointless and very obviously stupid. Nevertheless, Clay hoisted his shield and prepared to do just that.

But then Ganelon glanced over, stopping Clay in his tracks. Clay, in turn, held out an arm to stop Gabriel, and when his friend opened his mouth to ask why he told him, "Don't bother. I think it's over."

By the time he looked back it had already begun: Ganelon sprang forward, *Syrinx* chopping in sideways. The phantom matched the swing with one of his own; metal screamed and sparks bloomed like fireworks through which Ganelon was already moving, shouldering his opponent off balance as he whirled with the momentum of his deflected axe, slashing in from the opposite side. The double was already moving to defend itself—because it *was*, after all, a mirror of the man with whom it fought.

But what does a mirror know? What can it show us of ourselves? Oh, it might reveal a few scars, and perhaps a glimpse—there, in the eyes—of our true nature. The spirit beneath the skin. Yet the deepest scars are often hidden, and though a mirror might reveal our weakness, it reflects only a fraction of our strength.

Ganelon had been born into slavery. He'd watched as his mother was flayed to death, and had murdered seven men a day after his eleventh birthday. He'd crossed the desert on foot, without food or water, gorging himself on the flesh and blood of vultures foolish enough to think him dead. He'd hacked his way out of a sand maw's belly and slashed his way into a castle guarded by four hundred men. He'd killed 2 gorgons, 4 giants, 17 harpies, 1,978 kobolds (which accounted for nearly 1 percent of the entire kobold population) and had slain an innumerable legion of awful things besides. Oh, and he'd killed a chimera pretty much by himself. Ganelon had spent nineteen years frozen in the dark, alone but for his festering thoughts, counting dust motes as a nomad counts stars on an endless journey.

The phantom, however, had done none of these things, and so when Ganelon poured not only his strength, but his *power* into the blow that followed, *Syrinx* smashed through the southerner's shade as though it were a spiderweb made of glass. It shattered into smoke and was instantly, utterly, destroyed.

Which left Clay wondering why the fuck Ganelon hadn't simply done that in the first place. He might even have been foolish enough to ask had Moog not shouted suddenly from inside the fort.

"Larkspur, wait!"

Gabe's face went pale. "Did he just say—"

"He did," Clay confirmed, already slogging back through the breach in the wall.

It was dark in the courtyard, save for the smouldering fire and the eerie blue light of the forest moon. Moog was sitting on the ground beside Matrick, and Clay followed the aim of his out-flung arm to where Shadow was awake and on all fours, spitting out blood and a handful of jagged teeth. To where, more worrying, the daeva stood over him with the scythe in her hands.

Larkspur, or Sabbatha (Clay wasn't sure which of the two he was looking at now), reached out and closed her metal talons around the druin's sagging ears, yanking him upright. There was wild fear in Shadow's face, the horror of an immortal gazing into the empty void of oblivion. He opened his mouth as if to scream, but only gaped in terror.

"Sabbatha!" Clay shouted. He saw her hooded eyes flicker toward him for one instant, but in the next the wicked bone blade lashed out, beheading one of the very last druins the world would ever know.

Chapter Forty

Cinnamon Smoke

Clay had endured a great many uncomfortable meals in his life, most of which had come during the past months alone: supper with Kallorek and Valery, breakfast with Lilith and Matrick's host of illegitimate children, cold eggs and sausage on the morning Jain had robbed them (for the second time), not to mention a banquet hosted by cannibals. This particular breakfast, however, was chief among them.

They ate dry biscuits and jam, though Clay suspected the biscuits had been made with salt in place of flour, and the jam was filled with bitter seeds, one of which had lodged itself between two of his teeth and was threatening to hang up curtains.

Moog brewed tea and then settled down to pore over the contents of Shadow's many pouches. Gregor and Dane sat together (as if they had any choice in the matter) and discussed the curious dream they'd shared the night before. Matrick wolfed down his food before promptly falling back asleep, while Ganelon didn't bother to get up at all. Kit sat cross-legged beside the fire, staring down morosely at the broken halves of his batinting.

Clay felt bad for the ghoul's loss, but considering he'd discovered yesterday that the adversary against which the band had pitted themselves was in fact the Heathen himself, the loss of an instrument—even a rare one—seemed a petty thing.

Gabriel had buried Shadow at dawn, using *Vellichor*'s rounded blade to dig a shallow grave in the crumbling earth of the courtyard. Clay wondered if Vespian would have minded the legendary sword being used as a shovel this one time.

Now Gabe sat exactly where he had the night before, chewing slowly on his biscuit and glaring across the fire at Sabbatha. The daeva appeared not to notice. Shadow's weapon—the scythe he'd called *Umbra*—lay across her lap. She acted as if it was hers by right, and although Clay found that unsettling for any number of reasons, he wasn't about to try to take it from her.

No one said much of anything at all, which suited Clay just fine. He'd been content to merely sit and enjoy his salt cookie in uneasy silence, but then Sabbatha went ahead and ruined everything.

"Who is Larkspur?" she asked.

After a stretch of what Clay might have called *apocalyptic* awkwardness Ganelon, who apparently wasn't sleeping after all, finally answered. "It's you," he told her, rolling onto his back and rubbing at the rough whiskers on his face. "Your last name."

Clay watched the daeva's face carefully, looking for some outward signal of distrust, but she only nodded thoughtfully. "I was wondering why it seemed familiar," she said. And then, after a moment, she matched gazes with Gabriel. "I'm sorry I killed the druin. I didn't think you'd want him alive."

"Not just a druin," said Gabe quietly. "One of the few of his kind left in all the world. I killed one myself once, remember? It's a burden I would have spared you if you'd stopped to listen."

"He was too dangerous," she insisted. "We couldn't let him go—he would have come after us eventually. Or did you plan on bringing him along? Tell him about Rose and hope that black heart of his was still beating? Be careful making friends out of enemies," she warned, "lest they remember why they didn't like you in the first place."

Clay felt the appalling weight of irony drag his jaw toward the ground, but Gabriel only smiled placidly.

"As you say, Sabbatha." The tone in which he'd said her name sounded like provocation, and Clay saw the feathers on the daeva's back ruffle in annoyance. She opened her mouth to retort, but was interrupted by the sound of Moog clearing his throat noisily.

"Um, Gabriel?" asked the wizard. "How would you like to speak to your daughter?"

Clay and the others sat to one side, as spectators. Matrick insisted he wanted to watch despite looking as though he might fall back asleep at any moment. Using some sort of powdered herb he'd found in one of Shadow's bags, Moog fashioned two rectangular patches on the ground, six strides apart, one of which had a flagstone at the centre upon which Gabriel was instructed to stand. The wizard sat between them, scratching out runes on a pair of sticks. When he finished he scrambled to the fire and plunged them both into the glowing coals.

"Shadow was a smoke wizard," he explained. "An illusionist of sorts, and a very powerful one. Hence those shades we fought earlier, and the magic he used to conceal that scythe of his. Also, did you see his...um...face, after he died?"

Clay had, briefly. It was strikingly different from what they had seen before: hard angles and jutting cheekbones, pallid flesh crisscrossed with a web of pale scars. The skin beneath his mouth had been stained black, as if he'd eaten a necrotic heart for breakfast and hadn't bothered to wipe the blood off his chin.

"Smoke wizardry has any number of uses," Moog was saying. "Most of them are harmless, though a few, as we saw, are very dangerous indeed. Some are extremely useful. I once knew a young witch who could walk through walls, though unfortunately she could fall through floors as well. Poor lass broke her neck when she—"

"Moog," snapped Gabriel impatiently.

"Ah, sorry. They're ready, I think." He withdrew the smouldering sticks from the fire, using one to set the empty patch alight, and the other to ignite the patch beneath Gabriel. A wave of flame licked across either panel and went out, leaving a bed of bright red embers and a scent in the air that smelled faintly of—

"Cinnamon?" Matrick said, sniffing the air.

"Cinnamon, yes," Moog confirmed. "It's not essential for the ritual—I just thought it might be a nice touch."

"It smells delicious!" exclaimed Dane. His hideous smile stretched from ear to deformed ear.

He didn't say as much, but Clay agreed. It reminded him of the buns Ginny used to bake and then slather with sweet, sugary icing. His stomach growled despite the salty biscuit he'd fed it half an hour earlier.

Steam began to rise up around Gabriel. He shifted nervously on his flagstone and pushed a strand of soiled hair from his face. "Will she see me?" he asked.

The wizard nodded. "Yes, she will. But not clearly. You'll be indistinct. Smoky, sort of. Something like those *things* we fought last night."

Gabe nodded. He was hard to see for the haze around him. An hour-long minute ticked by. Matrick's chin drooped to his chest and Clay nudged him awake with an elbow. All of them watched the air above the empty patch, waiting.

At last a shape began to materialize in the smoke, then a man's voice spoke as if from behind a muffling curtain. "—*a disaster,*" it said. "*The roof collapsed, killing everyone inside. Thankfully the tunnel was blocked, so we needn't worry about the creatures using it to enter the city.*"

"*Thankfully? Vail's bloody cock, Freecloud—that was our best chance to get out of this hellhole.*"

Clay didn't recognize the voice, but Gabriel did. He gasped as her ghostly apparition formed above the opposite patch. "Rosie!"

"Rosie!?" The figure whirled. "Who the fuck—"

"Rose, it's me! It's Dad!"

Vague as her image was, Clay could almost see the incredulity on her face. "Dad? What are you doing here?" She took two steps without moving and extended her hand toward the spectre of Gabe as it appeared to her.

"Don't touch it!" blurted Moog, and Rose withdrew her hand.

"Who is that?" she asked.

"It's Uncle Moog, dear. Do you remember me?"

"Uncle Moog? I . . . of course I do. You used to sneak me cookies after Mom had gone to bed."

The wizard clapped. "Aha, yes! I'd completely forgotten about that! Gods, but Valery was a tyrant when it came to—"

"Moog," Gabriel cut him off. "Please. You said we haven't much time, right?"

"Right. Sorry." Moog pretended to lock his mouth closed and ushered Gabe to go on speaking.

"Rose, are you okay? Are you safe?"

"Dad . . ." His daughter bowed her head. The last time Clay had seen Rose she'd been no higher than his waist, brash and chatty, brimming with curiosity. A lot like Tally, except considerably less well behaved. He remembered thinking at the time it was because she was an only child, but had decided since then that Gabe and Val were just shitty parents. "I'm in Castia," said Rose eventually.

Gabe swallowed. "I know."

She looked up. "It's awful here. The city's surrounded. We can't fight our way out. We tried tunneling, but . . . well, we're trapped, Dad. Our food is almost gone, and I think something's wrong with the water. Half the city is sick with the plague."

"We saw," said Gabriel. "They poisoned the river."

"How do you..." she began, and then turned to someone they couldn't see. "I told them, didn't I? Go tell Arik to cordon off the reservoir."

"What'll we drink?" a voice asked.

"Our own piss if it comes to it!" Rose snapped. "Wine, ale—anything but water. Remember those orange trees we saw yesterday? Yeah? Well go make some fucking juice."

Gabriel interjected. "Rose, who's in charge there?"

"No one," she said, exasperated, and then chuckled darkly. "Me. Freecloud and I are leading what's left of the mercs, but the people here resent having more mouths to feed, and the Guard is giving us a hard time. They're hoarding supplies, and most of our injured died because we couldn't get them proper care. I'm afraid it might come to blood soon."

"Who is Freecloud?" Gabe asked. Clay had been wondering the same thing, actually. Fatherhood was a funny thing.

Rose glanced to her left. "He's my...he's just...someone I met on the way here. He's a good man, Dad. A great fighter. You'd like him."

Gabriel sighed into the smoke. "Listen, Rose. I—"

"I know," she broke in. "I should have listened to you. You were right. I wasn't ready for this. None of us were." Rose took a deep breath and pulled her hair back from her forehead. It was a gesture Gabe himself might have made. "I'm sorry, Dad, but I don't think we're getting out of this. I think..." She looked left again, at Freecloud, presumably. "I think we're going to die here."

"No, you're not." Gabe's voice was hard as stone. "I'm coming for you."

A disbelieving pause. "You're what? You're coming here? To Castia?"

"We're almost there, honey. Just east of the mountains. We'll be there in two weeks, maybe less. I need you to stay safe until then, okay?"

"Really?" Rose's excitement was palpable. She glanced around her. "Did you hear that? They're coming for us! The Courts sent an army to break the siege."

Gabriel interrupted a chorus of desultory cheers. "Rose, wait. The Courts didn't send an army."

"What? Who are you with then?"

"I, uh..." Gabe wrung his hands. "It's just me and the band, actually."

Rose's ghost wilted visibly. "What, you mean *your* band? As in *Saga*? Are you kidding me?"

"Well...no. But Rose, we're all here! Even Ganelon."

"Even *Ganelon*?" she echoed. "Oh, well, shit. Why didn't you say so in the first place? Hey everyone! Everything's going to be fine! Fucking Ganelon's on his way to break the siege!"

There were no cheers this time, but Clay heard Ganelon murmur under his breath, "Sounds about right."

Rose squared up to her father. "So what? You and four of your friends are coming to Castia? You know there's a bloody *Horde* outside? You won't even make it *near* the city. Hell, I'm surprised you made it as far as you have!"

Clay considered offering up the fact that it wasn't just Saga coming to her rescue, but a wine-swilling ghoul, an amnesiac daeva, and a half-blind ettin were along for the ride as well. Then again, if something sounded ridiculous in your head, then voicing it aloud rarely did it any favours.

Gabriel looked about to muster a reply, but his daughter rolled over him. "Dad, seriously, don't come here. Okay? Just... don't. There's nothing you can do. I..." She faltered, and when she spoke again her voice had lost its cutting edge. "I'm grateful you came this far. I really am. It was very brave. But I don't want you to die because of me."

Gabe snapped out of his stupor. "Rose, I—"

"Dad, *go home.*"

The words rocked Clay like a punch. He felt as though he might be sick, and he could only imagine what Gabriel was feeling. He had come so far, through so much, only to hear the one for whom he had done it all demand that he abandon her. Clay heard Sabbatha catch her breath beside him, and Moog, crouched in the space between Gabe and his daughter, looked much as he had in the chieftain's tent—as though his own heart were breaking all over again.

"Not long," urged the wizard quietly. "The spell will end soon."

Gabriel straightened. "Rose, listen to me. Do you remember the stories I used to tell when you were little?"

Rose looked down at her feet. "Of course I do."

"You never asked me if they were true. You believed whatever I told you, no matter how incredible it was."

The light beneath Rose was beginning to fade. Her apparition flickered as she spoke. "I was a little girl."

"And you're not anymore. I know that. But I need you to believe in one more story, Rose." If Gabe's voice had been stone before, now it was harder, colder, the mask of ice on a mountain's wind-scarred face. "I am coming to Castia," he said. *"I am going to save you."*

His daughter looked up, took a breath as if to speak, and vanished.

The light beneath Gabriel went out as well. He remained where he was, a wraith cloaked in a shroud of cinnamon smoke.

Chapter Forty-one

Out of the Woods

They left the ruins shortly after noon. Before doing so, however, Gabriel reached into his pack and withdrew one of the salt-scoured stones from the bottom. Clay recalled learning why he'd brought them in the first place: not as a gift, but an offering, something to lay on Rose's grave in case the worst should happen. Gabriel peered down at the stone, thumbing a cavity left behind by a fossilized shell. After a moment he sighed and tossed it to the ground, then upended the pack and dumped the rest at his feet.

Gabe found Clay watching as he looked up. He smiled—the expression for once unburdened by the weight in his eyes. "Those were heavier than they looked," he said before turning and setting out after the others.

Clay followed a short time later. Behind him in the empty courtyard, the stones of a distant shore were piled neatly on the druin's grave. Because even a misspent life, he reasoned, was worth remembering.

The road vanished, but Gabriel led them unerringly westward. If a bog appeared he waded into it without slowing. If the forest hindered their path he hacked through it with his sword, turning copses to corpses and pressing on. He cut short every stop for rest and roused them each morning while even the sun was snoring.

They were nearing the edge of the forest, and the denizens of the Heartwyld said good-bye in their own special way. They were set upon by a gremlin war party whose only aim turned out to be stealing the silver buttons from Moog's robe. They were ambushed by a clutch of old treants who fled after Ganelon felled the biggest with a single chop. They were attacked one sweltering dawn by something like a bloodred tiger with wings that hummed like a dragonfly's, prompting Matrick to ask after they'd driven it off, "Does anyone know what the fuck *that* was?"

Now and then they heard the surge of tidal engines as the *Dark Star* sailed overhead, still searching for its fallen mistress.

At last they stepped clear of the forest's black eaves. There was a bank of stone-riddled foothills ahead, humped like worshippers before the awesome glory of the Emperor's Mantle. It was said that four hundred years ago, after he'd led his exiled court through the perilous Wyld, the heir of Grandual's short-lived Emperor had stood upon the crest of these mountains and looked back, sighing in despair at all his father's hubris had lost him.

Clay craned his neck, gazing along the line of peaks from north to south. Whereas most mountains had imposing monikers like Hell's Talon or Soulreaper, the ones in this range were called things like Vigilance, Patience, and Trust, as if they'd been named by some commune of peace-loving Getalongs. Clay didn't know which peak was which. He was bad with names, after all.

Gabriel was glaring at the mountains with an annoyed smirk, as though they were a gang of thugs who'd stopped him in an alley and demanded a toll. "We're close," he said.

"Sure," Sabbatha quipped. "Just a few thousand feet of

snow and stone between us and a Horde big enough to wipe an entire city off the map."

Ganelon looked heartened by the prospect of violence. "So how you wanna do this?" he asked of Gabe. "The Nightstream might be fun." The Nightstream was a shallow river that snaked an arterial path through the heart of the mountains.

Kit raised his hand. "The Nightstream is infested by goblins. We'd have a thousand of the devils on us the moment we set foot inside."

Ganelon bared his teeth. "Sounds fun to me."

Sabbatha barked a laugh. She'd grown less timid since claiming Shadow's scythe for herself. She leaned on *Umbra* as if it were nothing more than a walking stick, but even still Clay found the weapon unnerving. His mind kept returning to the moment after the druin's death: The one-winged daeva standing over Shadow's corpse, clenching his ears in an iron fist.

"We could take Garric's Gap?" ventured Matrick.

Clay scratched at his beard. "The Gap closed, I heard. Landslide filled it in a few years back."

"Too far south, anyway," said Ganelon. "What about the Defile?"

"*Giants*," Matrick and Moog spoke in unison.

Ganelon shook his head, the beads in his braids clattering softly. "You two were a lot more fun twenty years ago, you know that?"

Gabriel drew his gaze from the mountains. "We're taking the Cold Road," he said, and when no one spoke he went on: "It's the fastest way."

"It's dangerous," warned Ganelon.

"*Too* dangerous," Moog added. "If it was winter, then maybe—*maybe*—it might be an option, but now it's just... it's crazy, Gabriel. I'm telling you. *I'm* telling you it's crazy— that's how crazy it is!"

"What's the Cold Road?" asked Sabbatha.

"It's a bridge," said Clay before either Kit or the wizard could spin their answer into a story. "A bridge made of ice. Wide enough to cross five abreast in winter, but now..." He shrugged. "If you fall off, it's a long way down."

Kit made the wet, gurgling sound that passed for clearing his throat.

"Also there are rasks," Clay said. "Ice trolls," he added, noting Sabbatha's confusion.

"Like Taino?" The daeva sounded mildly hopeful.

Clay shook his head. "I don't think anyone's like Taino but Taino."

"Rasks don't speak, or read, or play the drums," Moog told her. "They kill. And then they eat what they kill. That's pretty much all they do."

Sabbatha frowned. "So the bridge is a bad idea?"

"A terrible idea," said the wizard.

"Reckless," said Kit. "The Cold Road takes its toll. Always."

Matrick groaned and rubbed his face. "So which is it then? The Defile?" He eyed the ettin warily. "Not sure how we'll sneak these two past the giants..."

"My vote's for the Nightstream," said Ganelon, which earned him a sour look from Kit. "What? They're only goblins."

"We're not voting," said Gabriel calmly.

Moog wheeled on Clay. He jerked his head toward Gabriel as if to say, *Talk some sense into him*, and his eyebrows jumped as if to add, *Please*.

Gabriel was regarding him as well, and behind that placid stare Clay caught a glimmer of uncertainty. Gabriel *knew* the bridge was a bad idea. He knew, as well, that if Clay refused to follow him across, then so would the others.

The Defile was the safer choice. Giants were dangerous, sure, but easy enough to avoid, especially at night. And it wasn't as if every giant was a vicious killer—except the children. The children were nasty buggers. In general, however, they treated humans the way humans treated spiders, which is to say they were as likely to cup you in a palm and carry you to safety as they were to scream and step on you.

The Nightstream wasn't the worst idea, either. They'd lose a week or so on the journey, but it was a fairly straight path to the other side, and goblins—even in numbers—were a lot less scary than rasks. As well, spending a few days in the dark felt preferable to crossing a narrow strip of ice over several thousand feet of empty air.

So, yeah, there were safer ways to cross the mountains, but there was not, assuming they could cross the bridge without incident, a *faster* way. Clay might have weighed these things against one another. He could have taken into account the protests of the others, except that, in the end, only one thing really mattered.

You would come if it was me, right, Daddy?

Clay closed his eyes against the ache in his chest. He clenched his fingers, imagining he could feel his daughter's tiny hand in his. What would he give to see her now? To hold her in his arms and breathe her in? What would he risk to keep her from harm? What would he dare if her life were threatened?

Everything. Anything. Clay opened his eyes.

"We take the Cold Road," he said.

"No..." Moog's voice was barely a whisper.

"Moog, listen, it's the—"

"Impossible," breathed the wizard.

"Well, c'mon now, I wouldn't say..." He trailed off, since Moog was very obviously not listening to a word he was saying.

The wizard's expression slipped from shock to disbelief—the sort of amazed wonderment you'd expect from a child who'd begged for a horse for their birthday and was given an entire herd. He raised his arm and pointed a trembling finger past Clay's shoulder.

Clay turned to look. At first he saw nothing but a rising

slope littered with rugged brown stone, but then something *shifted* against the hillside, and he saw... he saw...

Matrick's voice broke over his thoughts. "Is that what I think it is?"

Clay squinted, shading his eyes from the sun. What he saw looked a great deal like a bear, except it was bigger than any bear he'd ever seen. It had grey feathers in place of fur, horned ears above a stubby black beak, and a pair of large eyes. Comically large, in fact, which spurred Clay to realize, at last, what exactly he was looking at.

"OWLBEAR!" Moog was dancing on the spot. "It's an owlbear! I told you, didn't I? I *told* you! It's real! I *knew* it!"

Ganelon smirked. "Then why do you sound so surprised?"

The wizard ignored him. "This is incredible! Nobody's ever seen an owlbear up close and lived to speak of it. Gods of Grandual, if that old bastard Katamus could see this!"

"What did you say?" Matrick asked.

"He was my professor of Biological Impossibilities at Oddsford. He didn't—"

"No," Matrick cut him off. "I mean about no one seeing one up close and living?"

"Well, *obviously*," said Moog, as though it actually *were* obvious. "Or else they wouldn't be considered a myth, would they? Also, did you see its claws? It could cut a tree to kindling with one swipe!"

He went on speaking, but whatever he said was drowned out by deafening and distinctly territorial *WHOOOOOOOT!*

Clay was hoping no one had seen him jump when Ganelon reached suddenly for *Syrinx*. The runes blazed to life and the axe muttered like a sleeper kicked awake. "It's charging," he announced.

Chapter Forty-two

Bards and Broken Bowls

"I still don't see why you had to kill it," said Moog sulkily.

"Oh no?" Matrick asked. "Why don't you ask the zombie?"

"Zombie? Seriously?" Kit shook his head in disgust, but then proffered his right arm, which had been savaged almost to the bone by the enraged owlbear. "Anyway, I fear killing the beast was our only recourse, Arcandius. The poor creature was... well, it was *angry*."

"It was only trying to protect its little ones," Moog grumbled. He wore Gabriel's old pack slung over his chest, inside which were the two cubs they'd found on the hillside after the Owlbear was dead. Their beaks were barely big enough to clamp down on a finger, but their eyes were huge, gold as the Summer Lord's beard, and seemed to ask, *Why did you kill my mother?* whenever Clay made the mistake of looking their way. They mewled ceaselessly, only growing quiet when Moog stroked the soft white down on their heads, as he did now.

"Well I was trying to protect *my* little ones," said Ganelon. He reached over to pet Matrick, who flinched away and self-consciously smoothed his thinning hair.

Gabriel glanced back over his shoulder. "I'm sorry, Moog. It was her or us."

The wizard sighed and looked down at his whining charges. "I guess so. But at least I can keep these two safe."

Safe? Clay almost scoffed. *We're going to the most horrible place in the world by the most dangerous route possible, but okay, sure.*

"Have you decided what to name them?" asked Gregor. Beside him, Dane giggled for no reason at all.

"Not yet, no." The wizard winced; Clay could see that bearing the cubs was taking a toll on his stamina. "Can we rest soon, Gabriel? They look hungry..."

"Soon," said Gabe without turning.

They'd been climbing all day. First the rugged foothills below, then the mountain itself, which Kit informed them was called Deliverance. Clay's legs were on fire. His right knee had started popping with every step, which might have troubled him more had he not heard Moog's and Matrick's knees clicking as well, so instead he just found it darkly amusing. Ganelon was unaffected by anything resembling fatigue. He climbed with the dogged gait of an automaton. Sabbatha appeared tireless as well, despite her heavy black armour. She'd gone quiet over the past few hours, stalking along beside Ganelon while *Umbra* bounced like a garish fishing pole on her shoulder.

But still Gabriel led the way, fueled by determination alone. Clay saw him falter several times. Once he tripped and went sprawling, but he leapt up as though drawn to his feet by unseen strings, a puppet dancing beneath the hand of its own indomitable will.

Up they went, until the forest resembled an ink-dark sea lapping hungrily at the mountain's feet. Up, until snow crunched beneath their feet and every breath plumed white before them. Up, until the air grew so crisp and cold that Matrick suggested they might turn the cubs into a pair of warming cloaks, and Moog proposed they slit Matrick open, unspool his guts, and take shelter in his belly for the night.

They found a cave shortly before dusk. It was empty but for a small table and two damp pillows, each of which was occupied by a decrepit skeleton. Between them was a moonstone Tetrea board bristling with beautifully carved figurines. The game was one in which two players waged a war between Grandual's gods: one controlled the forces of the Summer Lord and his daughter, Glif, while the other played on behalf of the Winter Queen and her son, Vail. It was a game of tactical foresight and cunning strategy—which was to say that Clay Cooper had never won a match in all his life, including an especially embarrassing loss to his nine-year-old daughter.

On the board below, one of the Winter Queen's pawns had been advanced two squares ahead.

"Brilliant," said Moog.

"These two were masters," Kit agreed.

Clay frowned, gleaning nothing of the sort. Stranger still: The skeleton of a cat was curled beside the table, as if the creature had been content to sleep itself to death while one of the so-called masters contemplated a move he would never make.

Ganelon grunted and scratched the whiskers on his chin. After a moment he stooped and slid a pawn on the opposite side forward.

Sabbatha grinned. "You sure about that?"

Ganelon glanced up at her, and if Clay didn't know better he'd have said the southerner looked intrigued. Ganelon motioned at the board. "Be my guest."

The daeva's grin turned feral. She kicked one of the skeletons aside and settled herself in its place. Ganelon grasped the other by the skull and flung it away.

If Clay thought the scene before had been strange, now it was outright bizarre. *A notoriously malicious bounty hunter and a peerless killer hunkered down at a Tetrea board*, he mused. *Now I've seen everything.*

* * *

Someone had brought up bards, which in turn led to a discussion about how they died, since that was what bards did best.

"Which one was William?" asked Matrick. The old king had found a flask somewhere—Clay wasn't about to hazard a guess—and took a swig, wiping his mouth with the back of one hand. "Was he the one that got gobbled up by a crypt slime?"

"That was Cook," Clay reminded him. They'd managed to gather a few bare branches from outside the cave, and he fed one now to the waning fire.

"Oh yeah!" Matty slapped his knee. "I remember Cook! Great kid. Terrible cook. Hell of a bard, though, and a decent pickpocket, too."

Not if that pocket belonged to a crypt slime, Clay mused. The boy had seen something glinting within the cube-shaped gel and plunged his hand right into it. But crypt slimes, not unlike people, rarely reacted kindly when someone jammed a fist inside them. Also, they were extremely corrosive: The young bard had been nothing but a dismayed-looking skeleton by the time they'd killed it, still clutching the worn copper coin that had cost him his life.

"Great kid," Clay echoed. "Anyway, William was the nobleman's son. We called him Sir Billy, remember?"

Matrick snorted. "Sir Billy! Gods, he hated that name. Arrogant little shit, wasn't he? Whatever happened to him?"

Gabriel was scraping his dinner bowl clean with a finger. Tonight's fare had been a disappointing mix of overcooked sausages and undercooked lentils, but Gabe had devoured it like a prisoner given salted steak after decades of gruel. "Castrated by a nymph," he said.

Matrick cocked his head. "What? How did I not know that?"

The frontman shrugged. "You drank a lot."

"Good point," said Matrick. He tipped his flask again, and afterward smiled wistfully. "Recca was nice."

Recca had been Saga's first female bard, and accordingly several of them—Clay included—had been madly in love with her. But Recca, unfortunately for everyone involved, had been in love with a bloodeater. It turned her, eventually, and Gabriel had been forced to drive a silver stake through her heart. They'd gone after the bloodeater next and made damn sure it suffered.

"Well, she was a whole lot better than Catrina, anyway," Matrick added.

Clay shifted from one elbow to the other on his roll, hoping to relieve the pain creeping into his lower back. It helped, for the moment. "Catrina . . . was she the moontiger?"

"Raksha," said Moog. "Not a moontiger."

"There's a difference?" asked Ganelon without taking his eyes from the Tetrea board. He and Sabbatha had been at it all night, eating supper where they sat, muttering quietly to one another between finishing one match and beginning another. Clay had no idea how many games they'd played, or who was winning, since they both approached it with the same fierce intensity with which they fought.

"Of course there's a difference," Moog was saying. "Moontigers are lycanthropes."

Matrick looked puzzled. "They can see through walls?"

"What? No!" The wizard shared a *my friends are imbeciles* look with the revenant before deigning to explain. "Moonies are people, just like you or me, except they turn into animals during a full moon. It's a disease, actually."

"Like drinking," Gabe clarified, throwing a smirk in Matrick's direction. "Mostly you're a man, but sometimes you're a monster."

Matty said nothing, but looked thoughtfully at the flask in his hand.

"Well, yes, I suppose it *is* like that," said Moog. "Now rakshas, on the other hand, are monsters, though they can make themselves *look* like people, as Catrina did. They're not evil, necessarily, but the vast majority of them are assholes."

Clay could attest to that. Though she'd posed as a bard, Catrina had in fact been an assassin hired to kill Gabriel. She'd seduced him first (not an especially difficult task) and then attacked him in his quarters while the band was at sea. Gabe had narrowly escaped and fled, stark naked, onto the ship's deck with the raging tigress hot on his heels. Clay had managed to fight her off until Ganelon arrived, and the southerner had tossed her, scratching and screaming, over the rail and into the sea.

Rakshas, it also bore mentioning, were not especially strong swimmers.

"Ah, here it is!" Moog, who'd been rummaging through his bag for several long minutes, now withdrew what looked like a seashell made of brass and wood.

Clay was trying to decide whether it was some sort of bomb when the wizard brought the shell to his lips and blew a few tentative notes through a grille on one end. *An instrument*, he realized—which didn't necessarily mean it wasn't *also* a bomb. Moog was Moog, after all.

"I traded a pair of old boots to a trash imp for this, straight up," said the wizard.

Matty looked dubious. "What does a trash imp need boots for?"

"He ate them," said Moog. When Matrick's expression slipped further toward incredulity the wizard added, "It's true. He filled them both up with mustard and ate them right there in front of me. I swear, a trash imp would eat its own offspring if there was mustard on 'em."

He blew another series of exploratory notes into the shell before slipping into what was surprisingly recognizable as a song. Matrick sipped at his flask and smiled appreciatively. Gabriel closed his eyes. Kit hummed as though he knew the tune, and Clay, who didn't, lost himself in the fire's fitful light. He heard the quiet clack of a moonstone piece.

"I take your queen," Ganelon announced, and Sabbatha swore under her breath.

"Again?" he asked.

"Again," she answered.

Clay went on staring, Matrick went on drinking, Kit kept on humming, and Moog played on and on. The air in the cave began to smell just a little bit like salt. The brisk mountain wind rolled in from outside, whispering in the corners like a wave spilling secrets to the shore. The shell's song was a mournful sound, and so it came as no surprise when Matrick, having sucked the last dregs from his flask, spoke as though their tiny fire was the pyre of a departed friend.

"What's the best part about being immortal?" he asked Kit.

The ghoul spent a long moment considering. "Fearlessness," he said at last.

One of the little owlbears stirred awake. Moog laid the shell aside and hauled the cub into his lap, stroking the silky feathers between its saucer-shaped eyes. "How do you mean?" he asked.

"You'd be surprised how many choices one makes due to the intrinsic nature of self-preservation," Kit said. "When survival is no longer an issue, well, all bets are off, as they say. My first few years as an immortal were especially reckless. I took risks no mortal ever could. I leapt from the dizzying heights of waterfalls and strolled like a sightseer through the carnage of battlefields. I spat in the face of death, and death could do nothing but rage in impotence as I worked up another mouthful of phlegm.

"And then of course there's the travel element," he remarked cheerily. "I've wandered the deep places of the world without fear of starving or falling prey to some awful monstrosity crawling around in the dark. And believe me, there are some awful monstrosities crawling around in the dark. I've explored the ocean depths without needing to come up for air. I've roamed coral labyrinths and walked the submerged streets of ancient Antica.

"I once explored the shores of a land to which no ship had ever sailed and met a tribe of blue-skinned barbarians who had never even heard of the Dominion—or of Grandual, even. They killed me, obviously, as barbarians tend to do with strangers in their midst, and offered my body as a sacrifice to their savage god. But when I refused to stay dead they decided to worship me instead."

"Sounds better than being a king," said Matrick.

Kit nodded. "It was—until a plague tore through the village and killed every man, woman, and child in the tribe. I was left alone to do whatever gods do once all who believe in them are dust."

"Such as?" Moog prompted.

"I did a lot of hiking, actually. And swimming. And I whittled things out of wood, though I never really got good at it."

"And what about the worst thing?" Matrick asked. "What's the downside to being an immortal?"

The ghoul chuckled. "Well for a start it's been hell on my complexion. I was a handsome devil once, though you'd hardly know it now." He fell silent for a moment, gazing thoughtfully into the fire while his eyelids fluttered.

"I suppose it gets a bit lonely sometimes," he said after a while. "There are occasions on which I'll laugh at some amusing memory only to remember that the person it concerns is a century dead. And companionship—let alone intimacy—can be a scarce commodity when you look as I do. Children scream at my approach. Men reach for swords to slay me, or torches to burn me, or holy symbols with which to smite me—it's all very tiring, if I'm being honest. And it goes without saying that with the exception of a few blessedly twisted individuals, not many women look longingly at a bloodless ghoul. There's only so far a rapier wit and extensive wine knowledge will get you when your...uh...*apparatus* is about as useful as a chocolate teapot." He winked at Moog. "Though that problem has since been remedied by a certain wizard and his magnificent phallic phylactery."

"You're welcome," said Moog, though his smile was sad.

"You should write a book," Matrick suggested.

Kit snorted. "Who wants to read the self-pitying lamentations of an old revenant?"

"There's your title right there," said Ganelon. He used one of his Tetrea pieces to knock down one of Sabbatha's, and the daeva hissed through her teeth.

"Again?" he asked.

"Again," she answered.

"Have you ever met a ghoul like yourself?" Moog asked.

Kit shook his head, tugging absently at the scarf that hid the wound on his throat. "Not like me, no. I knew an alchemist once who made himself a golem bride out of flesh and bone, but her brain was a cantaloupe wrapped in bronze wire, so she wasn't much of a conversationalist." The revenant sighed. "Alas, it would appear I am the one and only person fool enough to try and pet a phoenix."

"Well, I'm glad we found you, Kit." Matty clapped their bard on his bony shoulder. "Kit the Unkillable—isn't that what they call you? It's good to know you'll survive this. Us, I mean. I mean, even if we don't. Survive, that is."

The ghoul cracked a smile like a coffin's lid sliding ajar. "I'm glad you found me, too," he said. "It will be my honour to tell your story. It has been vastly entertaining thus far. I do hope it has a happy ending, though."

"It won't," Matrick murmured.

"It will," Gabe assured them.

"It might," Clay said.

Something woke him. The sound of a scuffle, the scrape of metal on stone. Someone growled, someone gasped, and Clay was fumbling for his weapon before he realized what it was he was hearing.

It seemed Sabbatha and Ganelon were finished playing games.

At first, the idea of intimacy developing between those two struck Clay as absurd. They'd said barely a word to each other during the journey and had little in common save an aptitude for violence. They'd tried to kill each other twice now. He thought back to their first encounter in Conthas, when she'd pinned Ganelon to the floor with the heel of her boot and declared she'd be the last woman he would ever love.

Okay, well, the more he thought on it the more fitting it seemed. And besides, she and Ganelon were young (or young-*ish* in Ganelon's case), and rushing headlong toward the brink of something terrible. Clay knew the feeling. He'd been there himself in days gone by. There was something about the night before a battle, or the anxious days before a tour of the Wyld, that brought on a feeling of . . . not despair, but a kind of help-less, hopeless freedom.

Ganelon's needs were easy enough to ascertain—the man had been rock hard for nineteen years. And as for Sabbatha? Far be it from Clay to guess the mind of any woman, let alone one as complex as she. He didn't know her past, but it was very obviously dark. There was an old saying: *One look at a bowl and you can guess if a goblin made it.* It meant—at least he *thought* it meant—that beautiful things were not made by an unkind touch, and the daeva was as warped a woman as Clay had ever met.

His own bowl was a brittle thing and would have bro-ken long ago were it not for Ginny, whom he very suddenly missed with a longing so fierce it burned like an ember in his chest.

By the time he smothered it, the cave had grown quiet again, but for the restless wind and Matty's droning snore, along with the occasional rasp of a turning page. Kit had no need of sleep. He sat outside the mouth of the grotto, reading one of Moog's old books by starlight.

Clay had nearly slipped back into dream when he heard the low rumble of Ganelon's voice.

"Again?" he asked.

"Again," she answered.

Chapter Forty-three

The Cold Road

Clay figured that whoever gave the Cold Road its name must have had a particularly sinister sense of humor. That, or they'd been stark raving mad, which would explain why they were taking the Cold Road in the first place. It was cold, sure, but it was most certainly *not* a road. In fact, it was anything *but* a road.

It began as a steep slope of crumbling shale that slipped and slid beneath your boots and just fucking *dared* you to try to use your hands to help climb. By the time he reached the top Clay's fingers were sliced near to ribbons. Matrick was limping, having turned an ankle partway up. He would have fallen if not for Ganelon, who'd held him by the collar until the old king found his feet.

When they topped the rise Matrick straightened his vest and smoothed his hair. "Thanks," he said. "Hey, how'd you fare on the Tetrea board last night?"

Ganelon shot him a questioning glare.

"Did you win any?" Matrick asked without any apparent guile.

Satisfied, Ganelon answered. "All of them."

The king blinked. "What?"

But the southerner was already turning. In a gesture of

magnanimity as rare as, well, an owlbear itself, he was carrying Gabe's old backpack, sparing Moog the burden of the orphaned cubs. The pair had grown mercifully quiet after the wizard fed them breakfast, though it still gave Clay a chill to recall Moog spilling porridge from his own mouth into their open beaks.

The next leg of the Cold Road was a climbing track that hugged the face of the mountain. Clay spotted a cluster of scraggly-looking goats perched on the incline above. One of them, its beard so long it reached the ground even when it raised its head, bleated to alert the others. *Look at these assholes,* Clay imagined it saying.

Several times their path was blocked by landslides, forcing them to stop and clear the way with their hands—a task for which the ettin was especially well suited. Gregor, with a sly wink for the others, sold it to Dane as "digging for treasure," and though each time the search proved fruitless, Dane's optimism remained untarnished.

"I hope we find gold," he exclaimed. "Or silver. Which is prettier, Gregor?"

"Oh, they're both pretty," said his brother. "But what I really hope we find is duramantium, Emperor of Metals!"

"Durmadantum!" Dane's mouth mangled the word, but his shattered smile bloomed as he said it. "The Emperor of Metals!"

They pressed on, and all at once rounded a corner into a blistering storm. Gabriel called a brief rest while Moog plumbed the depths of his bag for the cloaks and heavy furs that he and Kit had been tasked with buying back in Conthas. The wizard had put some thought into it, apparently. He presented Ganelon with a great black boar skin with pointed tusks sewed up the spine, and Matrick with a hooded fox-fur cloak complete with ears and a snout. "It's fake," Moog admitted. "And a bit tacky. And I'm fairly certain it was tailored to fit a woman."

Matrick smirked beneath the hood. "I like it."

Gabe's cloak practically had a whole white wolf slung across the shoulders, and Moog himself doffed a heavy sheepskin coat matched by an appropriately ridiculous fur hat.

The wizard handed Clay a shaggy brown bearskin before looking apologetically at Sabbatha. "I'm sorry. I didn't know we'd have company."

Before Clay could offer up the bearskin she waved him off, enshrouding herself in a cloak of sleek blue-black plumage.

"How's the wing?" Clay ventured.

"Better," she answered curtly, and stalked off.

"Excellent," he muttered at her back. "Good talk." She and Ganelon together was starting to make a lot more sense to him now.

When they set out again Gabriel dropped back to fall in step beside Clay, who was bringing up the rear.

"Hanging in there?" he asked.

"Hanging in there," Clay answered, his breath pluming before the chill wind could snatch it away.

"Listen, I just . . . wanted to say thank you."

"For what?"

Gabe was about to reply but laughed instead. Ahead of them, Moog glanced back and frowned, as though dismayed at having missed out on a joke. "Where do I begin?" Gabriel wondered aloud. "You came after me back in Coverdale. You pulled me off my knees that first night at Kal's place, and again outside Brycliffe. You fought a chimera for me."

"Got my ass kicked by one, you mean," Clay murmured.

A chuckle, puffing white in the freezing air. "Yeah, well, we all did."

"Except Ganelon."

"Except Ganelon," Gabe conceded. "Ah, but you did throw my ex-wife's new husband off a skyship . . ."

Clay shrugged beneath the heavy mantle of his bearskin cloak. "That's what friends are for, right?"

"Right." Another chuckle from Gabriel. He moved a step

closer, so their shoulders brushed as they plodded side by side and he could speak without contending against the wind. "I know you didn't want any part of this, Clay. You had a good thing going back home. When I asked you to come, you had a thousand reasons to say no."

Just two, thought Clay, though he didn't bother pointing that out.

His friend flashed him a tight grin. "But you came anyway. You're here, beside me. And because of you the five of us are together again. Because of you I have a chance, however impossible it might seem, of getting my daughter back. Yesterday..." Gabriel shook his head, glanced down at his trudging boots. "The others would never have taken the Cold Road if it wasn't for you. We'd be skulking through the Defile right now, or knee-deep in the Nightstream, weeks away from reaching Castia."

"They would have followed you," Clay said with a sinner's conviction. "They've followed you this far."

Gabriel looked over, squinting against the snow-flecked gale. "Followed *me*? Gods, you really believe that, don't you?"

"Well, yeah." Clay was trying to keep an eye on the treacherous footing below. The mountain sloped steeply on their left; a single misstep could lead to a dangerously unchecked slide. "You're the leader," he said.

"I'm the frontman," Gabe corrected.

Clay had a sudden recollection of huddling around a table in Conthas—what, thirty years ago?—with Gabriel, Matrick, and Kallorek, dreaming of glory and doling out roles in an as-yet-unnamed band. Gabriel was the face, Matty the hands. Clay had been the muscle for roughly half an hour, before Ganelon showed up. "Frontman, leader...same thing," Clay said.

"Is it?"

Clay opened his mouth, closed it, spent a moment considering whether or not what he was about to say made sense before replying, rather ineloquently, "Yeah?"

"Say we rescue Rose," proposed Gabriel, and already Clay was beginning to feel like an old, blind dog limping toward a loving hug, a merciful axe, and a shallow grave. Gabe had a point to make, but he was taking the scenic route. "Say we make it safe and sound back to Grandual, and afterward I ask the boys—Moog, Matty, Ganelon—to keep the band going. Maybe take on a few smaller gigs, or hit the arena circuit to warm up first, and then do a proper tour of the Wyld, or the Wastes up north."

"Good luck with that," said Clay, though he knew Gabe wasn't being serious. At least Clay didn't *think* he was being serious. It was hard to tell sometimes, with Gabriel.

"They wouldn't come," Gabe said. "Of course they wouldn't. And after all this is done I doubt they'd follow me to an outhouse if they had to shit. But if *you* asked them? If Clay Cooper walked alone into the Heartwyld, or the Brumal Wastes, or the Frost Mother's Hell itself...they would follow you. You know they would. And so would I."

Clay had never considered himself Saga's leader, and he certainly didn't now, regardless of what Gabriel said. For the entirety of his mercenary career he had gone where Gabe said they were going, killed what Gabe said needed killing, spent whatever coin Gabe tossed his way, and generally drifted, leaf-like and listless, on the shifting current of Gabriel's bluster.

Sure, from time to time he'd weighed in on some moral quandary confounding his bandmates, and every so often he'd taken the first step down a hard road when no one else seemed keen on doing so. There were even, admittedly, occasions on which he'd gone ahead and killed who needed killing without asking for Gabriel's permission. Kallorek, for instance.

Clay was still mulling over Gabriel's words a while later when their progress was once again impeded by fallen rock. This time, however, Dane actually did discover a treasure among the stones. "Durmadantum!" he declared, brandishing the ice-encased skull of some hapless adventurer.

Gregor made the best of it. "Indeed it is, brother! Well done. Let's take a closer look at it later." He took the skull from Dane and handed it to Gabriel, who handed it to Moog, who tossed it into the snow behind them.

The way grew more treacherous still. The path was sloped and broken, slippery with snow and ice. The wind got mean, tugging and prodding like a bully urging you to jump or be called a coward. The peak of Deliverance loomed into cloud on their right. On their left was the canyon known as the Defile. It cut a jagged, mazelike path from one side of the range to the other, and Clay, shivering despite the heavy bearskin, was beginning to wish he'd sided with Matrick before they started the climb. It would be warm down there, and the likelihood of falling to your death was comparatively slim.

Remember the giants, he told himself. *Giants are bad*. The thought managed to console him somewhat. Enough to keep his legs moving, anyway.

But then, through the curtain of swirling snow, he saw it: a span of crystalline ice arcing from one side of the gorge to the other. The last, lethal stretch of the Cold Road.

And quite suddenly giants didn't seem so bad.

The rasks hit them before they reached the bridge.

Clay was taking a turn at the front, doing his best to keep his eyes from wandering over the sheer drop on his left, when one of the creatures came skidding and shrieking down the steep cliff face on their right. He rushed to meet it, hoping to engage it as far from the chasm's edge as possible, and pinned it against the stone while the others hurried past.

Clay had never gotten a good look at a rask up close, and now that one was howling into his face he couldn't have said he was grateful for the opportunity. It was roughly the size of Clay himself, with bedraggled blue-green hair that clung like wet seaweed to its scrawny shoulders. The thing's eyes were pale as milk, its breath an unsettling mix of blood and peppermint. Its nose was long, sharp as an icicle, and pointed dangerously at his face. Clay had its long arms pinned below his, and he could feel its claws scratching against his chain shirt, without which he would have been disemboweled.

He pushed *Blackheart*'s rim into the monster's neck and heard it snap, but still the thing fought him. Clay called out to the wizard as he went by. "Hey, how do I kill it?"

Moog spun, one hand pushing his oversized fur hat from his eyes. "Fuck if I know!"

"Moog, I'm serious!"

"So am I! Fire would do it, but good luck getting—oh, wait!" The wizard went to his knees, frantically plumbing his bottomless bag. He came up clutching a coil of rope, which didn't explain why he was grinning as though he'd produced something useful, until Clay realized that the rope wasn't rope. It was firewire.

Clay caught movement to his right. Another rask dropped from the ridge above and was loping toward them. "Moog, hurry," he growled.

The wizard twisted a short length of firewire from the rest. He darted up beside Clay and touched the two ends together. There was a hiss, and Moog fed the suddenly glowing loop to the monster's mouth. The pitch of its scream shifted from rage to pain; its head melted like a candle set alight with dragonfire.

Well, there's one way to kill them, Clay thought.

He danced back as the firewire, now a circle of molten gold, landed on the ground near his feet, then turned as the second rask reached him, a flurry of grasping talons and gnashing teeth. Clay sidestepped, set his shoulder into *Blackheart*, and knocked the creature off the path and into the abyss below.

He and Moog hurried after the others. They entered a long corridor that Clay remembered as having been more a tunnel and less a terrace, but it had been winter when they'd been here last. Now rasks clambered in from above, slipping like thieves through gaps in the ice. More of the creatures were blocking the way ahead. He saw Gabriel hack through them without slowing. Matrick skulked in his wake, plunging knives into those still thrashing, while Ganelon and Sabbatha dealt with any who came in from outside. Between his axe and her scythe, Clay couldn't imagine a more dangerous place in all the world than within the deadly circle of their reach.

A snarl tore the air to his left. Clay whirled as a rask came at him feetfirst. He brought his shield up an instant too late. The thing's talons raked across his face. Pain flared, then fled, chased off by terror and raw adrenaline. Blood ran into his eyes, gummed in his ice-tipped lashes when he tried to blink, and fouled his sight. Clay caught a glimpse of the rask attacking and ducked behind his shield. He was knocked backward, and his head cracked hard against the cold stone wall.

Clay swiped the blood from his eyes, but his vision was still blurred. There were four rasks, then twelve, then one again, lunging toward him with talons that snapped like shears.

Something *bright* spun past. The rask's head rolled into Clay's lap. Its body slumped like a supplicant before him, and he saw that its neck had been neatly cauterized. A few feet to his left another disc of glowing firewire steamed in the snow.

"Did you see that throw?" Moog mimicked what looked to Clay like an old man tossing horseshoes with his grand-children. When the wizard looked over, though, his grin van-ished. "Sweet Maiden's Mercy, are you okay?"

Clay climbed to his feet. His ears were ringing, and he could feel the wind probing the wounds on his face with frigid fingers. "Sure, why?"

Moog frowned as he assessed whatever damage the rask's talons had done to Clay's face. "No reason. We should hurry."

They ran after the others, emerging from the tunnel mouth onto a precipice of bare stone. The storm had died down, but flecks of snow still rode the breeze, spinning like spring blossoms in the air.

The bridge was directly ahead, a depressingly vivid manifestation of everything Clay feared it would be. Broad at the base, it tapered at its highest point to a strip so thin they would need to cross in single file. The mountain opposite, whose name Clay hadn't bothered to ask, was wreathed in white mist.

"Shall I remind you this was your idea?" Moog asked.

"I'd rather you didn't," said Clay, as they caught up with the others.

Kit started up it first, creeping despite the fact that a fall from several thousand feet would be little more than an inconvenience. Gabe and Ganelon put their backs to the bridge, ready to hold off the pursuing rasks.

Gabriel waved behind him. "Everyone over. Quick but careful. Very careful," he added, looking up at Gregor and Dane.

Gregor nodded gravely. Dane giggled, likely having been convinced they were playing some childish game. "I'll race you, Gregor!" he shouted.

"I'll race you both," said Matrick, jogging toward the summit. Moog and Sabbatha started up after them, making as much haste as they could before the bridge narrowed dangerously and forced them to consider every step.

"Clay—" Gabe started. "Good gods, your face!"

Clay touched two fingers to the gash across his nose. It hurt, and they came away bloody. "Is it bad?"

Before Gabe could answer Ganelon flexed his fingers on the haft of his axe. "Here they come."

The rasks exploded from the tunnel mouth, yelping and screaming, dismayed that most of their quarry was getting away, giddy that three were still within reach.

Ganelon killed the first with a sideways chop. Gabe stepped in with *Vellichor*—the sharp scent of lilacs filled the air—and two more fell. Clay was ready at his shoulder. A thrust from *Blackheart* snapped the fingers of a grasping hand, a blow from his hammer cracked the skull above it. Gabriel's blue-green blade flickered out to take a rask's head off before Ganelon moved in again. He impaled one, kicked a second, punched a third in the face with a dragonscale gauntlet. *Vellichor* cut a rask into halves, and when another lunged at Gabe he dodged, tripping it toward Clay with an outstretched boot. Clay dropped, ducking beneath his shield before the thing landed on him, and then, every muscle in his back protesting, he stood and flung the creature off the precipice behind him. The look of grudging respect he earned from Ganelon made the pain worthwhile—for the moment, anyhow.

We will speak of this later, his lower back promised. *Oh yes we will.*

The next clutch of rasks were notably less enthusiastic about rushing the bridge, their hunger tempered by the only instinct that mattered more: self-preservation.

Ganelon turned on them. "You two go. I'll hold them here."

From anyone else those words would seem loaded with the dreadful freight of self-sacrifice. From Ganelon they were simply a statement of fact. He might have said *I'll put the kettle on* with the same casual certainty.

Gabe hesitated, torn between wrath and reason, then finally nodded. He and Clay started up the bridge, legs pumping, breath gusting white from their mouths. Matrick was over the arch and had turned to wait for Gregor and Dane, who were shuffling carefully along the thinnest stretch of ice. Clay might have prayed it didn't break, but he reckoned the gods were already watching and had placed bets on who would fall first. Safe money was on the eight-hundred-pound ettin.

Something lunged from the mist behind Matrick, a rask much bigger than any of those they'd faced thus far. A chieftain, Clay supposed, noting the loop of broken skulls slung around its neck. Its hair was spiked with frost, shorn to a strip down the centre of its head. It was on Matrick in an instant, tackling him and pinning him to the ice with a strangling claw. It raised the other to strike—talons splayed like a fan of knives—and Clay heard Kit's warning words echo in his mind.

The Cold Road takes its toll. Always.

Chapter Forty-four

A Grave in the Clouds

Gabriel swore. Moog was yelling something, but the wind was in Clay's ears and he couldn't make it out. Sabbatha stood at the centre of the bridge, not moving, not trying at all to save Matrick before the rask killed him. And it *would* kill him, Clay was sure.

And then suddenly the ettin was there. It snatched the chieftain's arm and yanked it into the air. The rask took a swipe at Dane's head, but the ettin caught its other wrist as well. The two monsters wrestled one another, arms outstretched, thrashing like something pinned to a crucifix.

Dane turned to ask something of Gregor, but they were too far away, the wind too loud, for Clay to hear. The rask curled up on itself, lashed out with a clawed foot, and opened a wide red gash in Gregor's throat.

The ettin teetered for a moment, then toppled from the bridge into white oblivion.

Clay's heart fell with them, but there wasn't time to grieve. The rask landed in a crouch. It began scrabbling toward Matrick again when Sabbatha's voice brought it up short.

"Come to me."

The creature turned its curdled gaze upon the daeva.

"Come to me," she repeated, so quiet the wind stopped

to listen, so compelling the mountains strained against the shackles of their roots.

In thrall to a will stronger than its own, the chieftain shambled over to crouch at her feet. The skulls around its neck clattered against one another, grinning like fools. Its expression twitched between fear and reverence, as though Sabbatha was the Winter Queen herself, dark and divine beneath the pale moon of her scythe.

Umbra came down like a guillotine, shearing away the top half of the rask's head. It managed something like a whimper before it died. It tumbled from the bridge and was swallowed by cloud.

Clay found himself a step away from the narrow span without knowing how he'd come to be there. He dragged his eyes from the sickening emptiness below. The daeva was turned away from him. The wind had returned, ruffling the plumage on her back, lifting her long black hair like a pennant.

Clay swallowed. "Sabbatha—"

"Sabbatha's dead," she said. Her right wing snapped out, scattering a handful of black feathers into the air. Clay was watching them whirl away, transfixed, when a shadow fell across his face. He raised his eyes slowly, slowly, like a man condemned gazing up at the executioner's axe, as the daeva's supposedly injured left wing extended into the sky.

Fuck, he thought. *Fuck, fuck, fuck.*

"Larkspur," he said gloomily. "Welcome back."

She turned on him. "Thank you."

Clay pulled his gaze from the not-at-all-injured wing and looked across at her. "How long?" he asked.

The grin that split her face was a feral thing, terribly beautiful. "Longer than you'd think," she said, which wasn't really the answer he'd been hoping for.

All that pointless deception, all those lies we told ... Clay's mind was reeling, struggling to grasp the implication of what she was telling him. *All this time she was playing us, patient as a circling vulture, waiting for a moment like this.*

"And now?" he asked, though he already knew the answer.

Larkspur's gaze drifted beyond his shoulder. Ganelon had not only held the rasks at bay, but had driven them off altogether. He arrived short of breath, but otherwise unscathed, and the daeva's smile broadened as her eyes met his. "Now I take your king," she said.

The southerner made no reply. Even Gabe had been rendered speechless, though Clay assumed his next words would be *I told you so.*

Something behind the daeva drew his attention: He saw Kit emerge from the fog on the far side of the bridge. His arms hung limp by his sides, and something—the rask chieftain, probably—had savaged his throat. He appeared lucid, however, and one look at Larkspur told him all he needed to know. The ghoul started up the bridge at a jog.

"So what now?" Clay asked, playing for time. "You'll fly him to Agria all by yourself? That's a long way, and dangerous."

"You've seen my ship in the sky, Slowhand. My *real* ship," she emphasized, "not that floating brothel you stole from Kallorek. Where is he, by the way? His wife said you brought him along. You didn't leave him on board to burn, did you?"

Clay mulled over a few lengthy explanations, none of which resembled the truth. He settled on "No."

The daeva's smirk returned, tugging at something in his chest. She'd been suppressing her allure, he realized. Smothering it so she would seem like less of a threat. But now it burned, and it was all Clay could do not to offer himself up to the flame.

"My men will find me," she said. "I'll make sure of that. Now step back, Slowhand. I like you, but if you try and cross I will cut you down."

Her threat drew a sour laugh from Gabriel. "You are unfucking-believable, do you know that? You'll *cut him down*? He saved your bloody life, Sabbatha."

The daeva snarled, "Sabbatha's—"

"Yeah, Sabbatha's dead. I heard you the first time. It's a pity, really, because this Larkspur character is a real bitch. I mean, honestly, how *evil* are you? After all we've been through, you'd really *kill* Clay? You'd drag Matrick all the way back to Lilith for a fucking *payday*? She'll kill him!"

Kit was edging around Matrick's prone body. Clay had no idea what the ghoul could do if he managed to reach Larkspur, but he hoped it would be enough to distract her, if only for a moment.

"He's doomed already," said Larkspur. "You all are. Because of you, Gabriel. Because you haven't figured it out yet."

"What's that?" Gabe asked.

"That this isn't a story," she told him. Her eyes climbed the cloud-mantled mountains around them. "There is no happy ending. And you aren't a hero. You're just a deluded old mercenary who—"

Clay started running the moment Kit hit her from behind. Larkspur stumbled forward, nearly falling from the bridge, but she beat her wings once and managed to stay balanced. She drove the butt of her scythe into Kit's chest, propelling him back, then launched an attack at Clay.

He dropped into a slide, arching backward on his knees with his arms flung wide as *Umbra* carved the air mere inches above his nose. Clay heard the vertebrae pop down the length of his spine, and all the pain in his back vanished in an instant. He sprang up to his feet, launched a savage punch with his shield arm that knocked the daeva onto her back. A step, and Clay was directly above her. *Wraith* was in his hand, so cold it seared the flesh of his palm, and he brought the hammer—

"Wait, *please*," begged Larkspur.

There was no power in the words. No compulsion. Only fear. A woman's desperate plea for mercy. And had the man above her been anyone but Clay Cooper it would not have been enough.

But it was.

He wavered, but Larkspur didn't. The scythe tore an arc between them and Clay watched, uncomprehending, as his hand fell off.

His jaw dropped as though it were cast in lead. He was dimly aware of someone yelling his name. He blinked, trying to focus, and saw blood on the pale skin of Larkspur's face, blood on the pure white snow, blood frothing from the stump of his arm with every slow beat of his heart.

His hand was gone. His hammer was gone. They slid over the edge and vanished from sight.

"Clay..." He saw Larkspur mouth the words, but it was Ginny's voice he heard. She made to rise and he staggered away from her, except one foot slipped on the ice and the other stepped onto nothing at all.

Clay fell headlong into white cloud.

And so the Cold Road took its toll.

Chapter Forty-five

A Song for the Dreamer

The end of Clay's childhood came suddenly, a wildfire that reduced the brittle forest of his youth to char. It began as such things always begin: with a seemingly innocuous spark.

Reaching across the table at breakfast Clay accidentally upset his father's cup. Even so early in the morning it was filled with wine, which splashed into Leif's lap. Clay had barely opened his mouth to apologize when the blow came, knocking him to the floor. There was a shrill keening in his ears and the taste of blood on his tongue. Tears boiled in his eyes, threatening to shame him.

"Don't you ever lay a hand on him again," his mother said. Her voice was quiet, but fierce. Clay had never heard her use that tone before. Even Leif looked stunned, but then he barked a harsh laugh and sneered.

"Or what?" he asked.

"Or I will leave you. I will take Clay with me and you will never see us again."

His father's ugly grin remained in place, but his eyes went slack. He said nothing, just got up and went out the door. He was gone all day, and when Clay went to bed that night he wondered if maybe his father had left instead. To his surprise, the thought of life without Leif was a pleasant one.

The sound of the door slamming jarred him awake. His father was home, and drunk. Clay could hear his ragged breath, the heavy tread of his bad leg as he tramped across the house. There was a hush, and Clay listened as his heart counted slow seconds in the dark.

Then it started.

Screams. The muted thud of pounding fists. Clay pulled his blanket up over his head, trying not to listen as the screams became sobs, as the sobs became muffled whimpers. He wanted to shout, to intervene on his mother's behalf, but he couldn't find his voice, let alone the courage to share the brunt of his father's wrath. So instead he huddled in his bed, paralyzed by fear and berating himself for a coward.

"Leave me, will you?" he heard his father ask.

"Wait, please," his mother begged. Words that would stop her son cold so many years later.

"Take my boy away?" Leif growled, and Clay realized that the voice in his head, the one that condemned him and cut him down, was not his own. It was his father's.

There was a wet crunch—a sickening sound—followed by another awful silence. Straining his ears, Clay heard the sound of his father weeping quietly, and then another voice spoke in his head. It was unfamiliar, quietly ominous. It reminded Clay of a forest cloaked in the deep snows of winter. This voice, he knew at once, was his own. Or a part of him, anyway.

"Rise," it said. And he rose.

When Leif finally stumbled, red-handed, through the bedroom door, his son was waiting for him. Clay had planted his feet and set his shoulders, just as he'd been taught. His grip on the axe was low, and he swung with all the strength he could muster.

Hit it like you hate it, Leif had told him, and that, Clay found, was the easiest thing about killing his father.

*   *   *

Come home to me, Clay Cooper.

He wasn't dead, apparently. And even if he were, Clay knew, those words would bring him back. Over mountains, through swamp and field and forest, across an ocean if need be, to her. Because home, for Clay Cooper, was not within the boundary of any realm. It wasn't Coverdale, or a house at the end of a long road. Home was where Ginny was, its boundaries defined by the circle of her arms. Hers was the hearth in which his soul burned, unquenchable. She was, quite simply, the only reason he was still alive.

Well, that and an exceptionally durable suit of armour.

Clay lost count of the times he hit the mountain on the way down, though to be fair he stopped counting after being rendered unconscious. The first impact, which came long seconds after he fell from the bridge, broke his left arm—which might have bothered him more were there a functioning hand at the end of it, but there wasn't. The second time he landed hard, but the *Warskin* was famed for being impenetrable, and so Clay hit the mountainside like an egg in an iron shell. He half-slid, half-tumbled down a long slope and then, after spilling over another sheer drop, cracked his head against stone and slipped into blackness.

Despite this, his prejudice against helmets remained unchanged. You had your pride, Ganelon had told him once, or you had nothing.

He awoke buried in a tomb of snow and wriggled free, since his right arm was strapped to *Blackheart* and the stump of his left wrist was shit for digging. The cold, at least, helped to slow the loss of blood to a survivable trickle, like sap oozing from an elm in winter. When he was free of the snow, Clay slung his shield over one shoulder and tore a strip from his bearskin cloak. Between his chattering teeth and a near-frozen right hand it took him forever to tie off the wound.

Afterward he spent a few minutes staring at his mutilated wrist, repulsed because it looked so grotesquely surreal, fascinated because how had he *not* known there were *two* bones in his forearm? He was pondering this when the faint sound of singing pricked his ears.

It's the concussion, he told himself. *You're delirious, Cooper.*

But then the singer coughed, fell silent, and started up again. And what was more: Clay didn't know the song.

He stood, fell sideways, and stood again. He tried to swipe the hair from his eyes but only clubbed himself with the stump of his severed hand. It was extremely painful and only slightly less embarrassing because no one was around to see.

Clay began walking toward the sound. After five or six steps he stopped, fumbled right-handed into his breeches, and relieved himself into the snow. *No blood*, he noted, admiring the stream. That was good.

His gaze scaled the wall of the Defile before him, the top half of which was stained red by the setting sun. Or the rising sun. Clay honestly had no idea how long he'd been out, but judging by how full his bladder was it had been several thousand years, at least. When he finished he ambled on, following the drift of song down the shadowed corridor.

He found the ettin lying among a heap of rubble. Its limbs were askew, Gregor's head was wrenched to a crazed angle. The wound in his throat had torn during the fall; his chest was stained by blood.

Dane, miraculously, was still alive. He'd been singing softly to himself, and when he heard the scuff of Clay's approach he raised his head wearily. "Hello?"

"Hi, Dane."

"Clay? Did you fly here, too?"

Clay might have laughed if his ribs didn't hurt so bad. "I did," he answered finally. "Bit of a rough landing, though."

Dane giggled at that, but then raised a finger to his lips. "Gregor's asleep," he said. "I was singing him a lullaby, like our mother did when we were little. I don't remember her, but Gregor says she was very pretty."

Clay had never seen a pretty ettin. He honestly doubted there were any. Even so, he decided to believe it anyway.

Gregor had been born a monster in a monstrous world, and had managed to find beauty in it nonetheless. He'd squeezed sweet juice from a rotten orange. He'd painted an old house pink. And what was more: He had given all this to his brother, as a gift.

"He's dreaming," Dane whispered.

Clay spared a glance for Gregor's gaping throat. *They share dreams*, he remembered. "You can see it?"

Dane nodded. "It's a pretty dream. A peaceful dream. I can see it in my head, like I'm there beside him."

You would have to be, thought Clay. *Unless ettins weren't ettins in their dreams.* Dane closed his rheumy eyes, and was silent for so long Clay thought he might have succumbed to his wounds, but then he smiled, teeth like broken columns gleaming in the twilight. "It's so beautiful, Clay. I wish you could see."

Clay was cold. He was tired and hungry and hurt. He'd been betrayed—they all had—by Larkspur, and Matrick was very probably doomed. She would take him east, and Gabriel would carry on to Castia; he was too close to turn back now. Ganelon would follow him. Moog would wring his hands and tug his beard, but he would go on as well, because what else could he do? The path behind would be swarming with rasks.

The band was broken. What little hope they'd had was lost. Rose, by her own admission, was damned, and the dark days to come would claim them each, one by one. *Except, perhaps, for me*, thought Clay. He alone was trapped in limbo, stranded between life and death, standing at heaven's door without a hand to knock.

He knelt, settling himself on his haunches, and crossed his arms against the cold. "Will you tell me," Clay asked, "about the dream?"

*   *   *

When Clay awoke it was morning. He'd fallen asleep on his knees, chin nestled against the cold chain links of his armour. A light snow was coming down, settling soft as benediction upon his shoulders. The ettin was dead.

Dane, he saw through bleary eyes, had died as he'd lived: with a great big ugly smile on his face.

It took an effort to rise. His back groaned, his ribs whimpered, his knees howled in protest, but he managed to stand, and stay standing, as he looked left and right down the Defile. No giants. Nothing but stillness and snow falling. For a moment Clay wished he'd insisted they come this way instead of taking the Cold Road. But no, he had long since learned that harbouring regrets was akin to stashing embers in your pockets: it was pointless and bound to hurt. Probably Ginny had told him that.

His gaze snagged on something to the east: a pall of smoke against the blue-white sky. *A signal,* he knew immediately.

My men will find me, Larkspur had promised him on the bridge. *I'll make sure of that.*

Clay chewed his lip, looking east. How long before the *Dark Star* passed near enough to see the smoke? *A day or so if I'm lucky,* Clay figured. *A few hours if I'm not.*

Hey, Cooper, another part of his mind chimed in, *you just lost your hand, fell down a mountain, and watched a friend die in the cold. How lucky are you feeling right now?*

"Fair point," he muttered, to no one at all.

Whatever happened in Castia, Clay's part in it was finished. The daeva had seen to that. He would never reach the city in time to help Gabriel. There was, however, a chance he could rescue Matrick before Larkspur's thralls arrived, assuming he could do anything at all with cracked ribs and a missing hand against the deadly hunter and her fabulous new scythe.

He started running anyway.

Chapter Forty-six

Deliverance

Clay's determined run had long since become a jog, which in turn degraded into a forward-leaning shamble barely faster (but somehow more exhausting) than a walk. When the rumbling stride of giants shook the ground Clay was grateful for the opportunity to collapse behind a boulder and catch his breath as they passed by.

The drum-deep voice of one drifted down to him from above. "I don't get it. So if I *literally* froze my balls off—"

"Then it would mean that your balls had *actually* frozen and fallen off," boomed a second voice. "What you really mean to say is that you *figuratively* froze your balls off."

"So I've been using it wrong all this time?" asked the first.

"Literally!" his companion groaned, and both giants fell to laughter.

Clay waited until their footsteps faded before moving on. Sometime after noon he emerged from the wide mouth of the Defile and began climbing the southern flank of Deliverance yet again. Sweat chilled on his skin, his ribs complained with every sucking breath, but still he compelled himself on, step by plodding step, desperate to reach the column of smoke before Larkspur's skyship arrived.

*   *   *

The *Dark Star* beat him there, but barely. Clay was near enough to see it descend. Lightning cracked from sail to sail, the engines slowing until only a single gyre whirled within each—enough to keep the dreadnought hovering just above the rocky ground. A ladder was thrown over the side and a handful of monks came clambering down. Their crimson robes whipped around them in the wind.

Clay was laid out behind a nearby ridge, propped on his good elbow. He watched as Larkspur started down the slope, leaving her captive trussed and apparently unconscious beside the remains of her fire. If Clay could free Matrick, then maybe they could escape into the Defile, where the skyship couldn't follow and Larkspur's flight would make her an obvious target for giants.

A bitter chuckle escaped him. *It's a terrible plan, Cooper, but it's all you've got. Now get up . . .*

He made to push himself up, but his arm gave way beneath him. Clay's jaw cracked against stone and his ribs muttered their displeasure. Breath fumed from his nose as he tried once again to rise. He failed. His legs were heavy as stone, and Clay could feel his heart shudder in panic at the thought of any more effort on its part. *Don't make me*, it begged. *You can't make me!*

"Fuck you I can't," Clay hissed. He dragged a knee beneath him, used it to push himself up. He swayed there a moment before staggering to his feet. A step took him onto the ridge behind which he'd been hiding, another took him over, and then momentum carried him down the pebbled slope toward Matrick. He glanced right and saw the monks abasing themselves at Larkspur's feet, their faces pressed to the ground. The setting sun threw his shadow almost to the daeva's back.

Clay stumbled to his knees between Matrick and the daeva's signal fire, hoping the veil of smoke might obscure their escape. The king looked up, bleary-eyed. He'd lost some weight over the past few weeks, and it showed now more than ever. He looked drawn, grey-whiskered jowls hanging loose on gaunt cheeks. "Clay?"

"The one and only."

"She said you were dead. She said you fell."

"I fell," Clay confirmed. "Not dead, though. Not yet." He tried on a grin that didn't quite fit.

Matrick scowled. "Where's Gabriel? Is he with you? Where are the others?"

"They're gone," Clay told him, and when Matrick's face paled he quickly clarified: "They went on ahead, I mean. It's just us now."

Matrick moaned. "You shouldn't have come. She wants me alive, but she'll kill you for sure."

"Thanks for the heads-up," Clay murmured.

"Gods, your hand!" Matrick pointed toward the stump as Clay went hunting for bindings beneath the dingy fox-fur cloak.

"What about it?"

"Where is it?"

"I lost it."

"You *lost* your hand? What do you mean you *lost* it? How—"

"Matty, I can't . . . Are you even tied up?"

"What? No."

Clay raked hair from his eyes, exasperated. "Where are your knives?"

Matrick patted the sheaths on his backside. "Right here, why?"

"*Why?!*" Clay forced the word though his teeth to keep from shouting. "Why are you still here? Why not run? Or fight?"

"What's the point?" Matrick shrugged helplessly. "We're fucked, Clay. Literally fucked."

"Figuratively."

"What?"

"Nothing. Never mind."

"We can't outrun her," Matrick sighed. He looked as tired as Clay felt, and near to tears. "We can't outfight her. We obviously can't outsmart her. I mean, all that Sabbatha stuff? She was faking the whole time! Best to just let her take me and have done with it."

Clay couldn't believe his ears. He'd been pushing himself all day. He had reached the very limit of his endurance and then pressed on for several hours more. He'd risked his life to rescue Matrick, and now Matrick *didn't want to be rescued*? It was too much. It really was. He closed his eyes, swallowed hard to keep the rage from rising in his throat, and said as calmly as he could, "Get up."

"Clay!"

"Get up!" he repeated, realizing too late that Matrick had been trying to warn him. Clay spun in time to see a monk burst through the curtain of smoke, wisps curling away from an outstretched foot. The kick broke his nose all over again and split the raw wound on his face, spilling fresh blood in an arc as his head snapped around. Clay crashed in a heap, pain blaring in his skull like a bad song played too loudly with the wrong instruments. Someone grabbed his legs, dragged him over grating stone. His fingers scrabbled without purchase and his eyes swam, searching for focus.

He glimpsed clouds dark as bruises against the orange sky, and the swirl of red robes—like blood in water—as the monks swarmed him.

Clay could feel fists and feet pummeling him. The *Warskin* soaked up the brunt of it, but even still his ribs wept like a grieving mother. He was kicked in the shin, punched in the neck, and was trying to decide which was more painful (the neck—definitely the neck) when Matrick cried out.

"Sabbatha! Tell them to stop! It's me you want! He was only trying to help. Let him go! Let him go and I'll come along nice and easy."

Silence from the daeva, and several more blows from her thralls. Clay curled in on himself, cradling his severed hand, good arm thrown up to try to protect his head.

"Stop it!"

A kick rolled him over and Clay saw Matrick leap to his feet.

"Stop, now!" he barked, but might have been a chirping squirrel for the attention they paid him. Between one kick and the next Matrick's expression went from helplessness to frustration, from frustration to livid anger. He reached beneath his cloak...

Please, please the knives.

...and withdrew a flask. He tore off the cap and threw it away, then tipped the flask to his lips. His throat pulsed as Matrick gulped down its contents, then he tossed it as well and shrugged the fox-skin cloak from his shoulders. He wiped his mouth with the back of one hand.

"There goes nice and easy," he growled, and finally, *finally*, out came the knives.

Gabriel killed with flash and flourish, Ganelon with the instinct of a natural-born predator. When it came to fighting, Clay tried only to keep himself and his friends alive. And Moog? Well, the wizard was full of surprises, most of them more distracting than deadly.

Matrick, on the other hand, was a cutthroat murderer. By the time Gabe finished toying with a foe or Ganelon wrenched his bloody axe from an enemy corpse, Matrick could punch holes in half a dozen men. He fought with a kind of meticulous fury, parsing out violence in short, frenetic bursts. Clay had once seen him go up against six men and come out on top. Of course he'd been much younger then, and a great deal faster, and not nearly as fat.

He didn't kill any of the monks when he leapt to Clay's rescue, but he slashed all seven of them at least once. They scattered like wolves driven off by a burning brand, but like wolves they came circling back, hungry for blood.

Matrick picked one from the pack and rushed him, ducking a chop aimed at his head and driving both knives into the man's chest. He yanked the blades free, whirling as his assailants closed, and used one of his favourite tricks to help even the odds: he flicked a knife at the nearest man's face. He didn't throw it—it wasn't an attack—but the blood on the blade spattered into the monk's eyes, momentarily blinding him.

A moment was all it took. Matrick opened the man's throat and moved on, slicing three fingers from the next monk to reach for him and ramming the other knife up under his chin, cutting short a scream.

Four, Clay counted, watching from the ground. *One against four*.

A kick sent Matrick rolling sideways, and he kept rolling, evading a stomp from one monk and taking the legs out from another. He came up slashing, fending off a flurry of blows with sharp-edged blades. He glanced over the shoulder of one attacker and grinned.

The man looked. Of course he looked, because nobody just *grinned* over your shoulder at nothing in the middle of a fight.

Except sometimes they did.

One against three, thought Clay as the monk hit the ground.

Matrick was dancing, bouncing on the balls of his feet, weaving like a snake charmed from the basket. He was smiling in earnest now, obviously enjoying himself, and when the next monk drew close Matrick only snapped his teeth and the fellow jumped back in fear.

"Ha." Matrick straightened and gave his knives a spinning flourish, and dropped them both.

Yep. Both.

Clay didn't see what happened next, since a woman's harsh laugh demanded his attention. Larkspur was standing over him, *Umbra* slung across her shoulders. Something about her gaze—sidelong, appraising—was distinctly avian.

"You're a hard man to kill, Clay Cooper."

Despite the nagging pain in his legs, back, feet, neck, head, and arms, and notwithstanding the sense of overwhelming hopelessness that bloomed like a black flower in his gut, Clay found it surprisingly effortless to fashion a dispirited smile of his own. "But I'm easy to hurt," he said.

Her face slackened. Her eyes drifted to the bloodied stump of his left arm. She opened her mouth, but clamped it quickly shut, as though afraid an apology might escape unbidden. He could see the muscles in her jaw working, and could imagine her knuckles whitening beneath those sharpened steel talons. She looked, for half a heartbeat, like the woman with whom they had endured the trials of these past weeks, and Clay wondered which of the two—Sabbatha, inquisitive and empathetic, or Larkspur, the cruel and callous manhunter—was the greater affectation.

Which are you, Ginny whispered in his head, *the monster or the man?*

Looking up at the daeva, Clay could see her struggling with the same question, the same self-defining choice. He could have said something, he knew. He might have urged her to spare him, and in doing so, to preserve whatever vestige remained of the girl she'd once been. But he knew as well that a wrong word could simply goad her into deciding too quickly, or else concluding, rashly and wrongly, that she had no choice at all.

One hand scraped down the length of her weapon's haft, a noise like a raven's claw scratching at a tombstone. The light went out of her eyes, and Clay suddenly wished he'd said something, anything, to forestall this moment.

"I—" was as far as she got before the bolt slammed into her chest, launching her backward. She crashed in a heap several yards away, unmoving. Clay gaped at where Larkspur had been standing a moment before; there were only feathers now, spinning on the wind as another skyship dropped from the sky.

The glare of gold sunlight forced Clay to shield his eyes. Squinting, he scanned behind him and saw Matrick wrestling with the last remaining monk. Their struggle lapsed as the shadow of the arriving ship enveloped them, but Matrick quickly seized the advantage. He wrested one of his knives from the other man's grip and knocked him out with its pommel.

"You boys need a ride?" someone shouted. The voice was gruff, familiar. And so, when Clay could finally see well enough to make it out, was the face to whom it belonged.

Barret was perched at the *Old Glory*'s rail. He was holding a crossbow, the source of the bolt that had nailed Larkspur seconds earlier.

"That depends," Clay called out. "You heading west?"

Vanguard's frontman looked despairingly at Ashe and Tiamax, both of whom loomed behind him. The arachnian waved four arms at once, and Clay raised his remaining hand in salute.

"I'm afraid so," Barret said.

Chapter Forty-seven

New Hands, Old Friends

Clay was leaning out over the *Glory*'s rail, watching the sky-ship's shadow ripple over snow and stone. The wind stung tears from his eyes, tussled his hair, and tugged fitfully at the fringe of his bearskin cloak. It was fiercely cold, and it made the wound on his face itch like the Summer Lord's flea-ridden beard, but *good gods* it felt great.

He was alive. Matrick was alive. They'd been improbably rescued by old and faithful friends and were now skyborne, speeding toward a reunion with their bandmates, who no doubt assumed they were dead.

Oh, and he had a new hand.

"I can fix that for you," Tiamax had told him shortly after takeoff. They weren't going far, since flying over mountains at night was about as safe as sharing a bathtub with an alligator, but they were in a hurry, and even a dying sun shed light by which to see.

Clay had been fussing with his makeshift tourniquet, which had soaked through with blood and constricted as it dried. "You have bandages?" he asked.

"Of course. But I meant your hand. You want a new one?"

Clay frowned, trying to decide if the arachnian meant that as a joke, but it was difficult to glean anything like mirth in those insectile eyes. "You can make me a fake hand?"

Chittering laughter. "I can *grow* you a perfectly new one."

Clay sat waiting for the punch-line, but Tiamax only watched him expectantly, so he decided to take the bait. "How?"

"The solution is complex, but the procedure is easy enough. You've been out of the game a while, Slowhand. We've come a long way since you and yours sheathed your swords. I can have the unguent ready within the hour if you'd like."

Either the arachnian was being serious or he was hopelessly inept at pulling off a joke. "What's this...unguent made of?"

Three pairs of segmented arms shrugged. "Quite a few herbs, actually, plus a bit of troll, a dash of starfish, and some people."

"People?"

"People," said Tiamax flatly.

"Is it magic?"

"It's *medicine*. Also, there's a pinch of orc to help the bones mature faster. Did you know an orc can grow more than two thousand teeth over the course of its lifetime?"

Clay hadn't, but he was too aghast to say so at the moment. Eventually he tipped his head to indicate the medic's broken mandible. "Why not use it on yourself?"

Tiamax made a clicking noise. "Doesn't work on us hatchers, I'm afraid. Besides, I think this makes me look tough."

Ashe, who was sharpening a blade on the couch across from Clay, scoffed quietly.

"How long will it take?" Clay asked skeptically.

"Several hours," said Tiamax. "I'll give you something to help you sleep. The regenerative process can be somewhat painful, I'm told. Also it's quite unsettling to watch, as you can imagine.

Clay sighed. He had little to lose in trying, he supposed, and if this miracle unguent spared him from explaining to

Ginny why he'd left the house with two hands and come home with only one, then it was worth a shot, no question.

"Then again," Tiamax mused, " '*No*hand' has a certain ring to it."

Barret, on lookout from the opposite rail, was the first to spot them. "There! Edwick, bring us down."

"Down we go," shouted the bard, his hands moving lightly over the steering orbs.

The airborne dhow swooped low over rugged foothills, and as it swerved to land Clay caught sight of his bandmates. Gabe and Ganelon stopped to watch, but Moog hiked up his robes and ran at a sprint to meet the craft as it touched down. The owlbear cubs loped behind him, nipping at one another in an effort to be nearest the wizard's heel.

Matrick loosed a whoop and leapt past Clay. He and Moog came together in a tangle of wild laughter and a great deal of jumping.

Clay eased himself onto the ground. Despite the medic's attention (and a junkie's helping of drugs to numb the pain) he was still in pretty rough shape. Tiamax had stitched his face up and set his broken arm with a splint and sling, but a dull ache suffused his entire body, and his head throbbed as if he'd drunk an entire keg by himself the night before. Then again, considering the fact that he'd fallen down a mountainside and spent the following day running halfway up it again, Clay had to admit he felt far better than he had any right to.

"Clay!" Moog bounded up to him, blue eyes glistening. "By the Tiny Gods of Goblinkind, I thought I'd never see that sweet face of yours again!" He spent a moment analyzing the arachnian's stitch job. "That hatcher is an artist with needle and thread, I'll grant him that. The things I could accomplish with four more arms than I already have. And your hand! May I?"

Clay shrugged, and the wizard stooped to examine the appendage.

"Fascinating," he breathed, then leaned in close and sniffed. "Is that starfish?"

Clay withdrew his hand as Kit shuffled over. "You've a bit of phoenix in your blood," said the ghoul.

Ganelon stepped up and clapped him on the shoulder. "You die hard, Slowhand," he grated, which, as Clay understood it, passed for a glowing compliment among stone-cold killers.

"But I break easy," Clay said, mimicking the words he'd said to Larkspur the day before. He wondered briefly whether or not the daeva was dead. When Clay had seen her last she'd been laid out, unmoving, with a long iron bolt jutting from her chest. And before that . . . well, he was fairly certain she'd been about to kill him. But even so, a part of him hoped she lived long enough to outrun the shadow of her past.

Ganelon chuckled, gave his shoulder a friendly squeeze, and stepped away.

Gabriel approached him last. "I thought—"

"I know."

"If you—"

"I know," Clay cut him off again.

Gabriel flung himself the last few paces, crushing Clay in an embrace so tight he could almost hear his ribs groan. Clay clamped his good arm around Gabe's neck and felt his friend draw a shuddering breath.

When Clay trusted himself to speak, he did. "I'm back."

"You're back," Gabe said into his shoulder, and then withdrew, taking in the rest of the band with eyes gone sharp and bright as diamonds. "And now we finish this."

"To be honest, I didn't plan on coming," Barret said. "Only my wife got sick of me moping around the house. She fairly put the sword in my hand and kicked me out the door!"

"Lies," Ashe cut in, stating the obvious.

Barret chuckled. "Anyway, my boys are in Kaladar for the War Fair, or I might have brought them along. They've got their own thing going now. The Wight Nights, they call themselves. Orc-shit name for a band if you ask me, but they didn't bother asking." He blew out a long sigh. "Ah well, can't imagine they'll be sorry they missed out on this little adventure. We hit a few pretty vicious storms on the way across, and had to land once and fill the engine with water that smells like a city sewer, but hey—we made it!"

"I'm happy to be here," said Piglet, crunching on a pretzel half as big as his head.

"Me too," said Ashe with a cutlass smirk. "It's some kinda thrill, I tell ya, starting a fight you can't win." She winked and sidled up beside Ganelon. "Makes my britches moist."

"We might win," squeaked Piglet.

Tiamax raised a glass. "Here's to moist britches and the boundless, irrational optimism of youth!" He looked twice at Matrick (well, *twelve* times, actually, if you counted all eight eyes and subtracted the two patched over). "You need a drink, Matty?"

The old king smiled politely. "No, thank you. I'm...all done, I think."

The medic made a sound between a hiss and a rattle that Clay took for disbelief. "Done what? Not drinking. Drinking?"

"Drinking, yeah."

"Well that's it, then," said Moog cheerily. "World's over."

They all laughed—even Ganelon—and Clay's mind went back to the night they'd spent in the mountain cave, when he'd pondered the bizarre sense of elation that so often suffused the eve of battle.

This is it, he thought, looking from face to face around the skyship's deck. Each smile a fraction too wide, every laugh a little too loud. There was something unreal about this moment, something *not quite right*, like watching a beard-spider dance or getting stabbed on your birthday. *This is the end. And every one of us knows it.*

"We didn't know where exactly to find you," Barret was saying. "But then we saw the smoke, and found these two scrapping with the manhunter and her thralls."

"Lucky for us," said Matrick.

"So Larkspur is dead?" Gabe asked.

"Probably?" Clay guessed, and saw Ganelon's eyes narrow a fraction.

"I'd forgotten about the War Fair," said Moog, absently stroking the feathers of the owlbear asleep on his lap.

"Biggest party in the world," said Barret. "I'll confess I'm a little sorry to be missing it."

Ashe swatted the air. "Pah! What's to miss? Just a bunch of wannabe mercs and washed-up heroes mucking about in some old ruins. Here's where the real party's at, eh Gabe?"

"All done," piped Kit. The revenant had been hovering over a low table for the better part of an hour, using chalkstone to sketch a detailed map of Castia and its surroundings. The members of both bands gathered to survey it.

"The city straddles the river, like Fivecourt, except it is built on a rise instead of a valley. There are two gates. East—" Kit used a slender grey finger to point them out on the map "—and west. The walls are thick and extremely high, which is why it has withstood the siege for so long already. You could go over—or under, I suppose—but there's no going through. This is the noble quarter here, and a wall surrounds it as well."

Gabriel scowled at the map with sour interest, as though it were a painting of his ex-wife naked. "So if the outer wall is breached, the survivors will hole up there?"

Kit shook his head. "The outer wall was made to protect men from monsters. It has flame throwers, shock turrets, and ballista towers every fifty yards. This inner wall serves to stop peasants from wandering into a senator's backyard. If they *do* manage to get inside the city, the Horde will roll over that second wall like it was a picket fence."

"Can we sneak in through the river?" Gabe asked.

"Lastleaf will have tried that already," Kit told him. "The river curves north here. It runs beneath the hill and is trapped in the city reservoir, but there are several gates barring the way. It was never used for trade, only a source of freshwater."

"Not anymore," Matrick said glumly.

Vanguard's bard, sitting cross-legged on his pilot's stool and tuning a mandolin, cleared his throat before speaking up. "Remind me again why we don't just fly in? I mean, we're here for Rose, right? Why not just snatch her up and be on our way? Maybe even catch the last days of the War Fair?"

"Plague hawks, rot sylphs, you name it," Moog answered. "We caught a glimpse of the city in my crystal ball before Gabe—" he caught himself. "Before it fell in the river. The sky was full of all kinds of awful. Also, Lastleaf has a wyvern matriarch with him, and her brood will be there as well. We'd get torn apart long before we reached the city."

"Fair enough," said Edwick, returning his attention to the instrument in his hands.

Ganelon pointed to a crude circle sketched to the west of Castia. "What's this here?"

"Teragoth," said the revenant. "Well, the ruins thereof. The Dominion road runs right through Castia, under the arch of the Threshold here, and up into the old city."

"Threshold?" Barret interjected. "You mean like the one in Kaladar?"

"Just so," said Kit.

Clay took a break from anxiously chewing his lip to add his own voice to the mix. "Don't forget about Akatung. Shadow said he lairs in a shrine there."

Barret frowned. "Akatung. Why does that name sound familiar?"

"Dragon," said Ganelon, and Edwick chose this moment to strum an ominous note on his mandolin.

The frontman's bushy brows nearly leapt off his face. "Say what now?"

"Never mind the dragon," Gabe assured him. "We're not going into Teragoth anyway."

"Yes we are!" Moog blurted.

Clay was back to biting his lip. *Here it comes*, he thought.

"I have a plan," the wizard announced, peering down at the map over steepled fingers. Laughter bubbled up his throat and emerged as a worrisome cackle. "And let me tell you, friends—"

"It's risky?" Gabe supplied.

Moog glanced up. His eyes wide and wild above a lunatic smile. "Verging on suicidal," he said.

Chapter Forty-eight

The Maze of Stone and Fire

"Suicidal is right," Ashe muttered. "I can't believe we sent Matty into a dragon's lair by himself."

"I should have been the one to do it," said Kit. "I've little to fear from a dragon, but Matrick—"

"—was once a thief," Gabriel told them. "And a damned good one. If anyone can pull this off, he can."

They'd entered Teragoth before sunrise this morning, giving Castia a wide berth and approaching the ancient ruins from the south. Edwick brought the *Old Glory* in low, so as not to draw attention from the Horde. Kit had offered an unasked-for narration as they navigated the derelict city, elaborating on its former glory.

"There's what's left of the akra track. I won a fortune there once, and lost it all on a single bet." He shook his head and pursed his bloodless lips. "I should have known a bird named *Sure Thing* was too good to be true. And look, the scroll house! It had a roof once, and a lovely patio from which you could see the entire city. They served the most incredible brunch: poached basilisk eggs and toasted bread with brown butter preserve. No one does a good basilisk egg anymore," he remarked sadly, and Clay heard Ganelon mutter under his breath: *What the fuck is brunch?*

They'd set the skyship down in what had once been a grand forum. Moog's plan—Moog's brilliant, desperate, utterly preposterous plan—required one of them to sneak into the old shrine to Tamarat, the apparent lair of the dragon Akatung. Matrick had volunteered, and so the rest of them sat aboard the *Glory*, hoping against hope that their presence in the city remained unnoticed by Lastleaf or his Horde.

Clay had been cautiously hopeful since the wizard had outlined his strategy the night before, but when the sun broke over the snow-mantled mountains he was offered his first glimpse—aside from what he'd seen in Moog's crystal ball— of Castia itself, rising like a white shoal in the midst of a poisoned ocean just a few miles east.

And suddenly every breath was a sucking gasp, every heartbeat a hammer blow. A part of Clay's mind begged him to turn away, to close his eyes, to look anywhere but at the writhing, crawling, clamouring monstrosity that was the Heartwyld Horde, but he could not.

Someone, probably Gabriel, had once told him that to be courageous you had to first know fear. As Clay saw it, he would need a reserve of courage in the hours to come that demanded more fear than he had ever known, and so he let the horror of what they were about to face wash over him, soak into him, clamp around his soul like an iron fist, and *squeeze* . . .

"He's been in there awhile," observed Tiamax. The arachnian had painted himself for war. His entire body was black, save for the tips of each spindly limb, which were bloodred, and he'd painted a red hourglass on his abdomen. Clay wasn't exactly sure why an hourglass should be frightening, but for some reason it was.

"I don't think we've been spotted yet," said Piglet, peering fearfully over the starboard rail.

So far, so good, Clay thought.

But then Ashe pointed down a debris-littered side street. "Gnolls!" she hissed.

Clay squinted down the alley. A pack of humanoid hyenas were skulking in the shadow of a ruined wall.

"Barret, Tiamax, Piglet," said Gabriel. "You three run them down. Ganelon and Ashe, circle round and head them off. The rest of us will stay and wait for Matrick."

To Clay's surprise Vanguard's frontman didn't blink an eye at taking orders from Gabe. He jumped over the rail and beckoned his bandmates to follow. "Let's get this done. If these bonesuckers run off and warn their friends this whole plan goes to shit."

Kit followed Ganelon and Ashe overboard. "I know the city," he explained when it looked as if the southerner would order him back. "I can help make certain they don't escape."

Ganelon nodded grudgingly and the three of them hurried off east.

One of the gnoll scavengers loosed a startled howl. Barret replied with his crossbow, cutting it short. He nodded at Edwick in the pilot's seat and then squinted up at Gabriel. "Don't go killing my bard."

Gabe's smile was stretched thin. "No promises," he said.

Barret chuckled, then turned to the others. "Let's roll!"

Tiamax went first, four of his six hands bearing some sort of weapon, one of which was a barbed javelin. He hurled it as he closed, impaling one of the scavengers, and then spun his abdomen toward the rest. A splash of white webbing burst from the spinnerets near his rear, trapping a few of the gnolls as surely as a net.

A sticky, super-gross net, thought Clay. He wrinkled his nose, wincing as the stitches in his face pulled taut. Needless to say, he was beginning to understand Ashe's reluctance to let the medic bed her, despite, as Tiamax himself had put it, the obvious benefit of having six hands.

Barret reloaded his crossbow on the run. He got one more shot off (the gnolls ensnared by webbing were easy prey) before he slung the weapon across his back and drew a pair of short axes from his belt. Piglet lumbered beside him wielding a square longshield and his father's spiked flail. Clay might have wondered if the kid could hold his own, except he knew Barret, and Barret wouldn't keep him around if Piglet were a liability, regardless of whether or not he was Hog's boy.

Gabriel stirred restlessly, and Clay recognised in his friend the same urge he was trying to quell within himself: to jump out there and join the fight. The impulse wasn't just mental, either. Clay's heart was thrumming in his chest. His fingers twitched with the craving to feel *Blackheart*'s familiar weight, or a weapon's heavy heft in his grasp, though *that* wouldn't be happening anytime soon—not while his arm was in a sling, anyway.

No doubt sensing their bloodlust, Moog shuffled over and crouched between them. "Pretty fat for a warrior, eh?"

"Huh?" He and Gabe expressed their confusion in unison.

"Elavis." Moog indicated the statue in the centre of the shrine's sunken plaza. It was in miraculously good repair, considering its age and the state of its immediate surroundings. Set upon on a plinth twice as tall as Clay, the ancient deity stood with his head bowed, one hand clasping the hilt of a huge broadsword planted between his feet, the other pointed east, presumably toward the heart of Dominion power. Also, as Moog had so keenly observed, he *was* pretty fat.

"He was a hero of the Old Dominion. One of their greatest warriors, in fact."

Clay frowned up at the statue. "I thought humans were mostly servants back then."

"They mostly were," Moog confirmed. "But Elavis was an exception. He made his name by challenging the champions of rival Exarchs to single combat. He died without ever having lost a battle. Too young, alas."

"Young?" asked Gabriel. "How did he die then?"

Moog scratched at one bushy eyebrow. "Well, you see how big he was. Apparently he broke through a latrine seat and drowned in the sewage below."

A shitty way to go, Clay was about to remark when a muffled shout echoed from beyond the recessed columns fronting the shrine. "Did you guys hear that?"

Edwick was cupping one ear. "It sounded like Matrick," he said.

More incomprehensible words drifted into the plaza. Gabriel slipped over the skyship's low rail and moved a few paces ahead. Clay looked down the side street; gnoll corpses littered the ground, but there was no sign of Barret and the others.

"...rt...ip!" came the voice from within the temple, still faint.

"That was Matty, no doubt," said Moog. "But the words... Gabe, could you make out any of that?"

Gabriel shook his head. "It sounded like—"

"'Aren't the shrimp'?" Moog guessed. "What the heck is he talking about? What shrimp?"

"'Start the ship,'" Clay said under his breath.

Matrick came bolting from the shadows between two columns. His legs were pumping furiously, and he was cradling something against his chest that looked like a white stone wheel. "Start the ship!" he shrieked. "Start the ship start the ship *start the fuckin' ship*!"

Gabriel spun. "Edwick—"

"Starting the ship!" yelled Edwick, already dashing toward his chair.

The entire front of the shrine exploded outward. Blocks of stone rained down on the plaza, bursting on impact into spinning shrapnel shards, and a dragon—a real live you-gotta-be-shitting-me *dragon*—came roaring from the ruin.

Akatung looked much as Clay remembered him: vast and malevolent, armoured in jet-black scales and bristling with enough horns and spines and spikes to hang every hat in the world. And what was more: he still looked fairly pissed about the *You guys nearly killed me* thing from way back when, so that was probably bad.

Matrick sprinted past the statue of Elavis.

The dragon burst through it without slowing.

Matrick took the steps to the square three at a time.

The dragon was up them in a single stride.

Matrick was halfway to the ship when a chunk of stone clipped his heel and sent him sprawling, huddled protectively around the relic in his arms.

"Stay here," shouted Gabriel, and took off running.

The dragon lunged at Matrick. Its jaw hinged open like a snake's, lips peeling back from a double row of razor fangs. Matrick was fumbling with something at his waist, but if he hoped to stop a dragon with a knife . . .

Not a knife, Clay registered. *Something else. A . . . horn?*

The blast Matrick blew made no sound at all, but a plague of insects boiled out from inside—bees and beetles, wasps and weevils; grasshoppers, moths, crickets, cockroaches, horseflies, butterflies, dragonflies, and fireflies that glimmered like stars through a veil of pestilent cloud—straight into Akatung's mouth. Its jaws snapped shut just short of the king. Its yellow eyes bulged, and then the dragon made a sound like a cat summoning a sticky hairball from the depths of its stomach.

Gabe helped Matrick to stand and the two of them stumbled on as Akatung began coughing plumes of insects into the sky. When they'd climbed aboard, Gabriel took the white wheel from Matrick and offered it to Moog. "Is this it?"

The wizard took it reverently, a look of astonished wonder on his face. "This is it. This is Teragoth's keystone! See this groove here? When you—"

"Moog."

"Yes?"

Gabriel pointed. "*Dragon.*"

"Oh, yes, sorry. Plan B, then?"

"Will it work, do you think?"

Clay looked from the wizard to Gabriel. "There's a plan B?"

Moog nodded determinedly. "We have to try," he said, before leaping over the opposite rail and taking off at a sprint toward the eastern gate.

"Where's he going?"

"The Threshold," said Gabriel. "Edwick, we need to keep that thing busy until he gets there."

"Can do," said the bard. "I'll take us up—"

"Not up!" Gabe told him. "Not yet. We need to find the others first. Stay as close to the ground as you can."

"But the dragon—"

"—will be the least of our problems if Lastleaf knows we're here."

Clay turned to Matrick. "What's plan B?"

"No idea," said Matrick, still gasping for breath. "But it can't be any worse than plan A."

Akatung, meanwhile, had fixed them with a baleful glare. His eyes were roaring, hateful hearths. He bellowed something in the incomprehensible tongue of dragonkind that Clay assumed wasn't a friendly greeting.

"We'd better move," Gabe warned. "Now!"

Edwick sent the onyx orbs spinning. The dhow veered sideways as the dragon pounced. They plunged between its legs, but a tail swipe clipped the stern and rocked the *Old Glory* onto her side. The skyship tipped like a riverboat hit by a tsunami, but Edwick managed to steer them straight. The engine frothed as they shot like an arrow down a branching avenue.

They soared over a pile of sloughing rubble, slipped beneath the arch of a towering waterway. Edwick dared a glance over his shoulder. "Is it following us?"

"I don't—" Clay looked back in time to see the street behind them detonate. Three stories of stonework burst like a sundered dam as the dragon charged through on a tide of billowing dust. "Yes," he answered. "Definitely yes."

They swerved onto a narrow lane. The ship bounced between walls and the sail pulsed with static discharge. Akatung came skidding around the corner. He shouldered through leaning pillars and stooping pediments as though they were drunks at the pub.

Another turn saw them speeding down a wide thoroughfare divided by massive plinths displaying a succession of sandaled feet. The statues to whom those feet belonged lay toppled to either side. The skyship swooped between them, left and right. Matrick snorted to himself, watching with amusement as Moog's owlbear cubs slid and scampered from one side of the deck to the other.

Clay risked poking his head over the rail. Akatung was gaining fast, loping like a dog on all fours, heedless of anything in his path. He saw the barbed fins on either side of the dragon's head flare open. "Turn!" he yelled at Edwick's back.

"Why?"

"*Turn!*"

They cut right as bright blue fire flooded the street behind them. The bard made a left next, hoping to throw off the pursuit. It appeared to have worked, so when Gabriel spotted Barret and his crew in an alley half a block over they doubled back, halting just as Tiamax cut the head from a gnoll with clashing swords.

"Get in!" Gabe shouted.

Barret was cranking the winch on his crossbow. "There's more of them!" He pointed at a gang of gnolls fleeing down the alley, but then Akatung's head appeared in the street beyond. There was a sound like ten thousand matches being struck at once, and the gnolls evaporated in a cone of blue-white flame.

"Never mind!" hollered Barret. He tossed his crossbow and scrambled inside. Tiamax gave Piglet a push up over the rail and leapt in after him. The dragon's breath funneled toward them, near enough that Clay could hear the howls it carried and feel the heat sear his face like a brand, but Edwick was already palming the orbs—they hurtled forward, weaving through a maze of tarnished splendour as fast as the *Old Glory* could manage.

Clay found himself thankful that Kit wasn't on board. *There's the art gallery*, he could imagine the ghoul droning on. *And here was the most delectable little bakery. I'll tell you one thing mankind has not improved upon in twelve hundred years: scones.*

"I see Ashe!" Barret pointed over Edwick's shoulder. She and Ganelon were pelting headlong down the avenue ahead. They were gaining fast on Kit, who had hiked his bedsheet robes to his knees and was shambling for all he was worth.

"Something's after them," said Gabriel.

Not gnolls, Clay thought. *There's no way Ganelon is running from gnolls.* He'd as likely see a wolf running from a flock of sheep.

His fears were confirmed as the *Old Glory* cleared the ruins. Akatung was there, long neck extended, the fins alongside his head fanning like a bellows.

"Hold on!" yelled Edwick. He grappled both orbs and kicked the lever that powered the tidal engine—it shuddered off, and the dhow went slewing sideways, angled so that Ashe and Ganelon, who saw it careening toward them, could leap over the lowered rail. Kit got clipped midwaist, but the *Glory* swallowed him anyway. Tiamax, who was already holding both owlbear cubs, managed to snatch the ghoul's ankle before he rolled out the opposite side.

The skyship kept on spinning until the bard wrenched the lever again. Every hair on Clay's body went rigid as the sail above him crackled with energy. The gyres roared to life, and the *Glory* straightened out as a wave of blue-white fire splashed by them on the left.

Gabriel stepped over Kit on his way to the pilot's chair. He put both hands on Edwick's slim shoulders. "Can you get us to the Threshold?" he asked.

"I can try," said Edwick, "but we're too slow to outrun that thing!"

"Too slow..." Gabe turned to survey the deck, then threw a questioning glance at Barret.

The frontman sighed. "Gods damn it. Dump the furniture."

Out went the couches, the chairs, the chests crammed with clothes and armour. Out went the mattresses, the barstools, the bar. Matrick himself tipped the booze cabinet over the rail, wincing as he heard it smash.

Clay caught Ganelon sizing up Piglet. "Hey," he said, drawing the warrior's attention, "no."

Ganelon at least had the grace to look ashamed.

They were out of the city now, racing east above the broad Dominion highway. The Threshold was directly ahead, a soaring black arch that straddled the road. And beyond that, across a wide, flat stretch of devastated farmland...a sight almost beyond comprehension.

Castia, and the Heartwyld Horde.

There were a pair of giants striding among the monstrous multitudes, and a whole mess of creatures Clay had never seen or couldn't discern from this far away. The sky above the city swarmed as well: plague hawks and long-necked wyverns turned lazy circles beyond reach of the city's formidable defences. Harpies, rot sylphs, bloodshot eyewings, and countless other flying atrocities frolicked among smoke and cloud.

The Horde didn't just fill the horizon—it *was* the horizon. It was *all there was to see*, and for a moment everyone on board the *Old Glory* simply stared at it over the prow.

Nine hearts shared a scale with the leaden weight of fear, and even the stoutest watched the balance tip against them. And then Kit, whose heart weighed less than an orange rind, and whose head was sticking over the rail, called out, "The dragon—"

"I know!" yelled Gabriel.

"It's right behind us!"

Leaning out as far as he dared, Clay saw that Kit was right:

Akatung was practically on top of them, so close that when the dragon roared Clay could smell the metallic char on its breath. He turned his face into the wind, and there was Moog, standing beside the Threshold, pushing the keystone into place.

"Where am I going?" hollered Edwick.

Gabriel's eyes were fixed dead ahead. "Straight through."

They sped below the empty arch, and in the split second they spent eye-to-eye Clay could have sworn he saw the wizard wink at him. Glancing back over the stern, Clay saw the dragon duck beneath the arch just as the space below it shimmered like the surface of a soap bubble.

And then Akatung disappeared.

The *Old Glory* banked sharply. Clay could see, though not rationalize, a huge volume of water surging from the west-facing side of the Threshold. Moog was standing just wide of the torrent, frantically turning the keystone with both hands as though he were shutting off a valve—which, apparently, he was. The deluge ended as abruptly as it began.

Clay and a few of the others sighed heavily. Edwick was chuckling like a madman, and Gabriel, behind him, wore an expression of exhausted relief.

It was Matty who broke the spell of baffled silence with a joyous hoot. "Hells yes!" he bellowed. "Let's hear it for plan B!"

Chapter Forty-nine

Immortality

There was a merman flopping on the wet earth. He gasped and gazed up at the sky, no doubt wondering where he was. He sputtered something at Clay and the others as they leapt clear of the dhow, but since none among them (not even Kit) spoke the liquid language of the mer-people, the poor fellow died, as so many of us do, without ever knowing the truth of why he was here.

Although the truth, in this case, was hard to believe.

Moog was beaming as they approached. "I opened a portal to Antica!" he said.

"What's Antica?" asked Piglet. The boy had produced a mangled pastry from somewhere on his person and was scooping the cherry filling out with two fingers.

When both Moog and Kit opened their mouths to explain, Gabriel cut in. "There's three of these things," he said, gesturing to the arc of black stone above. "One here, another in Kaladar, and the last in a city called Antica, which is at the bottom of the ocean."

Barret looked confused. "Antica? I thought that was—"

"It's not."

"So the dragon—"

"—had better be able to swim," said Gabriel, before turning to Moog. "Is it ready?"

"I believe so, yes."

"Good. Show Tiamax how to use it. You're coming with me. You too, Barret." Vanguard's leader nodded grimly. "The rest of you need to protect this portal, no matter what. It's a good bet Lastleaf knows we're here, and he might even guess we've got the key to Teragoth's Threshold. He will come for it with everything he's got, and if he succeeds—"

"He won't," said Ganelon.

Gabriel met the southerner's gaze. It looked as though he would say more, but he only nodded.

They moved to the eastern side of the Threshold. Clay surveyed the land between there and Castia: blasted farmsteads, the burnt-out husks of storehouses, gently sloping fields turned to mulch by the tread of foot, hoof, and claw. The city was three, maybe four miles distant, surrounded on all sides by the enemy. From here Clay could barely make out flashes of flame and arcs of lightning as Castia's defenders kept their airborne assailants from getting too near the city walls.

Moog inserted Teragoth's keystone into the smooth black stone of the Threshold and pointed out to the arachnian which of the engraved runes signified their intended destination.

Tiamax scratched beneath one of his leather eye patches. "How did you know which of the two was Antica?"

Moog shrugged, and then answered with unnerving sincerity, "Lucky guess."

Gabriel moved to stand before the portal, flanked by Moog and Barret. He smoothed his hair and rubbed a hand over his face. "How do I look?" he asked.

Barret grinned. "Old."

Moog glanced over appraisingly. "Tired."

Gabriel snorted a laugh. "Fuck you guys."

Tiamax turned the keystone; the air below the arc shone

with lucent colour, as it had just before the dragon had disappeared through it.

And then, a single, impossible step away, were the ruins of Kaladar, where every band in Grandual, every weathered merc and wannabe warrior, every man or woman looking to carve their name into history with a blade, had gathered for the War Fair.

Assuming they would be able to secure the keystone and open Teragoth's Threshold, this had been the second half of Moog's audacious plan. Everything now depended on what they were able to accomplish on the other side.

"Clay?"

Clay blinked, looked over to where Gabriel and the others were waiting. "What? You want me to come?" he asked.

Gabriel nodded. "I think I need you to."

The War Fair was, as Barret had mentioned earlier, the biggest party in all of Grandual. For three days every third year, the hills around the ancient Dominion capital of Kaladar were home to half the warriors in the world. There were Kaskar berserkers draped in heavy furs, silk-robed swordsmen from southern Narmeer, swaggering Phantran pirates adorned with ink and gold, and bowlegged Cartean plainsmen all mingling, laughing, gambling, shouting, and quite often fighting with one another. The older mercenaries and established bands came to rub shoulders and swap stories, while young adventurers and new bands sought to make a name for themselves and, ideally, land a gig that paid.

The ruins of an enormous theatre had been retrofitted as an arena, though there were plenty of less illustrious venues where fledgling fighters could test their mettle among themselves, or else square off with some captive creature brought in for the occasion. There was a makeshift labyrinth in which thieves seeking employment could showcase their skills by picking elaborate locks and evading (mostly) harmless traps, and even a nearby moonstone quarry where a storm witch or an alchemic sorcerer could really cut loose.

There were, naturally, several casualties during the course of the fair, but what was any good party without a few deaths?

Also, a gathering of so many warlike individuals meant that numerous other sordid types descended upon Kaladar like crows to carrion. All the usual suspects were present: claw-brokers, charm dealers, merchants selling arms and armour. There were more bards than you could count in half a day, and bookers prowled the grounds in search of ready-made heroes, because who knew if the next Saga-calibre band was out there, like chips of gold in a riverbed, waiting only to be sifted from the sand?

It occurred to Clay as he stepped from the Threshold into spitting rain that the War Fair was a great deal like Conthas, only with less rampant fire and considerably more pissing out of doors.

The Threshold in Kaladar was nestled in a copse of black pines and maples turned red by the Autumn Son's mouldering touch. There was already a crowd gathered, gawking through the portal at the scene beyond, and now that Clay and the others had come walking out, there were hundreds streaming in from the surrounding camps to see for themselves.

Gabriel was already speaking with some familiar faces out front, men and women Clay hadn't seen for years. There was Geralt Snakewater, and Merciless May Drummond, and Red Bob, whose illustrious locks had long since fled and left him bald.

Barret, meanwhile, beckoned a pair of youths from the crowd and introduced them to Clay. "These are my sons, Rogan and Syd. Boys, this here is Clay Cooper."

"A pleasure to meet you," said Rogan. He was older, bigger, and damn near the spitting image of his father, while the other was slight of build, with Avery's blue eyes and toothy smile. Both of them were wearing more eyeliner than a Narmeeri pillow boy and had bleached their hair platinum white.

"Our mother's told us a lot about you," said the younger one. "Every time we misbehave she swears she should have married Clay Cooper instead of the old man here."

Barret had a chuckle at that. "Fine by me. Whaddaya say, Slowhand, you up for swapping wives?"

Clay was about to politely refuse when a familiar voice shouted his name.

"Clay Cooper? Well slap my ass and call me sister! What're you doing this side o' the Wyld?"

Jain pushed clear of the crowd, followed closely by her gang, which seemed to have doubled in size since they'd last met in Conthas. They were all dressed in a plethora of silks and fine furs, though none seemed to care that the rain would do them harm.

Clay grinned. *You can take the girl out of Cartea...*

Jain gestured grandly at the women behind her. "Behold, the Silk Arrows!" she said. "Got a full quiver now, as you can see. You look like shit, by the way. What happened to your face?"

Clay shrugged. "I was born this way."

"Your momma keeps an axe in her womb, eh? Was thinking of trying that myself, to keep the boys out."

That got another laugh out of Barret. "Oh, I like this one," he said.

Gabriel, Clay saw, was arguing heatedly with one of the Skulk brothers. He broke from the crowd and physically dragged Moog out of conversation with May Drummond. "Fucking cowards," he muttered as the two of them drew up.

"They won't help?" Clay asked.

"They want us to *close the Threshold*," he said. "They think we should abandon Castia, forget that thirty thousand people are trapped inside! Geralt Snakewater said this! The man who knocked out a rock-hulk with his bare hands! And the Skulk brothers—they killed a dragon once, didn't they?"

"Small one," said Moog, holding two fingers an inch apart.

"Yeah, well, they won't come. They're afraid."

"Talk to them," Clay said.

Gabriel held up his hands despairingly. "I tried! I thought if I could get the stone rolling that others might follow, but—"

"No," Clay waved a hand to indicate the surrounding hills. "Talk to *them*. All of them. Forget Geralt Snakewater. You don't need washed-up heroes, Gabe. You need *new* ones."

"Damn right," growled Rogan, and his little brother smirked by way of agreement.

Jain straightened and tapped the butt of her bow against the ground. "I like the sound o' that," she said.

Gabriel looked unconvinced, so Clay went on. "When May Drummond or the Skulks see you, they see an old friend. They see the Gabriel that rode a horse up the Riot House stairs, or the one that got so drunk during the siege of Castadar he fell off the battlements."

"Priceless," laughed Barret. "We rallied out the front gate to rescue you and decided to break the siege while we were out there."

"Or maybe they see a rival. Maybe they think you got too big for your own good, which you did. Or that you were a loud, obnoxious ass, which you were." Gabe opened his mouth to protest, but Clay rolled over him. "But when these kids look at you . . . they see a *legend*. They see Golden Gabe, who killed the Crypt Queen and held the bridge at Trolltoll against a legion of lizardmen."

Gabriel cleared his throat. "Actually, that was Ganelon."

"Fuck it," Clay said. "Doesn't matter. All these others, these old names . . ." He trailed off, fumbling for the right words. "They're only candles, Gabe, and you are the *gods-damned sun*." He pointed to the pediment beside them. "Now get up there and shine."

For the span of five heartbeats Gabriel just stood there,

dumbfounded. Finally he blinked, as though a spell of despondency had lifted from his mind. "Right," he said, nodding to himself. "I'm the sun. Moog—"

"On it!" chirped the wizard. He scurried to the base of a nearby pine and back, pressing something dark and wet into Gabriel's hand.

"A pinecone?"

"Ha! Can you imagine? All this at stake and I give you a pinecone?" Moog's cackle died in silence, and everyone simply stared until he went on. "Okay, yes, it's a pinecone. But it's a *magic* pinecone. Hold it like this." He arranged Gabriel's arm so that the cone was near his lips.

Gabe looked skeptical, but he climbed onto the pediment at the base of the Threshold and shouted, "*Warriors, hear me!!!*"

His voice boomed from the trees all around them, so loud the pines shivered and the maples shed half their leaves at once. The grey sky came alive with startled birds.

"My name is Golden Gabe," he announced. "You know me—or you know *of* me—from some poem, or song, or story. You might have heard I slew the Crypt Queen Nazalin in single combat, or that I was first over the wall at Castadar." He winked at Barret. "Those things are true. Maybe your father told you he fought beside me once, or perhaps your mother said she met me in a tavern twenty years ago. Well...if you've got blue eyes and the wits of an ox, that might be true as well."

He paused while a ripple of laughter rolled up over the surrounding hills, then cast an anxious glance through the Threshold before going on. "I'm in a band, and you'll have heard of them too. Matrick Skulldrummer. Arcandius Moog. Slowhand Clay Cooper. And Ganelon."

He was dragging it out, Clay realized. Playing for time. As if on cue a wyvern came crashing through the portal, a tumble of burnished red scales and thrashing wings, screaming like a sickened eagle. The crowd scrambled back a few steps as the creature slid to a stop. Ganelon was with it, clinging tightly to its long, sinuous neck. The muscles in his arms bulged as he gave it a wrenching twist; there was a loud *crack*, and the beast went still.

Something like sixty thousand people stood in rapt silence as Ganelon got to his feet, rolled his neck against either shoulder, and stalked back toward the Threshold.

"You need help?" Barret asked as the southerner passed him by.

Ganelon dragged the axe off his back. Runes pulsed across the black steel, steady as a heartbeat. "Naw, we're good."

Gabe went on. "Some of you—hell, most of you—are too young to remember why we're famous, so let me give you a few recent examples. We rescued the king of Agria from his wife's hired assassin. We burned the Riot House to the ground. We brought down a chimera, and took the Maxithon for a spin." He waited as a spatter of laughter came and went. "We crossed the Heartwyld, though it wasn't easy. We walked the Cold Road, and we paid its toll."

The fingers on Clay's newest hand tingled as the ettin's lullaby drifted through the echoing corridors of his memory.

"We found a druin keystone," Gabe was saying, "and opened the Threshold behind me. And oh, yeah, we killed a dragon. Akatung is dead," Gabe announced, to the audible disbelief of those listening. Which was everyone now, since the very trees were carrying Gabriel's voice over the hills and beyond. When he sighed, the leaves shivered as though the wind itself had raked its frigid fingers through their boughs. "But I didn't come here to brag," he said.

"Could've fooled me!" shouted Red Bob, who looked mighty pleased with himself until someone else yelled, "Fuck off, Bob!" to ensuing laughter.

Gabe took no notice of the exchange. "In fact, let me start over. My name is Gabriel, and I need your help." He pointed through the Threshold. "That there is Castia."

Dark murmurs arose from the crowd. If any had wondered what it was they were seeing beyond the arch—or *where*, rather—they knew now.

"Some thirty thousand men and women are trapped within its walls," said Gabriel. "Once, they hoped for salvation. Now they pray for death. One of them is my daughter, Rose. But that darkness...that shadow you see between us and them...is the Heartwyld Horde."

The murmurs grew into a fearful babble. The blanketing multitude seemed to wilt like grass on fire. A nearby blade merchant rolled up his sodden carpet with the swords still inside and jogged off through the crowd.

Gabriel pressed on. "Every nightmare you've ever had, every monster you feared to find beneath your bed, is right there. And it brought a thousand friends. They've already crushed one army, and sooner or later Castia will fall to them as well. The Horde is hungry. It is cruel. Those inside will wish they had died on the battlefield before the end."

Barret shifted uncomfortably, no doubt afraid that Gabe was unravelling the threadbare glamour his earlier words had wrought, but Clay knew better. He and Gabriel had been friends for thirty-five years, and Gabe had been talking him into doing recklessly stupid shit for damn near all of them. He was a charismatic craftsman: every heart a furnace, every soul a blade.

And here comes the hammer, thought Clay.

At least he *hoped* there was a hammer, because even Barret's sons looked as dismal as the weather.

"Why did you come to here, to Kaladar?" Gabe asked. "Was it to show off the paint on your face? Your latest tattoo? The colour of your hair? Or was there something more? Did you come to find a band, or a booker? Did you want to make a name for yourself? Was it *glory* you were looking for?"

Something about that word stirred the embers in Clay's gut. It didn't matter that he was old, or tired, or that he'd drunk deep enough from glory's cup to slake a lifetime's thirst. Saying *glory* to a warrior was like saying *walk* to a dog—you got its tail wagging, sure as shit.

"Because you don't find glory at a fair. It isn't something that just lands in your lap. You need to go after it and take it for yourself. You need to risk *everything* for it."

There was a flurry within the Threshold. Ashe and Piglet were tussling with a pair of harpies; Ganelon was squaring off against something that looked like a centipede with tiny wings along the length of its body.

"But glory is a hard currency to earn nowadays. It isn't just wandering in a forest, or lurking in a cave. You have to *breed* it, keep it in a cage, and parcel it out so everyone gets their share. I've heard it said—and so have you—that all the great bands have come and gone." There was a smattering of unrest among his audience, and Gabe kept nudging. "People think the world has already been saved, that we don't need mercenaries anymore. They say heroes are a dying breed!"

That got them going. There was jeering, and shouts of "It's true!" and "Fuck that noise!" from everywhere at once.

"He's right," Clay heard Barret's younger boy admit to his brother.

"So what can you do?" Gabe asked them. "You tour from city to city fighting whatever sorry thing the local wrangler can drudge up. You dress up and dance while some beer-swilling asshole hopes a goblin gets lucky and slits your throat so that he can see some blood!"

Moog laughed at that. So did a lot of the older mercs. But the younger ones nodded, tight-lipped, or else yelled their agreement.

"*Who will remember you?*" Gabe asked. "What have you done?" He waved a hand toward the Horde and the city it besieged. "Tell me: does the world look safe to you?"

First there was grumbling, but then someone ventured, "*NO!*" and hundreds more followed suit.

"Castia needs fighters!" he shouted above the thunder of stamping feet. "It needs great and glorious bands!" he yelled over the percussive crash of sword and shield. "Castia needs heroes!" he roared, and they roared back at him. Barret's boys were grinning like jackals. Jain's girls were howling like wolves. "Are there any heroes here?" he screamed.

"*YES!*" bellowed ten thousand. Twenty.

"I said: *Are there any fucking heroes here!?*"

"*YES!*" bellowed thirty thousand. Forty.

The hills seemed to be rolling, rising beneath the back of conjured leviathans. Birds were circling the sky, spooked by the spectre in the trees.

Moog was bouncing excitedly on his toes, and Kit, who'd slipped through the arch sometime during Gabriel's speech, was peering over the assembly as though committing the sight to memory.

Clay thought of what the ghoul had told them in the mountain cave, about the marvels and horrors he'd seen throughout the course of his extraordinary life, and he wondered if their bard had ever seen anything quite like this.

"This day," said Gabriel, "this *moment*, is when you step out from the shadow of the past. Today you make your name. Today your legend is born. Come tomorrow, every tale the bards tell will belong to you, because today we save the world!"

Clay sighed in relief. There'd been a hammer, after all.

Gabriel tore *Vellichor* from its scabbard and leveled it at the encroaching Horde. "This is not a choice between life and death, but life and *immortality*! Remain here and die in obscurity, or follow me now and live forever!"

Chapter Fifty

The Battle of the Bands

Barret's boys were the first ones through. Three other youths (the remaining Wight Nights, presumably) came with them, each sporting the same dark-rimmed eyes and bleached-bone hair.

Jain's girls were next; the brigand turned bandleader gave Clay a touch with the tip of her bow as she passed.

"Long way from stealing socks on the roadside, eh Slowhand?"

"Long way," Clay agreed. "Stay safe, Jain."

She laughed and called over her shoulder, "Little late for that!"

Geralt Snakewater came after. The big man was too ashamed to look Gabe's way, but he spared a respectful nod for Ganelon, who was standing on the carcass of the flying centipede with one eye on the sky.

Next came a whole host of bands Clay didn't recognise, though many of them announced themselves to Gabriel as they went by. The men of Giantsbane were big blonde northerners, each wielding an axe almost as huge as *Syrinx*; Courtney and the Sparks bore southern scimitars and red silk skirts; the Silent Sons were ashen faced, mute as corpses as they marched into line; the Banshees ran past screaming;

the Dustgalls shouted greetings in a language Clay had never heard; the Renegades sported an array of black eyes, bloodied noses, and gap-toothed smiles, as though they'd already been in a scrap that morning and were eager for more.

Mercenaries were announced by their bards as they emerged from the portal: Layla Sweetpenny, Jasper the Creep, Brother Sandman, Hasdrubal Doomflayer. There was a man called the Blind Tiger who might actually have been blind, and another named Ben the Stalactian who looked as though there was giant's blood in his veins.

Plenty of old names showed up as well—Tushino the Wicked, Jorma Mulekicker, Queen-Killer Lysanthe—and a great many bands Clay was surprised to see still touring: the Dreamers, the Locksmiths, the Wheat Kings, Slade and the War-Dancers. Red Bob strode proudly toward the front, trailed by a frightened bard that looked as if he were contemplating a sudden retirement. Neil the Young hobbled by, leaning heavily on a gnarled staff, prompting Clay to wonder if the grey-bearded wizard went by Neil the Old these days.

They kept on coming, streaming from the Threshold like a river delta flooding into the sea. Here came Deckart Clearwater and his double-hafted hammer, followed by Hank the Beholder, whose shield, due to an elaborate contraption built into the grip, could spout fire from the red eye painted on its face. Here came the Black Puddings, the People Eaters, the Shewolves. Five men jogged past wearing the livery of Five-court guardsmen. Each one waved at Clay as if they knew him.

Here came the Sisters in Steel, barrelling toward the wing on sleek white horses. They looked considerably more deadly and significantly less glamourous than they had during the parade back in Conthas. Here came the Stormriders as well, one of which stopped to shake Gabriel's hand and mutter an apology for, as he rather flippantly put it, *that whole business with the chimera.*

Clay felt a prickle on his skin and caught some kid glaring

at him. It took him a moment to place where he'd seen that scowl before, but he finally did.

"The fuck you looking at?" he asked the platinum-haired frontman of the Screaming Eagles—the one who'd managed to provoke Ganelon into a fight in the Riot House back in Five-court. The young man bore a crooked nose as a memento of that ill-fated confrontation.

"A legend, apparently," said the kid, waving his band-mates by.

"Same here," Clay told him. The frontman nodded, obviously heartened, and trotted off.

Truth be told, Clay didn't even know the kid's name, but it never hurt to bolster someone's confidence before a fight, and who said Gabriel had a monopoly on kick-ass pep talks? Clay was watching the boy go when Gabe took his shoulder and turned him round.

Barret had taken Vanguard to the front already, and Kit was watching the endless stream of wild-eyed warriors still arriving from the fair-grounds in Kaladar, which left Clay and his bandmates alone for the first time since they'd raided Kallorek's compound more than a month before—something each of them seemed to apprehend at once.

Moog and Matrick put an arm around each other. The wizard slung his other behind Clay's back, while Matty reached up and placed a hand on Ganelon's broad shoulder. The southerner shifted uncomfortably but didn't shrug him off, nor did he shy away when Gabriel clasped his left wrist to complete the circle.

Clay had no idea how long the five of them stood like that, though afterward he thought it might have been an absurdly long time, considering the fact that the Heartwyld Horde was now bearing down on them. For a while no one spoke, because in the roundabout course of thirty-some years they had said just about all there was to say to one another, until finally Clay could bear the silence no longer and cleared his throat.

"I love you guys," he said, and gods-be-damned if his voice didn't sell him out at the end and crack like a boy of twelve summers.

Moog nearly choked on a sob himself. "I love you guys, too," he said, unashamed by the tears rolling over his cheeks.

"Me too," Matty croaked.

"I love you," said Gabriel, matching gazes with each of them one by one. "All of you."

Ganelon remained silent, but when the rest of them looked his way he rolled his eyes and loosed a sympathetic growl. "Okay, fine. You're the last four people I'd ever kill."

A smile slipped onto Gabe's face for the length of a long breath, before it slid like a sickle moon behind a wisp of sombre cloud. "For Rose," he said.

"For Rose," they echoed, and by then the first horns of war were blowing, loud and long and clear across the sky.

The battle for Castia was about to begin.

A battle, as relayed by a poet, is a glorious thing, full of heroic stands, daring charges, and valiant sacrifice. But a battlefield, as experienced by some poor bastard mired in the thick of it, is something different altogether.

The word *clusterfuck* came to mind.

At least it's clear who the enemy is, thought Clay, using *Blackheart* to deflect the spear of a charging centaur as Gabriel took its front legs off at the knee. The centaur's wailing face-plant might have been amusing were there not several hundred more of his kind galloping behind.

Although they hadn't seen Lastleaf or his wyvern matriarch as of yet, there was clear evidence of a mastermind behind the Horde's tactics thus far. A detachment of centaurs and mounted wargs had circled to the north in an attempt to flank Grandual's mercenaries.

Gabriel, exerting what little influence he could over his

ragtag army, sent the Sisters in Steel, along with every other rider at his disposal, out to meet them. Their orders had been to break off as soon as possible, while Saga led a few hundred mercs on foot behind. Centaurs could mount a devastating charge, but once engaged, especially in the close-quarters chaos of a battlefield, they were pushovers. Unlike typical cavalry, where if you injured a horse you still had to deal with its rider, the horse-men presented huge targets, and if you hamstrung one it was fairly easy to finish it off.

Once Saga and the others had locked down their foes, the Sisters and their mercenary cavalry rushed back in from the rear. Before long the centaurs were dead or put to rout, while the wargs, enraged by bloodlust, began to turn on friend and foe alike.

A fair start, Clay was forced to admit, but that was the last manoeuvre Gabe could hope to make. By now the two forces—the horde of monsters and the host of mercenaries—had crashed together into a brawling morass that sounded to Clay's ears like an ocean filled with several hundred thousand drowning people all screaming for help at once.

"This way," yelled Gabe. He slipped through a knot in the fighting and led Saga toward the centre. Clay followed as close as he could. His left arm was mending but was far from healed. It was still in its sling, leaving him little choice but to stay on Gabe's heels and weather whatever blows he could on behalf of his friend. Matrick skulked after them like an urchin, slicing open foes like they were purse bottoms in a market square. Ganelon hacked his way alongside them with *Syrinx*, and Moog, who had strapped a quartet of bandoliers to his chest, was lobbing vial after vial of volatile explosives into the enemy ranks.

Gods forbid anything hit him, Clay worried. One unlucky strike and the wizard would go off like spring fireworks. *And us with him, probably.*

Gabriel had been spot-on about one thing during his

speech back in Kaladar: the Horde was a nightmare made real. Every heinous and hideous thing you could imagine was present. There were goblins and rock-hulks, wild orcs, uncountable thousands of yapping kobolds, and rune-broken golems with glowing green eyes. There were horse-headed ixil and horned hoary murlogs, skeletons rattling in rusted armour, and way more giant spiders than Clay was comfortable with.

There were scorpions the size of horses, lanky trolls with eyes like smouldering pits, firbolgs in soiled loincloths swinging spiked clubs, and ogre-mages hurling bolts of lightning from brandished bone totems. Great shaggy treants roamed the battleground, their twisted boughs home to spriggans firing tiny barbed arrows into the crowd below. There were burrowing wyrms that swallowed men whole, and drakes breathing everything from fire and ice to clouds of noxious gas.

There were battalions of black-scaled lizard-folk carrying wicked billhooks, scores of gibbering grimlocks with clammy white skin and round iron helms pricked with tiny holes to shield their eyes from the light of day. There were direwolves, bloodboars, and plate-armoured death knights on the backs of mammoth bears.

There were witches with curling nails and filed teeth, and warlocks who'd carved runes of vile power into their very flesh. There were great apes like the one he'd seen back in Conthas, striped like tigers in colours so vibrant they looked unreal. These ones were a touch more savage, however; Clay saw one tear a woman into halves like she was a loaf of warm bread.

Which was not to mention the big boys: A pair of giants roamed unchallenged, levelling a dozen warriors with every step. Several cyclopes waded knee-deep among the mercenary ranks, so hideously deformed they'd have made Dane look like Gabriel in his golden prime. They swung flails and broad-bladed axes that cut bloody arcs through anyone in their path. Clay had seen a swarm of scuttling ankheg and known that somewhere in their midst would be a queen, bloated with the next clutch of mindless drones.

The sky belonged almost solely to the enemy. Clouds of giant bats swept down with razor claws, rot sylphs belched streams of acid bile, gargoyles plunged like stones upon unsuspecting heads.

There was another creature—Clay hadn't even known what to call it—that was some kind of enormous plant. When it wasn't spewing acid all over the place it was hoisting mercs into the air with its tentacle limbs and dropping them into what looked, disturbingly, to be a mouth *inside* of its mouth.

But then another monstrosity arrived: An argosy armoured in metal plates and powered by what looked like a pared-down tidal engine came roaring from the Threshold. The plant-thing's acid splashed harmlessly over its iron-plated carapace, and the massive war wagon responded by blasting liquid fire from a spout at its front before running its adversary down beneath nail-studded treads. The mercenaries rallied around the rolling behemoth as it ploughed into the mob.

Clay saw pale-skinned necromancers hovering above plagues of living dead, their frayed cloaks billowing on deathly currents. Demons wreathed in boiling smoke cackled like madmen as they struck down would-be heroes with blades of blistering fire.

One of them stood out from the rest, and not just because it was several magnitudes larger. Well, *mostly* because of that, but also because it bore a whip that instantly froze whatever it touched and carried a sword as long as a ship's mast, which it used to smash frost-rimed mercenaries to bloody fragments. The thing looked like a man-shaped mountain of jagged ice, its limbs encased in scraps of dull black armour. A pair of iron-sheathed, front-facing horns curved from its head above eyes like charnel pits.

Clay knew it for an Infernal the moment he laid eyes on it. He'd never seen one before—not beyond the confines of paintings or tapestries, anyhow—but he recognized it none-theless.

Clay remembered Shadow, the druin claw-broker, mention-ing that Lastleaf had spent years rallying the horde, traveling the breadth of the Heartwyld, rousing the beast-tribes of End-land, brokering pacts with some of the forest's most corrupted inhabitants. Judging by the size of the force he'd managed to assemble, Clay was surprised there'd been anything left to haunt the Wyld on their way through.

"Look alive!" Gabe called as a clutch of urskin jumped them.

Clay deflected a spear thrust and drove his shield into his attacker's froglike face. Ganelon plucked one of the things off his back and slammed it onto the ground at his feet. Matrick took a tongue thrust to the face and reeled as though punched, but before the creature could finish him Moog tapped it with a wand.

"*Kaza!*" yelled the wizard. The frogman stopped short, bewildered. Before it could recover Matrick jammed his knives to the hilt in its chest.

"What spell was that?" Clay asked.

"Spell?" Moog brandished the wand. "You mean this? It's just a stick," he said, and tossed it away.

The world's a changing place, Matrick had told him back in Fivecourt, and Clay knew he was seeing the fallout of that change all around him. Because so many bands had sought the artificial glory of the arenas instead of venturing out in search of the real thing, the denizens of the Heartwyld had been granted time to repopulate, to nurse their hatred of human civilization, the whole forest festering like an untended wound gone septic.

And potentially fatal, he thought, as Gabriel led them into the body-strewn wake of the armoured war wagon. The closer they got to the city the more evidence they saw of the Horde's months-long occupation: bodies impaled on blood-sheathed spears, fire pits and trenches heaped with bones. The enemy had constructed a number of shoddy siege engines, Clay noted. Nothing they could hurl would have done much harm to Castia's spell-warded walls, but as they passed near to one he saw the bucket was stained with gore, and he shuddered to imagine what these machines had launched in place of stones.

They were nearing the thick of it now: the chaotic centre of the miles-long battlefield. He had been involved in enough petty wars to know that battles like this were won and lost on the wings, but Gabriel seemed dead set on driving like a blade toward the heart of the Horde, and Clay thought he knew why.

If we can find Lastleaf . . . if we can somehow kill him, then maybe we can end this.

With only a shield to hand, Clay did his best to keep his bandmates from harm. When a gargoyle dive-bombed Matrick, Clay pushed him aside, planting his feet and slanting his shield so the thing didn't crush him. Thanks to the impenetrable *Warskin*, Clay shrugged off countless sword and spear thrusts meant for Moog, and *Blackheart*'s mottled face was spiked with splintered arrows. He hauled Ganelon from the rubble of a vanquished earth elemental, and even found time to step between Red Bob and an ankheg's gnashing pincers.

The mercenary murmured scant thanks and rushed off, only to be crushed a moment later by a giant's pounding foot. Bob's bard turned and fled, wailing and clutching his harp to his chest like a scholar saving a single book from a burning library.

Clay gazed up at the colossus. It hadn't taken notice of them yet, but a giant hardly needed to see you to kill you, did it? It stalked across the battlefield like a child treading over grass, wreaking unwitting devastation with every step.

Well, perhaps not entirely unwitting, Clay amended, as the giant's next earth-hammering stomp killed all five of the Skulks at once. *But what the hell can we do?* Killing a giant was possible, sure, but it took time, and proper planning, the right weapons, and a fair bit of good fortune. *You just can't . . .*

The giant's throat suddenly bristled with half a dozen shivering crossbow bolts. The brute looked as confused about that as Clay was, but then several more barbs sprouted amidst a spray of misting blood. The giant's eyes glazed over in death and it sagged thunderously to its knees.

Clay craned his neck to gape at the skyship soaring ponderously overhead, now banking, so that even though they were too far off to read clearly, Clay knew at once the bold white words stamped along the dreadnought's hull.

Larkspur had come to Castia.

Chapter Fifty-one

The Autumn Son

The mind, Clay had learned long ago, could witness only so much carnage before it ceased to comprehend. You saw it, still. You heard it raging like a rainstorm against a closed window, but it simply did not register. His capacity for slaughter was overflowing, like a cup filled to the brim with wine, or water. Or, more aptly, with blood.

Everywhere Clay looked was pandemonium. He saw Tushino the Wicked deflect a lightning bolt with his sword before cutting an arm off the warlock who'd cast it. The Reavers were chopping at the trunk of a faltering treant as spriggan archers spilled from its eaves. Neil the not-so-Young-anymore hurled a bale of fire into the gaping maw of a great wyrm. The thing exploded, and since half of it was buried, the ground above it ruptured, hurling kobolds like clods of earth behind a galloping horse. Deckart Clearwater pummeled his way through half a hundred undead and broke the skull of the crypt fiend compelling them. The ghost-blue fires in its eyes went out, and the rest of its shambling soldiers crumpled in an instant.

Elsewhere things weren't going so well. Clay saw Merciless May Drummond trampled by a boar and the Dreamers go down beneath a pile of steel-helmed grimlocks. The Blind

Tiger was killed by an arrow he almost certainly did not see coming. A stooping cyclops reached beneath the steel-plated argosy and tipped it over. The great machine floundered like a beetle on its back, fire and smoke spouting from either end.

Clay's eyes roamed the battlefield, hoping to determine Lastleaf's whereabouts, but there was simply too much chaos. He looked to the frenzied sky for sign of the wyvern matriarch, but he couldn't pick her out from so far away.

The *Dark Star* soared overhead, mist streaming from its tidal engines. Rot sylphs bounced from its prow. Bats scattered from its path or were burned to ash by its storm-wracked sails. The same pitch bombs that had laid waste to *The Carnal Court* were now unleashed upon the Horde, a hedgerow of thumping explosions that vaporized hundreds at a time.

At last the daeva and her red-robed thralls came spilling over the sides, gliding toward the battlefield below. Her minions were more numerous than Clay would have figured, and he was wondering if she'd left any on board when the dreadnought's inevitable course became apparent.

So, no then, he thought—or hoped not, anyway—since the *Dark Star*, its prow ostensibly crammed with more of those volatile bombs, ploughed straight into the second giant's face. The resulting explosion lit the sky like a second sun, a flash of blinding incandescence followed by a *BOOM* that rattled Clay's teeth in their sockets.

For a heartbeat, as scraps of burning skyship rained down, every soul on the plain stood struck by horrific expectation. The giant tipped forward, and the mercenaries trapped within its shadow looked up in despair, but then it rocked onto its heels, toppling backward, an avalanche of flesh and bone crashing down into the midst of the Horde. The battlefield heaved; men and monsters bounced like bowls on a table struck by a god.

Clay was thrown from his feet, and for a moment he simply lay on his back, gazing up at a sky that already seemed brighter absent the looming threat of two rampaging giants, until a glossy black feather drifted above his eyes. He rolled to his knees, surged to his feet, preparing (if not the least bit prepared) to bear the brunt of Larkspur's vengeance.

Her thralls hit the ground first, red robes fluttering as they tumbled through a tribe of wild orcs. They wasted no time joining the fight, hands and feet a blur as they secured a space in which their mistress could land in safety.

The daeva's wings fanned as she descended. Her armoured toes aimed like a nail at the earth below. The scythe in her hands gleamed dully, white as a winter sky, and Clay's new-born hand itched at the sight of it. If she bore any lasting injury from being impaled by one of Barret's bolts, it wasn't evident at the moment. Larkspur touched down, folded her wings, and made straight for Ganelon.

"Took you long enough," said the warrior.

"Fuck yourself," she snapped, and drove the butt of her scythe into the ground like a conqueror coming ashore in a heathen land.

The kiss that followed was sudden as lightning, fierce as a storm at sea. She seized his throat with an iron claw. He clasped her hair in a mailed fist, and Clay saw her bite down on his lip.

When they finally wrenched themselves apart, Gabriel loosed a loud sigh. "Spring Maiden's Mercy, I thought I was the dramatic one. If you two are finished ... ?"

"For now," said Larkspur. The look she gave Ganelon was that of a torturer setting bloody instruments aside.

Ganelon's grin was flecked with blood. "For now," he agreed.

Gabriel hefted his sword. "Good, now we need to find—" *Lastleaf*, he'd been about to say—Clay was sure of it—except Lastleaf found them first.

The wyvern matriarch hit the ground like an anchor dropped into shallow water, splashing blood and bodies in every direction. Ashatan's black wings thrashed to either side, spines and talons shredding mercs as though they were stuffed with straw. Her tail lashed out, punching into the chest of one of Larkspur's monks and lifting him from the ground. The poor man screamed until venomous foam came boiling from his mouth, and the wyvern shook him loose with a snap. She had another of the daeva's thralls pinned to the ground with her snout, and Clay watched, repulsed, as her jaws burrowed into his gut. The man was dead by the time she raised her head, pulling entrails from the steaming ruin of his chest.

To their credit, or at least as testimony to the potency of Larkspur's preternatural charm, her remaining thralls positioned themselves between their mistress and the matriarch. The area cleared by the daeva's arrival earlier remained wide-open, since Grandual's mercenaries were more than willing to pick fights elsewhere, and Lastleaf's minions cowered instinctively from the great black wyvern and the man upon her back.

Lastleaf, the Autumn Son.

He no longer wore the Duke of Endland's tattered longcoat. Now he was clad for war in a suit of skirted, silver-green scale. His left arm was sheathed in overlapping plates of red metal that joined seamlessly with the pauldron on that shoulder, and he was wearing, of all things, a helmet: sleek and steely green, like his armour, with flared casings for his backswept ears. A crest running front to back was plumed with what looked like long, red-orange leaves.

Truth be told, it wasn't the worst helmet Clay had seen. He might even have said it suited the druin in a splendid-sylvan-prince sort of way.

"Gabriel," Lastleaf called down from the wyvern's back. He gestured with a pale hand at the battle raging everywhere but their immediate vicinity. "I assume this is your doing?"

Gabe shook his head. "I wasn't the one who summoned an army in the first place," he said. "I didn't lay siege to Castia, or threaten the Courts with annihilation if they dared to intervene. This is your doing, Lastleaf. Or would you prefer I called you Heathen?"

The druin's air of conceit vanished like that of a debt-ridden king confronted by his creditors. He opened his mouth to speak, but then his mismatched eyes fell upon the scythe Larkspur had planted like a flag in the blood-soaked earth. Clay saw a slew of emotions warring beneath the Heathen's calm façade, but they remained below, subtle as sharks in shallow water.

"Ashatan," he said, and the wyvern bowed beneath him. The druin dropped to the ground, ducked beneath the arch of a leathery wing, then reached behind him and withdrew the topmost sword from its scabbard. Clay had seen this one before, at Lindmoor. *Scorn*, Shadow had called it: obsidian black, laced with molten fissures, so hot it folded the air around it with shimmering heat. In the same moment the matriarch loosed a screeching roar that reeked of rancid blood and made Clay's skin crawl with primal fear.

While her thralls rushed Lastleaf all at once, Larkspur looked to the sky, which was Clay's first clue that it was about to come crashing down upon them.

A brood of black wyverns was plummeting from the grey clouds above, a twisting, shrieking spiral of wings and claws and snapping jaws that touched down like a cyclone in their midst. The daeva sprang away as one hit Ganelon with the force of a collapsing roof. The warrior let go his axe and howled as the raptor's clenching talons tried squeezing him to pulp. Larkspur came out of a roll near her planted scythe, tore it free, and leapt to Ganelon's defense.

Thankfully, the spectacle drew a whole company of mercs to the clearing. Vanguard was among them, and so were Barret's sons and the other Wight Nights. Aric Slake, who Clay had last seen losing a card game in the Riot House, rammed his spear, *Hawkwind*, deep into a wyvern's breast. Jorma

Mulekicker, whose right eye was now a bloody hole, charged into the fray, and May Drummond, who had apparently survived being trampled by a boar after all, limped by his side.

Clay returned his attention to Lastleaf in time to see the druin plunge *Scorn* into the earth before him. The blade's bright fissures drained to black, and the ground beneath the charging thralls detonated. Slabs of stone and red-robed bodies exploded skyward on a swell of splashing magma. Those who weren't thrown clear staggered, some pitching into pools of molten rock. One monk tried without success to escape his burning robes, while another floundered helplessly in foot-deep lava. Clay swallowed a surge of bile as he watched the man disintegrate before his eyes.

Lastleaf left the searing sword buried in the ground and was reaching for *Madrigal*'s scabbard when one of Larkspur's more dextrous thralls got close enough to throw a punch aimed where the druin's throat should have been. There was a warbling sound as the second sword sang loose, and the monk was rewarded for his effort with a cleanly severed arm.

The man tottered, not quite dead, until the Heathen shoved him backward into the molten pool.

Matrick was on his back beneath another of the matriarch's brood, squirming from its talons, rolling clear of its stabbing tail, and jamming his knives up into its belly every chance he got.

Clay spotted Moog retreating from a trio of yellow-eyed orcs. He almost headed over to help, but the wizard pulled a weapon from his bag that looked like a blue staff and a white staff had been locked together in a closet with the lights off. Clay recognized the Twining Staff immediately as one of the few magic items Moog had crafted himself and could have pitied the orcs for what was about to happen. The wizard gripped the staff with both hands, shouted a string of esoteric gibberish, and then held on for dear life as the Twining Staff began beating the living shit out of the three unfortunate orcs.

Larkspur, meanwhile, relieved the wyvern attacking Ganelon of its head, shearing through its neck with *Umbra*'s sickle blade. The warrior rolled free of its grasp—dazed, but not outwardly harmed—and scrambled to retrieve his axe.

Mere heartbeats had passed since the black brood attacked, but Clay felt exceptionally useless for squandering them, so he was almost relieved when Lastleaf's voice demanded his attention.

"What else did Shadow tell you?"

The Heathen was stepping slowly around the glowing pothole between them. His eyes never left Gabriel, even when Deckart Clearwater came out of nowhere and swung his double-hafted hammer at his head.

He's got a chance, thought Clay, since surprising a druin was the only sure way to offset the prescience, but Lastleaf stepped just ahead of the blow. In one fluid motion he turned, long blade whistling, and chopped Deckart into halves.

For a moment it looked as though Gabe might rush him, trying (likely in vain) to catch the Heathen off guard, but Lastleaf was too far away still, and Gabriel had never been one to shy from a little prefight banter if it meant a chance to mentally unbalance his opponent. Clay wasn't confident that was an option here, but it couldn't hurt to try.

"He told me about your mother," said Gabriel. "About the sword your father made to bring her back from the dead. He said you stole it from him."

Clay's eyes wafted to the bone-white scabbard on the druin's back.

Tamarat.

"I nearly killed him with it," said Lastleaf. "You'd think he'd have happily given his life for that of the woman he claimed to love. But instead he fled and found you."

A snuffing sound urged Clay to look past Gabe's shoulder. A minotaur had found its way clear of the larger melee and into the clearing. In paintings such monsters were always rendered as huge, hulking beasts, but in truth they were a head shorter than most men, which was probably why they had such famously short tempers. They also, for reasons even a scholar like Moog could only speculate on, intensely despised the colour red, which just so happened to be the colour of Clay's armour.

This one was missing a horn and sported a wound in its abdomen that would probably kill it within the hour, but in the meantime it appeared to be sizing Clay up for an attack. With nothing but a shield to hand, there wasn't much Clay could do but watch his friend's back, so he edged nearer to Gabe's shoulder and kept an eye on the beast in his periphery.

"The truth is," said Lastleaf, who was getting dangerously close now, "Vespian didn't make the sword for my mother's sake. He made it for his own. So *he* wouldn't be alone. So *he* wouldn't have to—"

"Shut up," said Gabriel, deliberately provoking. He inched his left foot ahead of him, turned his right boot outward. His knuckles went white on *Vellichor*'s grip.

The Heathen, just strides away now, looked suddenly irritated. "It wasn't *Tamarat* my father was after. It was me. If he had taken it from me—"

"Shut up," Gabe repeated, smiling now.

"He would have killed me with it," the druin sputtered, "to bring her back."

"Nobody cares," said Gabriel, who was better than anyone Clay had ever known at pissing people off—and sure enough, Lastleaf's affected cool dissolved in an instant.

Clay was (yet again) trying to wrap his mind around the fact that the Winter Queen was real—that she would have been resurrected if Vespian had actually managed to kill his son with *Tamarat*—when the druin surged forward, and the fight that could very well decide the outcome of the entire battle—and possibly the fate of humankind along with it—began in earnest.

Which was, of course, the same moment that stupid runt of a minotaur lowered his head and took a run at Clay.

Chapter Fifty-two

Sheer Dumb Luck

Vellichor carved a swathe of waist-high, windblown grass as it rose to meet the druin's singing sword, and the two blades met with a sound like glass breaking. Clay moved into the space behind Gabe, aware that several more blows were being exchanged just beyond his shoulder. When the charging minotaur was just strides away he stepped out to meet it, angling *Blackheart* so the beast bounced off and went careening toward Lastleaf.

The Heathen leapt out of its path, muttering a curse in druic as his sword quietly echoed at his side. The minotaur's stumbling momentum took it right into the lava pit. It succeeded in getting an arm down before falling in, but bellowed in wordless agony as the limb turned to char and its mane caught fire.

Gabriel blinked, sparing a glance at Clay. "Thanks."

Clay shrugged. "Worth a shot."

"Did you know," said Lastleaf, as casually as if the three of them were rocking in chairs on a sun-dappled porch, "my father told me once that to die by *Vellichor*'s blade is the only way our kind can return to our own realm."

Clay recalled Shadow saying something to that effect back in the Heartwyld. *It is a key*, he'd told them, without realizing the only door it opened was death itself.

"You'll find out soon enough," said Gabriel.

The Heathen's harsh laughter pealed into the air above the battlefield. "I think not," he said liltingly.

Gabe feinted low, drawing Lastleaf's blade humming toward his knees, but when *Vellichor* stabbed suddenly high the druin turned so the edge missed his face by inches. By then the Heathen's own weapon was slicing toward Gabriel's side. Clay managed to get *Blackheart* in its path, and gasped when *Madrigal* sheared a corner of his shield right off.

"Son of a *bitch*," Clay swore, and then yelped as Gabriel shoved him hard.

The Heathen's sword went *shing*ing through what would have been Clay's neck had Clay not been tumbling backward onto his ass.

A thought struck him suddenly, for no reason, and was of no use whatsoever except to explain why a piece of his most treasured possession was lying near his feet: *The noise his sword makes . . . it's cutting the air.* His next thought was more of an observation, really: *Gabe just saved your life.*

Currently Gabriel was trying to save his own. With no one else to steal his focus, Lastleaf was pressing the attack, using the prescience to anticipate his rival's every move. The Heathen's sword was a howling blur, ringing in rapid succession against *Vellichor* as Gabe relied on instinct alone to defend himself.

From the ground it was hard to tell whether or not the battle was going in their favour. More than half of the matriarch's brood were dead, but so was Aric Slake, whose head was admiring his body from several feet away. He saw May Drummond die (again) on the tip of a wyvern's tail.

An unfortunate side effect of Moog's Twining Staff was that once it was done clobbering one's enemies it more often than not turned on whoever was holding it, at least until its enchantment wore off. The wizard was currently locked in mortal combat with his own weapon as each of them attempted to throttle the other into submission.

Matrick had somehow got himself onto the wyvern matriarch's back. He was straddling one of Ashatan's wings and attempting to push a dagger between her black iron scales. Ashatan herself was preoccupied by Larkspur, who scored a deep gash in the matriarch's head before taking to the sky. The wyvern roared again and vaulted up after her, forcing Matrick to abandon his efforts to harm her and simply hold on for the ride.

Clay didn't see Ganelon until *Syrinx* was cutting a seemingly inevitable path toward the Heathen's midsection. Warned by the prescience, Lastleaf turned at the last second and brought his sword chopping down with enough strength to spin the axe sideways before it hit him.

It still hit him, though.

The blow drew a breathless grunt from the druin. He lost his grip on *Madrigal* and was thrown several yards through the air, yet somehow managed to land skidding on the soles of his feet. His helmet had been knocked askew, so Lastleaf tore it off and tossed it behind him.

Watching it bounce away, Clay was shocked to see the minotaur who'd charged him earlier climbing doggedly to its feet. Its mane was singed to stubble, and its left arm fizzled at the elbow in a cauterized stump, but it seemed hell-bent on getting back in the fight.

Clay was more immediately concerned by the fact that Lastleaf was pulling the straps of all three scabbards over his head. He let the two empty scabbards fall and curled his long fingers around the hilt of his third and final sword.

"The gorgon told me why you've come," he said to Gabriel, who was using this brief respite to try to catch his breath. "If I kill you I will find her, this daughter of yours. I'll make certain she suffers."

It was Ganelon who answered, green eyes glaring over the edge of his axe. "If," he said.

The Heathen's sneer wavered, but so far as Clay could

tell it had less to do with the warrior's remark than with the prospect of unsheathing *Tamarat*. Lastleaf's hands were trembling, his white-furred ears pressed flat. He seemed genuinely reluctant to draw it, and Clay wondered if he'd had cause to do so since the day he'd used it to defend himself from his even more monstrous father.

But then Ganelon took a step toward him and Lastleaf had no choice but to pull *Tamarat* out for all to see.

Except that Clay *couldn't* see it—not really.

His mind told him the blade was black, a colourless void, as empty as a sky without stars. But when he looked into it there was simply . . . nothing there. Whereas *Vellichor* served as a window to a realm beyond this one, *Tamarat* was a fragment of utter oblivion.

Clay hoped to hell Ganelon could see it, because the Heathen took two running steps and leapt, snarling, at the warrior, his blade a black smear against the sky. Gabriel moved to Ganelon's left side, leading with *Vellichor*'s bright edge and forcing Lastleaf to fight on two fronts.

Let's make it three, thought Clay, surging to his feet, determined to help in whatever way he could. He hoisted his shield—

The minotaur hit him like a wagon full of rocks rolling downhill. Clay saw the battlefield blur, and the next moment he was slewing sideways on the ground. His ears were ringing, his jaw ached, and Clay wondered whether or not he'd hit his head—he couldn't remember, so probably yes.

"You fucking—" he managed to say before his assailant fell on top him. The beast was surprisingly heavy for something half his height and missing most of an arm. Its bloody snout pressed wetly against his mouth, and Clay's nostrils filled with the scent of burnt fur and overcooked cabbage.

Groaning with the effort, he used *Blackheart* to shove the minotaur aside, and then continued to hammer it with his shield until all but its twitching hooves had stopped moving.

He sat up, disoriented.

Saw Gabe and Ganelon trade strikes too fast to follow with the Autumn Son and his near-invisible sword. Saw Moog holding his staff by the tail as it walloped a flock of reanimated skeletons into ash. Saw Barret stomping on an orc's head and Tiamax the arachnian cracking a wyvern's jaws with the strength of six hands.

The stitches in Clay's face had come open again, and his left cheek was scraped raw. He climbed groggily to his feet, trying to reconcile in his head how he'd spin this story to Tally if he lived to tell it.

What's that, honey? What was I doing while Uncle Gabe was duelling a god with all of civilization at stake? Why, I was wrestling in the muck with an exceptionally tenacious cow.

He hefted his shield again and hobbled as fast as he could toward the only fight that mattered. He could hardly believe it was still going: Gabriel was among the fastest, most cunning fighters Clay had ever known, and Ganelon was the strongest, fiercest warrior . . . well, maybe *ever*.

But Lastleaf had been alive for more than a millennium, and had spent the majority of those years skulking in the Heartwyld, evading the pursuit of his father and imposing his will upon creatures that would give even the most stalwart hero a lifetime of sleepless nights. He wouldn't go down easily.

He might not go down at all, Clay was thinking, when a rough snort behind him made him turn to see the world's most obstinate minotaur attempting to rise.

"Oh, c'mon," he moaned. "Stay down. Just . . . please, stay down." He took an involuntary step toward it and the beast whirled on him, glowering with bulging, bloodshot eyes. It snorted again, louder this time, and distinctly more threatening. In another world Clay might have offered to buy it a beer and call it a draw, but it was stamping one cloven hoof and weaving its fire-scarred head from side to side, so instead he squared himself to it and sighed.

He thought briefly of Ganelon and what the warrior had done to those men in Mazala; of Larkspur's revenge upon the children who'd made her childhood a living hell; of Lastleaf and his war against a Republic built on the blood of so-called monsters; and of himself, who would likely have died a monster if it wasn't for one woman's love.

Two women, actually.

"You know what?" Clay said. "Never mind. You are what you are. So come at me."

Whether the minotaur understood him or not, it charged: broken horned and burnt, one-armed and weaponless; its hooves churned the bloody earth below as it bowed its head.

It would occur to Clay mere moments later that the fights that seemed to matter most weren't always the ones that did, and that sometimes the fate of worlds was decided by something so arbitrary as sheer dumb luck.

He dropped as the minotaur rammed its hoary head into *Blackheart*, then rolled onto his back and let the beast's own impetus propel it into the air, whereupon it, quite unintentionally, blindsided Lastleaf and sent them both pitching headlong into the magma pool.

Clay scrambled onto his stomach just as the druin began screaming, and an instant later the corpse of the wyvern matriarch slammed into the ground nearby like a giant's hammer. A veil of dust roiled out from where the creature landed, forcing Clay to squint as he rose and shambled over to where Gabe and Ganelon were standing.

The southerner was craning his neck, peering through the gale of grit at the sky above, and Clay saw him grin as Larkspur, holding a bloodied *Umbra* in one hand and a harried-looking Matrick in the other, came gliding down on widespread wings.

Moog was there by the time she landed. The Twining Staff had gone dormant again, and the wizard fed it into the mouth of his sack as he beamed at the sickly-looking king. "That looked fun!"

Matrick smiled wanly in response, and Clay recognized a man doing his damnedest not to empty his guts on the ground.

"Well done," Ganelon told the daeva, as Gabriel wandered off toward the glowing pool.

"You too," she said, taking in the jumble of corpses—both mercenary and wyvern—littering the nearby vicinity.

Clay shifted his wounded arm in its sling. "If you're looking for Lastleaf—"

"He's gone."

Of course he is, said the part of Clay's mind that knew the druin's death had come too easy.

Sure enough, when he joined Gabriel by the frothing edge of the pit and looked within, the only corpse Clay saw was the one belonging to the most stubborn, spirited, suitably bull-headed minotaur he had ever known.

Moog touched a bruise purpling around one of his eyes. "You didn't happen to ask him what a cathiil was, did you? It's been bugging me since the gorgon's place."

"He can't have gotten far," Gabe said, ignoring the wizard. "Let's finish breaking this siege, shall we?"

Ganelon used his axe to point over the frontman's shoulder. "I think it just broke."

Clay looked beyond the seething limit of the Horde at the city of Castia, whose gates were grinding slowly open. A pair of druin skyships emerged from behind the walls, rising like bloated bees from the corpse of a flower.

The siege was indeed broken. Those who had lived without hope for so long were coming, at last, to claim it.

Chapter Fifty-three

One Last Time

"It's Rose. It must be."

Gabriel was gazing at distant Castia. There were mercenaries streaming from the open gate, remnants of the once-mighty army shattered by the Horde. There'd been more than four thousand of them once, but gauging their numbers Clay guessed less than half remained. Those who did were sick and weary, but they charged out from the city like madmen. Or heroes.

Clay had no doubt at all as to who was leading them. Neither did Gabriel. His friend took a breath with which to speak, but Larkspur cut him off.

"Go get her. We're with you."

Jaw clamped, nostrils flaring, red-rimmed eyes brimming over with love, with pride, and with a father's fathomless gratitude, Gabriel nodded. "I know," he said. "Thank you."

He turned to face the city.

"With me, then. One last time."

With the Heathen vanished and his matriarch dead, the Horde began rapidly losing cohesion.

The cyclopes were starting to fall. Layla Sweetpenny

hurled a lance through the eye of one. The men of Giantsbane climbed another like ants swarming a spoiled picnic. A third cyclops, sitting and scooping the insides from the overturned war wagon, pulled an engineer from the wreckage and ate him. A moment later something detonated inside it, bursting its belly like a smashed pumpkin.

Gabe and Ganelon dashed between the legs of the last one standing. *Vellichor* clipped one heel, *Syrinx* the other. The monster collapsed, wailing in anguish, and Moog lobbed an alchemical grenade into its open mouth.

"Oopsie daisy!" he shouted. Its head went *boom*, and blood came spewing from its ruptured eye.

Gabriel pressed on, relentless. The rest of them followed, trailed by a dwindling number of young mercs: Courtney and the Sparks on the left, Jain and her girls the right. Clay saw the Stormriders as well, and Ben the Stalactian wading through the press with a gore-smeared axe in either hand. Merciless May Drummond, who Clay had seen die twice already, was holding her guts in with one hand and swinging a spiked flail in the other.

Something resembling a scarecrow with embers for eyes leapt into their path, but Barret came out of nowhere and smashed it to straw with his hammer. His boys were with him, blood and sweat matting white hair to their faces. Tia-max waved a few desultory arms, and Piglet tried on a disastrous smile. The boy had been crying, Clay noticed.

He glanced around as Vanguard and the Wight Nights fell in step beside them. "Ashe?"

"Gone," said Barret.

Gone. Clay nearly stumbled over the word. "Barret, I'm—"

"Don't be, Slowhand." He said no more, and Clay let it lie.

The sky itself was coming down on them again. Harpies hit the ground in feathered heaps. Plague hawks fell shrieking from above. A listing skyship crashed onto the battlefield, killing scores.

Clay saw the refugees from Castia attack the Horde from the rear, and was reminded of the cold autumn morning (several lifetimes ago, it sometimes felt) on which his father had led him into the forest in search of a tree. He remembered Leif showing him how to cut a wedge in the opposite side before you set to work on the other. With any luck, Rose and her ragged company would be that wedge, and if they just kept hacking, and hacking, and hacking...

Clay spotted the Infernal again, a winter-cloaked titan stomping across the battlefield. Wherever it went the host around it seemed renewed, driven to mindless rage by the demon in its midst. If Lastleaf were seeking protection, or someplace from which to rally and reestablish his grip on his crumbling army, he would probably start there.

Either Gabriel had come to the same conclusion or he was simply plotting the most direct route to Rose, because he was leading them right toward it. Their line was stretched hopelessly thin by now, a bright thread woven through the midst of a vile tapestry.

The Wight Nights got held up fighting giant spiders, while Courtney and the Sparks broke off to fight a bear the size of a Narmeeri elephant. Ben the Stalactian got the business end of a centaur's lance in his throat, and the Stormriders disappeared amidst a crowd of clambering goblins.

A wave of kobolds rushed in from the left, yipping like a hundred pint-sized dogs. Jain gave Clay a prod with her bow. "Get on, Slowhand. We've got this."

He lingered long enough to see the first dozen critters get a faceful of arrows before taking off after Gabe. He passed Barret on the way—the old merc and his two remaining bandmates were facing down a snarling, snub-nosed warg.

Once, Clay thought he saw the glint of Lastleaf's scale slipping through the throng, but when he looked again the druin was nowhere in sight.

"Rose!" Gabriel shouted, but his daughter was too far

away to hear. Her refugees were set upon by a mob of screech-ing white imps that reminded Clay of the rasks on the Cold Road, only smaller.

Clay could see Gabe's daughter clearly now, distinguished from those around her by two things: her hair, which was dyed a bloody red, and the fact that she fought like a Kaskar berserker who'd walked in on her husband in bed with her sister. She held a glowing scimitar in either hand and was whirling, twirling, eviscerating everything within reach.

Or not quite everything, Clay saw, though he could scarcely believe his eyes. There was a *druin* by her side, lean and lithe, wielding a longsword he employed almost exclu-sively in her defence. His hair was the washed-out green of a shallow summer sea, swept back behind tufted ears. He was taller and broader than Lastleaf, and he moved with strange, strategic economy, as though the battlefield were some vast Tetrea board and he'd anticipated every move.

The two of them—Rose and, Clay presumed, Freecloud—seemed invincible. The imps hit them like surf against a high bluff and broke almost instantly.

The Infernal glared down at the creatures scurrying into the safety of his shadow, then turned its bottomless black gaze upon Castia's refugees and the pair leading them.

"Fuck!" Gabe swore.

"I've got him," said Larkspur. She launched herself skyward, leaving Ganelon frowning amidst a flurry of black feathers.

Clay glanced over. "She'll be fine," he said, and found himself believing it.

"I know," said Ganelon, but his frown deepened anyway.

Gabriel urged them on. Clay took position on his right, Ganelon the left. Moog moved in their midst, while Matrick brought up the rear. They were alone now, the five of them battling through a maelstrom of claw and tooth. Arrows buzzed overhead like midges in marshland. Clay was roared at, screamed at, spat upon; he was jostled, kicked, pummelled, shoved—all the while doing his best to cover Gabriel's flank as his friend carved a path through whatever lay ahead.

Moog had a wand in either hand, both of which launched bolts of violet light that took erratic routes to their targets but never, ever missed. Matrick plied his knives like a parade drummer, his rhythm so fast his enemies didn't know he'd murdered them until their god asked them if they took milk in their tea. Ganelon killed with a brutal efficiency that humbled even Gabriel, because Gabriel left wounded in his wake, while Ganelon left the dead in pieces.

Clay was amazed at how little his back hurt, or his arm, or the ribs he'd broken fighting Larkspur's thralls. His face wasn't throbbing as it had been earlier. He was weary, of course: Every breath was bought with a gasp, and his heart hammered like a blacksmith late for supper, but he felt... good. *Really bloody good*, all things considered.

Strangest of all was the utter absence of fear. He'd been very afraid this morning. Afraid the wizard's plan wouldn't work, that the dragon would kill them. Afraid of going through the Threshold and coming back empty-handed. The Heartwyld Horde, in all its abominable might, had been the scariest thing he'd ever seen—aside, perhaps, from the look on Ginny's face when she hit her head on a cupboard door he'd left open by accident.

But now... all Clay felt was a sense of profound certainty, as if things—dire though they seemed—were exactly as they should be. He was among friends, shoulder to shoulder with his bandmates, who just so happened to be the four best men he'd ever had the privilege of knowing.

As individuals they were each of them fallible, discordant as notes without harmony. But as a band they were something more, something perfect in its own intangible way.

So no—he wasn't afraid. He was, in fact, grinning from ear to ear, basking in the music of the men around him, listening with bittersweet sorrow as the end drew near.

* * *

Clay saw Larkspur close with the Infernal. She banked wide as its whip thrashed droplets of frost from the air, then dipped below a swipe of its massive sword. Her scythe came spinning round, but the demon was armoured in hoarfrost so thick that *Umbra* did little more than strike icy sparks from its carapace.

The titan's minions were scattering in every direction. A torrent of imps crashed into Saga, and Moog went down, disappearing beneath the press of pale bodies. Matrick lagged, shouting the wizard's name and wading through imps like a man who'd lost his dog to a river's swift current.

Clay stepped in front of Gabriel, planting his feet and squaring his shield against the impish tide. The creatures were hardly bigger than children, stooped and scrawny, with horns curling back from pinched faces. They bore no weapons but sharp teeth and wicked claws, and while most were too fearful to harass Clay and the others, those that got close attacked them savagely.

Peering over the rim of his shield, he watched as Larkspur dove again. The Infernal's mouth yawned like a portal into the Frost Mother's hell, unleashing a freezing gale that blew the daeva backward. She spun out of control, wings pumping madly as she fought to right herself. Clay could see frost coating her armour, crusting her wings. She faltered in flight, but managed to shake the rime from her feathers and—

The whip hit her.

Larkspur's scream was cut short as she froze solid, plunging earthward like an icicle struck loose from an eave.

Clay looked immediately to Ganelon. Distress was plain on the warrior's face, but he clenched his jaw, said nothing.

"Go get her," Gabe told him.

Ganelon glanced over, incredulous. "You can't—"

"I can," said Gabriel, grinning. "Of course I can."

Ganelon appeared as though he would object, but instead

he nodded, turned, and began hewing a path toward the fallen daeva.

The Infernal was advancing on Castia's refugees. Already its whip was falling among them, entombing every victim in an icy crypt.

"Rose!" Gabriel hollered, and this time his daughter looked up.

"Dad!?"

"*Rose!*" Gabe tried to step around Clay and was nearly swept away by rushing imps. He growled a curse and fell back behind.

Clay tried to push forward, but the enemy were too many, too deep to give way. It was all he could do to stand his ground.

"Dad!" He heard two voices call out. The first was Rose, desperate and disbelieving, but below that, faint as a whisper, was another.

Tally.

In his head Clay heard his daughter murmur sleepily: *You would come if it was me, right, Daddy?*

If it was you . . .

His knuckles went white on *Blackheart*'s grip. His jaw clamped down on a scream until the scream pried his teeth apart and came out roaring. He set his broken arm inside the bowl of his shield and heaved against the current with the stubborn resolve of a plough ox yoked to the moon.

If it was you, Clay had told her, as the glimmer of candle-light constellations moved across her face, *then nothing in the world could stop me.*

His determination bought him a single step, a second. He surged ahead, yelling himself hoarse, and the sea of scampering imps broke around his shield like ice beneath a ship's prow. Suddenly he was stumbling clear, looking up to see the Infernal looming overhead.

Breath like a blizzard engulfed him. Clay closed his eyes

for fear they would freeze in their sockets. Snow and chips of ice blasted his face. Frost formed on his beard, caked his eyelashes, and set his body trembling. His shield was suddenly too heavy to lift with one hand. It dragged him off balance, and Clay watched hopelessly as the Infernal's whip curled against the grey sky above...

Gabriel shouldered him aside; Clay hit the ground as the whip thrashed the air above his head. Before it could recoil Gabe slashed it, severing it, and then squinted down at Clay.

"You good?" he asked.

"G-good," Clay managed through chattering teeth.

The demon straightened, a sound like an iced-over lake groaning beneath the weight of something titanic. Its eyes, deep and dark as winter wells, looked on as Gabriel approached, unhurried, *Vellichor* dragging a furrow in the black earth behind him.

Its sword came chopping down so fast Clay barely saw it. Faster still was Gabe, who stepped aside so casually he might have been sliding past someone in a crowded room. The Infernal grinned, clearly amused. A flurry of snow gusted between teeth like shattered tombstones.

The grin fell away as Gabriel began running.

The demon's growl was the rumble of a distant avalanche. It took a backward step, startled, shifting the grip on its sword so the flared tip would be too wide for Gabe to dodge as it came thrusting toward him.

Gabriel jumped. It wasn't graceful, and if he hadn't timed it right the sword would have sheared him clean in half. Instead it ploughed into the ground beneath him, and Gabe landed on all fours on the broad, frosted flat of the blade. He sprang to his feet, sprinting up the sword's length as the Infernal tried to wrench it free. By the time it did Gabriel was almost to the hilt, leaping as the weapon's momentum sent him soaring.

For Clay, the next half second spanned the lifetime of a glacier. Gabriel hung suspended in air, both hands on *Vellichor*'s grip, the blade rising behind him, bright with the bloodred sun of another sky.

Swung with every ounce of strength Gabe could summon, *Vellichor* split the ice at the Infernal's throat and cleaved deep into its neck. Snow and sleet erupted from the wound like a storm gusting through an open door. The demon staggered, swayed, and crashed in a disastrous heap.

Gabriel hit the ground running. He'd left his sword lodged in the Infernal, but it hardly mattered now.

Rose came rushing out to meet him, and once again it seemed to Clay as if the world itself ceased turning as the distance between father and daughter fell away. Only the two of them remained in motion, scrambling like swimmers in mirrored oceans, drawn inexorably toward the surface of each other by the very breath in their lungs.

Rose staggered, overcome by exhaustion. As she pitched forward Gabe went to his knees on the mud-slick earth, sliding beneath her as she fell into his arms.

And now it was they who huddled, frozen together in that single, singular moment, as the world around them went on spinning.

And spinning.

And spinning.

Clay found Lastleaf in the corpse-littered stretch between Gabriel's mercenaries and Castia's refugees. The druin had suffered horrible burns along one half of his body, where the scale of his armour became fused with the charred flesh underneath. Part of his jaw was missing, and his eyes—one gold-bright, the other scar-ravaged—gazed sightlessly at the cloud-torn sky.

He'd been trampled by his own Horde as they'd scattered in the wake of the Infernal's fall, and for a moment, despite all he had done to deserve an end such as this, Clay felt a pang of sympathy for the druin. *We are each what the past has made of us*, he had said on the Isle at Lindmoor, and Lastleaf's past had made of him a bitter, broken, terrible thing.

The Heathen was lying on top of his sword, which Clay figured he had better take before someone else did. He slung *Blackheart* over his shoulder and knelt, gingerly turning the body over so as not to—

No.

Clay's heart froze.

Please, no . . .

His mouth went dry. There was a sound in his ears like a deep drum booming. Clay felt his hand begin to tremble violently as his fingers closed around *Tamarat's* bloody hilt.

"Oh, Lastleaf," he whispered, as he pulled the void-black blade from the awful sheath it had made of the Heathen's heart. "What have you done?"

Epilogue

Home

The following is an excerpt from *The Same Old Song* by Kitagra the Undying, Court Bard to His August Majesty, Emperor Matrick of Castia, first of his name:

> *Should you wish to learn what became of those who survived the Battle for Castia, I suggest you visit either your local library or your favorite pub. What you find in the library might be closer to the truth, but what you hear in the pub will no doubt be the better story.*
>
> *If you insist on reading,* Born in Fire: The Rise of the Watch *is one of my favorites, as is* I, Jain, *which details the exploits of the brigand turned world-renowned mercenary after she left the Silk Arrows and began her solo career.* The Sound an Eagle Makes *gives a good summary of the battle itself, although the simply titled* Castia, *written by Syd (son of Barret) is widely considered the most comprehensive account of that auspicious day.*
>
> *The members of Saga survived the battle miraculously unscathed. For all they endured during their journey to Castia, they incurred little but bruises during the rout of the Heartwyld Horde. It was, incidentally, the last time all five members of Saga would fight alongside one another.*

Matrick Skulldrummer remained behind in Castia. He spearheaded efforts to repair the city, and when it came time to appoint a new governing body (most of the old one having succumbed to the plague), the people of Castia decided it was high time they had an Emperor after all. There was a vote, and Matty won by a landslide. He gave up drinking for good and arranged a peaceful separation from his former wife, Queen Lilith of Agria. He invited his children to visit him in Castia, and it surprised no one but their mother when they opted to remain by their father's side.

I need tell no one what became of Arcandius Moog, as he is among the most well-known and celebrated scholars of our time. Of any time, for that matter. In the aftermath of Castia's liberation, he paid another visit to the witchdoctor Taino. After months of study Moog returned to, and rebuilt, his tower east of Conthas, where he developed a drinkable cure for the rot.

It is the firm belief of this humble revenant that Arcandius Moog is one of the few figures in all of history (aside, perhaps, from Clay Cooper) possessed of the moral fortitude to do what he did next.

He gave the cure to everyone. For free.

Moog never remarried, and though I suspect his involvement in one or two covert liaisons, it is clear to all that his heart belongs, even after so long, to his deceased husband, after which he named his miraculous potion: "Freddie's Finest Curative Cordial."

Ganelon bid farewell to the band and made his own way back to Grandual. We must conclude that somewhere along that fraught and forlorn path he decided that the world to which he'd returned to was not a place where he belonged, since his first stop east of the forest was the prison in which he'd spent a long, dark decade trapped in stone. The keepers warned him not to venture below, but those who tend the Quarry are pale, frail, and all but blind, so they sure as hell couldn't stop him from doing so. He said to them, rather cryptically: "Wake me when she gets here," and then descended, alone, to the lair of the Basilisk Broodmother, whose gaze renders living flesh to stone.

Alas, Ganelon was sadly unaware that his coupling with Larkspur had produced a son. The boy is young, still, but I'm told he's got a bit of an attitude.

Gabriel's story is invariably linked to that of his daughter, Rose. Their lives, along with those of her partner, Freecloud, have been the subject of numerous songs and stories, so I will spare you the details here.

As for Clay Cooper . . . Two days after breaking the siege at Castia he stepped through the portal to Kaladar and walked home from there. He was accompanied most of the way by Jain and the Silk Arrows, and by Gabriel, with whom he had set out from Coverdale several months earlier.

I was not present when Clay and Gabriel parted at last, but Jain claims it took place while the sun was setting. She watched their silhouettes from a distance as they shared a few laughs, shed a few tears, and finally embraced. Afterward, she says, Gabriel took Clay's head in his hands and uttered something too quiet to hear, which one might assume was a heartfelt confession that he owed every happiness of his life thereafter to Clay and Clay alone.

To which, Jain tells us, Clay Cooper responded with a shrug.

On the long journey home Clay spotted several roadside plots that would be greatly improved by the presence of a modest two-storey inn. There would be a stable out back, he decided, and maybe a smithy, in case folk needed simple work done.

Inside, sturdy round tables with plush leather seats, and a fireplace far from the stage for those who wished to sit and enjoy the fire's warmth in relative peace and quiet. *Blackheart* would be mounted above, and if anyone asked what an ugly, charred, chopped-up piece of wood was doing up there on the wall, well, Clay might just sidle out from behind the bar, kick up his feet, and tell them a tale or two.

By the time he reached town the sun had nearly set. His shadow stretched out behind him, as stoop shouldered and weary as the man it followed down the beaten track that passed for a thoroughfare in Coverdale.

"Clay?" The voice was familiar, the tone incredulous. "Clay Cooper?"

He looked up at Pip, who had stumbled out of the King's Head with his helmet tucked under one arm. "I've been called worse," Clay said.

"Ha!" Pip attempted to slap his knee and got most of it. "'Called worse,' he says. Classic! Hey, when did you get home?"

I'm not home yet, Clay thought. "Just now," he said. "All's well, I hope?"

"Better than well, I'd say. You hear about Castia?"

Clay couldn't help but grin. "I did, yeah."

"Wild, eh? By the Holy Tetrea I wish I'd been there!"

Pip was young, and had likely never ventured any farther afield than Conthas, or maybe Oddsford, and so Clay forgave the boy for saying something so incredibly stupid. "They ever catch that centaur out by Tassel's farm?" he asked, changing the subject.

"Catch him?" Pip scoffed. "You mean you haven't heard?" When Clay shook his head, the lad went on: "Your girl killed it!"

"My..." Clay faltered, since his mouth had begun speaking while his brain was still trying to make sense of what he'd just been told. "You mean Ginny?"

"Not Ginny, no," said Pip. "Ginny was pissed as Glif!"

Clay grabbed the boy by the shoulders, perhaps a bit more roughly than he'd meant to. "I need you to tell me what happened, Pip. Right now."

Pip blew a sigh that reeked of stale beer. "Well, that bastard—the centaur, I mean—chased Karl—that's Ryk Yarsson's oldest boy—out of the woods and down to that marsh by your place. Your girl saw 'em coming, I guess. Tripped it up with a stick or something. Broke its neck. Crack!" he added, in case Clay needed reminding what a breaking neck sounded like.

"You're telling me that Tally...*my Tally*...killed a centaur?"

"She killed a centaur!" Pip said. "You've got a little merc on your hands there, Cooper."

This time Clay's mouth and mind replied as one. "*No fucking way,*" he said.

Pip laughed. "And what's more, young Karl's been on her like a wasp on a sweetcake ever since. Barely leaves her side, that one, and she seems to like it that way. Poor boy's fallen hard, I think."

He doesn't know hard, thought Clay. He pried his fingers from Pip's sleeve and forced a smile onto his face. "Good seeing you, Pip."

"Good to see you, too," Pip slurred. "I'm glad you're home."

Clay set out for the west gate. *I'm not home*, he told himself. *Not yet.*

He stopped to relieve himself on the road outside of town. It was true dark now. The stars above were incomprehensibly numerous, and so much brighter than Clay remembered. He craned his neck to look up at them, and despite everything he'd accomplished since seeing them last, he *still* felt beggared by comparison. It occurred to him that this would always be the case, and Clay decided he preferred it that way.

He walked on, listening to the crickets chirping in the grass, to the wind rustling through the trees, taking long, deep breaths of the chill night air.

And then he saw her, shadow black against the warm

light spilling from the open door. It seemed an impossible distance to the end of his lane, an immeasurable stretch from the edge of his yard to the stoop upon which his wife sat waiting for him. She didn't actually see him until he was a few yards out and Griff came hurtling from inside the house, yapping and scampering madly around Clay's feet. He knelt to pet him while Ginny stood, crossed her arms, and lifted her chin in that rural-imperious way of hers.

"You're alive," she said.

"I'm alive."

"And Rose?"

"Safe and sound."

"Good."

"Tally?"

"Fine. Asleep. You heard about the centaur?"

He nodded. "I heard."

Her back got a bit more rigid then. Her chin climbed higher still. "That girl doesn't pick up a sword, Clay. Ever. Do you understand me?"

"No swords," he assured her. "No axes, or knives, or bows. Not even a sharp stick, I promise."

That got the chuckle he was looking for. Clay took a step into the light and heard her breath catch.

"Your face . . ."

He stopped to graze a finger over his latest scar. "Yeah, well. I guess that makes you the pretty one now."

She laughed, and Clay could have wept for the sound of it.

Ginny reached out to him, and Clay stepped into the circle of her arms like a pilgrim come, at the end of his days, to the last house of the holy. Her scent surrounded him. A loose strand of her hair tickled his nose and gods-be-damned if he was going to scratch it now. Her breath was warm and soft as summer wind on his neck as she whispered, "You're home."

And finally, he was.

Acknowledgments

When you're an aspiring author you don't (or you shouldn't, anyway) write with the absolute certainty that your book will be published. It helps, however, to be surrounded by people who are absolutely certain you will be. As it turns out, I was the very last person to know my wildest dream would eventually come true.

The book that became *Kings of the Wyld* benefited from a great many patient and enthusiastic beta-readers. Chief among these was Devon Pipars, who read it three chapters at a time over the course of a year and always clamoured for more, and Eugene Vassilev, who read it as many times as I asked him to and was as critical and ebullient a friend as an author could ask for.

I would also like to thank those with whom I shared the journey of writing my first, flawed attempt at a fantasy novel: Hollis Steele, Deyna Dodds, and Kaili Grant were champions of a book that might never see the light of day. Still, I am so very grateful.

Also deserving of gratitude is Bryan Cheyne, who has been a friend, a writing confidant, and a fellow fanboy of You-Know-Who for longer than either of us would care to admit. I sincerely hope to find his name a few spines to the left in a bookstore someday.

I should also give thanks to Richard Anderson for a beautiful cover, Kristine Cofsky for an excellent photo, Shannon Boyd for reading it aloud while I took notes and laughed at my own jokes, and Natasha McLeod, who listened patiently to every idea that made it into the book and several thousand more that did not. Because of her I emerged from this process as a (relatively) functioning human instead of a shambling, bleary-eyed troglodyte.

I owe a huge debt to Sebastien DeCastell, who was accosted at a restaurant one night by a fan and aspiring writer who also happened to be his waiter. Sebastien was gracious enough to answer my questions on the publishing process and eventually commend me to his agent. I owe him a copy of this book, and so much more.

The process of getting an agent can be a defeating, soul-crushing slog: You leap for a precipice, and more often than not you are dashed to pieces on the rocks below. I will be forever indebted to Heather Adams, who caught me, pulled me up, and continues to guide me toward ever more lofty heights.

Which brings me to my editor at Orbit, Lindsey Freakin' Hall: Editor Extraordinaire and righteous champion of this book from day one. Her support has been invaluable, her wisdom instrumental, and her enthusiasm rivalled only by my mom's. I am so extremely fortunate that in pursuit of our own dreams we've found ourselves side by side on a road that I hope goes on for a long, long while.

Lastly, I must thank my taller, broader little brother, Tyler. You have played many roles for me, Ty: the Robin to my Batman, the Man-At-Arms to my He-Man, the Luigi to my Mario. And finally, if you would indulge me once more, the Clay Cooper to my Gabriel. You're a *good* man, Tyler Eames. And when all is said and done, I'd say it's fairly obvious which of us is the real hero.

extras

orbit

meet the author

NICHOLAS EAMES was born to parents of infinite patience and unstinting support in Wingham, Ontario. Though he attended college for theatre arts, he gave up acting to pursue the infinitely more attainable profession of "epic fantasy novelist." *Kings of the Wyld* is his first novel. Nicholas loves black coffee, neat whiskey, the month of October, and video games. He currently lives in Ontario, Canada, and is very probably writing at this very moment.

Author Interview

When did you first start writing?
In high school, while I was undoubtedly supposed to be doing
something else. When I eventually got busted, my teacher
sent it to a family friend of his (Ed Greenwood, the creator of
Forgotten Realms) who graciously read it and replied that I
"had the fire of a good storyteller." Encouraging as that was,
I sort of shelved writing (pun intended) during college, then
decided after that to try my hand at it again.

Who are some of your biggest influences?
First and foremost, Guy Gavriel Kay. Reading him was what
made me decide to take writing seriously, in hope of creat-
ing something that might affect someone the way his work
affected me. More recently, Scott Lynch and Joe Abercrom-
bie (for me, at least) sort of kicked open the door for infusing
fast-paced, dramatic stories with a sense of humor.

Where did the idea for* Kings of the Wyld *come from?
It all began when I was struck by lightning...Kidding, of
course. In fact I can't remember what sparked it initially, only
that I thought, *How cool would it be to read a book in which
mercenary bands acted (and were treated like) rock stars?* Also,
there's that saying floating around and that goes something

like, "Write the kind of book you'd most like to read." Well, this is it.

Blackheart *is such a cool weapon. What made you choose a shield as your hero's foremost weapon?*

To begin with, the weapons I assigned to each of the main characters were due to their assigned role in a metaphorical rock band—the most obvious being Matrick wielding a pair of "drumstick" knives and Ganelon using an axe, which is, of course, slang for "guitar." Clay was envisioned as the guy on bass whose name everyone forgets but without whom the song just doesn't feel right. The shield, originally, was a way of keeping him passive. As he developed, however, it became a huge part of his persona. Though he battles a violent nature, Clay is, at heart, a protector—someone who, due to certain events in his past, will never again be a spectator when the lives of those he loves are at stake.

The pursuit of glory is a major theme in* Kings of the Wyld—*what drew you to focus on that?

That was inspired by—surprise!—music. How many of us have heard someone say that the music of today pales in comparison to what came before? That phrase has always (and will always) make old people nod and young people snort with derision. I tried to apply that sentiment to the setting of *Kings*, wherein the mercenary bands of today try so very hard to outshine a past that feels, even to them, somehow more authentic.

This book goes from breaking your heart to being laugh-out-loud hilarious, sometimes within a single page. How did you make sure the balance was right between these two elements of the story?

The short answer? I listened to the sound advice of my agent and my editor, both of whom helped me find that sweet spot. The longer one? I set out to write a funny book. A ridiculous book. A book that didn't take itself too seriously (hence the goblins, the erectile dysfunction potions, and the fact that my antagonist has bunny ears). But the characters just...got away from me. I blame Clay Cooper.

Kings of the Wyld *has a phenomenal cast of characters. If you had to pick one, who would you say is your favourite? Which character was the most difficult to write?*

First of all, thanks for saying so. Favourite? Tough call. Moog makes me laugh, and Larkspur is pretty badass, but I've got to say Clay Cooper. He's honest, loyal, more clever than he gives himself credit for, and just so doggedly good. I mean, he'd die for you. Yes, you. And he barely evens knows you!

Most difficult? Probably Lastleaf. Though he's technically the bad guy, I find myself empathizing with him a lot—to the point that if our heroes failed and everything went his way it might not be such a bad thing after all. Making him suitably evil while giving him a perspective that a reader might relate to was tricky. Did I succeed? My mom certainly thinks so!

Kings of the Wyld *is the first book of the Band series. What's in store for us in future books?*

The second book explores a bit more of the wider world we barely glimpse in the first, and features the next generation of mercenary bands, who are desperate for the chance to outshine their glorious predecessors. Unfortunately for them, they get what they ask for.

extras

If you could spend an afternoon with one of your characters, which would it be and what would you do?

Pete—the guy at the bar in the Riot House. We'd sip our beers and talk about life, love, and the little things.

Lastly, we have to ask: If you could have any superpower, what would it be?

Besides perfect spelling? Hmm...I'd like to be able to stop time, because then I could finally read every book, watch every film, play every video game, and spend as much time as I want with loved ones without that pesky nuisance known as "dying of old age" rearing its ugly head. Wouldn't that be nice?

introducing

If you enjoyed
KINGS OF THE WYLD,
look out for

BLOODY ROSE

by Nicholas Eames

It was said Rose had killed a cyclops when she was sixteen years old. She hadn't been a mercenary at the time—just a scrappy young girl eager to escape the long reach of her father's shadow. There'd been no band to back her up, no bard to watch what transpired and record it in song. Only a handful of awestruck farmers were there to see it, but farmers spread gossip like seed, and word of Rose's exploit grew quickly. She'd become a celebrity almost overnight, earning herself the moniker under which she would live forever after: Bloody Rose.

There were those who didn't believe the story, who thought she'd found it dead or used her daddy's gold to hire mercs to slay the beast on her behalf. Tam, of course, had never doubted it was true. But here in the arena, seeing a cyclops in the pallid, towering, monstrous flesh, she felt a pang of uncertainty in her gut, because how could a sixteen-year-old girl—how could anyone at all—overcome *this*? How did you even begin?

By running straight at it, evidently.

Rose took the lead at a sprint. Her rune-inscribed gauntlets pulsed blue-green, and the scimitars at her waist leapt like spawning salmon into her hands. Freecloud raced behind her, clenching *Madrigal*'s scabbard in one hand and leaning as though he were running into a gale.

As Rose closed with the cyclops it aimed a clumsy kick in her direction, which she dodged without slowing. She sprang onto its other foot and stabbed one of her swords into its shin. She used the weapon's leverage to haul herself up, planting the other blade an arm's length higher. The cyclops barely registered the wounds. Tam supposed that years of harsh captivity in the dim cells below the arena had somehow inured it to pain. It pivoted on the foot nearest Freecloud, unable to locate Rose, who was stabbing her way up the back of its leg.

While she climbed toward the creature's waist, Freecloud made an obvious target of himself by standing directly in front of it. The druin still hadn't drawn his sword, but his right hand hovered threateningly above its hilt. The cyclops tried stomping him flat, but Freecloud—who'd seen it coming—stepped clear. He did so with unhurried ease, like a pilgrim making way on the road for a farmer's cart. When the beast tried again with the other foot, Freecloud ducked aside. Tam heard a shrill ring and caught the flash of sunlit steel as *Madrigal* finally left its scabbard. Gripping the sword two-handed, the druin brought it down across the monster's toes, which split like logs beneath a woodsman's axe.

Blood and noise followed. The cyclops roared in pain, and Tam heard one of the mercs behind her clap and yell, "Attaboy!"

Freecloud moved in a slow circle around it, *Madrigal* poised like a scorpion's tail above him. The cyclops tracked him warily. Red gore dripped in viscous strands from its open mouth, slopping over the swell of its belly and into the matted loincloth below.

Rose must have suddenly hit a nerve, because the thing yelped and slapped her with a meaty hand. She weathered the blow, gripping her hilts like a climber clinging to purchase above a yawning abyss. She was twenty feet from the ground now; a fall wouldn't kill her, but it would leave her prone, which could prove lethal.

Determined to recover the beast's attention, Freecloud darted in and chopped at its ankle. The cut was shallow, glancing off bone, but was enough to distract the cyclops, who spun around as the druin danced between its legs. It stooped to swat at Freecloud, who didn't bother trying to evade it—only stood there as the gnarly hand swiped through him.

The cyclops looked bewildered as wisps of green smoke curled in its empty palm. Tam was confused as well, until she spotted Freecloud standing beneath its legs, exactly where he'd been a moment earlier.

She'd heard songs about druic sorcery. It was said they could cast illusions and pass unseen by mortal eyes. The songs were true, apparently, though by this point in the day it surprised her not at all.

When Rose reached the monster's waist she let her swords tumble to the ground. Using the soiled loincloth for purchase, she clambered onto the creature's back as it bent to reach for Freecloud. There was a ridge of coarse blue fur running the length of its spine, which Rose climbed hand over hand with alarming dexterity.

Below her, Freecloud was forced to retreat as the cyclops lunged at him with both hands. Fast as the druin was, his adversary was simply too big to evade for long. In his effort to distract it from Rose, he was forced to put himself in jeopardy. He could no longer afford to counter the creature's attacks, and twice more was obliged to rely on illusions to save his skin. Tam watched as he narrowly ducked a blow from the beast, and when another came there were suddenly *two* of him: mirrored swordsmen in silver mail and swirling sky blue cloaks.

The monster picked one and punched, at which point both Tam and Freecloud learned—rather painfully, in the latter's case—that even a cyclops gets lucky from time to time.

Freecloud—the *real* Freecloud—went tumbling violently across the stone floor of the arena. Where he stopped, he lay unmoving. His illusory double vanished in smoke.

From all over the arena came the sound of breathless gasps. The cyclops loosed a chortling roar as it advanced on the crumpled druin.

Tam leaned into her brother's shoulder. "It can't kill him, right? They won't let it."

Kars shook his head. "Who's *they*?"

Tam looked to one end of the canyon, where a cordon of shield-bearing spearmen were stationed in case any of the arena's monstrous denizens made a break for it. None of them appeared eager to rescue Freecloud. In fact, she doubted they would challenge the cyclops even if it came right at them.

Rose was lost to sight on the monster's back. She might have guessed from the crowd's reaction that Freecloud was down, but what could she do about it?

No more than I can, thought Tam miserably.

She started as Kars laid a heavy hand on her shoulder. "Look away, Tam."

Look away.

So she did. She looked away, and found her gaze drawn to the face of Fable's old bard. Although Kamaris may have resented his previous band, he didn't *hate* them. He wasn't evil. And despite his earlier comment about Tam's first song as Fable's new bard being an elegy, his expression now was utterly desolate, the face of a farmer finding his crops destroyed by an early frost.

When she bolted from the cave window her brother probably assumed she had gone to retch or to spare hemself the sight of Freecloud's death. In truth, Tam had no idea *what* she was doing, except that at some point in the past few moments she'd decided that she should do *something*, even if it amounted to nothing.

She pushed through the press of mercenaries behind her, and rushed to the lip of the cave before remembering she had no weapon but the knife her mother had given her. Without thinking she snatched up a bow from against the wall, shrugged the lute case from her shoulder and replaced it with a bristling quiver. And then she was past the door guards, sprinting all-out down the stone ramp.

The sound of the crowd hit her like a physical force, a percussive roar louder than anything she'd ever heard. The quiver bounced painfully against her side, and the bow was so tall she had to hold it sideways so—

Gods fuck me, Tam thought, only now recognizing the weapon in her hand. *It's Jain's bow. I just stole Lady fucking Jain's bow!* The realization of this—more than the fact that she was charging out to fight a cyclops—almost turned her back.

507

Too late now, since she was on the arena floor, running as fast as her legs could carry her. She was already short of breath, because it turned out—surprise!—that playing at being a mercenary was more physically taxing than clearing glassware off tables. She cast a glance toward Freecloud, facedown on the stone, but then her gaze went up and up, and she found herself looking into the abysmal black eye of the cyclops.

She felt her knees threaten to buckle. She slowed her pace without meaning to, because every instinct was screaming at her to turn and run the other way. The creature was bleating at her, but Tam could barely hear it over the noise coming off the canyon walls and the rasp of her own ragged breath.

Having decided that the girl with the bow presented no threat whatsoever, the cyclops took another step toward Freecloud. One more, and it could crush the druin with a stomp of its foot.

Now or never, Tam told herself. She skidded to a halt, chose an arrow at random, and let the quiver fall at her feet. The sun was in her eyes, so she had to squint to see. On her first attempt to draw the bow, she barely bent it at all. With a newfound respect for Lady Jain's upper-arm strength she tried again, gritting her teeth, knuckles whitening as she pulled the fletching to the edge of her jaw. She aimed the point of her arrow at the only target she could think of, because when you fought something with one huge eye in the middle of its head, choosing something to shoot at was sort of a no-brainer.

Beyond her centre of focus, Tam saw Rose gain the giant's shoulder. Rose extended an arm—the bracer on her wrist glowing bright—and one of her swords sprang into her waiting hand.

Tam took a breath, trying in vain to keep her hands from trembling. The muscles in her arms were on fire. She could feel the arrow straining against her grip, like a trained falcon await-ing the command to kill.

She let it fly.

Tam awoke with the roar of the arena echoing in her ears, ris-ing and falling like a sailor's memory of the sea in a storm. Her head was throbbing, and her jaw ached as if she'd taken a punch from someone a great deal stronger than herself. She was lying on a cot in a large lantern-lit tent, the ceiling of which was lost to shadow. She could make out the sound of music and harsh laughter beyond the canvas walls. From nearby came the slow rasp of quiet breathing.

Still alive, then, thought Tam, whose last memory was of fainting the moment after she'd loosed the arrow.

"Your brother was here."

Easing her head to the right, Tam saw Rose seated beside another cot upon which Freecloud was laid out, unconscious or asleep. The mercenary's hair was drawn back from her face, tied into a haphazard knot at the back of her head. It might have made her look younger, except Rose's eyes were as hard and cold as a mountain in winter. They were, Tam decided, the sort of eyes that held a knife to your throat as they rifled through the pockets of your subconscious.

"Where is here?" Tam asked, propping herself on one elbow. Her head grumbled a warning that doing so had been a bad idea.

Rose placed a hand on Freecloud's forehead, frowning at whatever it was she felt. "Remember those big tents we passed on the way to the arena?"

"We're in the Fighter's Camp?"

She nodded yes.

And so Tam found herself in yet another place she'd never imagined being before today. From what little she'd heard, Fighter's Camp was sort of an after-party for mercenaries only, though select members of Ardburg's nobility were invited, and pretty much anyone clever enough to slip past the loose cordon of sentries was permitted as well. It was said the guards could be bribed with booze, sex, or silver, though paying with *actual currency* was generally frowned upon.

Tam looked to Freecloud. There was a series of small cuts marring one side of the druin's face, which Rose was gently patting with a dampened cloth. His chest was rising and falling with the slow cadence of deep slumber.

"Is he okay?" she asked.

Rose took a long breath before answering. "He will be," she said quietly. Her eyes roved to Tam, and she chewed a moment on her bottom lip. She appeared to be weighing her next words carefully. "What you did today was..."

"Stupid," Tam finished for her.

"Very."

"Reckless."

"Wildly so, yes."

"I'm a fool," said Tam.

"No argument there." Rose raised a hand to forestall further bouts of self-recrimination, then placed the other hand on Freecloud's chest. "But it was also very brave."

Tam's face boiled like a kettle. She swallowed, if only to keep the steam from spewing out her ears. "My mother—"

"Is going to kill us both," said Rose.

"I won't tell her," Tam blurted.

Rose laughed. A grin like spearing sunlight broke across her face. "You won't need to. I'd wager all of Ardburg is talking about the girl with the bow. These things get around, believe me."

"Did I kill it?" Tam asked.

Rose's eyes narrowed. "The cyclops? No, you didn't. I cut its throat."

Tam didn't know whether to be disappointed or greatly relieved. "So my arrow missed, then?"

Rose shrugged. "That depends on what you were aiming for." She stood, grimacing, and Tam saw a strip of bloody cloth binding her right thigh.

Tam bolted upright. She felt the heat leach from her face. "I shot you," she breathed.

"You shot me," Rose confirmed. "Did a piss-poor job of it, though. I've had slivers that bled more when I pulled them out."

"I *shot* you," Tam repeated dumbly.

Rose resumed her seat. "Yeah, well, good luck convincing anyone of that. According to some fifty thousand witnesses you killed a cyclops with a single arrow."

Tam was still in shock. "I shot Bloody Rose..."

Rose looked at her seriously. "Say it one more time, and I'll return the favour."

"Sorry," she said. The pain in her head was receding, crowded out by awe and disbelief. Tam swung her legs over the side of the cot. Her boots were on the ground beside the bed, along with Jain's longbow. A single arrow lay atop it, and she had no doubt at all as to whose blood stained its iron tip red.

Tam sat in silence while Rose soaked her cloth in a basin of water, then continued mopping the druin's brow. At last, she summoned the courage to ask whether or not she was fired, but only got so far as drawing the breath to say it.

"I almost killed him today," said Rose without taking her eyes off Freecloud. "I should have been more careful. We could have fought that thing together and brought it down, no problem. But I charged ahead, tried to take it on my own. I put us in danger."

"You were fearless…" Tam began.

"That wasn't fearlessness," she snapped, looking up. Her eyes were narrowed, accusing, though Tam had the sense her ire was directed inward. "That was fear."

Tam was about to ask, perhaps unwisely, what she meant by that, but then Freecloud stirred in his sleep. He murmured a string of sibilant words in a language Tam didn't recognize before slipping back under.

Rose stroked one of his twitching ears with gentle fingers. "You should head outside," she said. "Find Cura and Brune—they'll look after you. Be a shame to spend your first Fighter's Camp in bed." She glanced up again, the ghost of a grin haunting her lips. "In bed *alone*, anyway. And say good-bye to your brother," she added. "He's going west tomorrow, along with everyone else."

"But not us," said Tam.

Rose looked away. "No. We've got a contract in Diremarch and a tour to wrap up before that. We're leaving first thing in the morning. You can sleep on the argosy."

Guess I'm not fired, Tam thought. She pulled on her boots and threw her heavy cloak across her shoulders. After a moment's consideration she picked up Jain's bow, deciding she'd better return it, even if doing so felt like returning to a dragon's lair because you'd lost an earring while stealing its hoard.

She was almost to the exit when Rose spoke up behind her.

"They've named you, by the way."

Tam paused. She could feel night air trickling through the tent flap, cool where it licked her skin. Turning, she saw that Rose's back was to her still. She looked very small just now, crouched in the gloom like a solitary candle's fitful, futile flame—this woman the world called Bloody Rose.

"Named me what?" Tam asked.

Rose sighed, a sound like the cold breeze whispering in her ear. "Oh, I expect you'll find out soon enough."

introducing

**If you enjoyed
KINGS OF THE WYLD,
look out for**

THE DRAGON LORDS: FOOL'S GOLD

by Jon Hollins

*It's not easy to live in a world ruled by dragons. The taxes are
high and their control is complete. But for one group of
bold misfits, it's time to band together and
steal back some of that wealth.*

No one said they were smart.

Will stood, momentarily paralyzed by the vision of a cave full
of goblins.

Run! screamed a small and eminently sensible part of his
mind, but for some reason his legs weren't paying attention.
They, it seemed, were more fatalistic. They would only carry

him from so many attempts on his life in one day before simply giving up and accepting the fate as inevitable.

"Sorry," he heard himself. "Wrong cave. My one's a few entrances down."

He went to take a step away from the goblins but his cowardly legs were still not on the same page as the rest of him.

A low growl seemed to rise from every small mouth in the room, a whisper brought to the volume of a roar by the sheer density of the bodies packed into the space before him.

"I'll be off then," he said, more to his own anatomy than to the crowd. His knees shivered in response, but he thought the movement boded collapse more than any sort of horizontal traction.

Suddenly a bloodcurdling howl rose through the night. It hollowed out all of Will's resolve, left him a quivering shell.

He found himself thinking of the Pantheon. Of Lawl, father of the gods. Of Lawl's wife, Betra, mother to all. Of their children, Klink, Toil, and Knole—gods and goddesses of money, labor, and wisdom. Of Lawl's daughter-wife Cois, goddess of lust and desire. Of Betra's husband-son Barph, god of revelry. Who could he pray to? Who might, against all the odds, send him aid?

Fuck it, he thought. *I'll slaughter a whole damn army of pigs to the first one of you lot who helps me out here.*

Apparently the Pantheon had about as much faith in him as he had in them.

His arms, more cooperative than his legs, rose up over his head. His spirits almost rallied as he felt movement in his petrified legs, but it was only him sinking to his knees.

Wait, said the small voice inside him, the one that had advised retreat, *that howl came from behind you...*

Shut up! yelled the panicking component of his mind. *I don't have time for your shit. I'm busy dying, gods curse it.*

516

Something massive bowled past Will. He felt the wind of it as it passed him, the bass growl of its roar in his chest, the pounding of its feet through the rock beneath him.

Then silence. A moment of absolute silence.

Then wind. A violent swishing noise.

And then the sound of death.

Will had grown up on a farm. He had raised enough livestock to know that sound. The sound of flesh tearing, bones breaking.

But it wasn't coming from him.

He dared to open one eye.

Divine intervention. At first, that was the only explanation that came to his mind. That somehow his prayers had worked. That Lawl had really stepped down from the heavens and come to intercede on his part. That a divinity had finally come back to Kondorra. Just for him.

And then he got a look at the creature, and while there were stories of Lawl, and Betra, and Barph, and the rest of the Pantheon taking on some odd forms over the years, nothing he'd ever read was quite like this.

It was a creature perhaps eight feet tall, made entirely out of vast slabs of muscle, and spackled with cobblestone-size scales that glistened bronze in the firelight. It wielded a massive war hammer, the head of which scythed through the pressed ranks like a blade through wheat. Small bodies flew, anatomy distorted, fluids flying in great spraying arcs. The scent of blood and shit filled the air.

The goblins screamed, panicked, tried to flee back into the dull dead end of the cavern. A few brave souls leaked around the edge of the creature's arc of death, fled toward the entrance. They raced past Will, and he tracked them as they hurtled toward the night.

And that was when he saw her. The angel to pair with the demon deeper in the cave. She was etched in moonlight, sweat-slick hair pulled back into a haphazard ponytail, mouth set in a grimace of rage. She held a sword in one hand, a dagger in the other. She slit the throat of the first goblin that tried to get past her, cut the legs out from beneath the next. It collapsed on severed knees, screamed so hard it retched.

The vast lizard demon waded into the cave, splashing death upon the walls and floor, and the woman followed, ending the lives of those initial survivors one by one with sharp, careful precision. Like a surgeon following in a butcher's wake.

Could they be demigods? When the gods manifested, they usually had just one thing on their mind. Anyone unfortunate enough to fall under their glamour and be impregnated was rarely allowed to go full-term, though. The Pantheon's offspring—demigods—simply sowed too much chaos in the world. They were too powerful, too unpredictable. The balance of nations could be knocked askew.

This butchery, though. Its scale. Its efficiency. It still felt almost divine to Will. The pair were quiet in their work. After the initial howl of the charge, there were no more battle cries, no more declarations of righteousness. All around them the goblins screamed, but the pair worked with a grim set to their jaws.

But as he watched, Will decided, no. Not divine. While the scale and the proficiency of this slaughter was a new vista for him, this was still quotidian butchery. There were no lightning bolts, no quakes of telekinetic power. Just blade, and blood, and bone.

So who in the Hallows were they?

Eventually the slaughter was done. All about them were the dead and dying. The pair stood, panting, looked at each other, sighed, and shrugged.

"See," said the lizard monster in a voice that sounded like rocks grinding together, "that is being more fun than baking."

"Shut up and start looking for the purse," said the woman. She wheeled round suddenly, stabbed a finger out at Will. "You," she said. "Have you seen a purse?"

Will stared at her. His life did not make sense to him anymore. He remembered a metaphor his father's old lost farmhand Firkin had said to him, in one of his increasingly rare sober moments. He said it was as if the narrator of his fate had needed to step away for a moment and handed the reins to an angry toddler—a god's hand sweeping through the bricks of his life and knocking everything to the floor.

"Me?" Will said, to the woman pointing to his chest.

"No," said the woman, shaking her head, "the other helpful bystander standing just behind you."

Caught off guard, Will looked over his shoulder. There was no one there. Then his mind processed. He looked back to the woman, embarrassed.

He could see her better now. The goblins' torches littered the floor. Her face was angular, hard, flat planes coming to abrupt angles at her cheekbones and jaw. She was dressed in boiled leathers studded with steel. A hodgepodge of plate mail was strapped to her shoulders, arms, and shins. The sharpness of her features carried through to her eyes, bright and alive in this field of death.

Behind her, the massive lizard man was holding two dead goblins aloft by their ankles and shaking them. A few scraps of leather and dirt fell from them, along with a fairly large quantity of blood. There was no purse, though. The lizard man grunted and slung both bodies toward one corner of the cave. They landed with a crack of breaking bone that made Will wince.

A hint of sympathy entered the woman's face. "Not how you spend your typical evening?" she asked.

Will shrugged helplessly. "Not even a typical day."

The woman cracked a smile at that. The hard planes of her face transformed, curves appearing out of nowhere at her cheeks, and even a small dimple revealing its presence.

"I'm Lette," she said. "That's Balur."

Will stared at the lizard man. Balur. The word sounded foreign. He had the feeling that this was a moment when curiosity might equate to a feline fatality, but he couldn't quite help himself. "What is he?" he asked.

"An obstinate idiot," Lette said without a pause.

Balur shook out two more goblins and flung them at the corner. "You being flirting is not helping us find our purse any faster," he said without looking up.

"At least," she spat back, "my version of flirting is a little more sophisticated than whipping my britches off and proffering some coin." Without pausing for breath she turned to Will and said, "Get any ideas and I shall feed you your own testicles."

Will was still watching events through a thin haze of confusion. His head still hurt from running into the tree. He wanted to sit down and ignore everything in the hopes that it would go away. Except Lette. He thought Lette could stay.

He realized he had not introduced himself. "I'm Will," he said. "I'm a farmer."

Lette nodded. She looked back at Balur. "How about farming?" she asked the lizard man, apropos—as far as Will could tell—of nothing. "Working with your hands. Very physically demanding, farmwork can be."

Balur grunted. "Bad for reflexes. Ruin muscle memory," he said, leaving Will none the wiser.

Lette sighed, sank to her knees, and started rummaging through the possessions of the nearest corpse. Behind her, Balur had moved on to a different part of the cave. He shook out two more goblins, then, disappointed, flung them away to start a new pile.

As they landed there was a muffled yell.

Balur hesitated, arm still outstretched from his throw. "Got a live one," he said.

Will's stomach tightened, a sharp knot lodging near his kidneys. He looked back at the entrance to the cave. He could slip away. They wouldn't notice. He could...

He could what? Run into more trouble? It was unlikely he would come across any other well-armed strangers to brutally slaughter all of his problems. Given the many and various ways the world had tried to screw him over this night, staying with Lette and Balur actually seemed the safer option.

Lette had her short sword out once more and was advancing on the source of the sound, Balur by her side. They slowed as they came close. Then with a speed that surprised Will, Balur darted forward and grabbed something. It wriggled and writhed in the lizard man's massive hand as he held it aloft.

It was bigger than the goblin corpses littering the ground. And it was wrapped in ropes. Balur had it by its ankles, but it still took Will a moment to realize the massive scruff of hair at the bottom was a man's hair and beard.

"That's not a goblin," Will said, just in case stating the obvious would help.

"Might be in league with them," Balur said, eyes narrowed at the struggling form. Grunts and squeaks emerged, and Will realized that one of the ropes had firmly gagged the man. "Maybe be killing it just in case."

"In league?" Will said incredulously. "He's tied hand and foot."

Lette nodded. "Farm boy makes a compelling case."

"I am still thinking I should perhaps be squishing it. Just in—"

"I'm still thinking about spaying you," Lette cut in. "Put the poor bugger down."

Grudgingly, Balur lowered the man to the ground. Lette's knife appeared in her hand, apparently without having traveled through the intervening space between it and the sheath at her waist. The knife flashed in a single stroke, and the bonds fell away.

A dirty, disheveled man emerged from the looping mass of rope, shouting as he came. He was naked except for a pair of discolored undershorts, and a fairly thick coating of mud. He was rail thin, but with a small potbelly sticking out, as if he had at some point in the past swallowed a child's ball and it had obstinately stuck in his system. His arms too were more muscular than his frame might suggest, and his hands were disproportionately large. His face was almost entirely lost in a shock of hair and beard, long, tightly curled bristles standing out in wild clumps.

"Varmagants!" he was screaming. "Barph-cursed wotsits! Menagerie! Cursed and hexed vermin! Thy cannot prevent me. I am the inevitable! I am the word of the future that shall come! I am the inescapable odor!"

Both Lette and Balur took a step away from the man. Lette's sword was up once more.

It was rather a shock to Will that he recognized the man.

"Firkin?" he said.

Lette glanced at Will, quick and darting. "You know him?" she said fixing her attention back on the raving, half-naked man.

Will took a step toward him. And, yes. Yes he did. It was indeed his father's old farmhand, Firkin.

Memories flooded Will. Sitting with his father and the farmhands on a summer's day, all of them laughing at Firkin's tall tale. Up on Firkin's shoulders, his mouth full of stolen apple flesh, racing across a field, his father chasing and cursing. Watching Firkin tell jokes as his father branded the pigs. Passing bread out of a kitchen window while his mother's back was turned, Firkin gathering the rolls up in a fold of his shirt. Sitting and talking about dragons and dreaming of revolution. Watching Firkin tickle the cow's backside with a porcupine quill and then watching as the cow's kick sent him halfway across the yard. Laughing so hard he thought some part of him might rupture. Firkin and his father standing in the yard, yelling at each other, red-faced. Will and Firkin sitting slouched beneath a tree, daydreaming about stealing a dragon's gold from beneath his nose. Firkin drinking so much he fell off the table, and his father, not far behind him, laughing so hard he joined him on the floor. His mother slapping Firkin full across the face, the red handprint standing out stark on his pale skin. Firkin telling him that he didn't want company right now, and the first feeling of utter rejection in his life. Then riding a cow madcap down a hill, Firkin running behind full tilt, switching its behind. His mother holding him, sobbing and shouting at the same time. Asking his father where Firkin was. Days spent listless and wandering. Then a meal interrupted by a knock at the door, his father rising, words exchanged with an unseen man, voices rising, the scuffle of violence, and then Firkin framed in the doorway, his father on the floor, lip bloody, horror in Firkin's eyes. Then Firkin from a distance, a shadow shape that haunted distant fences. Riding with his father into town and seeing a man shouting at people who weren't there— he only recognized him as Firkin as they passed him on the way home. The moment when he realized he was used to that sight, not bothered by it anymore. His father's funeral—seeing that familiar shadow that used to haunt the fences. Watching Firkin being thrown out of the tavern again. Again. Again.

And now here. Firkin. The village drunk. The village crazy. A man who seemed to be waiting for everyone to forget why they gave him the dregs from their plates, the spare copper sheks they couldn't spare.

Firkin chose that moment to vomit noisily and messily over the floor. It was a practiced movement—tip and pour. He straightened, wiping his mouth. "Darn varmints," he said. "Gone went fed me some of the pootin'."

Nobody seemed up to the task of asking him what "pootin'" was.

Balur regarded the filthy, scrawny man and then shrugged. "Is looking goblin-y to me." He hefted his hammer.

"No!" Will yelled, darting toward the old farmhand. "No, he's not. He's a friend."

Firkin narrowed his eyes at Will. "I don't like you and your bunk," he said with surprising clarity.

"I am saving you from poor taste in friends," Balur said, not relaxing his grip on the hammer.

Firkin assessed the massive lizard man, stuck out his lower lip, and squinted with one eye. "You's a biggun," he said. "I like the bigguns. Carry more of the ale for me. Down to the merry lands, and we all drown happy like." He smacked his lips twice.

"We can't kill him, Balur," said Lette from behind Will and Firkin, sounding slightly exasperated. Will felt a wave of gratitude flood through him.

"We can be," said Balur matter-of-factly, causing the wave to break. "Be being simple. I be bringing down this hammer with speed of a certain amount. His head is going crump, and we are having a dead man there."

"Well, I know literally you can kill him..."

"Thank you," said Balur, readying himself once more.

"No!" Will shouted again. "He's my friend. He helped raise me."

Balur gave Will a skeptical look. "Maybe I should be killing him to be saving you from your poor taste in friends, then I should be killing you to be saving Lette from her poor taste in men. Everybody be being happier then."

"No!" Will said, starting to feel repetitive, but not sure what other words might save him from a homicidal lizard man at this point in the proceedings.

"If we're saving me from my taste in friends," said Lette to Balur, "maybe I should be killing you then."

The hammer blow continued to fail to fall.

"Look," said Will, reaching out to Balur, imploring, "he's just an old drunk, who the goblins found and tied up. Who knows how long he's been captive? He needs some kindness, not death threats." That, at least, seemed obvious to him. A little piece of the world he could have make sense.

"Was all part of my plan," said Firkin, tapping the side of his nose. "Right where I wanted them."

"You're not being where I want you," Balur groused, but he finally put down the hammer. The head rung as it struck the stone ground, a sonorous bass note. Will had no idea how he'd been able to hold the weight of it for so long.

"Let Firkin just stay for the night," Will said, turning to Lette, now that yet another threat had been averted. "He'll catch his death out in the rain, and you only just saved his life from the goblins."

Lette nodded. "Be a shame to put good work to waste. He sleeps downwind of me and there'll be no complaints."

Balur grunted. Possibly in agreement.

"Hey," Lette said as if struck by a sudden thought, putting a hand on Firkin's shoulder. "Don't happen to have seen a purse, have you?"

"I seen the world," said Firkin, eyes fixing on some far-off point. "I seen the plans. I seen the writing on a turtle's back. I seen the insides of a cow." He nodded, self-satisfied. "It was warm in there," he added.

"Right," said Lette. "I'll just look over here then."

As the search continued, Firkin drifted away toward the cave entrance. Will was worried he might wander into the rain, but he stayed standing there, half-sketched in moonlight, staring out into the night, muttering obscenities to himself.

Behind him, Lette and Balur seemed to be losing what little good temper they'd had.

"Where in the name of Cois's cursed cock is it?" Lette spat. "Where did that little fucker put it?"

"Maybe you were tracking him wrong. Maybe this is being the wrong cave."

"Oh, it's insulting my professional skill set is it now? That's how you're going to fix this situation? By pissing me off so much that I gut and skin you and sell your hide. Except, oh wait." She struck the side of her head with the heel of her palm. "It's fucking worthless. If I just hung a ball sack from a stick and carried it about with me it would be very little different from having you around."

Balur shrugged. "Be being a better conversation starter too."

Joining the conversation, Will realized, would be a little bit like holding his hand in a flame to see how it felt. Lette captivated him, but the piles of corpses around the room were a useful reminder that she could back up her threats if she wanted to. And then, despite all this sensible thinking, he found his jaw starting to move

"Could he be right?" he said, pointing to Balur. "Could there be another cave?"

Lette rolled her eyes and set her jaw. "Look around you," she said. "There are sixty-four corpses here. We left eighteen others back up at the mountain pass. That means they need to scavenge enough wildlife to support eighty-two souls. That means a range of twenty or more miles in any direction from here. That means that if any other tribe came within that distance they'd fight until the others were dead and their eyes boiled down to surprisingly tasty after-dinner snacks. Which means that unless I'm a complete fucking idiot who couldn't track her own grandmother from the bedroom to the privy, then this is the only fucking place the goblin that stole my purse could have gone. And yet that fucking purse is not fucking here."

Another dagger appeared as if by magic in her hand, and she flung it at one of the piles of corpses. It buried itself up to the hilt in a dead goblin's back. She spat after it.

There was, Will thought, something very sexy about Lette's competence. The area of expertise was utterly terrifying, but, on the other hand, it was significantly more exciting than butter churning, or animal husbandry, or any of the other interests the Village girls usually pursued.

"Could the thief have dropped it?" he said somewhat against his better judgment. He was trying to keep in mind that the moth tended to come out of confrontations with the flame rather the worse for wear, but it wasn't helping much.

Lette closed her eyes.

Balur grunted again. "Running pretty hard, it was," he said. "And it was being focused on not dying more than it was on being rich."

Lette groaned.

"It was being easy enough for us to miss," Balur continued. "We were being focused on the beast instead."

Lette clawed her hands down her face.

"Might be a drop even," Balur went on. "Someplace special hidden like. Be dumping the stuff there and be returning for it later when the coast has been cleared. Be throwing it up in a tree even. Makeshift drop."

"Shut up," said Lette. "Just shut up." She sank to her knees. "Gods' hex on it all."

Will almost reached out to her, to put a hand on her shoulder, but he saw Balur shaking his head.

"I had a coin once," Firkin commented from the front of the room. "But she left me. Cantankerous bitch."

It happened so fast, Will almost missed it. A roar of rage from Lette. The blur of her limbs. And then she was across the room, knife in hand, holding Firkin's collar by the other, pressing him up against the wall.

"You fucking—" she started to snarl.

"Excuse me?"

A new voice—the tone deep but feminine—brought Lette to an abrupt halt.

They all stared at the newcomer standing in the entrance of the cave. She wore a gray traveling robe, hood pulled up to obscure her features. Dark-skinned, long-fingered hands were clasped in front of her. Looking at them, Will found himself thinking of small blackbirds.

For a moment everything was very still.

"By Barph's ball sack," Lette said, not letting go of the squirming Firkin. "How many people are going to wander into this cursed cave tonight? Is there some gods-hexed sign I missed?"

"Like you were missing a goblin tossing all our gold," Balur murmured.

Lette whirled, pointed the dagger. "Don't you even fucking start."

"You know," said the figure, "I think this is the wrong cave after all." There was a tone of refinement to her voice that made Will straighten up a little, and run his hands down his shirt to smooth it. The action mostly served to spread the blood-stains out.

"I'll j-just be going," said the robed woman, and stepped away, back toward the sheets of rain that blanketed the night.

The tremor in her voice caught Will's attention, though. He saw water dripping from the front of her hood in an almost steady stream. Her robe swung heavily. She was soaked to the bone.

"Wait," he said. "You can't go out."

The others looked at him. Even Firkin, still pressed up against the wall.

"She's soaked to the bone." He pointed out to the room at large. "She'll catch her death."

"You be saying that a lot, I think," Balur said. "Unhealthy obsession."

Will stared around at the sixty-four goblin corpses. But, yes, of course, he was the one with an unhealthy obsession. Though, given the size difference between him and Balur, he decided to keep that opinion quiet.

Instead he just said, "It's been that sort of night."

Lette let out a small huff of laughter. She let Firkin go. The disheveled man collapsed away from her. "Come in then," she said to the woman in the cave's entrance. "Let's get a fire going and try to salvage what's left of this shit show of a day."

orbit

Follow us:

f **/orbitbooksUS**

𝕏 **/orbitbooks**

▶ **/orbitbooks**

Join our mailing list
to receive alerts on our
latest releases and deals.

orbitbooks.net

Enter our monthly
giveaway for the chance
to win some epic prizes.

orbitloot.com